Book Two of Ahab's Legacy

Hannah Rose

Book Two of Ahab's Legacy

Louise M. Gouge

RIVEROAK®

Good News in Fiction

COOK COMMUNICATIONS MINISTRIES
Colorado Springs, Colorado • Paris, Ontario
KINGSWAY COMMUNICATIONS LTD
Eastbourne, England

RiverOak® is an imprint of
Cook Communications Ministries, Colorado Springs, CO 80918
Cook Communications, Paris, Ontario
Kingsway Communications, Eastbourne, England

HANNAH ROSE
Copyright © 2005 by Louise M. Gouge

All rights reserved. No part of this book may be reproduced without written permission, except for brief quotations in books and critical reviews. For information, write Cook Communications Ministries, 4050 Lee Vance View, Colorado Springs, CO 80918.

This story is a work of fiction. All characters and events are the product of the author's imagination. Any resemblance to any person, living or dead, is coincidental.

First Printing, 2005
Printed in the United States of America
2 3 4 5 6 7 8 9 10 Printing/Year 08 07 06 05

Published in association with the literary agency of Les Stobbe, 300 Doubleday Road, Tryon, NC 28782

Unless otherwise noted, Scripture quotations are taken from the *King James Version* of the Bible. Italics in Scripture quotations are added by the author for emphasis.

Library of Congress Cataloging-in-Publication Data

Gouge, Louise M. (Louise Myra), 1944-
  Hannah Rose / Louise M. Gouge.
    p. cm.
  ISBN 1-58919-040-8 (pbk.)
  1. Widows--Fiction. 2. Slavery--Fiction. 3. Boston (Mass.)--Fiction. 4. Mothers and sons--Fiction. 5. Whalers' spouses--Fiction. 6. Ship captains' spouses--Fiction. 7. Women--Massachusetts--Fiction. 8. Ahab, Captain (Fictitious character)--Fiction. I. Title.
  PS3557.O839H36 2005
  813'.54--dc22

                        2004019120

Acknowledgments

I am indebted to the following people for their invaluable assistance in the development of *Hannah Rose*: Gloria Ganno, researcher extraordinaire, and Nan Slone and Kathy Clodfelter, all of whom provided character insight and research assistance; my critique group, Priscilla Burns, Lynn Meiseles, and Cindy Oldham, who went through my manuscript with a fine-tooth comb; the librarians at The Bostonian Society Library, who dug out some amazing research sources for me, including an 1847 almanac, enabling me to be historically accurate; and Stephen O'Neill, Director of Development, Pilgrim Hall Museum, Plymouth, Massachusetts, who corrected those pesky historical details that had slipped through our notice. As always, I dedicate this story to my dear husband, David, who is my inspiration and loving support.

Prologue

Clark County, Indiana, Spring 1847

"Timothy, stop fighting right this minute!" Hannah Ahab dashed toward the barnyard where two boys scuffled and yelped. But when she pulled her six-year-old son off his nine-year-old cousin, she discovered the boys were laughing.

"What's the meaning of this?"

"Aw, Ma ..." Timothy whined.

"We're just having fun," said Johnny. "Aunt Hannah, Timothy's a tiger. Tall as me and almost as strong."

Timothy grinned at the compliment.

"But we're leaving shortly, and just look at you." Hannah brushed dirt from his jacket. "Go clean up. Hurry."

"Yes, ma'am."

The two boys raced toward the house, and Hannah followed. Inside, she glanced around the bedroom she had shared with Cousin Willa through the winter. Now that she and Timothy would be traveling back East to Boston, she must be certain everything was packed in their trunk.

Pleasant memories warmed her heart as she recalled her relatives' welcoming arms after she fled Nantucket Island following her husband's death. Here, even the scrapes Timothy had with his cousin could not dishearten her, for they were far different from the very real fights he had encountered in Nantucket.

Many people there blamed Captain Ahab for the tragic loss of the whaling ship *Pequod*. Although only three years old when he last saw Ahab, Timothy was very much his father's son. When cruel boys called Ahab a murderer, Timothy fought back fiercely to defend his father's name.

But children's brawls were not the main reason Hannah had left the island of her son's birth. Rather, against community expectations that every boy should go to sea by the age of ten, she refused to let him be a whaler. No matter how much she had loved Ahab, she would do everything in her power to prevent Timothy from following in his father's footsteps.

Hannah often dreamed of Ahab—handsome, brilliant, daring, wealthy beyond imagining. Had he ever found peace with God, or had he continued to blame Him for the loss of his leg in a whaling accident? Surely, with godly Mr. Starbuck as his first mate, he had come to see the futility of his bitterness.

For her part, she had ceased praying altogether. Why should she cry out to God? Had she not done so all during Ahab's last, fatal voyage, to no avail? Over the months since learning of his death, she recalled the night she renewed her trust in God, committing both her life and Ahab's into His care. But that was almost certainly the very night her husband died. If her heartfelt prayer meant nothing to God then, why should she believe He cared anything about her now?

Henceforth, Hannah would consult only her own heart in deciding how to live, and the time had come for her and her son to embark on a great adventure. All her life she had longed to travel, and after a short visit with friends in Boston, she and Timothy would sail to Europe and perhaps Egypt.

After one last glance around the farm, Hannah bade her relatives good-bye, gathered Timothy, and began the journey eastward by coach, ferries, and trains. Along the way, she devised a daring scheme to protect her son. She would take her cousins' last name so no one in the seafaring community would know of their relationship to the infamous whaling captain who had madly, vengefully pursued a great white whale, dragging all his crew, save one, to their deaths beneath the ocean waves.

Chapter One

~

"*B*oston ahead, ma'am," the coach driver called down from his seat.

"At last." Hannah closed her volume of Shakespeare and gazed at her son sleeping soundly on the upholstered bench across from her. The sight of his black eyelashes against his tanned cheeks gave her heart a tug. He had nearly lost his baby looks, a good thing in light of his unusual height, but she would miss that cherubic phase.

She leaned forward and shook him gently. "Darling, we're almost there. Come look out the window."

Timothy rubbed his eyes and sat up with a smile before he was fully awake. Again Hannah's heart tugged. He had been such a happy baby, but after Ahab's death, he often wore a dark frown reminiscent of his father. After their Indiana visit, he once again wore a peaceful expression.

Now awake, he climbed on Hannah's lap. "Are we there yet? Are we at Uncle Jeremiah's?"

Hannah laughed. He had asked the question for the last two weeks of their trip. "No. Just another hour or so. Mr. Jones will ask directions to the mission. Let's look out and see the city."

She pulled the cord on the window shade to roll up its thick oilcloth. "Oh, it's bright outside. Do you think we'll remember how to walk after all these weeks of travel?"

Timothy gave her a look indicating the silliness of the question, then asked, "Do you think Aunt Ker ... Keren ... Ker ..."

"Kerenhappuch."

"Do you think Aunt Kerenhappuch is a good cook like Aunt Willa? Are you sure all my Boston cousins are girls? How long are we staying at the mission? What's our ship's name? When does it sail?"

Hannah laughed. "I'm sure the food will be fine. You don't remember, but Aunt Kerenhappuch was your nursemaid from the moment you were born until you were a year and a half old. She'll be so happy to see you again, and so will Uncle Jeremiah. All their children are girls, but not really our cousins. They're good friends, and you may call them Aunt and Uncle, not Reverend and Mrs. Harris. We'll stay with them while we plan our trip, and I don't know the ship's name yet."

As she finished her answers, happiness swept through her. At last her lifelong dream of traveling abroad would come true. From Timothy's infancy, she had read him travelogues hoping he would share the dream, and indeed he seemed eager to go.

They needed this trip, both of them. By the time they returned, any stories the *Pequod* survivor might have spread about Ahab would be forgotten, replaced by some other scandal. Her son would never have to bear the disgrace of his father's actions. Now she must prepare him for their new identities.

"We're going to play a new game."

His eyes twinkled, and once again his resemblance to his father moved Hannah. When Ahab had been happy, before he lost his leg, at the first, when they had fallen in love, oh, he had been magnificent. And when their son was born, Ahab's eyes had twinkled when he looked at her, just as that son's eyes now shone. How could she take away the pride her son should feel in his father, no matter how unwisely Ahab had behaved after his accident? But that unwise behavior now made it necessary.

"What's the game?"

"We're going to pretend. You know, just as when you and Johnny pretended to be soldiers."

"Can I ... I mean ... may I be the general?"

"Oh, we'll play soldiers later. This is a special game. We'll pretend to have a different last name, but not completely different."

A cloud seemed to pass over his eyes. "What name? Jacobs, like Mr. Jones keeps calling us?"

Not one to tell lies, Hannah pursed her lips. "Yes. We're going to call it our Indiana name, like our cousins. And since it's your own middle name too, it means you'll still be called Timothy Jacob, only with an *s* on the end."

"You mean we won't be Ahabs anymore?"

She winced at the double meaning of his words. No, through no fault of their own, they were not Ahab's family anymore. "No. Our name won't be Ahab now."

He stared out the window, frowning. Hannah's heart twisted. Was she making a terrible mistake?

He looked back at her sharply, again the picture of his father. "That's why the driver calls you Mrs. Jacobs?"

"Yes, even Mr. Jones is playing the game."

"Will everyone play it with us?"

"Everyone will play with us. But most people won't know it's a game."

He seemed doubtful. "So we have to see how many people we can fool?"

Again, she winced. Was she teaching her son to lie?

"It's not really fooling them, darling. It's more like playing hide-and-seek with words."

"Does that mean we want them to guess our name?"

Hannah could no longer meet his troubled gaze. "No. It's our secret."

He nodded his acceptance, then slipped off her lap and knelt at the low window. After a few moments, he spoke in a dark, troubled tone. "Boston is awful big. I hope Mr. Jones can find the way to the mission."

Thirteen years had passed since Hannah attended Miss Applegate's boarding school. More than ever, Boston teemed with life, as did most of New England's coastal cities. Thousands of European immigrants came to America every month for opportunities unknown in their own countries. As the carriage wended its way toward Jeremiah's mission in the North End, Hannah could discern Portuguese, French, and German being spoken on the streets. Regretting her lack of attention to language studies, she longed to understand them, yet they pleasantly foreshadowed her upcoming trip.

Soon Mr. Jones found the Grace Seamen's Mission on North Square, not far from the docks. The large, five-story clapboard building was painted a light, sunny yellow with white trim. Six gabled windows graced the top floor, and a cupola sat high atop the roof. Next to the building stood the Grace Mission Chapel, its charming architecture reminding Hannah of the Seamen's Bethel in New Bedford, where she and Ahab had said their marriage vows.

On the far side of the chapel stood a three-story clapboard house, also painted yellow and white. Dark green shutters adorned the windows, and lacy curtains were visible through the glass. The large, pretty house suited a young minister and his growing family, although Hannah felt some concern about his choice of neighborhoods in which to build.

Mr. Jones reined in his team of horses, jumped down from the driver's seat, and walked up the front doorsteps to announce their arrival. Soon Jeremiah and Kerenhappuch Harris came out the door, flanked by two little girls, the third daughter in her mother's arms.

"Jeremiah!" Hannah flung open the carriage door.

"Hannah, dear Hannah." Jeremiah came to the carriage to help her down, then pulled her into his strong arms. His sandy brown hair was tousled, his rolled-up shirtsleeves were rumpled, but his face beamed with joy. "Oh, how good to see you. And who is this fine young gentleman?" He released her and reached out to shake hands with the suddenly shy Timothy, who still stood in the carriage door. Jeremiah pulled back his hand and bowed. "Master Timothy."

Kerenhappuch held no such concerns. After embracing Hannah with one arm, she deposited her toddler in her guest's hands and pulled her former charge from the carriage. "Come here, my little man. Let me see how thou hast grown. Oh, how thou favorest thy father. Every inch as handsome as the captain too." Without waiting for his response, she set him down and reclaimed her youngest daughter. With the back of his sleeve, Timothy wiped his cheek where she had kissed him, but he also grinned.

"Mrs. Jacobs, shall I carry the trunk into the house?" Mr. Jones said.

"Mrs … ?" Jeremiah began.

Hannah gripped his arm. "Yes, Mr. Jones, if you could please. Jeremiah, could you direct Mr. Jones to my room?"

Jeremiah stared at her for a moment, then turned back to the other man. "Up the stairs to the second floor, if you please. The second door on the left. Dorice will show you." He nodded toward the serving girl waiting by the front door. Spying a young seaman who had just emerged from the mission, he called out, "Mr. Callahan, would you be so kind as to help the coachman?"

While Jones and Callahan lifted the trunk down from the coach and carried it into the house, Jeremiah swept his family and guests up the front stairs, through the front door, and into the great parlor. Once Hannah had settled into an overstuffed chair, one considerably softer than the thinly cushioned coach seat, Jeremiah confronted her.

"What's the meaning of this, Hannah? Have you gone and married again without my examining the credentials of your intended?" His tone was that of a teasing brother, but his eyes revealed his concern.

"No, not married, just ..." Hannah glanced toward the children.

Jeremiah traded looks with Kerenhappuch, who quickly sent the children to the kitchen for cookies with their young nursemaid Ellen. At the door, Timothy turned back with a glower, but the two girls grabbed his hands and dragged him away.

Once they left, the couple turned to Hannah. She stared down at her hands, busied herself removing her black kidskin gloves, and wondered how to begin. She might have more trouble explaining her lie to Jeremiah than to Timothy, for the discerning young minister had known her since childhood.

"It was very difficult for us in Nantucket after word got back about Ahab." She twisted her gloves in knots. "I just couldn't bear for Timothy to face any more ridicule for what ... for what ..." Hannah's eyes filled with tears. How could she expect them to approve of her lying?

Kerenhappuch sat on the arm of Hannah's chair and embraced her. "Dearest Hannah, how our hearts have ached for thee. That whaler's tale spread to every tavern on the waterfront and of course here to the mission. It caused us great concern. Then Mother wrote of thy departure from Nantucket and thy trip out West. Thy letter this past winter brought us great relief."

"But to take a different name ..." Jeremiah leaned toward her, pastoral concern radiating from his intense blue eyes. "I fear this sets a bad example for Timothy even as you try to shelter him. Perhaps we can find another way to protect him from stories about his father."

Kerenhappuch squeezed Hannah's shoulders. "Husband, thou knowest that I do not condone a lie, but can a person not change her

name without censure? The Scriptures tell us Saul changed his name
to Paul after his conversion."

"This is hardly the same. I'm concerned—"

"Shh, don't distress her further." Kerenhappuch hugged Hannah
again.

"He isn't. I'm just exhausted from the trip, and it's such a relief to
be with dear friends." She pulled a handkerchief from her sleeve and
dabbed her nose. "Is using my relatives' name so terrible?"

Jeremiah shook his head. "I cannot fully approve, but until we
think of another way to protect Timothy, what else can *you* do?"
He chuckled softly. "When I went out West ten years ago, I met
many men who had taken on new identities because of past
misdeeds. I don't mean to compare you to them, but I understand
your feelings."

Kerenhappuch nodded. "Hannah, thou must not give it another
thought. No one here knows thee, and we will keep thy secret."

Jeremiah nodded as well. "You can count on us. After all, we owe
all our happiness to you."

Despite the comfort of her down-filled bed, Hannah slept fitfully
that night. The sea air blew renewed dreams of Ahab through her
open window. He strode up a cobblestone street from the New
Bedford docks, his two long, powerful legs bringing him home. He
lifted her up in his arms and swung her around as they both laughed.
He lowered her to their marriage bed and showed her how happy he
was to be home. Then he stood, turned from her, and limped away
toward the Nantucket harbor on his ivory leg. *Ahab!* She tried to call
out to him, but no words would come. Then he was gone. She awoke
in a sweat, aching for his loving touch.

She arose, went to the window, and stared out at the sky. These
nightly visions had not tormented her for several months, for her
hard work on the farm had exhausted her and brought on dreamless

sleep. Perhaps to chase away useless longings, she should find something to occupy her time in Boston until her trip was arranged. In the morning, she would ask Kerenhappuch—Kerry, she corrected herself—for some useful work at the mission.

Kerry's Quaker upbringing had prepared her to participate as a full partner in her husband's work. Thinking back, Hannah recalled that Ahab had been captain of both his ship and his marriage. As much as she had loved him, she could not help but admire Jeremiah for seeking Kerry's counsel. The moment she thought it, she felt disloyal to Ahab. He had been a good husband and father, at least as good as he knew how to be.

After breakfast, Jeremiah invited Timothy to the mission. "You can meet some new friends and learn about our work."

Timothy turned an eager, questioning face to his mother. "Can I … may I, Mother?"

Hannah mirrored his expression, pursing her lips as she teased. "I don't know, darling. Should you disappoint the girls? They want you to play house."

He wrinkled his nose, sighing his disappointment.

"Hannah," Kerry said, "the girls have their sewing lessons with me this morning. We won't require Master Timothy's presence until later, will we, girls?"

The two older girls nodded their heads agreeably, and the boy looked hopefully at his mother.

"Of course you may go. I'm coming over too, as soon as I help Aunt Kerry."

Timothy rewarded her with a beaming smile.

After he and Jeremiah left, a vague uneasiness nagged Hannah. "Kerry, what kinds of men usually stay at the mission?"

"Do not worry thyself, Hannah. Jeremiah seems mild mannered, but he's firmly in charge of all the doings at the mission. And he has several good men working with him. One of them lives on the top floor with his wife and children. Timothy will be happy to see that they have boys for him to play with."

"Ah, how wonderful. He's been agreeable with the girls, but he's grown used to playing with his boy cousin. I'm also grateful for Jeremiah's influence on him."

"And Jeremiah will appreciate having a boy in the house for these few weeks. Though he would never say anything, I'm hoping this next baby will be the son I know he wants."

"Kerry, are you expecting again?" With closer study, Hannah could discern Kerry's expanded waistline beneath her morning gown.

The younger woman smiled. "Sometime in November. Isn't it wonderful the way God has blessed our little family?"

Hannah still felt stunned by the news as later that morning she carried a basket of homemade sweet rolls up the block toward the mission. Kerry had plenty of help for her household, but how long would her health hold up if she continued to have a baby every year? But then, Hannah could hardly rebuke Jeremiah when Kerry seemed so happy. Not only that, but she herself longed for another child, especially a daughter. What fun it had been to brush Lacy's and Molly's long blonde curls this morning, and how wonderful it had been to hold little Daisy in her arms. With a sigh for herself and an inward wish for Kerry's health, she rejoiced for her friends' quiver full of children and happiness.

She paused to study the outside of the mission building. The narrow flowerbeds along the front and sides gave the property a homey look, while the elegant Georgian pediment and double front door suggested a grand hotel. Jeremiah must have used much of his inheritance from his late father to give the mission its welcoming appearance. Seamen who might be put off by a more austere building would have no excuses for wasting their pay in tawdry waterfront bars when they could find rest and diversion at this attractive haven.

Climbing the three front steps, she put her hand out to the door just as Timothy flung it open.

"I'm already helping Uncle Jeremiah. May I take the basket to the kitchen?"

"Of course." She handed it to him and followed him through the front hall into a large, sunny dining room, where blended smells of bread, bacon, and pipe tobacco greeted them.

Several men sat at breakfast served by the mission staff. At the end of the long room, Jeremiah stood talking with another man who, like his host, wore a dark business suit. The tastefully groomed stranger was tall and muscular, with neatly trimmed, sun-bleached blonde hair. He was clean-shaven and had the tanned, weathered complexion of a seaman. He appeared to be in his late-thirties, perhaps five years older than his host.

When Jeremiah saw Hannah, he led the other man to her. As they approached, she felt a rush of panic, despite Jeremiah's tranquil expression. She knew this man and, far worse, he knew her. It was too late to flee. Soon every sailor and whaler in the room and every seaman in Boston would know her name.

"Hannah, here's an old friend I'm sure you remember."

The man took her hand, raised it to his lips, then lifted his gaze to her stricken countenance. "Mrs. ... Jacobs, how good to see you again. I've already become reacquainted with your fine young son." His broad, handsome face was lit by a guileless smile, and his clear gray eyes exuded kindness and understanding.

Tears stung her eyes as she struggled to regain her composure. "Captain Lazarus, how good to see you again."

Chapter Two

❧

You're the picture of health, Mrs. Jacobs. The credit is due to your trip out West, I suppose? I understand the Indiana air is invigorating."

Hannah and the captain sat on the window seat in the mission's large front parlor. Jeremiah had taken Timothy out behind the building to help stack firewood while Hannah visited with the man who had shipped as captain of her father's last vessel.

She smiled at his compliment. "I believe the country air and my cousin's cooking have done wonders for my health and Timothy's as well. But then it was not a lack of those things that caused us to leave … that is to say …"

"It must have become difficult for you on …" He glanced around. Several seamen sat reading or talking in other parts of the room, but the window seat was in a secluded corner at the front. He lowered his voice. "I should say, where you lived previously."

She nodded, staring down at her hands.

"I'm so very sorry for your loss. I understand how painful it is to lose your beloved."

"Yes. I believe you do."

"It has been a great source of comfort these past few years to recall that you nursed my wife and daughter as they suffered on their deathbeds. What consolation to know the last sight Eliza saw as she left this earth was your face, as gentle and compassionate as any angel she now sees in heaven."

Hannah studied his face. When she last spoke with him, only grief had been written there. Now he was at peace. "Thank you, Captain."

"But what of you, dear lady? How are you managing?"

She considered her words carefully, wishing to be honest with him but fearing to reveal how badly her faith had been weakened by Ahab's death. "A wise man once asked me how a person could endure adversity and suffering without God. When my grief threatens to overwhelm me, I consider my son and live for him."

He sighed. "How very sad that you received no support from the community—"

"Ah, well, the people of Nan ... the people of the community ... were horribly shocked. The sinking of the *Pe* ... the ship ... was an extraordinary event they discussed with great concern. Everyone admired my husband. You know yourself his exploits were legendary throughout the whole whalefishery. Before the sinking, most had nothing but admiration for him. The few who disliked or feared him did so because he demanded they give an honest day's work for their pay or be fair in their business dealings. After the sinking, those latter voices seemed the loudest in recalling all his faults. I simply could not stay there and have my son stigmatized by his father's one shocking act. But of course it *was* shocking, if the survivor's account is to be believed."

Captain Lazarus's kind expression brought tears to her eyes. He touched her hand.

"Permit me to tell you a story. Some sixteen years ago, when I was on my first voyage as captain, sailing for Mr. Gantvort out of New Bedford, I was nearly as green as any cabin boy. A mutiny was brewing on my ship, but basking in my own self-importance, I ignored the signs, certain all was well. A week's sailing west of Valparaiso, we gammed with the *Pequod*. Captain Ahab ..."

Lazarus lowered his voice and glanced around. "The captain came aboard and, finding out who comprised my crew, seemed in no hurry to be off. He made much of my vessel, the *Agnes*, saying she was a fine ship for an untried one, for we had not yet taken whale. He consented to stay for dinner, being swayed, I thought, by my boasts about my excellent cook. After dinner, he made an unusual request, wanting to ship my second mate, for his first mate had been lost at sea a month before. He knew my Mr. Winthrop and felt he would do for a first mate on the *Pequod*.

"In my pride, I thought I had trained the man well that he could bring such recognition, though he was older by ten years and should have been a captain himself by then, save for his temper. In any event, I spoke with Mr. Winthrop, and he declined the offer. However, Captain ... my wise friend ... took the mate aside, repeated the proposition, and offered some incentive I was not privy to. This time it was accepted, and the *Pequod*, its captain, and Mr. Winthrop sailed off on a tangent to our heading. Then one of my younger men from before the mast, a Christian boy, came to tell me all about Mr. Winthrop's mutinous plans. The lad had been unable to approach me earlier, for the mate had threatened to kill all who took my part if word was breathed to us. Still, the lad was determined to warn me at his first opportunity. Now there was no need. With their leader gone, the other men abandoned their murderous designs. On reflection, I realized the captain had discerned the impending evil within moments of stepping aboard the *Agnes* and had saved this green young fool for another day. I shall be eternally grateful for what he did for me. What an instinct—what a grasp of human nature—he possessed."

Hannah's heart lightened with happiness at his story. How true. Ahab had possessed great discernment. And this generous man told the story at his own expense. "And did you ever discover what became of Mr. Winthrop under my husband's command?"

"I seem to recall word eventually came back to New Bedford that he found a South Pacific island much to his liking and decided to jump ship there."

Hannah laughed. "Now that's a wonder. Imagine any whaler with mutiny on his mind leaving our captain's service."

"Precisely my point, dear lady."

Squeezing his hand, she whispered, "Thank you, my friend. How hungry I have been for stories of my husband's generosity and wisdom. As I said, it was his detractors who spoke the loudest after his death."

"Mrs. A ... Mrs. Jacobs ... you will never hear an unfavorable opinion from me about your husband, nor will I even harbor such a notion."

A comfortable silence came over them, interrupted only when Timothy ran in with a small, golden ball of fur.

"Mother, look what I found. Uncle Jeremiah said I could keep it if you say yes. Please say yes." He plopped to his knees beside her and laid a dusty, longhaired kitten on her lap. "It's very smart, and Uncle Jeremiah said it's a stray and nobody wants it and if we don't take care of it, it'll go hungry because the big cats get all the rats and mice, and can I have it, I mean may I? Captain Lazarus, do you like cats?"

"I suppose they're fairly tolerable creatures." Lazarus chuckled, as did Hannah.

"Oh, darling, he is a sweet little thing. But, don't you know, we won't be here long enough to give him a home. When we go on our trip, we'll have to leave him, and how can we burden Aunt Kerry when she already has three cats?"

"It's a she, and her name is Jemima, 'cause she has blonde hair and black eyes and looks like Jemima Starbuck." Timothy glanced at the captain. "Jemima's my friend in Nantucket." He petted the kitten, which purred with contentment in Hannah's lap.

She stroked the thin, sweet-faced animal while reluctantly

framing words to disappoint her son. "We're going away and can't take her with us."

Timothy stood, took his mother's face in his small hands, stared earnestly into her eyes, and spoke in an even more earnest tone.

"Mother, this cat needs me."

His intense, dark gaze seemed to penetrate her soul. Ah, how he favored his father. Even his young voice seemed to resonate with Ahab's deep inflections. Sighing, she squeezed his hands, then brushed his unruly hair back from his forehead. It was not the cat who needed the child, but the child who needed the cat. "Then you must care for her well, my son."

As suddenly as he had grown sober, he once again beamed with childish delight. Throwing his arms around Hannah's neck, he kissed her cheek. "I promise I will. Come, Jemima. There's milk in the galley." He scooped up the placid kitten and ran from the room. Hannah tried without success to shake all the loose dust and fur from her black skirt.

Lazarus at last gave vent to his laughter, and Hannah joined him. "Mrs. Jacobs, your son is the most enchanting little lad I have ever known. My heart could burst from the abundance of joy his antics give me."

"Another sign that his father could not have been utterly devoid of redeeming qualities?"

"Most assuredly, madam. And, most assuredly, a sign that his mother has loved him well. But I must hasten to ask, where are you going on your trip?"

"We're going to England, the Netherlands, France, Italy, and at last to Egypt. Our itinerary is not definite yet, but I will solidify my plans while my travel wardrobe is being completed."

"How interesting. But surely you don't intend to go alone, just the two of you?"

"Why, yes, although I might try to engage a serving girl to go along. Why do you ask?"

His concern was evident in his eyes. "I don't wish to alarm you, but in addition to a widespread epidemic of influenza, there is great upheaval in many parts of Europe these days, even England. And France has not been stable since the revolution over fifty years ago. If I cannot persuade you to postpone your journey until things have settled down—that is, if you're determined to go this year—surely you can find a group of good people with similar plans, or perhaps a tour guide who can navigate around the troubled areas."

"Perhaps I can. Thank you for the suggestion." Hannah paused, self-conscious in the face of his apprehensions for her. Still, her father had chosen him to captain his ship, the *Hannah Rose*, and Ahab had thought highly of him. Surely this friend could be trusted. And of course, there were those striking gray eyes, which exuded kindness and good will. His admonition simply displayed his Christian concern for a widow and her child. Yes, he was a good friend.

"Captain, we have only talked about me. Tell me about yourself. Do you work here at the mission all the time?"

His expression mellowed once again. "No, but I volunteer when I can. After the success of my voyage on the *Hannah Rose*, I began a shipbuilding and import business. It's doing well, and I have trustworthy workers, so I'm often free to help. Do you recall that I told you about my brother who worked in a seamen's mission here in Boston? It turns out that your good friend Jeremiah Harris was the founder of that mission."

"So your brother is the man who lives on the fifth floor with his family. What a charming coincidence. And how lovely that you have family here."

"Yes. And lovely friends too."

Her heart warmed at his compliment. How pleasant, how

peaceful, to sit in this man's company. She would be pleased to look into those kind gray eyes often.

He leaned back against the wall. "I suppose you've heard about our Friday evening social to raise funds for the mission?"

"A little, but I would like to hear more."

"The social is for soliciting donations. Some members of Boston society will be here, along with naval officers who will see the benefits of encouraging sailors to spend their leave time here. I'm sure you would enjoy the event."

"Kerry has informed me that I do plan to come."

"Wonderful. Who knows? You may find new friends among these fine people, all of whom, I think you will agree, are your social peers."

Hannah laughed softly. "Oh, Captain Lazarus, I have never cared much for society. Your remark reveals how little you know me."

"I stand corrected, and might I add that I hope to make up for that deficiency."

"You're very kind. But I've taken too much of your time. I must go see that Timothy is not annoying Jeremiah." She stood and reached out her hand. "Good morning, Captain."

He stood, gave a slight bow, and seemed reluctant to release her hand. "And a good rest of the morning to you, Mrs. Jacobs."

Chapter Three

ઐ

"You are a vision of loveliness in this gown, madam. Its delicate sea-green shade enhances the beauty of your emerald eyes. And your magnificent auburn hair, swept back in such artful curls against your neck this way, the dark against the light of your delicate ivory complexion … what a splendid contrast. Oh, madam, all eyes will be on you."

Shrugging off the dressmaker's extravagant praise, Hannah sighed as she studied her own reflection in the wardrobe mirror. The dress went well with the jade necklace and earrings Ahab had brought her from China long ago, but its light color seemed improper. Planning to wear only mourning clothes for the rest of her life, she had left her wardrobe in Nantucket except for six black dresses. But a winter of wear made them all useless for an important social event. Of course, she must attend this one, for perhaps she could set an example of generosity.

Hannah's limited experience told her that society people tried to outdo each other at such events with grand philanthropic gestures. Though hating to fuss about her clothes, she knew she could not influence other wealthy donors if her appearance did not measure up to theirs. And so she must have a new black gown.

Kerry's dressmaker, however, was in a flurry of busyness making summer wardrobes for wealthy city dwellers who would soon remove to their country homes for the hot days of July and August. With many apologies, Florence could only offer one nearly finished gown abandoned by a previous client. With a few alterations, it would do, even being long enough for Hannah's five feet eight inches. No one other than Hannah, not even Jeremiah, thought the gown's soft green color was in poor taste for a widow of almost two years.

"I'm not comfortable with this neckline." Hannah tugged the band of lace lying just off her shoulders and plunging to a deep V in the bodice's front.

"But, madam, décolletage is all the fashion today. Everyone admires it. To wear an evening gown up to here …" She placed her hand against her own throat. " … *that* would be ludicrous."

Hannah turned and glanced over her shoulder. The back neckline was acceptable, and pretty pale-green buttons extended from the edge of the lace border to several inches past her waistline. The slenderizing lines of the bodice were pleasing, but not the corset underneath. Though social convention dictated that decent women wear the dreadful contraptions, she had shunned the practice while on the remote Indiana farm. In the city, she must wear one again or risk her reputation. In any event, she did like the skirt, for it draped nicely over her petticoat hoops and trailed gracefully behind her.

"It will have to do. The social begins shortly. Thank you, Florence. Let me pay you now."

"Oh, no, madam. When I have your entire travel wardrobe finished, then you can pay me. Shall I bring my fashion plates and material samples here on Tuesday?"

"Oh, by Tuesday, I'll be ready for an outing. I'll bring my son, for he needs a travel wardrobe as well. Will ten o'clock be too early?"

"Ten o'clock, madam. I can provide every possible garment and accessory you may need. If I don't carry the item myself, I can contact a shop nearby to send it over." Florence packed her sewing basket, brought for last-minute alterations, and took her leave.

After she left, Hannah still fussed with the dress. Her dissatisfaction with the color was just a symptom of her overall displeasure. She had never cared for large socials, but she reminded herself this evening was not for her enjoyment, but rather to benefit Jeremiah's mission. She felt pleased to support his efforts.

The past few days had been hectic, but both Hannah and Timothy had shaken off their travel weariness to help prepare the mission. Timothy already felt as much a part of things as he had at the Indiana farm. Hannah's friendship with Jeremiah and Captain Lazarus gave her reason enough to assist. She did not feel as comfortable, however, with the rest of the Lazarus family.

She had learned that Jonathan and David Lazarus, sons of a New Bedford tradesman of modest means, had always been vastly different from each other. David began to move in polite society in his early teens after the whaleship owner saw his potential as a natural leader and future captain. His older brother, Jonathan, took after their father as a man of tools. He could build or repair anything, whether wooden or mechanical, but his social skills were lacking. At first meeting, he seemed to Hannah like a great hostile bear, with his massive stature, dark-brown hair, and a bushy beard streaked with gray. Her involuntary reaction to him must have been what caused David to mention later that scarlet fever in childhood had damaged his brother's hearing. His dark frowns indicated not anger but concentration. After that, Hannah trusted Timothy to his charge for short intervals.

Maria Lazarus, a short, plump, and pleasant woman with black hair and dark complexion, spoke with a thick Portuguese accent. She and her two daughters, sixteen and fifteen years of age, did all the cooking and cleaning for the mission. At twelve, the oldest son was away on his first whaling voyage. The two boys at home were nine and five, and provided Timothy with companionship.

Yet to Hannah, the poisonous snakes and wild animals near the Indiana farm seemed far less a threat to her son than the vast array of dangers in this untamed neighborhood so near the wharves where ships from all over the world docked. Hannah understood why

Jeremiah built the mission here; he wished to be near those to whom he ministered. But how could he bring Kerry and the girls here? Little Paolo and Estevam roamed freely, and no one seemed concerned about them. Further, she had seen the brothers slinging rocks at stray cats and laughing when they hit their unfortunate targets.

Hannah's musings were interrupted by the very boys who concerned her. Timothy burst through her bedroom door, flanked by his new companions, all three breathless.

"Mother, Mrs. Lazarus says Paolo and Estevam can spend tonight with me. I asked Aunt Kerry, and she said yes. Miss Ellen doesn't mind keeping an eye on us, so will you please say yes too?"

"Please, please," echoed the other two boys. Paolo emphasized his plea by jumping up and down along with Timothy, while Estevam, as the oldest, modeled a bit more decorum.

"I don't think …"

"We'll be good. You can count on us," said Estevam. The other boys nodded vigorously.

Hannah gazed at her son, and his pleading expression swayed her. "Very well, you may play together, but you must stay indoors. And when Miss Ellen tells you it is bedtime, you must obey instantly, or you will not be given this privilege again."

As they shouted their delight and ran from the room, she shuddered. Everything in this city seemed to conspire to disconnect her son from her. Even Jeremiah saw nothing wrong with neighborhood boys who hung around the alley behind the mission and played rough games. *Just wait until he has a son of his own.*

As Hannah followed the three out, she realized she had neglected to scold her son for bringing the other boys into her room without knocking.

After administering final admonitions to their children regarding good behavior, Hannah and Kerry left the house at dusk to join

Jeremiah at the mission. Looping her arm in Hannah's, Kerry seemed near to skipping as they walked up the street.

"This will be a wonderful evening," she said. "Jeremiah has worked so hard and used every connection possible to influence good attendance. Thou ... I mean, *you* ... will meet some dear Christians this night."

"Why, Kerry, why did you change to 'you' in place of 'thou' just now?"

"I've been trying to change recently. Because I am Jeremiah's wife and, of course, a member of his congregation, few people know I was raised in the Society of Friends. I worry my 'thee' and 'thou' may sound artificial to them."

"No one who knows you could ever think you artificial. You should speak as you always have."

Kerry smiled. "If my choice of words offends even one potential donor, then I can surely select words that make others comfortable. Among Friends, plain speaking demonstrates a true heart. But if what I call plain speaking sounds odd to someone else, then a barrier is created to ministry."

"But, dear, must you give up your heritage in order to minister?"

"Hannah, I am first of all a minister of Christ. It is my joy to become 'all things to all men, that I might by all means save some.'"

"Yes, of course." Hannah hid her annoyance with a smile that felt strained. Kerry seemed to solve every problem with a Bible verse, but since Ahab's death, Hannah had found life had brought problems and heartaches for which the Bible had no answers.

Their arrival at the mission prevented further conversation. Out of respect, Hannah stifled her feelings of resentment that Kerenhappuch should change both her name and her manner of speaking to accommodate other people. Such changes seemed a futile exercise. She herself had changed in many ways to try to save Ahab, and it had not helped at all.

Kerry excused herself to check last-minute details, and Hannah hurried into the mission, chiding herself for being cross about Kerry's willing self-sacrifice. In this mood, she would be no help to them at all.

Inside, she glanced around with approval, seeing that the simple decorations had survived the afternoon. That morning, she and Kerry had arranged fresh spring flowers from the gardens of generous donors and placed them in borrowed vases. Plain linen cloths covered the tables in the dining room, and a large, nondescript punch bowl decorated the buffet. Unlike more extravagant trappings, this economical use of gifts should impress donors.

In the great parlor, Captain Lazarus stood by the fireplace talking with a short, attractive woman in an elegant blue gown. The blonde woman's easy manner with the captain bespoke respectable friendship and warmth. Lazarus towered over her, yet he wore his height with casual indifference. Hannah could not help but wonder how such an attractive man could be so humble. He did not seem to realize how much the woman admired him. Hannah saw it, however, and the thought brought both discomfort and dismay, and confusion over her own reaction.

Upon seeing Hannah, the object of her musings motioned her to join them.

"Mrs. Jacobs, this is Mrs. Childers. She has been a good friend of the mission since its beginning."

Before Hannah could respond, the other woman exclaimed, "Hannah Oldweiler," and embraced her.

"Nan Bowers, I hardly would have known you. You've changed. My goodness, how you've changed." The once plump young girl with a baby face was now a lovely woman with just the right amount of roundness in all the right places—the very picture of a modern beauty.

"Only you and my dear, late papa have ever called me Nan. How good it sounds. I'm stuck with 'Antoinette' these days."

Nan glanced up at the captain, whose face wore a bemused expression. "When Captain Lazarus told me a friend was newly arrived in Boston and on her way to Europe, I had no idea it was you. My late husband, Mr. Childers, took me to Italy on our honeymoon, and it was truly grand. You must permit me to help you make connections there."

"I would be grateful. Oh, Nan, how good to see you after all these years."

"And you look exquisite, my dear. Even taller than when we were girls. And your gown. Green always was your color." Nan again glanced up at the captain. "I don't suppose we should keep our mutual friend in suspense any longer as to how we know each other. He had planned to save us both from boredom by introducing kindred spirits, never knowing we were mischievous little schoolmates at Miss Applegate's boarding school back in ... how long ago was it?"

"Why, only about thirteen years, I think. Yet it seems a lifetime."

"Yes, and for me as well. I understand you've lost your husband too." Nan held both of Hannah's hands and gave her a sympathetic smile.

"Yes. But we can discuss that later. This evening is for the mission." She looked up at the captain, who was observing their conversation with interest. "What a nice surprise, Captain Lazarus."

"I confess I'm curious to hear more about your being 'mischievous little schoolmates.' What possible mischief could two such proper young ladies do in a proper Boston boarding school?"

Hannah and Nan exchanged a glance and then giggled like the schoolgirls they once had been. Hannah quickly controlled herself, putting her fingers demurely over her lips, as if the stern Miss Applegate were watching. But her heart danced with merriment. It had been years since she had thought about her childish escapades.

"Am I to assume that this means you won't tell me?" the captain asked.

"Well …" began Hannah.

"Oh, let me," said Nan.

"No. Not until he promises not to tell my son any of it."

"Indeed, I do give my word, Mrs. Jacobs." His expression was grave. "I would never wish to encourage him to be mischievous and therefore a normal child."

"Oh." Hannah gasped at his comment, then laughed when she saw the twinkle in his eyes. "Why, Captain Lazarus, I would not have thought you one to tease."

"That's because you just don't know our Captain Lazarus." Nan tapped the man's arm with her folded fan and gazed up at him.

Hannah continued to smile, but for some reason, the merriment of the moment faded a little. Something indefinable in Nan's manner with the captain bothered her. Both were widowed, and their easy manner seemed to suggest more than friendship. But she would feel unfaithful to take the kind of interest in a man that Nan was demonstrating. Although Hannah had known of Ahab's death for over a year, she still felt married. How could these two so easily forget their spouses, whom they once loved?

Lazarus shook his head. "I think Mrs. Jacobs is right. We can discuss our various eccentricities at a later time. We're neglecting the other guests."

Chapter Four

ଚ୬

*H*annah glanced about the crowded room with mild indifference. More than a hundred guests wandered about the library, parlors, and galley, the latter being the seaman's term for the dining room. Some of the residents, such as mariner Seamus Callahan, escorted interested guests on a tour of the upper floors of the building, where up to fifty seafaring men could find a safe harbor while in port. Showing potential donors how their money would help minister to the seamen was an indispensable tool in winning their support.

The reception began at seven o'clock and would be followed at eight-thirty by a program in the chapel. By seven-thirty, Hannah had met many wealthy Bostonians but, after the first few, had not troubled herself to remember names. After all, she would not be staying in the city for long, so making connections would be pointless. She would have Nan to visit with and from whom she could learn about Italy.

A few other people interested Hannah. Mrs. Monroe was a descendant of Boston's earliest settlers and one of that exclusive society's prominent members. Her presence lent significance to the occasion, for she could secure assistance for the mission from the Seaman's Aid Society. The Burns family's more recent ascent to wealth probably made them eager to succeed socially as well. Mr. Burns had informed Hannah of his skill in parlaying each business success into something even more profitable. He now owned a large mill where raw cotton from Southern states was woven into fabric that found an ever-expanding market locally, nationally, and even overseas. Hannah wondered if he hoped to enhance his social standing by being seen as a philanthropist. If that should benefit the mission, she could hardly criticize him.

She eyed the refreshments laid out on a side table. Everything looked delicious, and she longed to eat one of the spiced eel finger sandwiches, but her corset was too constricting. The dressmaker had praised Hannah's small waist and, clearly meaning to keep it that size, had given the corset lacings an extra tug. Hannah hoped she would be able to take some sandwiches back to her room to eat once her corset was off.

With a hungry sigh, she glanced around to find someone with whom to chat and spied Amanda Burns, a sweet-faced girl of sixteen, who was nestled in a corner. When introduced to Hannah, she had curtsied properly and murmured a polite greeting, but her eyes were downcast, and her lips wore a shy smile. Hannah had noticed several handsome young naval midshipmen who sought to converse with Amanda, but she chose solitude in the corner. Her gregarious parents, whose well-made clothes could not disguise their country background, did not force her to socialize.

"Miss Burns," Hannah said, "have you tried the eel sandwiches? They're delicious."

Amanda appeared surprised. "No, ma'am, I haven't tried them. I've never even heard of eating eels. Are they simply horrible?"

Hannah leaned forward and whispered, "No, it's quite tasty. My father's cook used to make eel dishes of every description. It's served everywhere in Boston. You may as well try it now and get used to it."

The girl eyed her skeptically but followed her to the table. With an encouraging nod from Hannah, she picked up one of the finger sandwiches and, after a moment of hesitation, bit into it. She winced at the tangy taste, then raised her eyebrows, gobbling down the bite with enthusiasm.

"It *is* delicious. Oh, how divine." She lifted another sandwich to her lips. "We never had these in Kentucky."

Hannah chuckled at the girl's affected accents. "I'm glad you like them. There are always new things to discover when you move to a new place. I hope …"

She stopped, seeing she had lost Amanda's attention. The girl's eyes had suddenly widened, and a smile had spread across her face. Hannah turned to find out what sight had changed her demeanor so quickly.

At the door, a naval officer stood talking with Kerry and Jeremiah. He was about as tall as Jeremiah, standing nearly six feet, and his broad shoulders were enhanced by the golden epaulets on his deep blue captain's uniform. His dark brown hair was stylishly parted in the middle, with short curls gracing the sides of his broad, tanned forehead. His face was lively and handsome, and his bright blue eyes sparkled with condescending good humor. His posture was nothing less than regal as he bent toward Kerry with a courtly bow, cocking his head in a charming manner and smiling splendidly. Everything about him exuded strength, confidence, and authority.

His stunning appearance sent a nearly forgotten feeling through Hannah, and her face grew warm. Suppressing the unexpected emotion as best she could, she forced her eyes back to Amanda and hoped her young companion had not noticed her struggle. But the girl had eyes only for the man.

"Do you …" To Hannah's chagrin, her voice squeaked when she started to speak. After quickly clearing her throat, she began again. "Do you know that gentleman?"

Amanda nodded with enthusiasm, causing her long ringlet curls to bounce down to her shoulders. "He's Captain Duncan Longwood of the United States Navy. He's a war hero. He's only thirty-four but a captain already. Oh, and he's almost royalty too. You can see it in the way he carries himself. Isn't he just splendid?"

Surprised at her previously demure companion's sudden loquaciousness, Hannah shot a quick glance back at the captain. Every part of her agreed with Amanda's assessment of him. "But we don't have royalty in this country." How breathless she sounded. Her corset's fault, of course.

"Oh, no, of course not," gushed Amanda. "But he's the grandson of some Earl of Sherwood ... Sheridan ... or something, in England. His mother was born with a title—*Lady* Elizabeth. She married Mr. Longwood during the War of 1812. He was an American, but he was descended from a duke or something. They ran away from London together, and their ship was almost sunk by a British frigate, and they settled on Mr. Longwood's plantation in Virginia, and she gave up her title to become plain Mrs. Longwood. Isn't that romantic?"

Hannah glanced again at the captain, who himself was gazing about the room. Standing next to Jeremiah, who wore an austere black suit, he made the handsome young preacher look almost plain in comparison. She seldom had seen men in military garb and was surprised at how the uniform enhanced the appearance of an already attractive gentleman.

"Hmm. Yes. Very romantic." Hannah pretended to scan the crowd, but her wandering gaze often paused on the object of their conversation. She also noticed that fifteen-year-old Elana Lazarus, who was supposed to be serving punch, was instead staring at the same man as she stood in the galley doorway. Then there was Mrs. Burns, a happily married woman, who also could not keep her eyes off him. Hannah choked back a giggle. The attention of every woman in the room was focused, whether blatantly, casually, or surreptitiously, on Captain Duncan Longwood.

We women are such silly creatures. This man probably found himself the center of ladies' attention wherever he went and was therefore undoubtedly the vainest of individuals. But if his appearance at the social would cast a good light on the mission and influence the men under his command to find shelter here, she could find no harm in his being admired. What did she care? After all, she thought, giving a little sniff for no one's benefit other than her own, she had been married to the most magnificent man she had ever seen, bar none, one who also had been greatly admired by men and women alike.

Amanda's audible sigh, followed by a strangled squeal, brought Hannah fully back to herself. She was no longer an impressionable eighteen-year-old, as she had been when she met Ahab. She was a grown woman, married—rather, a widow—and no longer given to girlish emotions. If this dear girl beside her was infatuated with the captain, she would humor her.

The captain had moved to the center of the room and was now chatting amiably with Mr. and Mrs. Burns. No wonder Amanda had squealed. The parents, or at least the mother, would certainly do all she could to connect him with their daughter, who was fast approaching the marriageable age. True to Hannah's inward prediction, it was not long before Mrs. Burns took his arm and steered him to the refreshment table.

"Now, Captain Longwood, do try these excellent sandwiches. A local delicacy, I'm told. Why, Amanda, I didn't see you here. Captain, you remember my daughter."

The paradigm of male perfection kept true to form. He stepped up to Amanda and took her hand, leaning forward with that courtly bow of his to set a proper kiss upon her fingertips. "Why, Miss Burns, how truly delightful to meet good friends here. And might I add, you are a vision of feminine pulchritude." His words rolled out like warm honey, with his soothing Southern inflections intoned in a rich and pleasing baritone.

As Amanda curtsied, she lifted her dark brown eyes to meet his, with all modesty but without the slightest display of shyness. "Captain Longwood, I'm so glad you came," she purred. "This mission is such a worthy cause, and it will certainly benefit from your patronage."

Hannah struggled to keep from laughing. Amanda had not been hiding in the corner at all. She and her mother had plotted the whole thing. Hannah could think of no reason to stay near. She certainly would not put herself forward to meet this person, no matter how attractive he was. She would withdraw into the crowded room and find Kerry or Nan, leaving mother and daughter to weave a web to catch their prey, and much happiness to them. But before she could move, Captain Longwood turned to her.

"Miss Burns, may I have the honor of meeting your friend?"

Amanda's face fell for only an instant before she brightened it with a smile. "Captain Longwood, may I present Mrs. Jacobs, an old, old friend of Reverend and Mrs. Harris? Mrs. Jacobs, this is Captain Longwood."

Hannah could not tell if the girl had deliberately broken etiquette with the faulty introduction or if she simply did not know that the gentleman should be presented to the lady first. "How do you do, Captain Longwood?"

"Mrs. Jacobs, this is truly an honor. I believe I met your husband over by the door. Congressman Jacobs?" The captain gazed at her with an expression that was everything proper in a Christian gentleman, but with what seemed more than casual interest. His blue eyes were intense, yet kind, and filled with sincerity.

"That must have been Congressman Jackson, Captain. My husband is deceased."

"Oh, I am so sorry. Please do forgive me. What a dreadful blunder." He looked stricken.

"Please don't blame yourself, sir. How could you have known?" Hannah wanted to kick herself. She should have worn a black dress, even an old one, so that everyone could see she was in mourning. She turned to Amanda, determined to join the conspiracy to snare the man for her. "Amanda was just telling me how delicious the finger sandwiches are."

Amanda beamed. "Yes, Captain. Do try one." She lifted a platter to him as if she were the person responsible for preparing the delicacy.

"Why, thank you, Miss Burns."

As he took a bite, Hannah gave a gentle nod to the group.

"Excuse me," she murmured. Before she turned away, she noticed the captain's eyebrows go up in surprise, but whether it was from her sudden departure or the spicy taste of the sandwich, she could not tell. Had she been rude? She hoped not, but it was too late to go back. She would find someone else to visit with until the meeting in the chapel.

When she saw Captain Lazarus and Nan in cozy conversation on the great parlor window seat, a strange feeling tugged at her heart. Romance seemed to be all around her. Though time was beginning to ease the sting of losing Ahab, she missed the intimate conversations they had before he was wounded, before he changed. As she started to turn, Captain Lazarus looked up and saw her. He quickly stood and motioned to her, taking a step in her direction.

"Please join us. You and Mrs. Childers must tell me about your childhood mischief." He took her arm and gently settled her on the window seat between himself and their mutual friend.

Hannah smiled at Nan, but she also searched her face to see if his gallantry to another woman had created a problem for her. To the contrary, Nan seemed as pleased as Lazarus to have her company. She put her arm around Hannah's waist like the old school chum that she was.

"What do you think, Hannah? Should we confess our sins to this fine Christian gentleman? Won't he be scandalized?"

The warmth of their greetings set Hannah at ease. Seeing Nan's merry face, she felt the years melt away and was grateful to be in this place, with these friends. If she must forever be bereft of the intimate companionship of her husband, she would enjoy this generous fellowship.

"I have nothing to confess. But you, I seem to recall, were always leading someone astray."

Nan laughed. "Whose idea was it to skip church, hire a horse and carriage, and go sight-seeing all over Boston?"

"Hmm. I don't remember that. It must be someone else you're thinking of. I was always a model of decorum."

"Ha. I can see you now, on our picnic blanket in the Old Granary burying ground. You sat beside Paul Revere's tabletop tomb, complimenting the old patriot for his dashing courage in helping Sam Prescott and William Dawes to raise the alarm about the arrival on our shores of the British troops. Then you insisted that we go to the docks and—"

"You have your stories muddled," Hannah broke in. "It was you who praised Mr. Revere. I preferred to address John Hancock's grave and thank him for secretly helping to finance the revolution. His actions took courage too. And it certainly was you who wanted to go to the docks, for I was not permitted near the water, and I never, ever disobeyed my superiors."

Lazarus, who had been chuckling at their exchange, now broke into laughter. "I do believe you've been tricked into a confession, Mrs. Jacobs."

She laughed with him. "But I still maintain that Nan was the instigator. She was outlandishly bold with all her great ideas and schemes. I only went along when it pleased me."

"Hmm." Nan gave Lazarus a meaningful look. "That's not always a bad thing in a friendship."

"No, indeed," he said.

Hannah glanced from one to the other. A private joke, she assumed. No matter. Their entire demeanor bespoke her inclusion in their conversation.

A shadow fell across the group, calling all their attention to the naval officer who stood before them.

"I do beg your pardon, Mrs. Jacobs," said Captain Longwood. "I hope my grievous error was not the cause of your departure a while ago."

Hannah stared up at him, her face growing warm. "Oh, no, sir. Please set your mind at ease."

Lazarus stood to greet the newcomer, and Hannah made introductions. "Won't you join us, sir?" Lazarus shook hands with the other man and then pulled up a recently vacated wooden chair.

"Thank you, sir." Longwood sat down, adjusting the ceremonial sword at his waist so as not to pose a hazard to anyone. "May I ask, Captain Lazarus, if you are retired from the United States Navy or if your service was in the United States Army?"

Lazarus smiled blandly. "No, sir. I was a whaling captain out of New Bedford for some fourteen years."

"Ah. I see." Longwood paused and lifted his eyebrows almost imperceptibly, seeming to search for an appropriate comment. "Then we have you to thank for the fine oil lamps that make an evening like this possible without the smoke that tallow candles inflict upon us."

Lazarus gave a slight bow, and Hannah could see his lips draw into a thin line.

She must defend Ahab's profession, a profession that this charming naval officer seemed to think so little of, his praise of oil lamps notwithstanding. "My h …" she began.

"Captain Longwood," said Nan at the same time. "How good of you to support this mission. Tell me, do you have much trouble with your sailors getting into mischief when they come on shore?"

"I'm afraid so, even though it is my custom to exhort them sternly before they are permitted to leave the ship. But we officers can only do so much. We give admonitions and try to set a Christian example, but the men have their own free wills. Unfortunately, many prefer the temporary pleasures of sin over the eternal rewards of righteous living. More often than not, they return to the ship with no money to send to their families due to gambling, and much the worse for wear due to their drunkenness. Some are even beaten and robbed." He paused, frowning. "Forgive me, ladies. I should not mention such things."

"But we know these things happen. That's why we are here," Hannah said. "Jeremiah's mission provides a safe harbor for those who will seek it. I do hope everyone will give generously."

Lazarus glanced across the room. "It appears we will soon have an opportunity to do so. Reverend Harris is indicating it's time to go next door to the chapel so he can address the assembly about the financial needs of the mission."

"It's about time," said Nan.

"Mrs. Jacobs," said Longwood, "before we go, may I be so bold as to request that I might come calling on you?"

Hannah felt a sudden dizziness, but whether it was from her corset, her hunger, or the presence of this overwhelming man, she did not know. Nor did she know which surprised her more, his unexpected request or her own breathless response.

"Captain Longwood, I would be delighted."

Chapter Five

౸

Something cold and wet touched Hannah's nose, and a soft, purring mass brushed her cheek and settled against her shoulder. Hannah could hear her son's breathing close by, and she knew he was kneeling beside her bed, staring at her face in the dim morning light, and willing her to wake up.

"Good morning, Jemima." She stroked the kitten, now bathed and well fed. "What mischief have you and Master Timothy got into so early in the morning?" She smiled lazily and reached out to give her son a hug. "Good morning, my darling."

He hugged back and grinned at her. "May I go help Paolo and Estevam with their chores?"

"Isn't it a little early? You haven't eaten breakfast yet, have you?" She turned toward her two large windows. Around the edges of the dark drapes, slender cords of light sought entrance. She had slept long and well.

"Breakfast was a long time ago. Can I go?"

She caressed his cheek and tousled his hair before sitting up on the side of the bed. She felt mellow this morning, and no maternal instinct warned against giving him permission. "All right. You *may* go. But do not, *do not* leave the mission property, even if Paolo and Estevam do."

"Thank you, Mother." Still grinning, Timothy jumped up and ran to the door, then hurried back to plant a kiss on her cheek and endure another maternal embrace. "Will you take care of Jem? The big cats outside pick on her."

Hannah glanced down at the kitten now fast asleep on her pillow. "Yes, she may stay here. Go have fun with your chores."

He slammed the door a little too hard on the way out but poked his head back in for a split second to say, "Sorry," before slamming it too hard again. Hannah laughed as she heard him running down the hall and then the staircase.

She went to the washstand, where a pitcher of lukewarm water waited, and began her morning ablutions. Then she tied back the blue velvet drapes with their silver cords, unlatched and pushed opened the window, and took in a deep breath of sea-blown air only a little tainted by city and harbor smells. The day was beautiful, not too far spent, and it seemed to stretch out before her with many lovely possibilities.

Happiness. How long had it been since she felt it, truly felt it? She hardly recognized the feeling or understood why it now welled up inside her. The social, of course. All the right people had come, making it a success.

All the right people indeed, she thought as she began dressing. For too many years, she had been disconnected from her childhood, and reuniting with Nan had restored something of the long-ago girl she used to be. What dreams and schemes the two of them had concocted together. Somehow, despite being girls, they had decided they would find great adventures in life, just as all the young men in their social circles had been doing.

Yet both she and Nan had married at eighteen, swept away by attractive older men of the world who had captured their hearts. Now they were both widows and both wealthy. What was to stop them from taking up the adventure? Maybe she would be able to convince Nan to join her European tour. The idea was enough to make even a dreary day seem beautiful. How much more exciting it seemed on a bright, carefree day like this one, which by its very nature suggested one should embark on some sort of adventure.

Not only was Nan as pretty as she had been at fourteen, she seemed as healthy and every bit as energetic. She would be able to endure the rigors of travel with no difficulty. Captain Lazarus had suggested Hannah consider traveling with others. Perhaps she and Nan could form a group.

The thought of Captain Lazarus brought Hannah up short. Throughout the entire evening, she had not been able to comprehend why it had bothered her to see Nan and the captain together. She had no claim on Lazarus. True, she had enjoyed his company and would like to spend more time with him, but that was yet another thing she did not understand. And then there was the effect Captain Longwood had on her. What foolishness. Why were these men affecting her this way? These silly, girlish reactions must stop.

It did not help that both Cousin Willa and Kerry had tried to convince her it was not too soon to consider another marriage. Nor had it helped to see her cousins and her friends enjoying the sweet harmonies of wedded bliss. Even Mr. and Mrs. Burns, whatever social faults they might have, seemed to enjoy the intimate exchanges only happily married couples know. She had seen it in the way they leaned toward one another as they spoke, and the way their eyes revealed bonded spirits even across a crowded room. But she must not let that affect her. She had a son to raise and a world to see. Another hasty marriage, no matter how grand the love that compelled it, would only prevent the realization of her lifelong dreams.

She had finished dressing and was brushing her hair when a soft knock interrupted her thoughts.

"Hannah, are you awake?" Kerry called.

"Come in. I'm just fussing with my hair."

"Good morning, dear." Kerry breezed in, shooed away Jemima, and picked up the scattered bedcovers to spread on the bed.

"Oh, Kerry, don't do that."

"I don't mind. I like to keep busy."

"Then let me help." Hannah hurried over to the bed. "How are you this morning? You seem a little tired."

Kerry placed a hand at her waist. "It's to be expected. I'll feel better soon. Don't worry about me."

"How can I not?"

Kerry gave her a knowing look. "The same way I keep from it. Besides, what good does worry ever do? But I didn't come up just to wake you. You have a guest."

"A guest? I had no idea he would come this early in the morning, or even today. Oh, dear." She sat at the dressing table, distressed by her bland appearance.

"Shall I take your regrets?"

"No. Just give me a minute. I'll be down."

"All right." Kerry wore a smile as she left the room.

Hannah stared once more into the mirror, trying to still her hammering heart. No use denying it. Captain Longwood's attentions delighted her. But would he be as interested after seeing her today, dressed in these widow's weeds rather than the more flattering green gown she had worn last night? Wondering did no good because she had nothing brighter to wear. But then, if seeing her this way cooled his interest, she would not change to please him. She had changed far too much for Ahab, to no avail. Yet, after last night, she saw no harm in ordering at least one green day dress from Florence.

Descending the stairs, she heard a familiar masculine voice coming from the great parlor, one lacking Longwood's genteel Southern accents. Without the slightest twinge of disappointment, she realized Captain Lazarus had come to call. Then, as she entered the room, two guests stood to greet her.

"Nan, Captain Lazarus, how good of you both to call. Please sit down."

After pleasant greetings and inquiries about each other's health, they sat in a grouping of furniture beside the unlit fireplace. Lazarus leaned back on the long divan and stretched his long legs out in front of him, as one would in the home of an old friend. Nan, true to her character, sat on the edge of her seat, indicating she was as anxious as Hannah to erase the years since they had seen each other.

"I have plans for you," said Nan. "You are not going to Europe—at least not yet."

"What?" Hannah stared at her, then at Lazarus, who shrugged and shook his head.

"Listen to me, dear," Nan said. "You have no business taking your child, whom I have yet to meet, I might add, and going off to you-don't-even-know where, with all that rampant influenza and who-knows-what-else abroad these days. First, you need to settle down in a home of your own, one right here in Boston where you have friends who love you, and I have just the place for you."

"I know you mean well, but why purchase a home and then be gone from it for at least a year? I won't even have time to make it a true home before leaving."

"But that's just the thing. You won't buy it; you'll lease it from me. Later, when you make your trip, the current staff will be perfectly capable of keeping it up."

"Oh, Nan." Hannah turned to Lazarus. "Was this your idea?"

He chuckled. "Mrs. Jacobs, when did our Mrs. Childers need anyone else to give her ideas?"

Hannah nodded ruefully. "How true. Oh, Nan, I'm not certain Boston is the place to raise Timothy."

"And not Indiana, and not Nantucket, and not New Bedford." Nan stood and came to a chair nearer Hannah. "What place on earth will be good enough or safe enough for your son?"

"Nan—" Hannah said.

"Mrs. Childers—" Lazarus said.

Nan shrugged. "You know I've never been one to hold back the truth."

Hannah squeezed her hand. "I appreciate your concern more than words can express. And I have an idea. You consider going to Europe with me, and I will consider leasing your house."

"Me? Go to Europe with you?"

"Yes. Don't you think it would be grand? We could revive all our girlhood dreams and visit all the historical places we read about in school."

"When you put it that way ..." Nan cocked her head and gazed into space. "Oh, *wouldn't* that be grand?" Then she sighed. "Unfortunately, I couldn't be gone for a year." She glanced at Lazarus, then at Hannah. "No. I couldn't possibly be gone for a year."

"But what keeps you here?"

"I have work to do here—things no one else can attend to."

"Work? But I thought your husband ... oh, forgive me, that's not ..."

"No, that's all right. Yes, Mr. Childers *and* my parents left me well cared for. The work I do is charitable."

"You mean like helping with the mission."

"That, and other things that cannot be taken care of by anyone else."

"I see." Hannah decided not to pry.

"Which is not to say I won't ever go anywhere again. Oh, dear, you certainly have stirred me up about traveling." She frowned, then brightened again. "But for now, why don't you postpone your trip. Lease my house, and we'll think about the tour of Europe for the future."

"I don't think so. I want to go soon. This June. That's a good time for sailing across the Atlantic, or so I'm told. Isn't that true, Captain?"

Lazarus sat up, clearly pleased to be invited into the conversation.

"For the most part, it is, although that's when the season of hurricanes begins. But then, sailing is always unpredictable. If one must sail, June is as good as any other time."

"Lazarus, you are such a coward," Nan said with a laugh. "You've cleverly refused to take sides in this discussion despite the fact that you don't want Hannah to travel right now any more than I do."

How could Nan talk that way to her suitor? But then, perhaps the captain was not pursuing Nan. And how strange that the speculation pleased Hannah. Perhaps it was time to divert the conversation.

"Have either of you been to the mission this morning?"

"All right, go ahead and change the subject." Nan was still laughing. "I'll not rest until you've postponed your trip."

"I stopped by early this morning," Lazarus said. "Why?"

"I was just wondering if anyone made donations last night after I left," Hannah said. "Wasn't it just like Jeremiah not to take up a collection? Most other preachers would have pleaded for cash on the spot, or at least wrung out a written pledge of future donations from each person. How can he expect to support the mission if he does not strike while the iron is hot?"

"But he just left it to each person's conscience to donate to the mission as they are led by God," Nan said. "Most of those who attended are good-hearted Christians with plenty of money. They'll do what's right."

Hannah studied her, nonplussed. In their younger years, Nan had questioned her family's spiritual beliefs even more than Hannah, but what did she think now? And what other surprises would her old friend come up with?

"I believe Mrs. Childers is right," Lazarus said. "One must think of the benefactor as well as the beneficiary. It does the unwilling soul no good to give a generous gift. Rather, it can cause great resentment against religion." He stared at Nan meaningfully. "Any good work must come from a willing heart."

Nan glared at him with annoyance but then softened her expression. "You are right, of course."

Once again, a knowing look had passed between the two that Hannah did not understand. Sitting with them during the service the night before, she had noticed several of those traded looks punctuating Jeremiah's message, but she had not been able to decipher them. Of course, her full attention was not on what the minister was saying. At the time, she could only notice that despite Captain Longwood's interest in her, he sat with the Burns family.

"Excuse me, Mrs. Jacobs." The housemaid appeared in the parlor doorway.

"Yes, Dorice."

"You have another visitor, ma'am, a Captain Longwood. Shall I show him to the small parlor?"

Hannah's heart seemed to jump to her throat. "Oh, no. Please show him in here."

"Hmm." Nan stood and gathered her reticule and parasol. "Since I don't have the patience for …" She gave her head a little shake. "I mean, I suppose I had better be going. Lazarus, will you come along?"

He stood slowly, his expression bland. Before he could respond, Hannah said, "Please don't go. Both of you stay."

"I truly must go, Hannah, but I'll come back next week some time." Nan gave her a quick embrace, then sailed out the door, tossing "Good morning, Captain Longwood" over her shoulder as she swept past the new visitor.

"Captain Longwood, how nice to see you." Hannah lifted her hand, hurrying to make up for her friend's abrupt departure.

"Mrs. Jacobs, I am honored that you have agreed to receive me. And may I say, you look lovely this morning." Longwood took the offered hand and bent forward with a courtly bow.

"Please sit down. As you can see, Captain Lazarus and Mrs.

Childers have been gracious enough to visit me this morning as well."

Longwood now noticed Lazarus and stepped across the room to shake his hand. "Ah, good morning, sir. And how are all the whale ships today?"

"Good morning, Captain Longwood." Lazarus sat back down on the divan and leaned back as if he were at home, while Longwood regarded him with raised eyebrows.

Hannah took her seat between the two men, and then wished she had sat across from them. This arrangement could become very awkward if she turned her gaze from one to the other and back again. And she must ignore the girlish thrill that surged through her. All this masculine attention must not cause her to act like young Amanda. Rather, she must smooth the social waters before the conversational ship sailed into choppy seas.

"Captain Longwood, perhaps you did not know that Captain Lazarus is no longer in whaling. He now owns a shipbuilding and import business here in Boston. In fact, he imports cotton from our Southern states, perhaps from your very own Virginia."

"Indeed? Then you've given up the sea, sir?"

"No, sir." Lazarus's tone was bland. "I sail one of my ships down to Norfolk several times a year. I like to be closely involved in all segments of my business."

"Ah, an excellent practice, one which I myself observe when my service to our country permits."

"Yes, you mentioned last night that your family owns a plantation near Richmond. Do you grow cotton?"

"We do have some cotton acreage, but tobacco is our main crop."

"Interesting. I suppose you keep many workers employed in your fields."

A slight frown crossed Longwood's handsome brow. "I am sure you know who works our fields, Captain Lazarus. Our people have been with my family for many generations, and they are very well cared for. In fact, we consider them family."

"Hmm."

The room was silent for several moments. Hannah had no idea what to say. An attractive man sat on each side of her, and she dreaded slighting either. A queasy feeling stirred in her stomach, and she realized with dismay that not only had she missed breakfast, but she had not remembered to bring back sandwiches the night before. If she did not appear pallid, she certainly was beginning to feel it.

"Mrs. Jacobs, I won't take more of your time this morning," said Longwood. "I came by to ask if I might have the honor of escorting you to the Boston Museum on Tremont Street near Boston Common on Monday afternoon. There is a display of Egyptian artifacts that is said to be exceptional."

"Ah, I do like Egyptian artifacts. I would love to go."

"Then Monday at one o'clock. I shall bring a covered buggy to carry you there so the sun will not strike your delicate complexion. Will that be acceptable?"

"Certainly. Thank you."

"I'll take my leave of your charming company until then." He stood and took her hand, kissing it once more. Turning to Lazarus, he nodded shortly. "Good day, sir."

Lazarus stood. "Good day."

After Hannah had seen Longwood to the door, she returned to the parlor to find Lazarus standing at the front window.

"My goodness, it's been a busy morning."

"Hannah … forgive me, Mrs. Jacobs …"

She came to the window. "We are old friends. You may call me Hannah. And, if I may, I will call you David."

"Yes, please do." He turned to her, sorrow written in his eyes. "Hannah, you realize, do you not, that your Captain Longwood holds his workers in unpaid bondage?"

"Unpaid bondage? I don't understand."

"Slavery, Hannah. He keeps his workers in slavery."

Now his stare bored into her, and his tone demanded a response. She felt her face grow warm.

"Of course he has slaves. All Southern planters have slaves. How else could they produce the crops you import? But you heard him. They treat their slaves like family. They provide food, clothing, and shelter in exchange for work. What's wrong with that?"

Lazarus relaxed his posture, and his face softened. "It sounds simple, doesn't it? Perhaps you've never considered what an evil institution slavery is."

His gentle tone encouraged her to be honest with both him and herself. She turned away and sat down on the divan. "No, you're right. I've never thought much about it. I'm not even certain I've ever seen a slave, although many free Negroes live in New Bedford, and one often sees Negro whalers in Nantucket. Ahab shipped more than a few dark-skinned whalers on the *Pequod*. But slaves? No. In fact, Nantucket has never permitted slavery, even long before it ceased to be legal in the rest of Massachusetts. The Society of Friends would never permit it."

Lazarus sat down beside her. "A worthy viewpoint, don't you agree?"

She looked up into his kind gray eyes. "I never thought much about it."

"But you must think of it. Would you enslave another person? Would you beat that person if he didn't please you? Would you keep him in shackles or sell him if it were no longer profitable to keep him? Would you sell a wife away from her husband, a child away from his mother?"

"Stop," she cried. "Who would do such things?" She turned away, disturbed by the images his words brought to her mind.

"Your Captain Longwood is a slave owner. If he has not directly done those things, someone in his family did at some time in the past. Someone ripped *his* people *or* their parents *or* their grand-parents away from their homes in Africa and shipped them to this continent and sold them as slaves. And someone bought them. Bought another human being. Even if Longwood inherited this 'family' of his, he perpetuates the evil."

She turned back to him, glaring. "I will not believe Captain Longwood is evil. He cannot help what his family has done."

"But he perpetuates it. Otherwise, he would free his slaves and pay them for their work. That is, if they chose to stay with him because they also consider *him* family."

"I believe you are being too hard on Captain Longwood. He is serving our country. He's a respected naval captain. I believe he is a good man, a Christian man, just as you are."

"Christians can be mistaken. Many Southern ministers justify the continuation of slavery by citing the practice of it in the Bible. They appease their wealthy parishioners to keep their Southern economy solvent."

"I don't think you're being fair."

With a sigh, Lazarus stood. "I won't trouble you with this anymore. At least, not today. But I will ask you to think about what I've said."

Hannah stood up and rested a hand on his arm. "You're a good friend, David. I will think about it."

Yet after she saw him out, she thought of a contradiction between David's words and his actions: he condemned slavery but he, too, helped perpetuate it by doing business with slave owners.

Chapter Six

෪

Timothy's dark eyes sparkled with interest as he studied Captain Longwood's elegant uniform. Hannah could see that her son was trying to keep from touching the shiny saber at the captain's side. When he had answered her summons to come meet a new friend, he had dashed into the great parlor as though chasing his cousin into the Indiana barn. But he had quickly recalled his manners when he saw the captain.

Hannah glowed with maternal pride to see Timothy act according to his height instead of his age. People expected him to be a responsible nine-year-old rather than the playful six-year-old he was, yet instinctively he always seemed to meet the challenge. Despite Lazarus's cautions about Longwood, she was proud to present her son to this man who showed such interest in her. If the captain passed the test of accepting her son, and the son accepted him, she could receive the captain's attentions without reservation.

"How do you do, Master Timothy?" Longwood stood and reached out to shake the boy's hand.

Timothy stood straight and offered a crooked smile. "I am well, thank you, sir."

Hannah could see he was pleased to be greeted with a handshake instead of hair tousling.

The captain sat down to be at eye level with the boy. "Did you attend Sabbath school yesterday morning, my fine young man?"

Hannah suppressed her annoyance. Christian gentlemen always asked children that question, perhaps because they lacked knowledge of children's interests. Still, she should appreciate Longwood's concern for her son's spiritual education. *David is wrong. This is a good man.*

"Yes, sir, I attended Aunt Kerry's class."

"Do you recall the text of your lesson?"

A shadow blinked across Timothy's dark Ahab brow, but he stared steadfastly into the captain's eyes. "'Choose you this day whom you will serve ... but as for me and my house, we will serve the Lord.' Joshua twenty-four fifteen. There's more words in the middle of the verse, but that's the part Aunt Kerry wanted us to learn."

"Very nicely done, Master Timothy. Mrs. Jacobs, you are to be commended for raising such a fine boy."

"Thank you, Captain. He never disappoints me. Timothy, do you recall Saturday when I told you Captain Longwood invited me to visit the museum this afternoon?"

"Yes, Mother."

"Do I still have your permission to go?"

He nodded cheerfully. "Yes, ma'am."

"You're sure you don't want to go too?"

He wrinkled his nose and shook his head. "I'd rather stay and help Estevam and Paolo with their chores."

She brushed a kiss on his cheek. "Then run along and help them."

He spun around and ran toward the door, then stopped and spun back to face the two adults. "Sorry." He ran back to the captain and grabbed his hand to shake it. "I was very pleased to meet you, sir."

With pursed lips and twinkling eyes, Longwood nodded. "It was my honor, Master Timothy."

As the boy once again raced from the room, Longwood turned to Hannah, chuckling. "My, what a fine boy. You must be very proud of him."

"Yes, extremely proud."

"And he would rather do chores than go on an outing? Astonishing."

"I think his little friends convinced him that museums are boring. And the chores are more like games. Mr. Lazarus is teaching the boys how to work with wood—carpentry and that sort of thing."

"Mr. Lazarus? Do you speak of that, eh, your friend, the whaling captain?"

"No, his brother. He works for the mission."

"Hmm. Woodworking could prove very useful to the boy in the future. But I declare, he does not favor you at all. Does he get those dark, handsome features from his father?"

"Yes. He has resembled my late husband from the day he was born, not only in his features, but also in his unusual height. My husband was a very tall man." For some reason, despite a strong urge to tell him that Ahab had been a whaler, she could not form the words. She had long known of the universal disdain other mariners felt for whaling men. But to begin such a discussion might lead to giving away far more information than he needed to know, and the very child they were discussing might suffer because of it.

Abruptly, Longwood became serious. "Mrs. Jacobs, I do not wish to be rude, but I would protect you from any potential scandal." His piercing blue eyes locked intently on hers.

"Scandal? What could you possibly mean?"

"I do not wish to be insensitive to your feelings, but seeing you are wearing widow's weeds, may I ask how long your husband has been deceased?"

"I'm sorry, Captain. Perhaps when you came calling on Saturday and saw me in mourning clothes, you should not have asked me to the museum."

"Dear lady, please forgive me if my question was rude. I only mean to protect you. In the circles in which I was reared, widowed ladies do not hasten to resume social activities until at least a year after their husbands have died lest a scandal be attached to them." He shook his head and brushed his hand across his clean-shaven jaw. "I fear I am not doing this well at all."

Hannah stifled a laugh. This moment of embarrassed confusion made him all the more charming. "Don't be concerned, sir."

"But don't you see? It is all my wrongdoing, a grievous error. I should never have given in to my impulse to seek your company on Friday evening until I had inquired ... that is to say, I found my desire to meet you wholeheartedly irresistible."

"How flattering."

He chuckled contritely. "It was not intended as idle flattery, I assure you, madam. When I entered Grace Seaman's Mission and saw you across the room, I was overwhelmed by your beauty."

Heat began to rise in her cheeks.

"I am not an impulsive man. A naval officer must be disciplined to the highest degree. So let me quickly assure you that when I saw you, I was not drawn to you by some indelicate passion stirred by your outward appearance—which was the epitome of modesty, I might add. Rather, my heart felt as if it had been struck by lightning—as if some voice thundered within me that you are all that is excellent in a woman. I felt compelled to meet you by whatever means I could, and having met you, I was not the slightest disappointed in the nature of your character. And now I see that your sweet humility only proves you to be all the more beautiful, both within and without. Ah, but if it is too soon to call on you, I shall retire until a more appropriate time. And I will pray that no other suitor will begin to court you in an untimely manner."

Hannah drew in a deep breath. Captain Longwood's fervor was nearly overwhelming, but his lovely words, poured out on the honey of his Southern drawl, rang with sincerity. As a young girl, she had been courted by many young men whose extravagant flattery annoyed her. As a young woman, she had fallen quickly, deeply in love with the magnificent Captain Ahab, who never flattered her at all. Yet now, Captain Longwood's compliments certainly stirred her.

She looked down at her gloved hands. Her wedding ring made a ridge in the black doeskin glove on her left hand. Tonight she would remove the ring and tuck it away with her other few mementos of Ahab, perhaps someday to give to Timothy for his bride.

"My husband died some seventeen months ago, Captain. I believe that even in Boston, no one will frown upon our attending a display in the museum."

Longwood expelled a great sigh of relief. "Thank you, dear lady. And I shall promise to cool my ardor so as not to overwhelm you."

Too late for that, she thought. "Then shall we go?"

The Boston Museum's first-floor exhibition of Egyptian artifacts consisted of a variety of items from hieroglyphic tablets to painted pottery to one mummy, whose desiccated body and startling death-grin caused Hannah to turn quickly away. Captain Longwood gripped her elbow and moved between her and the glass display case. He glanced back at the mummy and grimaced. "Forgive me. I'm certain this must assault your delicate sensibilities. I should not have brought you here."

Hannah laughed lightly. "Oh, not at all. I'm truly not all that squeamish. But I could not help but think how sad it is for the person who once inhabited that body, now exposed for anyone to gawk at."

"Ah, yes, I see what you mean. What a thoughtful observation. I agree, one dislikes to think of one's own bones being on display like that. But here's something more interesting." He led her to a poster on the wall near the entrance. "There is a stringed quartet in concert in the theater upstairs. Hmm, it began at two, so they've only just begun. Shall we ascend and hear how well they execute Bach's challenging scores?"

"Oh, lovely. Let's do." Hannah did not have to pretend interest, for she enjoyed music. Perhaps, after their European tour, she and Timothy could take up piano or some other instrument.

They found seats at the back of the auditorium and settled in to listen. But, although the performance gave Hannah additional incentive for her musical aspirations, Longwood murmured his disappointment. He whispered that the violinist was too young or perhaps too thick-fingered for the intricacies of Bach's arduous runs, while the very thin, very long-legged cellist could not keep his instrument in place, thus marring his performance. In short time, despite Hannah's unspoken disagreement with Longwood's review, the captain suggested they seek other amusements. They left the theater, going out into the sunshine on Tremont Street.

"Have you visited the King's Chapel burying ground, Captain?" Hannah nodded toward the cemetery as they strolled past it. "When I was a Boston schoolgirl, I loved to read the tombstones of our Pilgrim ancestors who settled these shores and to imagine what their lives must have been like."

"I must admit," he said, "that such a pastime for a delicate young lady is rather shocking, but I do understand your interest in our ancestors. Their stories can be quite inspiring, can't they? And, of course you know we'll pass another historic burying ground on the other side of the street. Shall we cross?"

Hannah looped her arm through Longwood's and permitted him to lead her across the street. At the Tremont House, he stopped and suggested refreshments. In the hotel dining room, she declined one of the sumptuous desserts but accepted a cup of tea.

She glanced out the front window toward the large building across the street. "Tremont Temple. That's the church my friend Mrs. Childers attends."

Captain Longwood frowned. "Indeed? Why, I must say I'm appalled to hear of your friend's choice."

Hannah regarded him for a moment. "But why on earth? This is a prominent church here in Boston—"

"Have you not heard? Has your friend kept you in the dark about the nature of the congregation in that establishment?" His voice was filled with disdain, and his handsome face marred with a slight sneer. "Why, whites and free Negroes sit side by side for worship, as if they were equals. Can you imagine? It is unconscionable that the founders established this church for the very purpose of violating scriptural law."

Hannah stared at him, unwilling to make excuses for her child-hood friend. His revelation surprised her, but Nan was an adult and a widow. Why should she not choose a church to her own liking? As to his comment about scriptural law, she would have to ask Jeremiah if his assertion was correct.

Longwood shook his head and leaned toward her. "I know you're shocked, and I realize it will undoubtedly affect your friendship with her. But please do not let it spoil our day. There is so much more to see."

Relieved that she did not have to respond to his censure of Nan, Hannah made a benign comment about the weather being perfect for their outing. He returned with a comparison between the weather in Boston and in his home state of Virginia, recommending the fresh air of his plantation over city smells.

They walked past the Granary burying ground, each commenting briefly on the Revolutionary War patriots buried there. Since he had been shocked by her previous confession regarding burying grounds, Hannah wondered what he would think if she told him about her mischievous girlhood picnicking on John Hancock's tomb. But his serious and reverential demeanor toward the heroes warned her, he might not take it as lightly as some others.

They continued toward the nearby Common, where people hurried about with their daily business. For Hannah and the captain, the day seemed right for a pleasant stroll among the flowers that blossomed in the Public Gardens on the southwest end of the Common. When they stopped to enjoy the fragrant blooms, Hannah tilted her parasol and looked up at Longwood.

"Captain, it's my understanding that you will soon be involved in the current war with Mexico. But I have also heard there have been significant victories recently in that conflict. How is it that more people must be sent to fight?"

"We must ensure victory by reinforcing and refreshing our troops. In fact, when I received the assignment to my new warship, I had hoped to sail to Mexico immediately. But now I believe Providence has given me this extra time in Boston while the USS *Lanier Wingate* is being fitted for battle."

Hannah turned away from his intense gaze. "Then you do not know how long you will be here?"

"No, not precisely. My ship's preparation is a priority at the Charlestown Naval Yard, of course, for every warship is needed to assure an American victory. And the marines we will transport there are still in training.

"I shall be pleased to join the war, for it is my duty, but I will also regret leaving. We in military service struggle with divided hearts— love of country and love of homes and families. But homes and families must be protected by a strong military force, and I have chosen to be a part of that protection."

Hannah's heart surged with admiration. She ventured another glance his way. "Oh, how courageous of you, Captain. But then who manages the affairs of your plantation when you are away at war?"

His smile revealed his pleasure at her questioning.

"My father and older brother keep things well in hand as far as the crop production is concerned. And my mother manages the household much as her mother managed Sheridan Woods, the English estate where she was born."

So Amanda Burns had given an accurate history of the captain's family, though the young girl's description had been a little effusive. Still, despite the fact that the United States had no royalty, one still could say that Captain Longwood and his family were very like true, old-world aristocrats. Hannah wondered if he realized many would not consider her pedigree equal to his, but he seemed to have no such concern.

"Shall we stroll up the hill to the State House, dear lady?" Longwood indicated the great edifice across the Common. "There is a site you must see, or you have not seen Boston."

Soon they stood in Doric Hall on the second floor of the Massachusetts legislature's home, admiring various portraits and sculptures on display. Longwood touched Hannah's arm to draw her attention to a particular piece, a tall, white marble statue by Sir Frances Chantrey.

"George Washington." Longwood gestured broadly, and admiration beamed from his face. "Now you must agree he was a truly great man. Even before he was our first and greatest president, it was his military leadership that made it possible for our troops to outfight the French, and then the British. Why, without him, Mrs. Jacobs, this country could not have come into existence. Other than my own father, who was not a military man, there is no one I admire more."

Hannah stared up at the life-sized statue, whose proportions seemed even greater because it stood on a six-foot granite base, accentuating the greatness of the man it represented. She turned back to her companion.

"What drew you to the military, Captain, and why the sea? Was there someone in your family who served in the navy before you?"

"None that I know of. At least not in the Virginia branch of the family, though my English relations have distinguished themselves in many ways throughout the centuries. No, it's difficult to explain the lure of the sea that gripped me when I was a boy and my father took me on a grand tour of Europe. The sights were magnificent on the Continent, but it was the voyage there and back that inspired my love of the maritime life. I'm sure that to a fair lady like yourself, the prospect of climbing the rigging of a ship while it rolls about on the high seas must seem frightening, while I consider it the supreme adventure."

Hannah glared at him with mock indignation. "So you think that just because I am a woman, I should prefer tea parties and ordering new gowns." His amused, almost condescending shrug goaded her to continue. "That I would never wish to experience adventure. That I should be kept at home and protected and ..." She stopped, surprised at her own rising annoyance, which she saw had brought mild alarm to his expression.

"I'll have you to know I just returned from a trip out West with my son. We traveled to Indiana and back again, just the two of us, and I have every intention of taking *him* on a grand tour of Europe as soon as our travel plans can be completed."

"Ah, such a spirited reply. I would not have thought ... that is, when I saw you across the room the other evening, and again Saturday morning at the minister's parlor, there was such a fragile air about you. Even now, that quality inspires me to wish ... yes, to desire ... only to protect you. Dear lady, I can't imagine that you could withstand the rigors of either land or sea travel or that you could keep up with an active boy."

She looked away from his intense gaze to keep from giggling. Both prior times he had seen her, she had been so hungry she had felt close to fainting. No wonder he thought her to be in delicate health. "Dear Captain, I assure you, I am not the slightest bit fragile. If that is what attracted you to me, I fear your interest is misplaced."

He chuckled. "I must say, Mrs. Jacobs, you certainly do not respond as one of our Southern ladies would. And I hasten to say that I appreciate your straightforward manner. And now, as I regard your lovely complexion after our invigorating walk up the hill, I can see that your cheeks do seem to glow with health, and it is most attractive."

"I am in excellent health, and I shall walk up and down many a hill during my upcoming trip. It is my son who will have to hurry to keep up with me."

"Ah, I see you are determined. Well, then, I shall do nothing to prevent you and all I can to assist you in your plans."

"Indeed? You truly will not try to discourage me, as all my other friends have done?"

"Not at all, dear lady. Not at all. So high is my esteem for you that I would not see you deny yourself any pursuit that might delight you. Please tell me how I can be of service in making your dream come true."

"Thank you. I will let you know if I think of something." Once again, Hannah turned away from the intensity of his gaze, this time glancing up at the statue of Washington. "Do you wish to emulate our first president, Captain?"

Longwood stared up at the statue, his blue eyes sparkling with admiration for the man it represented. "Surveyor, plantation owner, patriot, military strategist, president—a true father of this country. Any man worth his salt should wish to emulate him. Any man who seeks to be a leader could find no better example to follow."

"I agree, and I'm so glad you suggested we visit here. I might never have been aware of it otherwise. But I do need to return to my son. My hostess has enough work on her hands without looking after him any longer."

"I regret to end our lovely afternoon, but I commend your diligence toward your maternal duties. Shall we go?" Longwood took her elbow and guided her toward the door. "If it is not too soon to ask, may I have the honor of calling on you tomorrow afternoon?"

Hannah glanced up at him as they passed through the doors of the State House into the fading sunshine of a late Monday afternoon. "I'm sorry, Captain. My son and I are to spend most of the day at the dressmaker's choosing designs for our traveling clothes."

"Ah. Then another time?"

"Yes, I would like that." Yes, she would like to see this fascinating man again, but she could not help but notice that, after spending an afternoon with him, she was not quite as overwhelmed as she had been earlier in the day. Perhaps now she would be able to discern her true feelings, rather than being swept away by his elegant manner and almost irresistible charm.

Chapter Seven

∞

*H*annah awoke early the next morning discomfited and cross. Once again, she had dreamed of Ahab, and now, as a new day dawned, she scolded herself for accepting the attentions of another man. She must not fall into the deep, dangerous well of love again. If she did, she feared she and Timothy would never reach Europe, despite Captain Longwood's promise to help with her travel plans. She would accept that help, but keep his attentions at arm's length.

After all, she barely knew him. She would not be in Boston for long, certainly not long enough for a proper courtship. And he would not be here long either. As soon as his ship and crew were prepared, he would be sent to the war in Mexico. That alone should be enough to cool her interest. Never again would she accept a long-distance marriage or such an engagement. Even if she were to find herself caring for someone, she would choose the time to come and go. And now was certainly the time to go.

While she washed and dressed, she redirected her thoughts toward her upcoming adventure, considerably cheering herself for a morning at the dressmaker's.

The extensive clothes fittings exhausted both Hannah and Timothy, but it also exhilarated Hannah. Not only did Florence convince her to order a modestly colorful, fashionable wardrobe, but she also demonstrated skill in designing children's clothes that made allowances for rapid growth. Hannah felt satisfied she and her son would be appropriately dressed for any occasion during their travels.

After dinner at noon, they both rested until Timothy roused Hannah and begged to go find his friends. With only a moment of hesitation, Hannah consented, reassuring herself that she would soon whisk him away from the Lazarus boys' influence. With growing excitement over their coming trip, Hannah rose from her nap and sought some task to help Kerry. Even with several servants, the Harris household could always use an extra pair of hands to keep things running smoothly.

The house seemed abnormally quiet with Ellen in the kitchen helping Dorice polish the silver, Cook out shopping for supper, and the girls still napping. Even Kerry was lying down for a longer than usual rest. The day was warm, and most of the windows had been opened to let the early May breezes cool the house. Outside, horses' hooves and carriage wheels clattered on the cobblestones, and in the distance, street vendors hawked their wares. None of the sounds was intrusive.

Hannah searched for something to put her hands to and found Kerry's mending basket in the small parlor. Every evening, the young housewife mended her family's clothing and socks before small tears could become larger. Unlike her, Hannah had let Ahab's wealth spoil her. For years, she had given torn clothes to charity. That is, until she had spent the long winter with her cousins. Willa soon restored her to more frugal practices, which Hannah herself had once followed in her father's house. In helping Kerry, she found that old skills quickly returned.

Amid stockings and shirts, the most pressing need was to secure loose buttons on the girls' frocks. Needle and thread in hand, she began to stitch, and her mind returned to travel plans. But before the calm solitude of the parlor gave rise to either dreams or dreads, Dorice appeared in the parlor doorway.

"Mrs. Jacobs, Mrs. Childers has come calling. May I show her in?"

"Good afternoon, Hannah. Sit still, dear, I'll just make myself comfortable." Nan had followed the housemaid into the parlor. "Dorice, be a good girl and bring us some coffee. Mrs. Jacobs and I have some things to discuss." She plopped herself down in the chair next to Hannah's, set her reticule and parasol on the coffee table, and drew up a small white stocking to mend from Kerry's basket. "Now, when can you move into my house in Louisburg Square?"

Hannah could not keep from laughing despite Nan's deliberate display of bad manners. How reminiscent of their boarding-school days when their doors were always open to each other, with no formalities needed before they got down to the business of sharing secrets and dreams.

"And may I counter? Have you ordered your traveling wardrobe yet? I ordered mine and my son's just this morning."

Nan laughed merrily and then sobered a little, reaching over to squeeze Hannah's hand. "My dear friend, it's as though these past thirteen years have simply melted away. You haven't changed, at least not in ways that matter most."

"And you are still *my* dear, spirited friend, always out for adventure. That's why I don't understand why you won't go with me. What charity could possibly hold you here? What work that only you can do?"

Nan regarded her for a moment, and then busied herself pulling a child's stocking over a white, glass, darning egg. She threaded a needle and began to stitch around a tiny hole in the stocking. "Did it ever occur to you how strange it seems that our Captain Lazarus was not scandalized by our confessions of childhood mischief?"

Hannah watched her. So it was true. They were courting.

"I suppose that in his travels he saw many far more scandalous things than two naughty schoolgirls putting crickets in the teacher's wardrobe or even skipping church for a lark." She thought for a moment. "My husband always told me the whaling life is not for the faint of heart."

"No, indeed, I would not imagine so." Nan looked up from her sewing, her expression thoughtful. "Tell me more about your dear husband, Hannah."

Hannah studied her mending. To her surprise, her eyes began to burn.

"Oh, dear, see what I've done," Nan said. "I'm so sorry. I thought perhaps it had been long enough …"

"No, it's all right. I would love to tell you about him." She pulled a lace-edged handkerchief from her sleeve and dabbed her eyes. With a sigh, she gazed out the parlor window. "He was the most magnificent man I have ever seen."

"More magnificent than that Captain Longwood?" Nan shot her a wicked grin.

"Oh, hush. You asked me about my husband, so let me answer. He was very tall, which of course was wonderful for me. So many of my suitors were just my height, or even shorter, and I did so want to marry someone tall. Someone to look up to, literally. Silly, wasn't it? But very characteristic of the romantic girl that I was. He had broad shoulders, dark, piercing eyes, and the blackest hair, not a trace of gray except for a bold white streak above his left eyebrow. And oh, how handsome his face, like a Greek statue. He wore a chin-curtain beard and no mustache, and there was a …" Hannah paused. How could she explain that the vicious scar etched from Ahab's forehead down to his chest had made him all the more attractive, as if it were a noble badge of courage from some horrific battle? Who could understand the way she felt about it? So she said, "He had a way of smiling that made me feel warm all over."

She glanced at Nan to see if she were scandalized. But her friend nodded, her eyes soft with understanding.

"Oh, yes, I know just what you mean. And, oh, how I do miss my dear Henry. It never mattered to me that he was so much older because he was so jolly and so good. But tell me more about Mr. Jacobs. What was his first name?"

"A ..." Hannah stopped. What was she doing? She must not let herself be lulled into confiding her awful secret, even to Nan.

"A?" Nan's face was a study of amused confusion. "What kind of name is that?"

"Amos."

"Oh, Amos. The same as your father."

Hannah nodded mutely. Now she had lied, and to her dear, old friend. How far was she going to take this? How far would she have to take it to protect Timothy? And with this bold-faced lie between Nan and her, how could she expect to travel with her or even enjoy the close friendship just starting to be rekindled?

"Now it's your turn. I want to hear all about Henry."

"Yes, Henry. Now there was a man for you. For me, I mean." Her grin became a tender smile. "Oh, my. I was so blessed to have such a good man to love me. To finish raising me when my own parents had spoiled me so. He wasn't tall like your Amos. He was short, just a couple of inches taller than I, not as tall as you. He had a sweet, round face, mutton-chop sideburns, and a pug nose. And the cutest little grin. He was just right for me. He was so patient with my headstrong ways. And what a deep thinker. Do you remember how you and I used to question everything our parents taught us? And everything we learned in church? Henry did not scold me or tell me I was a lost soul, as some would have done. He let me say everything I was thinking, and when I finished talking, he asked me wonderful questions to make me think some more."

Hannah nodded, recalling how Ahab had encouraged her to question what she was taught and to reach her own conclusions.

"And then, instead of preaching at me and telling me what he expected his wife to believe ..." Nan paused, her eyes shining at the memory. "He showed me God."

"What?"

Nan became wistful. "Sounds odd, doesn't it? But it is the only way I can describe his goodness to me. To everyone. He was so unselfish. Generous to a fault. No, not a fault. Just amazingly, sweetly generous. He helped me understand that, just as our Savior did not live or die for Himself, our purpose on this earth was not to live for our own pleasure but to live for others. So many people suffer great hardships in this world, and he said we, he and I, were given advantages so we could help them, not so we could sit idly by amusing ourselves. He had such a great heart, a heart that gave out just over two years ago while he was involved in a ... eh, a charitable work he had started, the charitable work I am continuing today. The work I so much want you to be a part of. Oh. I didn't mean to blurt that out."

Hannah was so struck by the cause of Henry's death that she barely noticed Nan's last few comments. He had died while helping others. No rage. No mad revenge against a mute beast. No dragging other men to their deaths. Just a weak but noble heart giving out in the midst of his good works.

"But weren't you ... weren't you angry at God for killing such a good man?"

Nan blinked with surprise. "I was angry about my loss, I suppose. But God did not kill Henry. He took him home. The man who was with him when he died said he had the most peaceful expression on his face. His last words were, 'Why, there You are, Lord. How good to see You at last.'"

Hannah dabbed her eyes with her handkerchief. "How wonderful."

"Yes. How kind our Lord is. I could not hope for a better last memory to have of Henry."

Bent over her sewing once more, Hannah struggled to control her thoughts. What different last memories they had of their loved ones. Yet Nan had not deliberately chosen what to tell her about Henry, and it was clear David Lazarus had not told Nan about Ahab. So why did Hannah compare the two men?

As she tried to think of some way to change the subject, sounds of scuffling and boyish voices raised in anger shattered the quiet house. She dumped her mending and dashed to the parlor doorway just in time to see Ellen trying to separate Timothy and Estevam.

"Quiet, you wicked boys. Mrs. Harris and the girls are still asleep."

Estevam quickly released the younger boy, and Timothy caught himself against the wall. Five-year-old Paolo stood near Ellen, a worried look on his sun-browned face.

"In here. Now." Hannah dragged her son into the parlor, then turned on him, hands on her hips. "What's the meaning of this?" She glanced beyond him at the Lazarus boys in the doorway. This would be the last time she permitted her son to play with them.

Timothy glared up at her, his fists at his side and his dark Ahab eyes defiant. He had never before defied her this way. Behind her, she heard Nan clear her throat, struggling not to laugh, and her anger grew. What could Nan possibly know of the difficulties of motherhood?

"Mrs. Jacobs," Estevam said, "it ain't Timothy's fault, but I had to help him out."

"No, you didn't," Timothy growled. "I coulda licked 'em. They deserved it."

"But they's street boys. Rapscallions. They ain't got no home, and they's mean as the devil. 'Scuse me, ma'am. I don't mean to swear." Estevam shrugged his shoulders apologetically, and Nan snickered again.

"What are you talking about?" Hannah demanded, and both boys tried to answer.

"They were killing cats," said Timothy, while Estevam asserted, "They can lick anybody and put 'em in bed for a month of Sundays."

Horror darted through Hannah. Had she almost lost her son to street ruffians? As she swayed with fear-induced dizziness, Nan came next to her and put a steadying arm around her waist.

"All right, now, boys, one at a time," Nan said. "Estevam, you're the oldest. You go first."

"Yes, ma'am." He stepped forward obediently and stood tall. Even in her shock, Hannah could see the honesty in his eyes. He looked much older than his nine years.

"There's these mean boys, older than us by a long shot. They like to do bad things to anybody or anything smaller. Most times, grownups on the street keep 'em from bullying little kids, but nobody cares about stray cats. These rascals, well, I won't tell you what they do, 'cause it's awful ugly."

"Just a minute, young man," Hannah said. "I have seen you throwing rocks at cats too."

"Yes, ma'am, I use to. But that was before Tim here told me and Pal not to. He told us about the farm animals he took care of out West and how we's responsible to take care of all critters and not be mean to 'em. We never thought about it, I reckon, 'cause the only animals we have around here is dogs and horses and them stray cats. What Tim said made sense." Estevam grinned. "I can tell ya, my ma and sisters liked hearing him say that."

"But that still doesn't explain why you and Timothy were fighting."

"When Tim here saw these street rascals tyin' something to a cat's tail, he jumped all over them. Lit into 'em like a wildcat and whupped one of 'em."

"I coulda licked 'em all too," Timothy muttered.

"No, you couldn'ta." Estevam's tone was paternal. "Those three big rascals coulda broke your head." He looked at Hannah. "So Pal and me dragged him home, fighting all the way." He jerked his head toward his brother, then stared down at his feet. "Sorry for the ruckus."

Hannah gave a great sigh of relief, which was mixed with a measure of remorse. She had badly misjudged these two boys. She sat and pulled her son close. "Thank you, Estevam. Thank you, Paolo." She brushed her son's dirty cheek and found a small patch of blood near his temple— just a scratch.

"Ow!" He pulled back as if she were killing him, but he was not badly hurt. He had survived numerous such scratches doing farm work.

"Are you boys all right?"

The two brothers traded looks and nodded. Then, to her chagrin, all three boys giggled.

"That was a good scrape," Timothy said. "Can I go now?"

Nan laughed, Ellen shook her head and glanced heavenward, and Hannah put her face in her hands with another sigh of relief. After a moment, she glared at her son.

"Go wash your face first, and ask Miss Ellen to put some ointment on that scratch."

"Yes, ma'am."

"And you stay away from those bad boys."

"Yes, ma'am."

"Go see if Mr. Lazarus needs some help."

"Yes, ma'am," the three boys chorused. As they ran from the room to obey her orders, she rose and followed them into the hallway. "Estevam."

He stopped and turned to her.

"Thank you."

His large, innocent eyes and boyish grin transformed him back into a nine-year-old.

"Yessum," he called over his shoulder as he ran to catch up with his playmates.

Returning to her mending, she could not keep from smiling even as she shuddered. "I do hope Timothy learned a lesson from that."

"What a beautiful son you have, Hannah." Nan's eyes shone with admiration.

"Oh, dear, I didn't even introduce you. Please forgive me."

Nan shook her head to dismiss the apology. "Of course. There were more important things going on." Then she sniffed, shook her head again, and focused on her sewing.

"What is it, dear?"

Nan glanced up at her. "My son would have been almost Estevam's age."

Hannah drew in a sharp breath. "Oh, my dear ..."

Again, Nan shook her head, this time shaking away her own sadness. "But he's with his father, so it's just fine." She thought for a moment and then added, "No, it's just fine. No matter what we may think, God never makes a mistake."

Hannah studied her friend's expression. She would ask no more questions now, but one day she would insist on knowing how Nan could accept her loss with such a peaceful spirit.

After Nan left, Hannah searched the house to see if Kerry had risen from her nap. She found Ellen in the kitchen feeding Daisy, while Cook doled out sweets to Lacy and Molly. The three little girls were quiet and mellow after a long nap.

"Is Mrs. Harris up yet?"

Ellen shook her head. "No, ma'am. She's not feeling too well this afternoon. I just sent Dorice over to the mission to tell Reverend Harris."

"Goodness. Do you think she's still sleeping, or would it be all right if I look in on her?"

"No, ma'am. She not sleeping, or at least she wasn't just a few minutes ago."

Ellen seemed as if she were trying to keep worry from her voice. Molly and Daisy were too young to be frightened by grownup talk, but Lacy now looked from one adult to another, her eyes wide. Hannah smiled at the three-year-old to reassure her.

"I'm sure she just needs a little extra rest. I'll check on her." Despite her words, Hannah was concerned. Kerry never stopped working, and in her delicate condition, it was beginning to wear her out.

She tapped lightly on the master-bedroom door and heard a faint response. Inside the large, darkened room, she blinked to adjust her eyes, crossed to the bed, and whispered, "Kerry, are you ill?"

Kerry tried to shake her head, but a look of pain darted across her face. "No. I'm all right. Just a little tired."

Hannah sat on the side of the bed and brushed damp strands of hair from Kerry's face. "No, you're not all right. You're burning with fever." She reached to the nightstand and poured water from a dainty pitcher into a small glass. "Here. You need to drink this. Can you sit up?"

Kerry struggled to lift herself but quickly dropped back, pressing both hands against her temples. "Oh … oh …"

"There, there. Don't overdo. Let me help you." Hannah set the glass down, gently scooped Kerry up against her own shoulder, and offered the water again. Kerry could only take a few sips. The heat from her body burned into Hannah like fire, but she was loath to lay her friend back down on the sweat-soaked sheets.

"We need to get you changed. Your gown is damp."

"No, I'm sure there's no need … Ah." Her hands once again pressed against her temples, and she began to shake.

"Oh, dear," Hannah cried, but then forced down her alarm. If she panicked, she could not help. "I'm going to lay you down for just a moment while I get Jeremiah." She covered her with two blankets and ran to the door just as Jeremiah entered.

"Kerry." His long legs took him to the bedside in two strides. "Darling, is your headache worse?" He sat beside her, touched her face, and felt the bed and pillow. "Dear Lord … my darling, you're soaked."

Hannah returned to the bedside. "We must change her. She had a chill just before you came in."

Kerry turned her eyes toward Jeremiah but seemed unable to focus. "Didst thou help Seamus?"

"Shh, don't be concerned, darling. Seamus is fine."

How like Kerry to fret about others, even in her own misery. Hannah hurried to the wardrobe for a fresh gown. Clean sheets would be needed as well, so she went to the hallway, where Dorice and Cook wrung their hands.

"Fresh bedding?" Hannah asked Dorice.

"I'll get it."

"Cool water and some clean cloths, please."

"Yes, ma'am." Cook hurried away to obey.

Hannah helped Dorice bring bedding from a hallway chest, and Cook returned with a pitcher of water and a basin. Back in the sick room, Hannah's heart ached to see the fear written on Jeremiah's face, but she once again squelched her own anxiety.

"Here, let's wrap this blanket around her, then you take her to the couch. Sit and hold her while we change the bed. Cook, please wring out a cloth for him to cool her."

Jeremiah did as Hannah instructed, holding his trembling wife and wiping her face while the women stripped the bed.

"Even the mattress is wet," Dorice said.

"Do you have any oilcloth?" Hannah asked.

"Oilcloth?" Jeremiah said.

"To put under the sheets to keep the mattress dry."

"Yes, ma'am, we have some," Cook said. "I'll fetch it."

"We'll turn the mattress," Hannah told Dorice. "Here, let's lift it from this side."

"Hannah, it's too heavy …" Jeremiah began.

"Nonsense." Hannah forced a bright tone into her voice. "We'll have it all fixed up in no time. Heave-ho, Dorice."

Dorice gave a little laugh, then quickly stifled it. Once the mattress was turned and fluffed, Hannah patted her on the shoulder. "Very good. You're a strong girl." Dorice beamed her appreciation.

With the bed prepared, Hannah sent Jeremiah outside the room while the women bathed Kerry. The cool water brought her fever down a little, and she was able to take in some liquid. Soon she was drifting off to sleep, her still-damp hair brushed back from her flushed face.

Cook and Dorice returned to their duties, but Hannah saw Jeremiah's reluctance to leave his wife. He had pulled a small chair beside the bed and now leaned across the pillow, caressing Kerry's brow.

"If you need to get back to the mission, I can stay with her."

His blue eyes glistened as he gazed at Kerry, and Hannah's heart went out to him.

Dear God, don't You see how he loves her? Please, please, I beg You, have mercy on these precious ones. Yet she feared by her very asking, the answer would be no.

"Go, Jeremiah." Hannah touched his shoulder. "I'll call you if we need anything."

He glanced up, as if surprised to see her standing there. As his eyes focused, he nodded. "Yes. All right." He caressed Kerry's brow again. "Do you think I should get the doctor?"

"That's a good idea. It's probably just a little fever, but it never hurts to get a doctor's opinion, especially because of her condition."

He kissed Kerry's cheek, then stood and faced Hannah. "I don't know what we would have done without you."

"Never mind. You just go get the doctor. I'll be here."

He glanced once more at Kerry and, with obvious reluctance, left the room.

Hannah sat in his abandoned chair and leaned over her sleeping friend. "I'll be here, dearest Kerry," she whispered. "I won't leave, not until you're well. I promise."

Chapter Eight

❧

The doctor had no specific diagnosis and so prescribed bed rest, broth, and a mild dose of laudanum to be given whenever Kerry's headaches were severe. She resisted all but the broth but was forced by both fever and headaches to submit to the other two. To Jeremiah's relief, Hannah repeated her promise to stay until Kerry could leave her sickbed. Except for Cook, the household servants were too young and inexperienced to be left without supervision, and Hannah had managed households with great skill since she was fourteen years old.

Each morning after breakfast, she assigned chores. Once the day's menus were decided, Cook needed no further instructions. Ellen helped where she could, though she had her hands full with three little girls who could not understand why they were forbidden to see their mother. Dorice proved her mettle by trying to keep the home's three floors clean. The housemaid also helped Hannah bathe the patient and freshen her bed. Even Timothy and his two friends were put to work hauling wood, sweeping the front and back porches, and running errands. When the boys finished their chores and ran off to play, Hannah's newfound trust in Estevam relieved her mind of worry for her son.

Everyone worked hard to keep the household running smoothly, but by Friday, everyone was exhausted, none more so than Jeremiah, who ministered at the mission by day and tended his wife at night.

"We must have help," Hannah told him while they rested in the parlor after supper. "You can't go on like this. None of us can."

He nodded his agreement. "You're right, of course. How I wish Charity lived closer. She always comes when Kerry has her ..." He colored a little and gave Hannah an apologetic glance.

"Her lying-in? How can you be embarrassed to say that to me? You were right with me when Timothy was born."

He smiled at the memory. "In the next room praying, while your beloved husband and that extraordinary Tishtega delivered ..." He cleared his throat. "Really, Hannah, we shouldn't discuss such things."

She laughed. "I must say this: you would never manage on the farm. How *ever* do you minister to salty seamen? Why, even the Bible discusses births, and far more than that."

He shook his head, but still smiled. "But aren't we more useful servants of God if we follow the manners of society and refrain from what is considered indelicate conversation?"

"Oh, yes. Being all things to all men." She waved her hand in annoyance. "But how silly not to talk about the realities of life."

Jeremiah sighed, closed his eyes, and laid his head against the back of his chair. "I've never won an argument with you, and I'm too tired to try now."

"Oh, dear. I've made you cross, and I am too. I suppose we're both wrung out. Do let me ask Nan to recommend someone to help."

He gave her a weary nod. "Yes. Do it. I trust your judgment."

Early the next morning, Hannah sent their request, and Nan arrived at midmorning full of ideas and with no qualms about conversation.

"Since Mrs. Coffin usually comes for Kerry's lying-in, you should send for her right away. I'm sure Kerry would prefer to have her own mother over anyone else. In the meantime, I know just the person to help out. She's a midwife, but she also knows other medicine and doesn't mind doing whatever else is needed around the house." She nestled into her customary chair in the parlor and picked up a shirt from the nearby basket. "My, this mending does pile up, doesn't it?"

"It certainly does." Hannah also took up a garment. "I wish Kerry would hire more help for every day. She has a washerwoman on Mondays, but that's all. I can understand that she wants to be frugal so there is more money for the mission, but she does far too much of the work herself. I'm glad you know someone who can help. Is she available right now?"

"She's free at the moment, although she was bound to another family for some time." Nan giggled. "Yes, she's quite free."

"Why is that funny?"

"Private joke."

"Indeed? When did you begin to keep jokes from me? I could use some laughter too."

"Oh, I hear the front bell. I saw Dorice go upstairs, so shouldn't you answer?"

Hannah listened. "You're just trying to change the subject. Oh. Now I hear it too. It's difficult to hear in this part of the house." She set down her mending and hurried out the door and up the hallway to the front entry. When she saw Captain Lazarus through the door window, she chirped a happy "Oh" before flinging open the door.

"David, how nice to see you. Do come in."

He removed his tall beaver hat and entered, bending over her with a gentle expression. "You're looking well, Hannah."

She shook her head. "Thank you. I'm sure you mean to be kind, but with all our difficulties, I must be showing my lack of sleep."

"Difficulties? Good heavens, what's happened?"

"Haven't you been to the mission to see Jeremiah?"

"No, not for several days. Hannah, are you all right? Is Timothy … ?"

She could not miss the deep concern clouding his eyes, as if … as if what?

"Oh, no. We are both well. It's Kerry."

"How distressing. What's the matter?"

"She has a fever and has been in bed most of the week. We're all pitching in to help out." Though she would have liked to keep his visit to herself, conscience demanded that she tell all. "Even Nan has come over to help with the mending and to advise us on hiring more servants."

"How like her to help. Where is she?"

Hannah guided him though the hallway to the small parlor, where Nan glanced up with a cheerful grin.

"Sit down, Lazarus, and grab a needle. We're working on Kerry's mending."

"Nan, what a thing to say."

"Not at all," Lazarus said. "On those long voyages around the Horn, every man takes needle in hand to do his own mending."

"Even as captain?" Hannah could not imagine Ahab sewing.

"Even as captain." He did a visual search of the basket and shook his head. "But I do think these stockings are a little too small for my large hands."

Hannah gazed at him for a moment. What an interesting man. He actually had considered helping them with such a domestic chore.

"Hannah and I were just discussing how best to help Kerry and Jeremiah. I thought our friend Mattie McClure, being free right now, might like to earn a little money. What do you think?" Nan winked at Lazarus.

He coughed, and Hannah thought he was stifling a laugh. So this was another private joke they shared. She felt a little left out but managed to disregard her shock over Nan's wink.

"But we also thought Kerry would like her mother to come, so we're going to see about sending for her. How long do you think it would take to send word to her in Nantucket and then for her to make arrangements to get here? The *Moss* used to sail every day when the weather was good, and I would imagine it still does. That would get her to New Bedford. But do you know if there is reliable public transport from New Bedford to Boston?"

He did not answer right away. Rather, he rested his chin on his fist, furrowed his brow, and stared at the floor. After a few moments, he nodded decisively.

"There are railway trains between the cities, but they might be rather unpleasant for a woman of her age. On the other hand, I have a ship ready to set sail for Norfolk. Weather permitting, it would take just a few days to go to Nantucket instead and bring Mrs. Coffin here."

"Oh, David, how generous," Hannah said. "How very good and generous."

Nan nodded. "Just like you, Lazarus. Never think of time or expense. Just do whatever works to solve the problem."

He dismissed their praise with a wave of his hand. "One can never do too much for friends."

"But you say you were about to sail to Norfolk." Nan stared at him, her face showing concern. "Will this delay picking up a shipment of cotton?"

"No, not seriously. One must always plan for the unexpected, and our, eh, our appointment has a broad enough time span to allow for an extra week."

"Ah. Very good."

They were talking in their own private language again, yet Hannah felt pleased that she sensed nothing romantic in it. But she also felt a little confused. *I'm just like a silly schoolgirl. Surely my fatigue is causing these selfish feelings.*

"Very good. We have a plan. But before weighing anchor …" David chuckled. "I suppose I should ask Jeremiah if he wants me to fetch his mother-in-law."

Nan and Hannah laughed.

"Of course you should ask him," Hannah said. "I must warn you both though, you are to call her Aunt Charity. Everyone in Nantucket calls her that, and she will think you do not like her if you address her any other way."

"Ah, yes. I recall that from her visit last year. Well, dear ladies, if I am to accomplish this mission in a timely manner, I suppose I should leave your gracious society and seek our young minister's approval for our plans."

"Good sailing," Nan said, as Hannah rose to see him out.

At the front door, he turned to shake her hand. The warm strength of his callused palm felt so comfortable, she did not want to release him.

"How lovely of you to call, David. And so fortuitous. I know Jeremiah will appreciate your kindness." Hannah stared up once more into his gentle gray eyes, marveling at the peace she saw there, and the way that same kind of peace seemed to fill her heart when she was with him. He did not withdraw his hand, and it seemed natural to rest hers there.

He returned her gaze, a slight smile on his lips. "Will you make me a promise?"

"Oh, yes. Anything."

"Don't sail for Europe while I'm gone."

"Of course not. How could I leave Kerry now?"

His smile broadened. "No. I didn't think so. You have a good heart, Hannah." He paused. "I came this morning ..." He frowned a little, then gently let go of her hand and shook his head. "It can wait."

She stepped back and opened the door, wishing to keep him there but knowing the urgency of his mission.

"I'm so glad you came. Safe voyage, David. And God bless you."

Chapter Nine

&

By noon, the mending basket was empty, and all the clothes were in a kitchen hamper to be washed the following Monday. Nan stayed through dinner, leaving with a promise to bring over her friend Mrs. McClure following church the next morning. After having his meal with Kerry, Jeremiah checked with Hannah before returning to the mission. Though his face still revealed weariness, his steps seemed lighter.

"What a miracle this household hasn't fallen apart. All your doing," he told Hannah as he left. "Yours and the Lord's."

Waving him off to work, Hannah returned to duty, encouraged to know she could help. Kerry's illness distressed everyone, but they were managing to survive with only a few problems. Lacy became fretful at naptime, but the two younger girls went right to bed. Ellen rocked the three-year-old to sleep and then helped Dorice with the myriad of chores still to be done. As soon as Hannah washed Timothy's face and settled him down for a rest, she made the rounds of the house to be sure everything was in order. With only a twinge of guilt, she stole a few moments for herself to read in the great parlor.

She had found no time to keep her promise to Lazarus to consider what he called the evils of slavery. So when she found *Narrative of the Life of Frederick Douglass, an American Slave* on Jeremiah's bookshelf, she settled down to read it. The author was Mr. Douglass himself, who once had come to an antislavery convention in Nantucket. Timothy had been an infant at the time, so she could not attend the meetings and, in fact, had as little interest in the abolitionist movement then as now. But everyone who heard Mr. Douglass address the assembly spoke of his natural skill at oratory and the wisdom of his words, despite his recent escape from bondage.

She opened the leather-bound book and found all the page edges had been carefully slit open. Either Jeremiah or Kerry must have read every word in this book. Before she could begin, however, the front bell jangled, echoing through the entryway by the front staircase. She quickly set the book on the coffee table and hurried to answer before the visitor could ring again and waken the children.

Through the front glass, she saw Captain Longwood, and an involuntary gasp escaped her. What a striking man, especially in that handsome uniform. Without another thought, she flung the door open.

"Captain Longwood, how lovely to see you. Do come in."

For an instant, he appeared surprised. Then he doffed his hat and gave her a courtly bow. "Mrs. Jacobs, how exquisite you look this afternoon." He smiled, his blue eyes sparkled, and the May breeze rearranged his hair into charming curls across his forehead.

As he stepped through the doorway and came to take her hand, Hannah tried to catch her breath, but her corset held her fast. When he bent to kiss her fingertips, her face felt on fire, and when he straightened, they gazed at each other for what seemed an eternity. At last, as if someone had given a command, they each stepped back and remembered their manners.

"My dear lady, why are you answering the door? Where are the servants?"

Hannah wished for a fan to cool her flaming cheeks. What had he just said? Servants? Door? Why should she not answer the door?

"Do come into the parlor, Captain Longwood." She led him toward the large front room. "The children are sleeping, and I fear our voices may waken them."

"But don't they have a nursemaid to tend them?"

"Yes, but she's helping in the kitchen now." She waved toward a large wingback chair. "Please sit down." As he adjusted his saber and took his seat, she sat on the adjacent divan. "The house has been in upheaval this week due to Mrs. Harris's illness."

"My dear ..." He stopped and frowned. "I do hope it's nothing contagious. If you should become ill because of your generosity in staying here to give assistance, when servants should be capable of managing things, I shall greatly despair on your behalf and that of young Timothy. Should you not seek other accommodations until this disease has passed?"

She shook her head, not knowing whether to be complimented or annoyed by his zealous concern. "The doctor assures us that Kerry is not contagious. He feels that the fever is due to her ... her ..." Remembering her conversation with Jeremiah, she felt heat rising in her face again.

"Ah, yes. I understand." He rescued her from having to say more. "I am relieved that you and your son are in no danger. Fevers and the like will be my paramount concern for you as you travel abroad. As to the current influenza epidemic, I will be certain you are provided with a list of precautions that you must follow stringently. I will also provide you with several medicines that one is wise to carry along to less healthful climes."

He took a small writing tablet from his jacket pocket and leaned toward her, his eyes bright with enthusiasm. "Also, on that matter, I have taken the liberty of making this list of seaworthy passenger ships sailing for England in the coming weeks. I have only listed sailing packets, for I am unconvinced that these Cunard Line steamships can be trusted, despite the favor many people of note give them. Now when you have chosen your date of departure, I shall investigate the captain to learn if he is reputable and then interview him myself to ascertain his character.

"Of course, England is the best and safest place to begin and end your European tour. My mother's family has an estate not far from London. I shall contact my cousins, and they will be more than pleased to show you every hospitality. Knowing them, I would not be at all surprised if several of them decided to join your tour. I have even designed an itinerary for your approval." He leaned back, a pleased smile gracing his lips.

Hannah sat stunned for a moment. She had not given one thought to her trip since Kerry became ill.

"Dear Captain Longwood—"

"Dearest Mrs. Jacobs." He reached out and took both her hands. "I do so want you to enjoy this journey. I would do anything within my power to bring about your happiness." He raised her hands to his lips and held them there for a moment, gazing into her eyes, until a shadow crossed his face.

"Ah, you seem reticent. I see I must beg you to forgive my lack of attention recently. Please understand there have been many official duties that only I could attend to these past few days, or I would have come calling. Perhaps you thought I had deserted you when I did not call after our wonderful day together … was it just this past Monday? It seems an eternity ago, so much did I wish to be in your company. Unfortunately, duty to our country always preempts personal desires, or I would have been at your doorstep every day. You must have felt neglected, so your reticence is understandable. But, as you can see by the plans I have made for you, you were ever in my thoughts." His brow furrowed, and he stared at her with a hopeful, vulnerable expression, still refusing to release her hands.

She felt breathless after his long speech. Indeed, she had barely been able to breathe since seeing him through the front-door window. But the dizziness she felt came as much from his stunning efforts to fulfill her dreams as from lack of air. How amazing to meet someone at last who understood her need to see the world and have adventures all her own. "I hardly know what to say. You have my deepest gratitude."

"Then you have only to give me the word, and I will make all the arrangements. That is, if I am forgiven for my neglect?"

"There is nothing to forgive." She gently took her hands from his. "Perhaps I should get us some lemonade."

He reached for her hands again. "I would not have these delicate hands serve me, dear lady. You must always be the one who is served. Ring for the maid, won't you?"

Hannah shook her head. "Nonsense. I'll see to it." She pulled away and rose, and he followed suit.

"Very well. This time." He gave her a slight bow.

She laughed softly as she walked to the kitchen. Cook, having heard the front bell, had already made a pitcher of lemonade and was preparing to bring it to the parlor.

"Do let me carry it, ma'am."

"Not this time, Mrs. Cook."

"But it's heavy."

"Nonsense." She lifted the silver tray, found a comfortable balance, and proceeded back through the swinging kitchen door into the hallway. Nearing the parlor, she tried to think of some humorous remark to lighten the intensity of the conversation. But when she entered, Captain Longwood stood by the fireplace, and a scowl marred his handsome face. In his hands, he held the Douglass book.

"Please tell me you have not been reading this seditious, wicked foolishness." His tone revealed no anger, only disappointment.

She did not respond right away, but slowly placed the tray on a side table and filled a glass for each of them. By the time she handed him a drink, she had decided this was her opportunity to answer David's challenge concerning slavery.

"Why, no. I only just picked it up. May I assume you don't

recommend it?" She sat on the divan, gave him her sweetest smile, and then sipped her lemonade.

Relief washed over his face. "Certainly not. And I'm disappointed that Reverend Harris permits it in his home, right here within the reach of innocent women and children and ill-advised parishioners who might read it and be deceived."

"But perhaps it belongs to Kerry. As you may know, she was raised in the Society of Friends, and they are adamant in opposing slavery."

"Nonetheless, it is her husband's responsibility to shield his family from lies." He tossed the book on the mantle, as if to put it out of reach. Then he sat beside her on the divan, close beside her, with one arm draped behind her.

"Mrs. Jacobs," he murmured near her ear, "the Quakers are good-hearted but misguided people. They disparage a way of life they don't understand."

Despite the coolness of the drink, she felt heat rising to her face once again. She turned halfway toward him, held the glass with both hands cupped in front of her, and leaned back. "The day is a trifle warm, don't you think?"

He quickly moved back from her, his eyes radiating under-standing and contrition, which only enhanced his winsome appeal. She had to look away to keep her composure. How easy it would be to surrender to his charms. She must direct this conversation to a proper path.

"Of course I would expect you to feel that way. In fact, I myself know little of slaves—"

"I do wish you would not use that word."

"I beg your pardon?"

"'Slave' is a harsh, indelicate word. If any term must be used, we prefer to say chattels or, in my home, *family*. My dear lady, listen to me. You admit that you know little of the Southern way of life, so let me tell you about it. Learn the truth from me, not from some foolish

book put out in the name of an ignorant Negro being used for iniq-
uitous purposes by Northern politicians."

"An ignorant man … ?"

"Why, yes. You surely don't think a Negro has the capacity to think
and reason enough to write a book."

She thought for a moment. "I do not know. I have only had passing
acquaintance with Negro shopkeepers, drivers, and such. They
seemed capable enough." She would not mention knowing of a few
very capable black whalers, for then he might quiz her about her past.
Still, she could not help but think of one little Negro boy—what was
his name?—who had lived a short time on Nantucket Island and
dreamed only of sailing with Captain Ahab. Pip. That was he. And
with his Captain Ahab, he had gone down aboard the *Pequod*.

"And I have known many Negroes very well all my life. When I
first told you we consider them family, did you think I said it only for
your Captain Lazarus's benefit? All the people who live and work at
Longwood Plantation are greatly loved and cared for, white and black
alike."

Once more, she saw the sincerity in his face. "I don't doubt your
feelings, but I must question your definition of family. Can your
'people' come and go as they wish? Can they decide to move away
and live somewhere else, or set up a business to earn their own
way?"

"Of course not." He spoke in a gentle tone, instructing her. "But
neither can a child. Our Negroes have minds like children. They
never have a thought beyond the simplest reasoning. They would
never be able to take care of themselves. They cannot read. They
cannot count or understand money. They simply have no capacity
for such things. Although it is true that some few of them have
skills to be blacksmiths or barbers or carpenters, it would be
madness to let them set up their own businesses. They are simple-
minded and trusting, and unscrupulous men would cheat them out

of everything they might earn. That is why it is my father's and brother's responsibility, and mine when I am there, to take care of them, to provide for them. And they, in turn, earn their keep through their labors."

What he said seemed to make sense, but questions still plagued Hannah.

"But I have heard that slaves—for that is what they are called by most people—that slaves are often beaten. How can that be? How can one beat a member of one's family?"

He gave her a knowing look. "Do you ever spank your son?"

She gasped. "Why, no. Never. There has never been any reason to do so."

He sighed. "Then he must be a perfect child or you too gentle a mother. My father tanned my hide more than once when I was a rascally little lad, and I'm a better man for it."

"And I suppose your 'people' are better for being beaten." She could not keep emotion from her voice.

He glanced down, appearing wounded by her tone. "Some children require more correction than others. But you must not think of these things. If you think me so evil for having chattels, let me persuade you otherwise. Do you know that many Southerners, fine Christian people, believe that Negroes possess no souls at all? I am not entirely of that persuasion. We require our entire family to attend church services every Sunday, and we endeavor to bring every person to salvation, black and white alike. Would to God I could do the same for the men who serve aboard my ship. But I find many of them far more hard-hearted than those who serve on my plantation. No, but our Negroes, having childlike reasoning, receive the Gospel as little children, just as the Scriptures say. And if, indeed, they have no souls, we have still done our duty by them."

Hannah set her empty glass on the coffee table. "I suppose it's good to be persuaded in your own thinking."

He leaned his elbow against the back of the divan, propping his head on his hand in a winsome pose. "But I have not persuaded you?"

She sighed. Could she voice this one last concern without tears? Perhaps not, but still she must try.

"Captain, do you sell children away from their mothers and fathers?"

He sat erect and frowned. "Have you not heard a word, dear lady? We do not sell our people. They are our family. While the parents work, the children are kept in the care of the older women, in their own house on the grounds. At an appropriate age, each child is trained for those duties for which he or she seems best suited."

"But I know some slave owners sell children ..."

"Yes. And how like you to be so tenderly concerned that they might grieve as you or I would. But when I was just a boy, I asked the same question of the master of a neighboring plantation. He told me the children adapt quickly to their new homes, and the parents grieve no longer than a mother dog when her pups are taken away. Given a year or two, they would not know each other. As for the men, most have no paternal sensibilities at all, except with regard to their master's children. The Negroes are not like us, Mrs. Jacobs. Even if they have souls, they are not fully human. If ever you truly looked at a Negro and studied the inferior design of his appearance, from face to form, you would perceive this."

She stared into his eyes, reading again the sincerity there. If what he said was not true, at least she could see he believed it to be.

"You've given me a good deal to think about."

He reached over, patted her hand, and held it. "That is all I can hope for. And now may I ask, could we escape this quiet room and go for a stroll? We both could benefit from some fresh air ..."

As if to respond to his question, a series of thumps sounded on the staircase, and soon Timothy peered into the parlor. His shirt buttoned in the wrong holes and his shoes unbuckled, he gave his mother a crooked grin. Then he ran to lean against her, flinging his arms around her neck. She pulled him up into her lap, grateful for the distraction, and grateful he had not outgrown their after-nap custom.

"Hello, my darling. Did you have a good rest?"

"Mmm-humm." He rubbed the sleep from his eyes. Seeing the empty glass on the coffee table, he reached for it.

"Permit me." Longwood took the glass and filled it with lemonade, bringing it back to the boy.

Timothy's eyes were wide open now, and he stared up at the captain as he took the glass and lifted it to drink.

Hannah set her hand on her son's. "What do we say?"

"Thank you, sir." He drank noisily before eyeing his mother and correcting his manners with quieter sips.

"You are most welcome, young man." Longwood sat down beside them again, gazing at the boy.

Hannah brushed Timothy's unruly hair back from his forehead and kissed his brow. Fully awake now, he moved away from the kiss, and she glanced at Longwood with a shrug and a rueful smile.

He nodded with understanding. Then, noticing the boy's shoes, he lifted one small foot to his lap and fastened the buckle, repeating with the other foot. Timothy submitted to his ministrations with a shy smile, nestling close to his mother once the shoes were secured.

Longwood sat back. "Master Timothy, would you like to go aboard my new ship? Would you like to see how the United States Navy goes about defending our great country?"

Timothy swung around, staring at Hannah with large, round eyes and a wide grin. "Mother, can I go? Can I go see the ship?" He swung back to the captain. "Do you have cannons and sails and lots and lots of sailors?"

"Oh, yes, all of that and more." Longwood chuckled, turning his gaze away from the boy to seek Hannah's approval. "And, of course, you are invited too, Mrs. Jacobs. I would be mightily pleased to show you where I fulfill my duty to our country."

"You have to say yes, Mother. Even Estevam has never been on a navy ship."

Hannah shook her head in amazement. "I must say, you have a way of making a little boy very happy. How could I refuse? But we cannot go today. I must wait until Mrs. Harris's mother arrives from Nantucket. Perhaps one day next week?"

Timothy wiggled happily in her lap, and the captain reached over to shake his hand in celebration.

"Next week it is. I'll make the arrangements."

Reaching over to correct the ill-buttoned shirt, he began to tell Timothy more about his ship, but Hannah could only gaze at the captain in wonder. What she saw in his gentle expression made her heart seem to stand still. His eyes shone with genuine fondness for her son, a boy he barely knew.

Surely he was a good man. No matter what cruel things other plantation owners did to their slaves, she would never believe evil of Captain Duncan Longwood.

Chapter Ten

ॐ

In all her life, Hannah had never seen a person with such dark skin. Even little Pip, whose sweet, smiling face she had dreamed of the night before, had not been so very deep brown. But it was the eyes of this woman of color that held Hannah's stare. Despite obvious trepidation, perhaps at being in the home of white strangers, Mattie McClure gazed at Jeremiah with astuteness and unmistakable self-possession.

She was of medium height, with straight posture and a strong but slender build. Her dress was a well-made gray muslin Sunday gown with black grosgrain ribbon adorning the bell-shaped sleeves and fitted bodice. Her wavy black hair was parted in the middle and pulled back under the matching bonnet, which was lined with white ruffles and therefore made the wearer's face seem all the darker. Hannah could not guess her age.

In the front hallway, Nan stood beside her friend and beamed. "Reverend Harris, Mrs. Jacobs, this is Mattie McClure. Mattie, Reverend Harris will be your employer. Mrs. Jacobs is a friend of the family who is managing the household while Mrs. Harris is confined."

Jeremiah appeared mildly surprised, but he put out his hand. "How do you do, Mattie?"

She stared at his hand and then hesitantly touched it with her own gloved fingers. "Thank you, sir. I am well." Her rich alto voice had a melodious accent, Southern, it seemed, but different from Captain Longwood's. She gave Hannah a respectful nod. "Ma'am."

"Come in here, and let's discuss the terms of your employment." Jeremiah led the party into the great parlor and indicated a chair. "Please sit down."

Mattie's eyebrows rose, and she looked at Nan.

"Let's sit down and get comfortable." Nan took a seat and patted the one beside her. Mattie followed her lead and sat down.

"Mrs. Childers tells me you have extensive experience in nursing the sick," said Jeremiah, "and that you are not averse to performing other household duties. We all pitch in to help here, so that's exactly what we need. I would like you to begin right away, and we have an empty room for you on the third floor that I'll furnish with a bed from the mission."

Mattie sat forward in her chair. "Sir, are you going to hire me right out? Don't you want to ask me some questions?"

Jeremiah blinked and then crinkled his face as if in thought. If Hannah had not been so astounded by the situation, she might have giggled at the sweet, boyish expression that skipped across his countenance. She could see Nan's choice of nurses may have surprised him, but it had not caused him the slightest concern.

"Mrs. Childers's recommendation is sufficient for me. Hannah, do you have any questions?"

She had expected him to seek her advice during this interview, but now she was nonplussed. Not only was the woman's race a shock, but also she was nothing like the Negroes Captain Longwood had described. Though a little apprehensive, she had a forthright manner and an amiable expression. While her features were large, they had a pleasing symmetry. Her full, well-shaped lips, both upper and lower, bore a thin gray scar on the left side, as if from a single injury. When she spoke, Hannah saw that, beneath the old cut, two upper teeth and a lower one were missing. What could have caused such a wound? But Mattie's eyes, black opals set in clear, white pools, exuded intelligence and grace, and that, above all, captured Hannah's gaze and persuaded her she was a competent woman and one to be trusted.

Hannah scanned the group. "As Reverend Harris said, Mrs. Childers's word is sufficient."

Jeremiah tapped his hands on the arms of his chair. "Excellent. It's decided. You can start at once. Today. That is to say, will you accept the position?"

She smiled, her eyes glowing. "Yes, sir, I would be pleased to." She glanced at Nan, who gave her an encouraging nod. "May I meet the missus before I go fetch my things?"

"Certainly. I'll take you up. After that, you're in Mrs. Jacobs's hands. She'll give you further instructions." He stood and showed her out of the room and up the stairs.

"I must say, that's work well done." Nan had not stopped beaming since entering the house.

Hannah leaned toward her friend. "Aren't *you* pleased with yourself."

Nan drew back, surprised. "If you have any objections, you had better voice them now. Once she has given up her current residence, I'll not have my friend embarrassed by being let go and put out on the streets."

"I didn't say I had objections. It's just that you never bothered to mention she is a Negro."

Nan stared at her, a look of puzzlement on her face that was soon replaced by one of maternal indulgence. She bent toward Hannah and patted her hand. "My dear, the day will come in this great country of ours when no such explanations will be necessary."

If Jeremiah and Hannah were satisfied to welcome the new employee to the household, the same could not be said for the other three servants. Cook had the maturity to control her annoyance, but at suppertime it was clear to Hannah that she did not like having to prepare food for Mattie. Nursemaid Ellen, being educated and having expressed a wish to be elevated soon to governess, made no excuses for snubbing the Negro woman. And Dorice did everything she could to avoid helping Mattie learn where household supplies were kept, until Hannah took the house-maid to task late Sunday evening.

"I'm disappointed in you, Dorice. Why are you acting this way?"

The girl tried to hide her sullenness, but her pouting lips betrayed her. "If you needed extra hands, Mrs. Jacobs, my younger sister is ready to go into service. She's as strong as me and works full chisel."

"But does she know nursing? Has she ever attended in a sick room?"

The girl studied her own feet. "No, ma'am. But we coulda helped you find someone who has. I would prefer not to …" Her voice died away, and she shrugged.

Hannah regarded her for a moment. Who would think that Mattie's being in the house would cause a disturbance? In her expe-rience of managing households, she had never dealt with difficult servants, but in Nantucket she herself had felt great resentment toward her husband's housekeeper. That is, until she and Abigail had formed an alliance to help him after he was wounded. But now she must bring this house back into the harmony Kerry had estab-lished.

"I must ask you to think of Mrs. Harris above your own prefer-ences. She has been very good to you, hiring you at only fourteen and with no experience. She has been generous in your salary and free time, as well as days off. But if you insist …"

Dorice's head shot up, and her eyes widened with fear. Hannah stopped, wishing back her words. She had not meant to threaten the girl. Kerry never would have threatened. How could she retreat without undermining her own authority?

"… if you insist on being rude to Mattie, it will disturb us all. Mrs. Childers promises she is a good, skilled worker, so you must look for her good points *and* learn from her experience. Regard this as an opportunity to advance your own skills."

Relief washed over the girl's face. She gave a quick curtsy, her head bobbing in agreement. "Yes, ma'am, I never thought of it like that. Yes, ma'am. May I go now?"

"Yes, you may go." Hannah dismissed her with a nod. But as Dorice left the parlor, the echo of Hannah's own words came back to her. She, too, had been less than warm to Mattie. Perhaps Captain Longwood's words had influenced her. Perhaps she thought the nurse was … was what? Not fully human? But contrary to his assertion, Hannah had perceived that behind those remarkable dark eyes there was indeed an intelligent mind. The days ahead would provide ample opportunity for her to discover whether she could retain that opinion.

Sunday night, Mattie stayed in the sickroom, sleeping on a cot to be near her charge. Jeremiah moved into the second guest room with Timothy, and for the first time since Kerry had become ill, he reported to Hannah the next morning that he had slept all night.

"Kerry is feeling a little better today," he said over breakfast. "So I think I'll go to the docks and greet incoming ships. We have a much better opportunity to draw the sailors to the mission if we meet them personally rather than depend on the tracts and posters. If you need me, send Dorice over to tell Jonathan. He always knows where to find me."

Then, according to his daily custom, he gathered his household and prayed for them by name, asking God's blessing upon each of them and for each to feel His presence as they went about their duties.

Hannah loved these quiet moments. When Jeremiah prayed, it was the only time she could truly feel God's presence. Many years had passed since she had heard him preach or pray. Now, being reunited with this friend who had always been like a brother to her, she longed for her own faith to grow stronger. For after his parting prayer each day, the house seemed like a peaceful, holy sanctuary, at least for a short time.

This day, however, she was determined to bring about lasting peace among the servants, all of them. It was the custom for Cook, Dorice, and Ellen to rise early and eat together in the kitchen before the family arose. Then Ellen sat at the dining-room table with the family to help with the children. With Kerry sick, family breakfast had become chaotic, so Dorice was needed to help feed the little girls in the kitchen while Cook served Jeremiah, Hannah, and Timothy.

That morning, Hannah had checked on Kerry before coming downstairs. Mattie had brought breakfast up for the patient, had fed and bathed her, and had somehow managed to look fresh herself. But at prayer time, Hannah detected fatigue in the nurse's face. After Jeremiah left for work, she gave instructions to the assembled household.

"Ellen, I'm concerned that my son is forgetting his lessons. Will you take him along with you to the nursery and have him write his letters and sums, please?"

"Yes, ma'am." Ellen bounced baby Daisy on her hip, clearly pleased with her new assignment.

A mumbled protest coming from Timothy's direction was cut short by Hannah's stern stare, but then she softened. "Timothy, you must help Miss Ellen with the children." His pout turned to pleased confusion, and she stifled a laugh. If he thought he had an important job to do, even one as distasteful as helping take care of pesky little girls, he might be more willing to do his lessons. Little Molly and Lacy cast adoring glances in his direction, and he gave them a crooked grin.

"Dorice, after you have gathered all the clothing and bedding for the laundress, please make certain Mattie's room has all the necessities. Then you must trim the candlewicks, fill the oil lamps, and do the floors and dusting. If you cannot finish by noon, we can see if Mrs. Lazarus will spare Elana to come over and help you."

The serving girl curtsied, obviously schooling her face into a pleasant expression. "Yes, ma'am. I can manage."

"Mrs. Cook, Mattie needs a substantial breakfast if she is going to have the strength to care for Mrs. Harris. Please be certain she has ham and eggs and some of your exceptional biscuits every morning. She is to eat with the rest of you so we all can get on with our day as soon as Reverend Harris leaves."

"Yes, ma'am." Cook nodded, her face devoid of expression.

"Mattie, today I will sit with Mrs. Harris until you've finished your breakfast. If you need anything for your room, tell Dorice, and she will get it for you."

"Yes, ma'am." The nurse's eyes shone with gratitude, and a soft smile graced her lips.

Hannah glanced about to see if there was anything she had left unsaid. "Very well then; you all may go."

Cook sighed. "Come along then, girl. I'll get your breakfast."

As they all dispersed, Hannah released a controlled sigh of her own. She had sensed a hidden message in Jeremiah's prayer for her this day, and it was clear God had seen fit to answer it. But then, even before he became a minister, Jeremiah had seemed to have special influence with God.

Kerry lay in bed gazing out the window when Hannah entered the room, and she turned to greet her. "Maybe I'll be able to get out of bed for a while today."

"Has your fever gone?" Hannah touched Kerry's forehead. "I don't think so. You're still warm."

Kerry sighed. "I know. And my head still hurts when I sit up too long. But I can't bear to be away from the girls any longer. When the doctor came yesterday, he was certain my illness is not contagious. Don't you think it would be all right to let them come in to visit?"

Hannah shook her head. "I don't know. It might be too much for you. Did you ask Mattie?"

Instead of answering, Kerry studied Hannah's face for a moment. "What do you think of Mattie?"

"I think it's more important what you think of her."

"She's wonderful. Very maternal. In many ways, she reminds me of Mother, always pressing on despite adversity. When I couldn't sleep in the middle of the night, we had a long conversation. She's had a difficult life, but things have been improving for her since she came to Boston."

"Difficult?"

"Yes. Didn't Antoinette tell you?"

Hannah shook her head. "She told me Mattie had worked for another family until recently but that she was free to work for us now."

Kerry began to giggle, wincing a little as she did. "Oh, dear. Antoinette can be humorous, can't she?"

"Shhh, don't laugh. It's making your head hurt."

"But laughing lifts my spirits too. You know, 'a merry heart doeth good like a medicine.' We are such a merry family, and I miss the laughter."

Hannah patted Kerry's hand. "I'm sure you do." She saw her friend's face relax. The pain was subsiding. "But what's so funny about what Nan told me?"

"Hannah, I don't want to say it out loud. We are not certain of Dorice's or Ellen's opinions about certain things, and I don't want them to hear anything harmful. Just think for a minute about Antoinette's words."

"She said she was bound to another family but free now. Oh, don't make me guess … Oh. Oh! *Bound.* Do you mean she's a—"

"Shh." Kerry winced again. "Yes. She came from somewhere in Georgia or Alabama, I'm not sure which."

"Oh, my word. Does Jeremiah know?"

"Of course."

"Then you two are …"

"This is the first time, but I think it won't be the last."

Hannah was still staring at her friend, mouth agape, when Mattie entered the room and came to the bedside.

"Mrs. Jacobs, I can take over now if you need to do something else."

Now Hannah stared at Mattie, and the woman backed up a little, her eyes wary.

"Is something wrong, ma'am?"

Hannah shook her head, trying to gain control of her sudden tears. Now she understood the scar on Mattie's lips and the missing teeth beneath it. *Some children require more correction than others,* Captain Longwood had said. But what kind of person had thought Mattie needed to have her teeth knocked out?

"No, no." She cleared her throat and forced a smile. "We were just wondering if the girls could come see their mother this morning. What do you think?"

Mattie gave her a doubtful look, but nodded. "Yes, ma'am. I think that would be very good for Missus."

"Wonderful. I'll go tell Ellen to bring them down as soon as they're freshened up from breakfast."

"Don't forget my dear Timothy," Kerry said.

"Oh, good. I know he'll want to come. That is, if you're really up to seeing him too. He prays for you every night at bedtime."

"Ma'am, you set still. Let me fetch the children." Mattie looked at Hannah for approval.

"Why, thank you. Please do."

As soon as she was out the door, Hannah turned to Kerry. "Now, for you, Miss Kerry." She didn't know whether to laugh, cry, or be angry. "How did you know you could trust me? How do you know I won't tell someone you're harboring an escaped ..." She stopped, remembering Kerry's caution about the servants.

Kerry gazed at her with a beatific smile. "Because I know your heart, dearest Hannah. I know you'll do the right thing."

Chapter Eleven

&

"A unt Charity." Hannah stood on the front porch holding the frail old woman in a gentle embrace. "It's so good to see you. Are you well?"

"As well as ever, and that's very well. Now let me take a look at thee, my dear Mrs. *Jacobs*." Aunt Charity pulled back and silently, lovingly admonished Hannah with her brown eyes.

Hannah's face grew warm. She glanced beyond her old friend to acknowledge Captain Lazarus. It had never occurred to her that bringing Kerry's mother from Nantucket might expose her true identity, yet he had protected her. At her grateful smile, he doffed his seaman's cap and gave her a slight shrug, as if to deny any irregularity. Still, his eyes shone with understanding. Then he turned and nodded to another woman behind him, reaching out to urge her forward.

"Tishtega," Hannah cried. She released Aunt Charity and grasped the hands of the tall Gay Head Indian. "Oh, Tishtega, how wonderful to see you. And what a surprise."

"Miss Kerenhappuch is not well. Where else would I be?" Her gruff words did not match the light in her eyes.

"Indeed," said Aunt Charity. "Now let me see my daughter. Tishtega, come along."

The two women hurried into the house, their spry steps belying their advanced years. Hannah turned back to Lazarus, and her heart overflowed with an unexpected profusion of emotions.

"David, we're so grateful to you. What other man would go to such lengths to help friends, as you have done?"

He shook his head. "I won't refuse your gratitude completely, but many men do far more for their neighbors."

His kind gray eyes and guileless expression imparted to him an angelic glow. How utterly selfless he was. They stood for a moment, at home in each other's quiet presence. Then he cleared his throat and looked down to brush invisible lint from his cap. "I suppose you will be completing plans for your trip abroad now that Aunt Charity is here."

"Why, I haven't thought about it, not even when the dressmaker brought some of my new gowns the other day."

"But now you will have time?"

"You know, I just don't feel comfortable leaving until Kerry recovers."

"Ah, interesting. And so good-hearted."

She gave her head a dismissive little shake. "Oh, well, Europe will always be there. But good friends ..."

"I understand."

They stood in comfortable silence until Hannah gasped. "Goodness gracious, where are my manners? Won't you come in for tea? You must be exhausted from your voyage."

"No tea, thank you, but I can spare a few more moments before I return to my ship."

They soon were seated in the front parlor, sipping tea despite his mild refusal.

"I wanted to ask you something, David, if you don't mind?"

"Certainly, you may ask me anything." His pleasant gaze encouraged her.

"I have been thinking about the issue of slavery, as you suggested, and it seems to me that if the wise men who founded our country had felt slavery was wrong, they should have abolished it at the very beginning, or at least when they composed our constitution. But many of them were slaveholders, even George Washington." She felt a little foolish invoking the first president's name, as if David might know that she had received her idea from Captain Longwood.

David nodded thoughtfully. "This is true. But tell me, did you study our nation's history at boarding school?"

"Yes, we were required to read about our American revolution. But my main interests were the antiquities—Roman, Greek, and Egyptian, as well as older literature. I fear I neglected our own recent history."

"Or perhaps your instructors neglected to stress the importance of knowing all that went into our country's founding. I would not attempt to make up for that deficiency, but I would ask you to investigate two things to make certain my information is correct."

"You sound like my father. Rather than tell me what to think, you would have me research ideas for myself."

"Yes, for such research requires more thought on your part than simply memorizing lessons you are taught."

She raised her eyebrows and nodded her agreement. "And when I come to a conclusion about my research, the ideas are truly my own instead of someone else's. Or at least I have always found it to be so."

"I thoroughly agree." Admiration shone in his eyes.

She felt her face warming. "Now tell me the two things I must search for."

"First, read about our Constitutional Congress. I believe you will find that there were those who tried to abolish slavery at the outset, but the Southern states would not accept that. And without their compromise on many such serious issues, we would never have become this great country. Second, look into the life of our first president, and I think you will find an important surprise: in his last will and testament, George Washington freed his slaves."

"He did? Truly?"

David chuckled. "Truly. But don't take my word for it. Find the information yourself."

"I'll certainly do so." Hannah nodded vigorously. Would Captain Longwood wish to emulate *this* aspect of Washington's life? Did he even know about it?

"But now, please forgive me for I must return to work. It takes several days to prepare for the voyage to Norfolk, and I cannot postpone it any longer."

"Do stop over at the mission and see Jeremiah. And perhaps you could come to supper before you sail." She already felt the loss of his leaving.

"Thank you. Your invitation means the world to me."

At the front door, he lifted her hand, gently brushing her fingers with his lips. "Good day, dear friend."

"Good-bye, David. I shall do as you suggested. Have a very good day." She watched him descend the stairs and walk toward the mission. Halfway there, he glanced back, grinned, and waved, as if pleased to see her still on the porch. What a good friend. What a dear, good friend.

If Mattie's employment caused consternation among the servants, Tishtega's presence proved intimidating. She was at least six feet tall, with broad but womanly shoulders. Her frame was lean and muscular. Thick, waist-length white hair framed a rough, wrinkled, but still handsome brown face, and her piercing black eyes exuded an almost mystical power.

Dorice and Ellen stared wide-eyed when introduced to her, and Cook hurried back to the kitchen as quickly as possible. Only

Mattie seemed to take her presence in stride, conferring with her amiably about their patient.

"I must make certain these white doctors know how to care for Miss Kerenhappuch. She is one of my children," Tishtega proclaimed.

Mattie nodded her understanding, but Hannah quizzed her with a look.

"All are my children whose births I watched over."

"How do you keep up with all of them?"

The other two women traded glances. "One always knows her own," said Mattie.

Tishtega hummed her agreement. "Of course, some are more memorable than others. Where is my son Timothy?"

"I think he's in the nursery with Ellen and the girls," Hannah said. "I'll go—"

"Why is he not with the men?" Tishtega's deep voice rumbled through the room. "Is there no true man in this place who will make a man of him?"

For a moment, Hannah felt a little of the disquiet the servants experienced. As tall as she was, she still was forced to look up to Tishtega, and in more ways than one. Beyond her height, the woman possessed an earthy, practical wisdom. Ahab had always trusted her without hesitation, and she had never disappointed Hannah.

But recently, as the days passed and Hannah's mind was occupied with household duties, she had kept Timothy closer so as to have one less thing to worry about. When did he last play with Paolo and Estevam? When did he last practice woodworking with Jonathan Lazarus? Still, she resisted losing control of her son, and Tishtega's question annoyed her.

Before Hannah could respond to the challenge, Mattie set a calming hand on Hannah's arm, her expression betraying surprise that Tishtega would scold the lady.

"Miss Hannah has so many things to fret over, taking care of the whole house. 'Sides, those street boys are no good. I would keep my son close by too, if he was here."

"But you wouldn't send him to the nursery with the baby girls ..."

"No, ma'am, I wouldn't."

Their brief exchange gave Hannah time to control her temper. "Perhaps you're right. I know how you love Timothy, and I appreciate your concern. And there are good men around here to influence him. Captain Longwood has offered to show him his ship. Now that you and Aunt Charity are here, I can accept his invitation."

"Who is this Captain Longwood? Is he a whaler? The boy needs a whaling man to teach him."

Now Hannah laughed. "Spoken like a true Nantucketer. No, he's not a whaling man. He is a captain in the United States Navy, and his ship is a man-of-war."

Tishtega grumbled out a grudging half-approval. "Better to follow his father and be a whaler, but this one is a seafaring man. He will have to do, I suppose."

With the addition of two more adults, the house began to feel crowded to Hannah. But unlike the similarly crowded Indiana household, this group's members were more disparate than her relatives, which created confusion. Sharing her bed with Aunt Charity, she lay awake most of the night fearing she would roll over and injure the frail old woman. And though Jeremiah would never say anything, Hannah felt certain the weary look she often detected in his eyes was caused by sleeping next to an active little boy. Even Tishtega's remarks caused her to wonder if she should leave this house full of women. Perhaps it was time to take Nan's suggestion and rent the house in Louisburg Square until Kerry mended.

When Captain Lazarus came for supper the night before sailing to Norfolk, he commended her decision. Seated adjacent to her at the dining table, he said, "I'm sure you will enjoy the house. It's roomy, and there is a small park in the square where Timothy can play with the other boys in the neighborhood."

Hannah glanced across the table at Tishtega, who responded with an almost imperceptible nod. Hannah turned back to Lazarus. "That sounds wonderful. And Nan tells me she already has a housekeeper and full staff."

He leaned closer to her. "Will you be there when I return? My voyage will take over a week, perhaps a fortnight."

His tone seemed casual enough, but his eyes seemed to hold some silent message.

"David, I promise I will not sail without consulting with you. And remember, Kerry must be completely well too."

"Good." His eyes reflected his satisfaction with her response. "I would like to—"

"Excuse me, Mrs. Jacobs." Dorice rushed into the room to the table and quietly bent near Hannah, her eyes shining with excitement. "That handsome Captain Longwood is in the great parlor. He asked to speak to you for just a moment. What shall I tell him?"

Lazarus grunted. "Longwood? Is he still coming around?"

Hannah felt her face grow warm. "Why, David—"

"Forgive me. That was unnecessary."

"Dorice, tell Captain Longwood I will be with him in a moment."

"Yes, ma'am."

While the girl skipped out to obey, Lazarus reached over to touch Hannah's hand. "Have you had a chance to research the things we discussed?"

"No, not yet, but I have been reading a book by a remarkable man named Frederick Douglass, a former slave. When you return, perhaps you and I and Captain Longwood can come together and discuss this slavery issue in greater depth."

An uncharacteristic laugh of surprise exploded from him, and he sat back in his chair to shake his head and stare at her. "You always think the best of people, don't you, Hannah? Even when they don't deserve it."

"Will you share the joke?" Jeremiah called from the other end of the table, where he had been chatting quietly with Aunt Charity.

Hannah shook her head. "There is no joke. Now if you'll excuse me, Captain Longwood has come to call on me." She pushed back her chair and rose, as did the two gentlemen.

"Captain Longwood." Timothy jumped down from his chair and raced from the room before Hannah could stop him.

"Since we're up," Lazarus said, "why don't we all go?"

"Indeed. A grand idea," Jeremiah said. "I want to commend him for encouraging his sailors to attend our mission services each Sunday. We've reached several lost sinners through his efforts."

Hannah felt her face burning. "Shall we go then?"

In a troop, Hannah, Lazarus, Jeremiah, Aunt Charity, and Tishtega marched through the hallway to the great parlor where Longwood knelt on one knee beside Timothy, showing him his ornate ceremonial sword.

"This saber is for my dress uniform," he was saying. "We have another sword to use in battle."

When the group entered the room, Longwood looked up sharply, appearing shocked for only an instant. "I do beg your pardon, Reverend Harris. I certainly did not mean to disrupt your supper hour."

"Not at all, Captain." Jeremiah strode across the room, his hand extended. "I've been meaning to write you a letter of praise for all your evangelical zeal with your crew."

Longwood rose and shook Jeremiah's hand. "And I must thank you for returning to me better men than I sent you."

"A work well done, we both agree." Jeremiah turned to the others. "Mother, may I present Captain Duncan Longwood of the United States Navy. Captain, this is my wife's mother, Mrs. Coffin, whom Captain Lazarus so kindly brought up from Nantucket. She insists everyone call her Aunt Charity, so please don't break custom."

"Aunt Charity." With extreme gentleness, Longwood took her fragile hand and bowed over it.

"Captain Longwood, it is a pleasure to meet thee."

"And this is Tishtega, also from Nantucket."

Longwood assessed the woman for only an instant before giving her a polite nod.

"And, of course, you know Captain Lazarus."

"Of course." Again, a polite nod. "And good evening, Mrs. Jacobs. I hope I find you well." He stepped up to her and kissed her offered hand. "I do hope none of you will think me rude. My purpose in coming this evening is to find out if you, Mrs. Jacobs, and young Timothy here can join me tomorrow for that promised tour of my ship." He reached over and pulled Timothy to his side. "The lad says he's never been aboard a naval vessel, and I'm eager to remedy that deficiency. In fact, our plans seem to have coincided with a little ceremony going on at the Charlestown Navy Yard, and I would be honored if you two would be my guests."

"Oh, Mother, you must say yes." Timothy struggled to keep his feet planted firmly on the ground, but still he bounced with excitement.

Longwood gave him an indulgent, paternal look, and then turned to Hannah. His eyes sparkled, and the smile he gave her was charm personified. "Yes, Mother. You must say yes."

Standing next to Lazarus, Hannah could hear a long, soft sigh escape him, even as she felt Longwood's smile to the very core of her being. Her face felt so hot she wondered for a moment if she had caught Kerry's fever. She took a quick, shallow breath to stave off sudden dizziness. "I see no reason why not. He's been looking forward to this for days. Yes, we'll go."

Timothy jumped to his mother's side and threw his arms around her waist. "Thank you, Mother."

Longwood chuckled. "Very good then. And now, our country's duty calls me." He bowed to the party, shook Timothy's hand, and kissed Hannah's once more, this time with elaborate formality. "I shall call for you tomorrow morning at ten." After taking his leave of the rest of the group, he retrieved his sword, which the boy had left on the floor, and gracefully returned it to its scabbard.

Hannah walked him to the front door, where he took her hand again.

"Dear lady, you are a vision of loveliness this evening, as always. It's so difficult to leave you. Won't you sit out on the porch with me for a few moments?"

Once again, his imposing presence and handsome face, lit by his warm smile and dazzling blue eyes, ignited a fire deep within her. She glanced away, certain he could read in her eyes how much she was attracted to him, or at least to his impressive masculinity. With a measure of composure, she looked at him again and shook her head.

"Like you, I must tend to duty. But I am eagerly anticipating tomorrow's outing."

He slumped against the doorjamb, and his face took on an attractive, boyish pout, which he could only maintain for a few seconds before regaining his courtly posture. "I live for the moment I see your beautiful face again." A last kiss on her hand, and he was gone.

Hannah returned to the parlor and found the supper party

dispersed. Only Tishtega remained, standing in the center of the room with arms folded.

"There, you see, a good, strong man to influence my son."

Tishtega broke her stolid pose, strode past Hannah, and stopped at the parlor door. "With this one you would replace our Ahab?" Before Hannah could answer, she disappeared up the front staircase.

And when Hannah searched for David Lazarus, she learned from Jeremiah that he had left by the kitchen door.

Chapter Twelve

&

The next morning at ten o'clock sharp, Captain Longwood arrived in an elegant landau driven by a liveried Negro servant and drawn by four handsome bay horses. With much excitement on Timothy's part and much curiosity on Hannah's, they proceeded across town, chatting happily about the day's coming events, the details of which Longwood seemed reluctant to reveal. Just a simple ceremony, he insisted.

No rain had fallen for almost two weeks, and the air was dry. The horses' hooves stirred up dirt from the streets, but the passengers were enjoying their trip too much to mind. The dust could be easily shaken off when they reached their destination.

As they crossed the river to Charlestown, Hannah felt a moment of trepidation. Their carriage was at the edge of the traffic-crowded bridge, the same bridge she and Timothy had crossed as Mr. Jones had driven them into Boston. Somehow, his covered coach had seemed much more secure than this open carriage. With difficulty, she pushed away her fear that the landau might be jostled and toppled through the rails into the water below, for indeed the large conveyance must be as sturdy as the coach and sound enough to keep its balance.

So Hannah sat back to enjoy her son's antics. Timothy had spied the Bunker Hill monument across the water and was extracting a promise from Longwood to accompany him one day up the inside stairs to the top of the obelisk.

Once across the bridge, the carriage found its way through the streets to the narrow gates of the Charlestown Navy Yard, where Captain Longwood received salutes and permission to enter from the uniformed marines on guard. Longwood then instructed his driver to take them down to the stone wharf.

On that short drive, he pointed out some of the many stone buildings that were spread about the twenty-five acres of leveled land on the banks of the Charles River. One long, massive brick building was called a rope walk, so named for the endless miles of rope made there that would provide rigging for the ships being built in the yard.

Another building held the navy store and another barracks for the sailors and marines. The large smithy building supplied hardware from its twelve forges. In one part of the naval yard, marines paraded in ranks across the green lawns. And atop the highest point in the yard stood the commandant's house where, Longwood informed his two guests, a reception would be held after the ceremony.

Timothy, finely dressed in his new blue short jacket and gray-striped trousers, could not see everything fast enough. He stood to watch the sights, his dark eyes shone with excitement, and he kept grabbing at Hannah's hand to cry, "See, Mother. Over there ..." By the time she located the item of interest, he had found a new delight, the most important being Captain Longwood's new command.

The warship was enormous, larger than any sailing vessel Hannah had ever seen, perhaps three times the size of the *Pequod*. Even sitting in its berth in the navy yard with its massive sails tightly furled to their spars, the USS *Lanier Wingate* was an awe-inspiring sight. But it was the vast number of people on the wharf that surprised Hannah.

Countless sailors and marines in various types of uniforms stood in their assigned ranks on ship or dockside, while crowds of spectators clambered for an advantageous spot from which to view the ceremony. The Stars and Stripes flew from numerous flagpoles, and red, white, and blue banners fluttered in the mild breeze. Adding to the festive mood, a marine band played stirring military tunes. On the dock near the ship, a platform had been built for both civilian and military dignitaries. A brisk breeze infused the scene with salty sea scents that mingled with animal and human odors typical of a warm, sunny, late-spring day.

Timothy, seemingly unaware of the crowds, begged for an immediate tour of the ship, pelting Captain Longwood with endless questions until the commander put up his hands in surrender and begged for mercy.

"We'll go aboard after a bit of ceremony, my lad. Then you will learn all you wish to know. But we must not be late, for punctuality is of prime importance in military affairs."

The carriage stopped, and Longwood lifted Hannah and Timothy down and escorted them toward the dais. Her hands full of her son, her shawl, and her parasol, Hannah was gratified to see that the wooden docks had been swept clean, even scrubbed, making it unnecessary to lift her new tan linen skirt to keep it from being soiled.

Amid all the busyness, she soon became aware that her host was a prime target of attention. As usual, the captain was elegantly dressed in his dark blue naval uniform, complete with brass buttons, golden braiding and epaulets, and ceremonial sword. But his posture, often relaxed in the pleasant homelike setting where he visited her, had regained the regal bearing of the first time she had seen him. He looked like a grand duke or perhaps even a prince. Though he seemed unconscious of the teeming crowds, she could see that, not only was every feminine gaze on him, but every man's as well. Beyond attention to his exceptional appearance, however, was the deference with which the dignitaries treated him, and now her, as he introduced her to various acquaintances.

While they awaited the opening of the day's events, she stared at his flawless profile until he turned and gave her a charming but controlled smile: his formal face, she decided, necessary for this solemn, official event. How could she have failed to realize what an important man Captain Duncan Longwood was? And to think, he was courting her.

The long ceremony included numerous speeches given by various public figures. Then at last, the Secretary of the Navy, who had sailed up from Washington, rose to take the podium. Hannah listened intently as the secretary related an incident some six months earlier when Captain Longwood and his crew had happened upon two Mexican pirate ships off the Atlantic coast of Florida. In his small sloop-of-war, Longwood had pursued them to their lair— the tiny, abandoned old Spanish Fort Matanzas, near St. Augustine—and had thoroughly routed them, putting an end to the terror they had inflicted on both American and foreign merchant ships.

The Secretary of the Navy had come to officially announce that due to Captain Longwood's great leadership, he would now receive his new command, a large ship of the line, the greatest of all U.S. warships: the USS *Lanier Wingate*, which they would now commission into service.

Hannah reached for her fan to cool her excitement. The ceremony, which Longwood had labeled "small," now proclaimed him the great hero of the day, punctuating the honor by placing under his command a much larger ship than his previous vessel. Yet, when he made his own short speech, he attributed the successful endeavor to every man doing his duty for the sake of honor and country. He then asked everyone in attendance to pray for the brave soldiers and sailors fighting the current war against Mexico, for which he and his crew must soon set sail.

During the two-hour event, Hannah grew more and more amazed. Not only was she learning things about the exceptional Captain Longwood he might never tell her, but Timothy was so fascinated by it all that he did not fidget for a moment. Then mother and son watched in further amazement as the wife of the Secretary of the Navy broke a bottle of "best brandy" against the ship's hull, thereby christening the USS *Lanier Wingate* into service. Cheers went up from the crowd and the assembled crew aboard the vessel.

After the closing remarks and a prayer by a local minister, Hannah waited while the captain received congratulations from numerous people. When at last he rejoined her, his face glowed with modest pride.

"Now the tedious part is over. Shall we join some others for reception at the commandant's house?"

Timothy, who had watched him with shining eyes, jerked his gaze to his mother's face.

"But we haven't seen the ship yet."

"Soon enough, my lad." Longwood placed a reassuring hand on the boy's shoulder. "I fear we adults must go through more boring formalities to make this all official. I would imagine you must be hungry, and the commandant's wife will take offense if we do not attend her buffet dinner."

The mention of food seemed to divert Timothy, and he happily walked between his mother and the captain as they made their way among the dignitaries crossing the navy yard.

Although Hannah lifted her skirts enough to climb the stairs to the red-brick mansion, she was gratified to see they had been swept as clean as the docks, and the scooping back hemline of her linen skirt would not be soiled before she entered the elegant mansion.

Inside the house, they were welcomed by the commandant and his wife and sent to mingle with the other guests. Once again, Hannah could see that every gaze and stare seemed to rest on Longwood, and once again the assembled dignitaries accorded great deference to him. How remarkable and a little unnerving to realize his courtship included parading her before those responsible for his future.

In short time, his appetite satisfied, Timothy reminded the captain of his promised tour of the ship. When Hannah started to correct her son, Longwood chuckled. Bending down to whisper, he confessed to being a bit bored with the reception, though Hannah could see he was not.

"So let us go, my lad, and inspect my new ship."

After taking their leave of their host and hostess, Longwood offered one arm to Hannah and took Timothy by the hand, walked them back across the expansive navy yard, and guided them toward the gangplank of his warship. As they neared, the blue-uniformed officer of the deck gave orders. A sailor in a spotless uniform of white trousers and a blue-collared white frock blew a signal on a high-pitched pipe and then raised his broad-brimmed black hat in a salute. All the sailors and side boys, and the marine guard, sprang into formation to join the salute to their captain as he boarded the ship and began the tour with his guests.

To Hannah, the most notable qualities of the ship were its order and cleanliness. Every piece of equipment was secured to its place, and she could have run her white lace gloves over any surface and found no soil or dust. She particularly admired Captain Longwood's spacious second-deck cabin, which was a model of organization.

Her son wanted to understand how everything worked, and Longwood patiently answered his questions. Timothy examined cannons, rigging, muskets, brig, galley, and storage for supplies and ammunition. He ogled sailor uniforms, begged for one of his own, and tried on the hats of willing donors, crusty seamen whose eyes beamed with instant affection for the boy.

When at last the captain lifted the exhausted child and his tired mother into the landau for the ride home, Timothy was asleep before the four-horse carriage conveyed them out of the Charlestown Navy Yard. Once home, the captain carried Timothy up to his bed, helped

Hannah remove the boy's jacket and shoes, and closed the drapes to darken the room.

Back downstairs, he reluctantly refused Hannah's invitation to sit in the parlor for refreshments. "There is nothing I wish more than to remain in your company, my dear lady, but I can see you are exhausted, so I will take my leave. Perhaps I could return tomorrow for some of that excellent lemonade Mrs. Harris's cook prepares."

"That would be lovely. Oh, dear. Tomorrow I am leaving ..."

"Leaving? But where will you go? You're not prepared to sail, are you?"

"Oh, no. I'm only going to Louisburg Square. I'm leasing a house from a friend." She did not mention that the friend was Mrs. Childers.

"Ah, good." His relief shone in his eyes. "But then, you'll hardly have time to get comfortable before your travels abroad."

"Sadly, I must postpone my voyage, at least for a short time. I cannot bear to leave until my dear Kerry is well."

He gazed at her for a moment, shaking his head in wonder. "Everything you do makes me lo ..." The captain, who an hour before had been a model of self-possession, appeared slightly befuddled. "That is, I, eh, I find cause to admire you more and more every day."

"I might say the same for you, Captain. Today's events revealed to me much of who you are. I must tell you, I'm impressed."

He lifted her hand to his lips, and his gaze intensified. He leaned farther forward and placed a gentle kiss on her cheek, pausing only a moment before placing a second, slower one near the corner of her lips.

For a moment, she swayed, unable to breathe, as her body remembered other pleasant sensations from long ago. Recovering with a quiet gasp, she moved back, her face flaming.

"Captain Longwood!"

He stepped away, his eyes sparkling and an impish apology in his grin. "Mrs. Jacobs," he crooned, just before sailing out the door.

Florence completed some of Hannah's order, and because the new clothing required more luggage, Hannah sent Seamus Callahan to purchase a large trunk and portmanteau. The baggage filled with the new wardrobe, Seamus conveyed them to Louisburg Square.

Nan brought her one-horse buggy to carry Hannah and Timothy across town to their new home. The small, four-wheeled phaeton had a closed, rectangular box under its leather-covered seat, which, Nan explained, kept her purchases dry should she be caught in the rain while out shopping. When Timothy remarked it would make a grand place to play hide-and-seek, Nan laughed merrily and told him he was a bright boy.

Halfway through their drive along the busy Boston streets, Nan handed the reins to Hannah, pleading an injured finger, pricked while she mended Kerry's stockings. "You told me you drove a buggy out in Indiana. Let's see how well you handle the laces. Belle has a soft mouth and a sweet temperament. If you like her, I'll leave her and the phaeton for your use."

"Housekeeper, staff, and now my own conveyance. You think of everything, don't you?"

"I do try." Nan waved away flies with her scrimshaw fan.

The day was hot and still, with no breeze to mitigate the stultifying humidity. Soon after leaving the Harris house, the three passengers became drenched with perspiration. On their faces and clothes clung a muddy veneer of dust, stirred up by Belle's hooves as she clattered along the dirty cobblestone streets. Stale odors of fish, horses, and humanity hung in the air, adding another layer of unpleasantness. Along the way, vendors hawking their wares called out crossly, as if to scold passersby for neglecting to spend their hard-earned money. Dogs on the street yipped and barked, creating a trial for

Timothy, who labored to keep Jemima from leaping out of his tight grip. Despite these circumstances, the three travelers arrived at Louisburg Square in high spirits and just in time to witness a noisy confrontation at the front door of Hannah's new home.

"I'll not have ye draggin' them crates acrost me newly shined floors, and that's the sum of it." A slender young woman with a bushy mass of bright red hair stood blocking the doorway, while Seamus stood on the steps clinging to one of the heavy trunks to keep it from sliding down the concrete stairs to the sidewalk below. Despite his cumbersome load, he was laughing.

"And I'm sayin', Miss Irish herself, that I'll be doin' what I was told by the new lady of this here house, and that's bringing these trunks inside and up the stairs to her ladyship's quarters."

"And I'm sayin' ..." The girl stopped, lifted her slender frame into a triumphant pose, and pointed toward Nan and Hannah. "'Tis her ladyship, herself."

"Goodness." Hannah began to envision more servant troubles.

"How delightful." Nan chuckled. "Now why didn't I think of it before?"

"What on earth are you talking about?"

"Why, those two, of course. They're perfectly suited to one another."

"Nan."

"Shh. Just watch."

Seamus nodded to the two women. "I'll have it upstairs in no time, Mrs. Jacobs." He pulled the trunk up the last step and, with its attached ropes, hiked it up on his back, bending forward to balance the weight. "And now, my lovely miss, if you would be so kind as to let me pass ..."

The girl's jaw fell open, and a grin of admiration spread across her pretty, freckled face. "Saints above. 'Tis Hercules himself."

"The door, please, Miss," Seamus said with a grunt.

"Oh, to be sure. To be sure." She pushed open the large front door and stood back to let him pass, turning to watch as he crossed the entry.

"Oh, Bridget," Nan sang out. "Come, dear, and give us a hand."

The girl swung around, blushing furiously. "Yes, Mrs. Childers." She ran down the half-dozen front steps and across the brick sidewalk. "I'm so sorry, mum."

"That's all right. Just secure Belle's line to the post there and give us a hand down."

Once Bridget had followed orders, Nan made introductions.

"Hannah, this is Bridget O'Neal, newly over from Ireland. She is an experienced housekeeper with impeccable references for such a young woman, and I know she'll not let you down. Bridget, this is Mrs. Jacobs. You'll be responsible to her from now on." Nan then introduced Timothy, and even his tiny companion. "And this is Jemima, Master Timothy's little friend. She may be a bit skittish at first, but do try to keep her near. It shouldn't take long for her to get used to her new home."

"Aye, mum." Bridget curtsied. "Welcome, Mrs. Jacobs, Master Timothy, and Miss Jemima. I would be pleased to show you the house, if you wish."

"I'll take her around. You just tell the rest of the staff to come meet their new mistress in the great parlor. Oh, and make sure Seamus— that's his name, Seamus Callahan, a fine Christian boy, and, as you could tell, Irish too—you make sure Seamus puts the rest of that baggage in the right rooms." Nan waved toward the wagon where the rest of Hannah's belongings sat.

"Yes, mum." Bridget curtsied again and hurried up the stairs to find Seamus.

Hannah had liked the neighborhood the moment the phaeton had turned into Louisburg Square. The red-brick houses sat in two rows on either side of a narrow park. On one side, the residences had four stories, and on the other, five stories. Each home was attached to its two neighbors, yet each was a single-family dwelling and had large, white-framed windows with green shutters. The front door and windows above sat back from the rounded front of the facade. On the sloping roof, dormer windows with classical pediments provided light to the attic rooms, which, Nan explained, were the servants' quarters. Hannah was reminded of the Greek Revival architecture so popular in her hometown of New Bedford.

The solid front door had a shiny brass knocker in its center, and on both sides of the door were sidelights—long, narrow glass panels that provided an outdoor view. Inside the entry, a narrow but elegant staircase rose from the left side up to the second floor, with a right turn at the top. From the center of the entry, a hallway ran toward the rear of the house, with the servants' staircase near the back. On the right was the great parlor, with the second parlor adjoining to the rear.

While Timothy dashed up and down the stairs chasing Jemima, Nan proudly showed Hannah the town house's elegant rooms, which were bright and airy due to several tall windows at either end of the house. Large sliding pocket doors of mahogany allowed the space to be used as one or two rooms, depending on the resident's needs and wishes. The rear parlor could also be used as a formal dining room. Both parlors were painted a soft green, and colorful wallpaper bordered the upper portion of the walls. Each room had a black mahogany mantel above its fireplace. Several pieces of graceful, finely upholstered furniture provided seating, with a variety of small mahogany tables placed conveniently nearby. Although the room had been furnished with enough seating, tables, drapery, crystal chandeliers, and several oil lamps, only a few pictures and other embellishments graced the room.

"I thought you might prefer to select your own," Nan said. "And, by all means, if you want to find other furniture—"

"I won't be here long enough to make buying furniture worth-while, and you know it."

"Hmm. We'll see about that." Nan turned away, fussing with a silver cord hanging on the wall near the fireplace. "Here's the bell pull." She swiped her hand across the unadorned mantel, checking her glove and then holding it up to Hannah. "See how clean every-thing is?" She studied the mantel for a moment. "What would you think of putting a large clock right here in the center?"

"And what would you think of our sailing for England in August? Maybe you'll find a clock you like over there."

Nan's eyes twinkled. "I may think about it. Now, let me show you the upstairs. Oh, in a minute. Here are the servants."

Three gray-uniformed servants entered the parlor, a man and two women, all dark-skinned of varying hues. Hannah glanced at Nan, who in turn watched her.

"Mrs. Jacobs, may I present Patience Hancock, your cook." Nan indicated the woman of medium height on her right. "She will simply amaze you with her culinary skills. And she will see that you put a little meat on your bones."

"Patience." Hannah nodded to the woman, ignoring Nan's last remark. The woman curtsied and nodded back. Patience's deep brown complexion reminded Hannah of Mattie, but unlike Mattie's, her large brown eyes exuded great self-confidence.

"And this is Leah," Nan continued. "She is just sixteen but nonetheless is wonderfully diligent in her housecleaning abilities. She never misses a spot of dust or dirt."

The slender young girl had paler skin than the other two, and her amber eyes could not quite meet Hannah's.

"Leah." Hannah gave her an encouraging smile, and the girl returned a shy smile. Why had Nan not mentioned Leah's last name?

"And this is John McAdam, your man of all jobs. He will take care of Belle and the phaeton, for they must be stabled down the street.

He will also meet with delivery men in back and tend to any outside work."

"John." Hannah nodded to the graying man, who stood about her height, with a stocky, almost stout frame.

"Miz Jacobs." He bent forward with a slight bow, then gave her a serene gaze.

"I'm pleased to meet all of you," Hannah said.

"Bridget, Patience, and Leah have the two rooms on the upper floor, and John has a small room in the basement, which we call the first floor," Nan explained. "Now, all of you run along, and I'll show Mrs. Jacobs the rest of the house."

Hannah marveled at the arrangement of the rooms, for the Louisburg Square houses were tall and narrow with space for only two large rooms on each floor. On the first floor, the entry of which was beneath the front steps, were the kitchen and family dining room, along with several storage rooms and John's tiny quarters. Above the second, or parlor floor, were the third-floor master bedrooms and two smaller chambers. The fourth floor was meant for a nursery, a child's room, and a guest bedroom. And, of course, the attic was for the servants.

Behind the house lay a small yard that sloped toward an alleyway where tradesmen made deliveries. A privy stood at the back of the property. Looking out the back window, Hannah noticed that some of the lots were divided from their neighbors by brick privacy walls, though no such edifice had been built between her new home and the house on its right. Since Timothy probably would be playing in the yard, she hoped her neighbor would not mind his boyish antics.

After examining the house's clever use of so small a property, Hannah announced that Timothy's room would be on the third floor beside hers. Used to having him nearby, she could not think of putting him in a room one floor above hers.

"Oh, Kerry, the head housekeeper is such a sweet little Irish girl. I could listen to her charming brogue all day long." Hannah sat at her friend's bedside the following week, describing her new household. "And not only that, Nan has employed three other servants, all of them Negroes, which, by the way, surprised me because I didn't realize how many Negroes live here in Boston. In any event, it was lovely just to move right in without having to hire my own staff, though I can't see why one would need a housekeeper and three servants for a town house. The only reason I can think of is that she wanted to give jobs to people out of work."

Kerry sat resting against her pillow, her thin, pale face showing the ravages of her illness. But her gentle spirit shone in her eyes. "Antoinette is very generous, isn't she?"

"She is a dear. But see here, I'm wearing you out. And where is Dorice? She should have been back with tea a long time ago."

As if to answer Hannah's summons, Dorice entered the room carrying a silver tray of refreshments. The housemaid moved gracefully, setting the tray on a side table and pouring the tea.

"We all miss you, Mrs. Jacobs." Dorice gently placed a bed table over Kerry's lap and set her tea on it. "Me, Ellen, and Mrs. Cook miss little Master Timothy too. Will you be bringing him by for a visit soon?"

"Thank you, Dorice." Hannah took the offered tea. "When Mrs. Harris is better, I'll bring him." She paused. "It's kind of you to give Mattie a break. I understand she was up all night so she needed to sleep a few hours today. Do you know where Tishtega is?"

Annoyance flashed across the girl's face. "That one is out with Mrs. Aunt Charity."

Hannah traded looks with Kerry. It was no longer her place to scold, but maybe Kerry would tell this girl what Tishtega meant to them. However, before Kerry could say anything, the usually quiet Dorice spoke up again.

"You know, Mrs. Harris, I wanted to tell you there's papers posted up all over town about runaway slaves. A person can get some real money finding them and telling the slave catchers where they are. So I just thought I would keep an eye out. And you should too, Mrs. Jacobs. Imagine, some Negro slave running away from whoever they belong to and trying to hide out here just because Massachusetts is a free state. As if we didn't have laws about that. As if we couldn't see what they are for their colored skin. No good and lazy is what they are."

"Thank you for the information, Dorice." Kerry's voice was soft, and she gazed at the girl with a tender expression. "That will be all."

Hannah could barely control her rage until Dorice left. "How dare she! That was a threat, and you know it."

Kerry sighed. "Yes, I suppose. She hasn't been happy since Mattie came. And of course Tishtega was just about the end of her. You know our Tishtega doesn't say much, but when she does, it's short and to the point. It got to where Dorice refused to help her in any way, so Jeremiah had to speak to her. Don't you know how difficult that was for him, with his tender heart?"

Hannah nodded. "I'm sure it was difficult. But why don't you just fire her?"

Kerry gazed at Hannah with the same expression she had given Dorice. "Because she's a lost soul whom God has sent to us. If we can show His love to her, maybe she will learn how to love others."

"But what if she tells the authorities about Mattie?"

"We must pray that she doesn't."

Hannah expelled a sigh of exasperation. "Oh, Kerry, I wouldn't keep a servant like that for anything. Fire her and *then* pray for her."

Kerry set her weak, shaking hand on Hannah's. "But we could

never do that. Her father is very ill, and she is supporting her family. What would they do without her income?"

Her gentle words stung Hannah more than an angry rebuke. "I didn't realize ... but still, she's like a serpent."

Kerry struggled to sit up a bit higher. "Think of how blessed we are, Hannah, two girls of modest means who married wealthy men. Neither of us has ever known what it is to be truly poor. But it's much harder for many other people of English descent, those like us whose families have been here since the earliest colonial days, but who never have prospered. With so many Irish and Negroes coming now and taking many of the jobs, they must feel their livelihood and their very lives are being threatened. No wonder Dorice is angry. But did you notice how well she does her work? Many servants in these circumstances might become lazy and careless, but since Mattie came, Dorice tries all the harder to be the perfect employee."

Hannah leaned over to kiss Kerry's cheek. "Your goodness never fails to be an example to me."

"If there is any goodness, it is God's. And God will take care of Mattie. She is His child."

Again, her gentle words struck with all the force of a stern rebuke. Hannah was not thinking about Mattie at all, but only how Dorice's insolence had offended her.

Chapter Thirteen

ॐ

"It's a charming town house, Mrs. Jacobs, well-built and in an excellent neighborhood." Captain Longwood had finished his inspection of Hannah's new abode and now sat in the great parlor enjoying his tea. "I shall reserve judgment about the staff, but if the condition of the place is any indication of their performance, I believe they will do."

Hannah laughed softly. While she had showed him about, he had assumed his military bearing, inspecting furnishings and servants with a critical eye, as though inspecting his ship and crew. "I'm glad you like it. It is quite a lovely place. As for the staff ..." She stopped, not wishing to revive an old discussion. In truth, she had found each of her servants to be not only competent, but very intelligent, contrary to his opinion about the capabilities of Negroes.

"Yes, I was going to remark about that. I could not help but notice that though you have a well-rounded staff, even a man for the back-yard work, you have no lady's maid. May I ask why you have not retained such service?"

His personal question surprised her, but his tone was so amiable that she felt compelled to answer. "But I've never had a lady's maid. I wouldn't know what to do with one."

"Never had ..." He stopped, shaking his head. "To think you appear so elegant, so flawless in every detail, no matter what time of day I come calling or whether you are expecting me. And you do it all yourself. Remarkable." Again he shook his head. "Forgive me if I am speaking indelicately, for I must admit I know little about ladies', um, wardrobes. But wouldn't you like to have someone to tend to your personal needs? I don't know what I would do without my body servant. Cyril's been with me since I was twelve. Even went along to West Point with me. He's indispensable on shipboard for keeping my things in order." He chuckled and stuck forward one black-booted foot. "Surely you don't think my half-boots are this shiny through my own efforts." His smile was attractively self-deprecating.

"Goodness, how interesting."

"Your eyes betray you. You're not the slightest bit impressed." He put on a wounded expression.

A short laugh escaped her. "I just wouldn't know what to do—"

"Aha! I have a brilliant idea. I'll write my father, no, my mother, and have her send up one of our own to show you how a lady should be cared for. If you like, you can take her on your tour of Europe. You'll soon discover she will become your right hand."

For a moment, Hannah could not speak. He was offering to give her a slave, or at least to lend her one. Her face began to burn, but whether from anger or embarrassment that he would offer such an unwanted gift, she could not tell.

"Thank you for your generous offer, but of course I must refuse." Her voice wavered as she tried to control her emotions. "If I decide I need help, I will hire someone."

He sat back, frowning. "I did not mean to offend—"

"No, of course not." She would never be able to explain how oddly his offer had affected her. She must divert his thoughts. "But perhaps I'm a little concerned about …"

"Ah, yes, of course. Here in Boston, how could you feel otherwise? But I assure you all of our people are loyal and would never consider deserting you, no matter what foolish things they might hear."

"I'm concerned …" She raised her voice a little to make him listen. "… about appearances. Your offer is far too personal. And while I'm on the subject of appearances, as pleasant as it is to have you call, I must ask that you restrict your visits to once or no more than twice a week. And never in the evening, as you did last week at the Harrises' house."

His frown deepened, and he leaned forward. "My dear, dear Mrs. Jacobs, how have I offended you?" His soft, deep murmur seemed a rebuke to her forceful speech. "And what can I do to rectify it? I will do anything—"

She shook her head and glanced down at her hands, wishing for a moment she still wore the protection of her wedding band. "I only meant to say, being a woman alone now, rather than chaperoned under the roof of a friend, I must be careful."

"Oh, thank heavens. I thought perhaps … yes, yes, I fully understand." He put his hand on his chest and pledged, "I shall guard your reputation with my life."

His relief, clearly written across his face, appeared so charming, she offered him her sweetest smile. "Yes, I believe I can trust you to do that." Then, to change the subject, she thanked him again for the enjoyable time she and Timothy had aboard his ship. "He has not ceased talking about it and vows he will be a sailor."

"I do hope you admire the profession sufficiently to encourage him to keep that vow." Happy again, he gazed at her with twinkling eyes.

"Oh, he must decide for himself what he wants to do, and children are always changing their minds." Why had she even mentioned it? *Her* vow had always been that she would not lose her son to the sea as she had her husband.

"But perhaps he will be like me and always wish it. Do you know we now have a naval academy at Annapolis, Maryland? When the time comes, if he truly wants to serve our country in the navy, I will use my influence—"

"Oh, please." She could hear the strain in her own voice. "He's only six. Please don't threaten to take him away from me already."

She stood and strode to the front window, surprised at another unpleasant turn of the conversation, one far worse than the first.

He came to her, gently gripped her arms, and whispered near her ear, "I fear my visit today has distressed you, and I don't know why."

His deep tones sent shivers down her side. How easy it would be to surrender to such pleasant feelings. With her quickly fading annoyance her only defense, a frown her only shield, she turned to break his hold, and stared up into his sorrow-filled eyes.

He reached out to touch her cheek. "If you could understand the depth of my feelings for ... I mean to say, my fond affection ..." He gazed into her eyes and seemed to sway toward her.

With a slow, deep breath, she moved back, fearing he would kiss her, and fearing she would like it too much, as she had the other night. "My son and I always enjoy your company. If he were not visiting his new little friend down the street ..." Her words died away.

With a rueful smile and bright blue eyes still darkened with sadness, he, too, retreated. Even Ahab, in all his magnificence, had never possessed such boyish winsomeness, and she reached out with a peace offering.

"I have always been fond of picnics. Perhaps, if you would like to see me more often, I could meet you someplace, perhaps on the Common, and bring a basket ..."

Joy burst across his flawless face like the sun breaking through dismal rain clouds. "... or I can have my ship's cook prepare something. Would you like that?"

"That would be lovely."

"Then a picnic it will be. And I will live for that day, my dearest lady."

"Excuse me, Mrs. Jacobs." Bridget stood in the parlor doorway. "There's someone to see you at the back door."

"Indeed." Longwood's posture straightened, and he glanced at Hannah. "Surely you don't permit tradesmen to interrupt—"

"No, not always, but this time I must." After only a week, Hannah had learned to read Bridget's face, and she could tell the matter was urgent. But to send the captain away in favor of a tradesman would be a dreadful offense. "I'll be right back. Please sit down and finish your tea. Bridget can bring more hot water."

"Very good then. I will eagerly await your return." Despite his genial words, he frowned and stood at his post by the window.

Hannah followed Bridget down the hallway toward the back entry.

"Why, Mattie, what brings you here? Is something wrong? Is it Mrs. Harris?"

The woman shuffled her small valise from one hand to the other, her face filled with fear, which she struggled to conceal. "Mrs. Harris is as well as can be expected, and no worse. But she said I should come over here for a spell."

"Of course you may. But why … ? No, don't tell me. Dorice."

Mattie winced. "I don't mean to cause you trouble, Mrs. Jacobs."

"It's not the slightest trouble," Bridget interrupted. "We can … Oh. I mean …" She looked quickly at Hannah. "Sorry, mum. I wouldn't have bothered you if I had known what she needed. That is …"

Hannah stared at first one, then the other. "What are you talking about?"

Bridget met her look with a serene gaze. "Sometimes folks need help, and so we help them."

The girl's confidence broke at the sound of heavy footsteps in the hallway. In an instant, an unwelcome specter appeared in the doorway, with martial law in his rigid stance and a cold, commanding glower on his face.

"What have we here?"

As deftly as a rapier thrust, his sharp tone pierced Hannah's heart. Her charming suitor once again became a ship's captain, like Ahab, a man of power, used to striking terror into subordinates when necessary. But before fear could conquer her, anger charged to the fore. She had survived Ahab's rages and would never again permit herself to be afraid of any man. With an artificial air of pique fueled by her very real fury, she lifted her chin and met his stare.

"It seems all my friends have the same idea about what I need. Mrs. Childers has taken the liberty of sending me a lady's maid."

She glanced back at Bridget, whose bland expression revealed nothing. Mattie, despite her trembling, rose to the occasion by staring at the floor and curtsying.

He scanned the faces of the three women and relaxed his posture. A pleasant smile replaced the grim line of his mouth. "Ah. Splendid. You will accept, of course."

With a sigh of relief disguised as annoyance, she shrugged. "I suppose there's nothing else I can do."

"Dear lady, you really must learn to appreciate being waited on." His eyes raked over Mattie, inspecting her as he had the furnishings of the house. "Mrs. Childers's thoughtfulness raises my opinion of her."

"Hmm. Bridget, please bring us more tea." She glanced toward Mattie. "Then you can tell her where to put her things." She marched past Longwood, her fists clenched. To regain her composure, she drew in slow, deep breaths, thankful she was wearing a morning dress the design of which permitted her to leave off her corset. By the time they were seated once again in the great parlor, she had managed to put on a pleasant face.

"You're right, of course. Nan was very thoughtful to find someone for me."

"I must caution you, however; these Northern Negroes sometimes lack training." His resonant voice seemed to carry beyond the room. "Our people have grown up in service and can anticipate your every wish. If she does not please you, you must not keep her simply for the sake of your friendship with Mrs. Childers."

Hannah glanced toward the doorway. "Captain, I have not known you to be rude. I hope she didn't hear you."

He shrugged. "It would be good if she did. Your servants need to know someone is looking out for you. Otherwise, they'll take advantage of your goodness."

"Looking out for me?" All the emotions of the morning bubbled out of her in an uncontrolled, girlish giggle. "Is that what you are doing, sir?"

He nodded solemnly, but the twinkle had returned to his eyes. "Why, Mrs. Jacobs, I certainly do hope so."

Hannah could not decide which distressed her more, Bridget's mysterious admission about helping people, Captain Longwood's assumption he had a right to "look out for" her, or her lie to him about Mattie. Though his courtship was flattering, his aggressive advances concerned her. Even Ahab, with all his self-confidence, never assumed she returned his affections. And now she found herself lying to Longwood. Still, she would never tell him Mattie was a runaway slave. Or even a freed slave. Better that he continue to think the woman was from Boston. But with this lie between them, how could she continue to receive his attentions? Surely she would accidentally betray Mattie.

Only one of her concerns could be dealt with immediately. As soon as Longwood left, Hannah returned to the front parlor and pulled the bell cord by the fireplace. Bridget soon appeared in the doorway.

"Yes, mum?"

Hannah regarded her for a moment, during which time the girl's serene expression did not fade.

"I must know what you meant when you said you help people."

"Why, mum, when a hungry man comes to the back door, I have him sweep the steps or fetch a package, then give him a bite to eat for his efforts."

Again, Hannah studied her. This couldn't be all there was to it, could it? Unless Bridget understood who and what Mattie was, she surely would not have gone along with their charade.

"Then why did you interrupt me when I had a caller?"

Bridget's eyes widened a little, and she stared down. "Ah, well, you see, mum ..." She paused and looked up. "Why, she asked to see you and only you to give you a message from Mrs. Harris. It seemed urgent, or I wouldn't have disturbed you and that exceedingly handsome captain. Goodness, mum, he certainly thinks the sun rises and sets with you. There's no mistaking that. And him surely a battle hero and no less. Faith and begorra. He must be fiercesomely brave."

Hannah almost laughed at the girl's cheekiness. This must be some of that famous Irish blarney she once heard Seamus mention, a tool to divert attention from the subject at hand. But how did one deal with such insubordination in a servant? She who had been so ready to see Dorice fired now wanted to hug Bridget for her subtle impudence.

"We were not speaking of Captain Longwood, Bridget. We were speaking about helping people."

"Yes, mum." The girl looked down again, working to hide a mischievous grin.

Hannah pursed her lips and gazed out the window. She must speak with Nan before discussing it further with Bridget, so she simply added, "Helping people is a good thing. I believe you should continue."

Bridget's smile opened like a morning glory at dawn. "Yes, mum."

"In fact, I believe I've seen you 'helping' Seamus Callahan one or two times."

Now the girl's face turned scarlet under its many freckles, and her smile faded. "Aye, mum. He was coming around for a day or two after helping you move in. But he's got work aplenty over to the mission, and they can feed him from now on."

"Why, Bridget," Hannah teased, "you were so interested in complimenting my gentleman caller, and yet you turned away your own. Why?"

Bridget shrugged. "It's the drink, mum. The curse of the Irish."

"Oh, dear. I didn't realize. But he's getting help. Reverend Harris is helping him, I'm sure."

"If he can help him, then Lord bless him. But I've never seen a man once smitten with the bottle who can give it up for good."

"But, Bridget, every man has faults. My dear father had an occasional glass of sherry, yet he was the kindest, most generous man I've ever known."

"Meaning no disrespect, mum, but I guess we all have our limits." Bridget's voice grew soft, but her sad gaze remained steady. "There's faults to be overlooked, and there's faults not to be abided. We all have to decide what we can live with. I've seen a man more in love with the drink than with his own wife. I've seen a man fight, willing to die, for the right to have his liquor and sell his own child to pay for it."

Hannah gasped. Bridget's eyes said what her words left out. She was speaking of her own father. "Oh, my dear ..."

"Now, if you'll permit me, mum, I've still got to see to the linens."

"Yes. Yes, of course. Thank you, Bridget."

Chapter Fourteen

ॐ

Seated at her vanity table, Hannah pondered her conversation with Bridget. The Irish and Negroes vied for the same jobs, so why would she keep quiet about Mattie? There was a slim chance she did not know the black woman had escaped slavery. Or, if Bridget's father truly had sold her into some kind of bondage, perhaps she, too, had escaped. That would certainly account for her willingness to help Mattie.

Just what kind of household was this? And why had Nan brought Hannah and her son here? Since moving, she had seen little of her childhood friend and had assumed that charitable work kept her busy. Now Hannah wondered more than ever what that work entailed.

She studied her reflection in the vanity mirror. Now that she slept more, the dark circles had vanished from under her eyes, greatly improving her appearance. The same could not be said for poor Kerry, whose pale face seemed to grow thinner with each passing day. At the thought, Hannah longed to see her friend. She would make the trip first thing tomorrow morning.

Hannah had promised Kerry she would visit every day, but with the Harris household now so full, twice a week seemed more fitting. And of course on Sundays, she and Timothy still would attend church at the mission, for she always enjoyed Jeremiah's soul-soothing sermons. Since her prayers for Ahab had gone unheard, those messages were all that connected her to her childhood faith.

Now, however, home duties called. Hannah rang for Bridget, finished her hair, and then met the housekeeper at the bedroom door.

"Have you settled Mattie in her room?"

"Aye, mum. She's to share with me, as Leah and Patience's room only has the two beds."

"And you don't mind that?"

"No, mum. It's not the first time I've shared. There was nine of us growing up, and me and my sisters, the six of us, slept together."

Hannah studied her expression and could not detect the slightest bit of displeasure. How remarkable.

Bridget looked at her expectantly. "Is there anything else, mum?"

Hannah shook her head. "Not right now. But I do want to talk to you again soon."

"Talk to me?"

"Yes, dear, talk to you."

Bridget grinned and stared at the floor. "Yes, mum." She curtsied again, and hurried away.

Early the next morning, Timothy went to spend the day with a neighbor boy. The child's mother, young Mrs. Atwood, had called the day after Hannah moved. The well-bred young woman possessed an education befitting a banker's wife, and her son displayed impeccable manners. After several visits back and forth with her neighbor, Hannah felt comfortable letting Timothy play with eight-year-old Charles. Despite her improved opinion of Paolo and Estevam, she preferred a more refined playmate for her son. Or perhaps just cleaner, for after a day with his old friends, Timothy often needed to be scrubbed from top to toe. Now Charles's governess, Mademoiselle Trudeau, took the two boys down the street to play on the grassy Common, and their games left them exercised but free of street dirt.

With her son in good hands and her servants given their instructions, Hannah sent John to hitch up her phaeton for a visit across town.

"Let's go, Belle." Hannah clucked to the horse and flicked the buggy whip near her rump. Only a light touch motivated the mare to obey. After several visits across town, she seemed to know just where to go and clopped along at a steady pace, which, if not energetic, was consistent. With remarkable intelligence, she maintained an attentive watch on the busy traffic before her.

Midmorning heat bore down on Hannah. She could not drive the phaeton and hold her parasol at the same time, but the buggy top kept the sun from her face. Yet bonnet laces trussed her neck, and a black dress, a corset, and numerous undergarments pressed against her body with relentless heat. Her new, lighter gowns were in the laundry, and she was still awaiting delivery of the rest of her wardrobe. However, Florence recently lost a seamstress to marriage, which postponed their delivery, including some of the summer garments. For now, Hannah must make do with what she had. Held up for a few moments as a milk wagon lumbered across Belle's path, Hannah idly wondered if Mattie could get work as a seamstress.

As she neared the North End, she saw Jeremiah entering an apothecary a half-block away. She reined Belle close to the sidewalk to wait for him.

Soon he appeared again, stuffing a small package in his pocket as he walked. But before Hannah could hail him, a young woman advanced toward him with a bold gait, caught his upper arm in a familiar grip, and moved her body close. He drew back in surprise.

"Hello there, Mr. Preacher Man." The girl spoke in a loud, coarse voice. "I hear your wife is laid up in bed these days. You must be awful lonely. How about letting me keep you company for a while?"

Hannah wished she were close enough to lash the insolent tart with her buggy whip. But just as she started to urge Belle to Jeremiah's rescue, he fixed an intense gaze on the girl. Hannah pulled back on the reins, happy to watch this disgusting sinner get her just deserts.

Jeremiah's face seemed to glow like Moses's did as he was coming down from Mount Sinai. He grasped the girl's arm and held her away from his body, but his grip also prevented her escape, and his stare imprisoned her eyes. She tried to pull away, her eyes wide with rage.

"Let me go."

"Forgive her, Father. She doesn't know what she's doing." Jeremiah's voice resonated, as from his pulpit.

"Let me go."

"God loves you, child. Let Him show you the way of salvation."

The girl struggled so hard to break his grip, if he had let her go, she would have fallen to the pavement. But he held her fast.

"The way of salvation?" She spat near his feet. "That's what I think of your salvation."

Again, Hannah itched to strike her with the whip. *If only I were closer.* But Jeremiah's eyes exuded sadness and that gentle, saintly radiance through which he always viewed lost sinners.

"Stop struggling, and I will release you."

With her free hand, the girl tossed her long, tangled hair over her shoulder, then straightened and, with reluctance, stood still. He loosened his grip, and she jerked back and adjusted her gaudy, low-cut red dress, which had slipped off one shoulder. She stamped the ground defiantly and glared up at him as if to defeat his kindness, as if to force him to brush her aside.

"So the preacher man's gonna save me, eh? How's about I save you?"

"You're always welcome at the mission, Clara. We can help you—"

"I don't need help!" She spun around, strode a few yards away, and then turned back. "I don't need help." But her protest, though shouted, rang uncertain the second time. She turned again and ran away.

Jeremiah lowered his head and sighed. Hannah knew he now prayed for the girl, and she felt ashamed. In the midst of all his suffering, he still ministered to the wayward, even this horrid, wicked girl. How good he was, and how deserving of happiness.

Dear God, please heal our beloved Kerry. Don't take her away from him. Please, please don't let her die. Tears filled her eyes as she slowly drove Belle closer to Jeremiah. Why would God bother with her prayers?

When Jeremiah looked up and saw her approach, his eyes still radiated an almost angelic glow. "Hannah."

"Jeremiah, I saw that … that awful girl. How dare she touch you! How could you let her do that without pushing her away?"

He seemed perplexed by the question, but only for a moment. "Isn't that what our work is all about? Our Lord commands us to minister to unfortunate ones such as Clara."

Just the answer she expected. He even knew the girl's name. She heaved a sigh, hoping he didn't see her tears. "Unfortunate? Yes, of course. Well, she's gone now. Let me drive you back to the mission."

He joined her in the buggy but gave her one of his disappointed, older-brother looks. "Here, let me drive. I can see the heat is a bit much for you. Are you sure you feel up to visiting us today?"

"I'll be fine once we get there."

"Yes, I'm sure you will. You're strong, Hannah. And so fortunate. Not like some …" He glanced her way and then turned his attention to driving Belle. After a moment, he continued. "You can see how deeply troubled she is. Kerry often visits her home and takes a basket. Just last month, Clara's mother and younger sister became ill. The mother takes in laundry and mending and tries to provide for the girls, but it's difficult. When she can't work, they have nothing. Clara's father ..." He glanced her way again. "He died at sea. Clara must feel her, eh, work is the only way she can help her mother provide for the three of them. But, Hannah, she needs prayer and love, not judgment. That's up to God. She also needs our ministry in her life, even if she won't admit it yet. And I just wonder if you're the person to minister to her."

Hannah stared out at the crowded streets, annoyed. It was one thing to repeat a prayer for such a girl, another to minister to her.

"You could help her, Hannah."

"Of course. I'll pray for her." *Pray she'll keep her dirty hands off of you.*

"You know I mean something else."

She could not ignore him. Not Jeremiah, her lifelong friend, the only person besides her father who could see into her soul and make her feel ashamed. If she refused to do God's will with her life, he seemed to imply, was she any better than the girl she so quickly condemned?

"I wouldn't know where to begin."

"Your prayers are a beginning. But lately we, Kerry and I, have been wondering, what if these desperate girls found a better way to provide for their families? Kerry told me Clara's home has few furnishings and is not well kept. These girls have so little, not even housekeeping skills. If we could open a school and train them, they wouldn't have to resort to such a ... um, dubious career." Excitement shone on his face as he spoke, and he gazed down the street toward the harbor as if looking into the future. But Hannah refused to be swept up in his dream.

"Perhaps I can make a donation to your school. I'm sure anything you and Kerry decide to do will be worthwhile." *I have Timothy to rear. We're going to travel. Jeremiah, don't do this to me. Don't make me feel guilty for not being like you.*

He focused on her again, silent for a moment. Then he gave her a sad smile. "You've been given so much, Hannah. When are you going to start using your gifts for God?"

"If you're suggesting I invite wayward girls into my home for housekeeping lessons, I'm not interested. Wouldn't that be the talk of Louisburg Square?"

"When did my Hannah become concerned with the opinions of others?"

"I'm not," she snapped. "I just can't live out your dream. I have my own."

He sighed. "I know you do. And this one is actually Kerry's dream. I suppose it will just have to wait until she ..." his voice caught. "... until she's well."

"Oh, dear, I didn't even ask how she is today."

"No better." The sudden sorrow written across his face told her how severely Kerry suffered.

Hannah looked away to hide her tears. Where was God when such a sweet, good woman lay suffering so much, a woman who lived every moment for other people?

When they arrived at the mission, Jeremiah summoned Seamus to see to Hannah's horse and buggy. Then he escorted Hannah to the house, which hummed with quiet activity. While the girls napped in the nursery, the servants performed their duties, and Aunt Charity read her Bible in the back parlor. After greeting the older woman, Hannah sat beside her, and Jeremiah took the medicine upstairs to Kerry.

"She'll want to see thee, of course," Aunt Charity said. "Thy visits always lift her spirits."

Hannah nodded her gratitude. At least this old friend would not condemn her. Aunt Charity's Quaker beliefs taught that each person should be guided by an Inner Light rather than sermons. But even as Hannah remembered this fact, another thought darted across her mind. Aunt Charity spent every day of her life serving others, and she spent her paltry earnings to buy hymnbooks and ginger tea for the countless whalers who sailed from Nantucket. Her whole life was a sermon.

She shook off her guilty thoughts. "How is she this afternoon?"

"She's in the Lord's hands, and Tishtega is doing what she can. With all her years of midwife experience, she's never seen anything like this. The fever comes and goes, the weakness and headaches remain." Aunt Charity's eyes filled with tears. "Would to God I could take her pain away."

Hannah pulled her friend into her arms. How frail, how fragile she was. Why couldn't God just heal Kerry and bring joy to this dear old saint's last years? Surely God could do that, couldn't He? But why wouldn't He?

"Hannah." Jeremiah peered into the parlor. "Would you like to go up now?" He focused on the two weeping women, fighting his own tears. Then he came close, knelt before the divan, and took them both in his arms.

"Beloved heavenly Father, look down upon us, Thy children, and give us grace to be strong for Kerry's sake. We are Thy servants. Do with us as Thou wilt. We long for Kerry's healing and for the child …" He choked back a sob. "… yet not our will, Father, but Thine be done. In the name of our blessed Savior, our Lord Jesus Christ, who suffered more than we ever could, and all for us. Amen."

Hannah resisted the impulse to bristle at his prayer. Just like her father, Jeremiah never fought, never demanded. How could he surrender so easily? But then, what choice did he have?

"Amen," she whispered in unison with Aunt Charity.

"Would you like to see Kerry now?" Jeremiah said.

"Oh, yes." Hannah gave Aunt Charity another hug, wiped her

eyes with her handkerchief, then hastened upstairs. As she tapped on the door and opened it, she willed her face into a cheerful smile. "Hello, my dear Kerry. How are you today? Good afternoon, Tishtega."

Tishtega stood by the window, adjusting the drapes to let in more light. She turned and nodded. "Mrs. Hannah."

"Oh, Hannah, it's so good to see thee." Kerry's soft voice sounded raspy, and her porcelain complexion now had a gray cast to it. "Come sit by me and tell me about my little Timothy. Did you bring him with you?"

Tishtega came to the end of the bed. "Yes, where is my son Timothy?"

"Oh, I'm so sorry to disappoint you both. He's visiting with a neighbor boy today. I'll try to bring him next time."

Kerry nodded her acceptance, but Tishtega clicked her tongue in disapproval.

"Estevam and Paolo come and beg for him every day," Tishtega said. "You must bring him here or take them home with you. They are good boys, good for our son. Who is this neighbor boy?"

Hannah never knew how to answer her, for she seldom approved of what Hannah did. But how could she argue with one who loved Timothy so much?

"I'll bring him next time." She turned to Kerry. "And what about our three little angels? Do they get to spend much time with their mother?"

Kerry's eyes brightened a little. "Ellen brings them in right after their naps when they are quietest. They're doing very well." She looked toward the foot of the bed. "Tishtega, thou hast been with me since morning. Please go get some rest. Hannah will be here for me."

"Yes, Mrs. Kerenhappuch." Tishtega shot another disapproving glance toward Hannah and strode from the room.

Hannah gave an involuntary sigh of exasperation and then shrugged. "Goodness, she's certainly disagreeable today. But when was she not disagreeable?"

Kerry managed a soft laugh. "Oh, forgive her, Hannah, dear. She's not angry with you, just frustrated by my illness, as are the doctors."

"I suppose so. But you haven't told me how you feel today."

"No better. Maybe this medicine I just took will help. But I want to talk to you about something else. Jeremiah told me about seeing Clara."

"Oh, that awful girl. Can you imagine? She ..." Hannah stopped. Surely Jeremiah did not tell Kerry how the harlot grabbed his arm in such an indecent way.

"Her hunger drives her to desperation. But her mother spends endless hours in prayer for her, and God always hears the prayers of a weeping mother."

"But surely this mother could stop Clara. What kind of mother would permit her daughter to continue as a ... a woman of the street?"

Kerry touched Hannah's hand. "I must tell thee about Clara's mother. Don't despise her. Her husband was a Nantucket whaler, a good man. But the sea can do strange things to a man, as well thou knowest. Over time, he changed, coming home after each voyage less and less like the gentle-hearted man she married. His last voyage was ... oh, Hannah, I despair of telling thee this, but I must. Dearest friend, he was on the *Pequod's* last voyage."

Hannah drew back with a gasp. If Kerry had slapped her, she would not have felt more harshly struck. Was there no end to the harm Ahab had caused?

"Oh, dear Lord. ..."

"But thou must not blame the captain for Mr. Macy's evil ways or his death. He chose his own wrong path. He chose his own isolation from those who loved him. He chose his own isolation from God." A gentle desperation emanated from Kerry, and her color rose as she continued. "Hannah, thou must go to Clara. Thou must try to reach her through this common bond."

"But I could never tell her about Ahab. I must never let anyone know he was my husband. She might even blame me for her father's death."

Kerry faded back into the bed, her pale cheeks matching the white of the pillow. "Think of her immortal soul, dear one. Then decide what thou must do." With another surge of delicate energy, Kerry reached up and touched Hannah's cheek. "Beloved, ask thyself, what would thy Father have thee do?"

Hannah enclosed the fragile hand in her own, distressed by Kerry's plea, yet unable to escape it. Her father would have given his last penny, his last breath, to save Clara. How could she do any less?

Chapter Fifteen

ઠ૭

Seamus will be happy to accompany you. He always drives Kerry out to deliver food, so he knows where the Macys live." Jeremiah escorted Hannah to her buggy, carrying a basket filled with Cook's delicious fish chowder and brown bread. "Clara may not be home, but perhaps her mother can tell you when she will be."

"Hmm. She might not be home. I hadn't thought of that. But I'm probably not that fortunate." Hannah unlatched the buggy's box cover so he could place the food inside.

Jeremiah chuckled as he secured the basket and closed the lid. "Now, Hannah—"

"Oh, don't preach at me. I'm going, aren't I? But I'll only take the food. I refuse to tell them about—"

"Good afternoon, Mrs. Jacobs." Seamus approached them and doffed his seaman's cap, bowing to Hannah. "It's a fine thing you're doin', mum, takin' on Mrs. Harris's charges while she's laid up."

"Thank you, Seamus. It's nice of you to help too." Hannah knew her voice lacked enthusiasm, and she glanced at Jeremiah. His sweet smile and saintly glow seemed to mock her. "As for you ..." She shook her head. "Good day, Reverend Harris."

"Good-bye, Hannah. I'll be praying for you."

"What a surprise," she muttered. Her displeasure notwithstanding, she accepted his offered arm and climbed into the phaeton.

Seamus picked up the reins, cooed to Belle, and snapped the

whip gently. Hannah sat back to enjoy the ride and Seamus's merry whistling.

The stocky, red-haired man seemed to be in his late twenties, although he might be younger. Mariners often appeared older than their true ages, their faces being weathered by incessant sun and ocean winds. Other than that, and contrary to Bridget's assertion, Seamus's hearty, healthy appearance gave no hint of too much liquor, unlike hardened drunks she had seen staggering about Nantucket. No, in fact, he exuded youthful energy and enthusiasm, and he never refused even the most menial job. No wonder Jeremiah let him stay at the mission without charge.

A happy plan darted across Hannah's mind. She would join Nan's matchmaking plans. After all, this young man deserved happiness.

"Seamus, it's so nice of you to drive me to the Macys' house."

"Glad to do it, mum." Seamus kept his eyes on the traffic ahead, but he grinned broadly.

"Maybe you could help me with something else."

His eyebrows went up, and he gave her a quizzical glance before turning back to driving. "Aye, mum?"

"You see, I never knew anyone from Ireland before meeting you and, of course, my housekeeper, Bridget. You always seem so sunny and happy, and so did she, so I assumed you Irish were all a jolly people. That is, until just the other day. I'm not sure what it is—"

"Is Miss O'Neal unwell?" His grin disappeared, and he stared at her, his bushy red eyebrows forming a V above his hazel eyes.

Hannah pursed her lips and gazed off toward nothing in particular. "Oh, is that the way to the new Revere Hotel? I always seem to lose my direction in this part of Boston."

"Uh, no, mum. You're thinking of the other side of town. Mum, begging your pardon, but is Miss O'Neal doing poorly? I mean, is she ailing?"

"Who? Oh, Bridget. No, she's not ailing, but she seems a little down in the mouth. Hmm. Isn't that a nice breeze cooling us off a bit, very refreshing for a June day."

"Down in the … ? Oh, you mean …"

"A little depressed."

"Is that all, mum?" Both his knit brow and hangdog frown turned upside down, and a twinkle came to his eyes. "Depressed, eh? Well, saints above …." He chuckled and then began to whistle again.

Hannah stifled the giggle that bubbled inside her. The last time she had so much fun was when she played matchmaker for Jeremiah and Kerry. The moment of humor cheered her considerably for this unwanted mission to the Macys'.

The ramshackle house sat among numerous similar dwellings on dusty, rutted Mumford Lane. No paint had ever touched the weathered clapboard exterior, and the roof appeared loosely attached, as if an afterthought. The fragile chimney threatened to topple should a strong wind arise, and the ill-fitting front door offered no protection against intruders.

Hannah knew of many similar shanties on Nantucket, but the island saw so little crime, its single jail cell rarely held a prisoner. On the other hand, with countless, varied immigrants coming to Boston every month, the city's crime rate had soared in recent years. In this waterfront area of town, especially, no one could safely walk the streets at night, for who knew what sort of criminals hid themselves among the latest shipload of newcomers? Why would a mother bring two daughters to such a hovel? Surely they could live somewhere else.

Seamus helped Hannah down from the buggy and took out the basket. "I'll just be waiting here, mum, to be sure Belle doesn't stray."

Hannah regarded him for a moment. Did he mean someone might steal the horse? "Very well. Thank you, Seamus."

She took a breath for courage, and instead drew in the stink of wastewater lying about the neighborhood. With a shudder, she gathered her skirts with one hand, held the basket with the other, minced around the muddy filth toward the house, and knocked, eager to hasten through her ordeal.

A slender waif dressed in a flour-sack dress peered out. She brushed aside her dull, thin, matted hair and spied Hannah's basket. A grin blossomed across her face, and she threw open the door. "Mother, Mrs. Harris ..." She froze, her smile vanishing. "Oh, you're not Mrs. Harris." Her large round eyes exuded a sudden wariness beyond her years, and Hannah felt a violent tug in her heart.

"Who is it, dear?" a raspy voice called from within.

"Please tell your mother Mrs. Harris sent a friend to visit." Hannah tried to sound cheerful.

The girl disappeared for a moment and then returned. "My mother will see you now." She spoke with quiet, strained dignity, and once again, Hannah's heart lurched in her chest. How could this sweet, brave child be related to that awful Clara?

She stepped into the front room of the dimly lit shanty, determined to treat the inhabitants as Kerry would. With difficulty, she endured a strange stench emanating from someplace near the small iron stove, a metallic smell that seeped into her mouth and made her want to spit. Instead, she swallowed hard. The one-room house was divided in two by the remnants of a tattered canvas sail, and Hannah followed the girl around its edge into the back area. When her eyes adjusted to the darkness, she could see a woman propped up on a crude wooden cot.

"Mrs. Macy? I'm Mrs. Jacobs, a friend of Mrs. Harris. She asked me to come see you and bring ..." Did she sound patronizing? Dear Lord, had she forgotten how to be kind? "This is that wonderful chowder Cook prepares. Would you like ... ?"

"Oh, yes. Thank you so much." Mrs. Macy's eyes shone with gratitude, understanding, and … hunger? "Please sit down." She indicated the room's one chair. "Jewel, please fetch us some bowls and spoons."

While Jewel hurried to obey, Hannah set the basket on a small table and removed its contents. "She sent some brown bread too, just baked this morning. I think it's the best I've ever had. But fresh bread always tastes wonderful, doesn't it?"

"Oh, yes." Mrs. Macy searched Hannah's face, as if she were determined not to appear too hungry. "Will you join us? Mrs. Harris sometimes has her lunch with us."

"No. No, thank you."

A blush of shame appeared on Mrs. Macy's cheeks, and she stared down at her hands, so Hannah quickly added, "I've just eaten. Next time, I'll wait and join you." She was rewarded with a shy smile and a nod from the other woman.

Jewel returned with two small brightly painted crocks and two iron spoons. Hannah looked about with feigned nonchalance, seeking something to comment on, resolved not to watch the two starving people struggle to eat with a semblance of dignity. Perhaps Kerry ate with them to distract herself from staring at their plight.

Her gaze lit on a patched woolen blanket that covered the room's one small window and blocked out some of the sun's baking heat. At the foot of the medium-sized bed sat a seaman's chest, and in the corner stood an unfinished wooden wardrobe and a few indescribable bundles. A worn but cheery quilt and a second pillow graced the bed, indicating Mrs. Macy shared the bed with one or both of her daughters. At last, Hannah's eyes lit on a Bible she had almost covered with the basket.

"Oh, how nice." She admired the well-worn book. "It reminds me of my father's Bible, almost worn out from years of being read."

Mrs. Macy swallowed and daintily wiped her mouth with her

ragged sleeve. Glancing at Hannah, she blushed and began to search her bed and the nearby table. Hannah pulled a clean linen handkerchief from her sleeve and held it out.

"Please, take it."

The two women stared at each other for a moment. At last, Mrs. Macy reached out, took the lace-edged cloth, and touched it to her mouth. "Thank you." Her words came out in a strained, shamefaced whisper.

Hannah smiled, studying once again the Bible in her hand. What would Kerry do now? What would she say to put this woman at ease?

"When Mrs. Harris comes, she reads to us," Jewel said around a mouthful of bread. "Mother can't see to read anymore, and I can't read all that good."

"I would be delighted." Hannah let the Bible fall open, wondering where to begin. "Do you have a favorite story?"

"Who are you?" A loud, harsh, familiar voice startled Hannah. "What do you think you're doing here?"

"Clara, don't ..." Mrs. Macy began.

Hannah turned and lifted her hand toward Clara. "How do you do? I'm Mrs. Jacobs, a friend of Mrs. Harris."

Clara stared at Hannah's hand and then crossed her own arms. "Oh, yeah? So what?"

Hannah withdrew her hand, thankful Clara must not have noticed her that morning on the street. "Mrs. Harris was concerned for your mother's health and asked me to visit." She glanced at Mrs. Macy, who now scolded her older daughter with a look.

"We don't need you coming down here, and we don't need Mrs. Harris. Here, Mother." Clara threw a handful of coins on the bed. "I found some money on the street. Now Jewel can go get us something to eat ..." She noticed the food, and for a moment, weakened. But she raised her chin and sneered. "So we'll get breakfast with it. Now you can leave."

"Clara." Mrs. Macy's voice sounded quiet but firm. "You will not be rude to our visitor."

Clara snorted, spun about, and strode around the canvas divider. "Mrs. Macy, I'm sorry ..."

"Mrs. Jacobs, I'm sorry ..." The two women began to speak at the same moment. Hannah nodded in deference to the older woman.

Mrs. Macy gave her a sweet, sad smile. "Clara is ..."

"I understand." Hannah noticed that Jewel was huddled on the floor in the corner. Perhaps she was trying to ignore what just transpired. "Jewel, tell me about yourself. How old are you?"

The girl came to life. "Ten. Almost eleven."

"And you don't read yet?"

"I want to go to school, but it never works out."

"Did you make that dress you're wearing? It's very nice." Hannah reached out to touch the long sleeve of the simple, well-made garment. "See these close stitches? It takes a great deal of patience to sew stitches like that."

"No, ma'am. My sister made it. When she can get the cloth, she sews real good. She made that there quilt and the pretty red dress she wears all the time. I love the red. It's so fancy and makes her look beautiful. Someday, I want a red dress like that." The child's pride in her sister beamed from guileless eyes. "She's teaching me, but I don't have the patience for the little stitches yet."

Hannah chuckled. "I had trouble with that when I was learning to sew too."

Jewel grinned. "You did?"

Hannah gave her an understanding nod. What could she do for this child? Maybe some books ...

"Mrs. Jacobs, I must tell you something." Mrs. Macy claimed Hannah's attention. "My daughter—Clara, I mean—hasn't always been … rebellious." She studied her empty bowl, shamefaced once again. "Her father died at sea, and she was devastated. Jewel hardly remembers him at all, but Clara doted on him. Then when she heard the horrible story about his death, it changed her."

"Oh." Hannah's throat constricted. She did not want to talk about this.

But the woman continued. "He was a whaler. It's a hard life, and dangerous. But he was strong. Oh, if he'd had a chance, it would've been different. But he was murdered by a crazy, one-legged captain chasing some particular whale. They say that captain murdered the whole crew."

"Murdered?" Hannah could hardly breathe. That was what some Nantucketers said.

"No, not murdered. Oh, I don't know. Clara heard the story from another whaler's woman, who heard it going around the whalefishery. One man from the ship survived. He came back and went round to all the taverns, telling how this crazy captain made his crew torment some large whale until it attacked his ship and sunk it."

"Oh, dear," Hannah broke in, her words coming out in a rush. "Yes, I believe I heard that rumor too. But who can say what really happened?"

"And even knowing the truth won't bring my husband back."

Hannah saw the suffering in Mrs. Macy's face and felt it to her core. "Nor mine."

"Yours? Why, Mrs. Jacobs, are you a whaling widow too?"

Hannah nodded and sighed. She could not, would not, tell the rest of her story. "But, as you say, nothing will bring our husbands back. We must do what we can for our children now."

"And what's my mother supposed to do for us, sick as she is?" Clara once again appeared in the doorway, an angry, menacing presence.

"But you ..." Hannah turned and looked her up and down. "You're healthy. Why don't you get an honest job?" The words flew out before she could stop them. She never should have come. She was only ruining things. Behind her, she could hear Jewel whimper and Mrs. Macy gasp. But she could not back down now. An apology would only spoil things further.

Suddenly aware again of that horrid smell permeating the house, Hannah tried to inhale inconspicuously to steady herself, but her corset clenched her ribs. Clara's formfitting dress revealed she wore no such device, leaving her free to huff her anger at Hannah's question. Still, the girl gave no answer, only stared at her accuser.

"I'm deeply sorry for your loss, Miss Macy. Having lost my father at a young age myself, I can certainly sympathize with you. But surely there is another way you can earn your living. Do you think your father would have been pleased to see you this way?"

"Ha," the girl spat out. "What could he say? What he didn't spend on drink, he spent on girls just like me. He might even be proud of me."

"Clara," cried Mrs. Macy.

Jewel gawked at her sister with innocent confusion.

Glancing at the mother, then back at Clara, Hannah shook her head. "Surely you misjudge him. But even if not, he's gone now. You must think of your mother. And Jewel. Do you want her to earn her living the same way you do?"

Clara's defiant look disappeared, replaced by a haunted expression as she stared at her sister. "Not if I have anything to do with it." Along with her defiance, her confidence also seemed to vanish.

"Then we must make certain it never happens." What impulse, what madness had prompted such a statement? Again, Hannah could not back down. But she must find something in this girl, some quality by which she could be redeemed, if for no other reason than Ahab had been her father's captain.

"What do you mean 'we'? What does a society woman like you want with me? I know your type. You come down to our end of town at Christmas and Easter, all dolled up like a grand duchess or even Queen Victoria herself. You smile and give us baskets of food and clothes, but all the while, you look down your noses at us …"

"Let's get one thing perfectly clear." The vehemence in Hannah's tone startled them both. "I am not a society woman. I am just an ordinary woman. Like you, I've seen great sorrow in my life, but I will not permit that to defeat me or drive me to a life of … a questionable life. Yes, my life has been easier than yours because my husband left me a little money, but that only puts a greater obligation on me to help others. If you are willing to stop this life of yours from this moment on, I will help you find a decent occupation. But don't waste my time with empty promises or lies."

Clara studied the wall and tugged at her sleeves as though trying to shut out distractions while she considered the offer. A series of expressions crossed her face: annoyance, anger, despair, and then a glimmer of hope as she turned back to Hannah.

"What do I have to do?" Her voice held only a hint of suspicion.

"Be willing to show up on time and work diligently at an honest job. Don't drink liquor. Be honest with your employer and with me."

"That's all?"

Hannah studied the girl up and down. "Take a thorough bath and wash your face and hair. If you don't have the means to do so, you may come to my house, and my housekeeper will help you. Throw away that dreadful dress. I'll find something for you to wear that isn't so … so …"

"I have another dress, a good one."

"She made it herself." Jewel jumped up and rushed to embrace Clara. "I told you she could sew."

Clara hugged her sister and gazed down at her with a tender

expression. "Yeah, I made it myself. And your dress too, my little Jewel."

The deep love between the sisters warmed Hannah's heart. The child had won over the young woman, not she.

"Come to my house tomorrow morning at ten. I should have an interview arranged for you by then."

"I might."

Hannah glanced at Mrs. Macy, whose face wore both tears and a smile.

"Oh, you'll come."

Clara nodded once.

"Good day then, Mrs. Macy, Jewel, Miss Macy." Hannah turned to leave.

"Mrs. Jacobs ..." Clara reached out but then pulled her hand back, as if ashamed to touch her new benefactor.

Hannah stopped. "Yes?"

"My pa ..."

"Yes?"

"He did drink. But he never went ... never visited girls like me. Down on the docks, people talk, so I know he didn't, at least not after he married my ma."

Hannah nodded. She wanted to say, "I didn't think so," but decided to let Clara have the last word.

How silly for society to scorn ladies who whistled, for during the trip back to town, whistling was exactly what Hannah wished to do. Her heart bubbled over with happiness because she had not shamed Kerry and Jeremiah after all. She had no idea what to do with Clara tomorrow, but she would think of something. For now, with things going so well, she must try for another success.

"Seamus, do you mind taking me back home to Louisburg

Square? I'll have John drive you back to the mission, but I would like to get home to my son now."

Seamus nodded. "Oh, surely, mum. Reverend Harris instructed me to take you home, and the walk back to the mission is exactly what I need to stretch me limbs."

"Oh, good. Then after you take the carriage around to the stable, be sure to come back and have Bridget pour you some lemonade. You've earned it for all this time you've spent in the sun waiting for me."

"Why, thank ye, mum." Already as carefree as a lark, Seamus now grinned broadly and launched into whistling another tune.

Joy surged through Hannah again, and she resisted the urge to giggle as a sweet memory came to mind. Her father often whistled, especially when he came home from one of his countless good deeds. No wonder she wanted so much to whistle now.

Chapter Sixteen

ᘓ

*M*other, I might hit Charles." Timothy lay in bed, an earnest expression in his dark eyes.

Her stomach did an anxious turn. "I know. Sometimes little boys, and big ones too, feel as if they must wrestle around to see who's strongest. I know it's all in fun."

"But it's not fun. Charles is mean." His face scrunched up in confusion. "Today, he kept poking me and yanking my hair when Mademoiselle Trudeau wasn't looking. Once, he stepped on my foot real hard with his heel on purpose. It really hurt."

Hannah drew a quick breath and uncovered his feet. The top of his right one bore a ragged, purple bruise, but the skin was not broken. Rage rose up inside her, and she struggled to hide it. Instead, she lifted his foot and bent to kiss the injured spot. He giggled and squirmed away. "Mother."

Relieved, she laughed too. "It must not hurt too much if you won't let me kiss it. But I suppose Charles isn't a very good play-mate. You don't have to play with him anymore."

Instead of greeting her pronouncement with pleasure, he shook his head. "Don'tcha think it'd be better if I just went ahead and hit him back real hard?"

"Timothy."

"Estevam always says that's the best way to stop a bully, unless they're lots bigger than you. Then you can get yourself killed, or at least hurt real bad."

"Oh, my goodness. But I can't in good conscience give you

permission to hit another boy. It's best just to avoid people like that."

His forehead crinkled. "But he's not all bad. We had fun when Mademoiselle took us to the Common. We raced, and I beat him. Maybe that made him mad 'cause he's older than me, but I'm bigger and faster. Maybe he'll be better tomorrow."

She brushed his hair back from his forehead. Maybe he was right. Maybe Charles would improve. Still, Timothy's revelation helped her understand what Mademoiselle Trudeau said when she brought Timothy home that afternoon: *Oh, Madame Jacobs, if you ever need a governess, I will be so happy to have the charge of such a wonderful child as your son. I am not under the contract....* Then she had shrugged apologetically and hurried back to her employer's house.

So placid Mrs. Atwood's little angel actually behaved like a beast. Hannah would have to be diplomatic about this problem.

"But if he's not better, can I hit him? Just once? Real hard?" At her exasperated sigh, he added, "Maybe not too hard?"

"Oh, Timothy, I ..."

Clearly frustrated, he took a turn at heaving a big sigh. "I need to ask Captain Longwood. He can tell me."

Captain Longwood. Was it just yesterday morning he paid his unnerving visit? And she still had not talked with Mattie. What eventful days these had been.

"Or you could ask Uncle Jeremiah or Captain Lazarus."

"No, Captain Longwood. He's a navy hero and knows all about fighting."

"Hmm. I see you've thought about this. Well, we can't do anything about it right now, so you get a good night's sleep."

After a kiss, which he did not refuse, she tucked him in and went down to the parlor to address another problem. She pulled the bell cord and waited for Bridget. The housekeeper soon appeared.

"Yes, mum?"

"Bridget, I must speak with Mattie. I hope she's had a chance to get settled since yesterday morning."

"Aye, mum, she has a bit, but I must say she's still frightened. She hasn't eaten a bite since she arrived."

"Oh, dear. Please go tell her to come down."

Mattie soon appeared, her eyes red and puffy. Hannah's heart ached to see the fear written across the woman's face.

"Please sit down." Hannah indicated a chair across from her own.

Mattie hesitated before lowering herself into the elegant brocade chair, where she sat erect and stiff. "Yes, ma'am?"

"We didn't have a chance to talk at the Harrises' house, but I want you to know I am aware of your circumstances, and I will not betray you."

Mattie's eyes welled up with tears, and she stared down at her clasped hands. "Thank you, Miz Jacobs." Her soft voice cracked as she spoke.

Weariness from an already emotional day and empathy for this woman brought tears to Hannah's eyes as well. Somehow, she must gain control of herself, or she would be no help to Mattie.

"We survived a scare yesterday, didn't we? Aren't we just as clever as can be?"

"Ma'am?" Then Mattie chuckled. "Yes, ma'am, we did." Her face relaxed, and she sat more comfortably in her chair.

"Our good friend Mrs. Childers has failed to inform me of exactly how I'm supposed to help you, so we'll just wait until she sees fit to tell us."

"I was supposed to go to Canada right away when I came to Boston last month, but I asked to stay a bit and ask around about my boy. You won't recall this, but I have a son."

"Of course I remember."

Mattie hesitated, a shadow crossing her face, as though she feared she had offended.

"Please go on." Hannah nodded her encouragement.

"My boy, he come North some few years ago. Mr. Douglass arranged for him to come. He's free, not a slave like me and my daughters."

"Mr. Douglass? The one who wrote the book I've been reading?"

Mattie's eyes widened, and she gave Hannah a shy smile. "I know he write a book, but I didn't know you been reading it."

"I started it at the Harrises and brought it here with me to finish. Now tell me about your daughters. Were you forced to leave them behind?"

"One of them, yes, ma'am. Pearl is still on the plantation, but she has babies she wouldn't leave. I wanted to stay, but she told me go. Missus has a mean streak, and she has the man hit me a lot, but Pearl gets along with her all right, and Missus likes Pearl's babies."

Hannah shuddered. That explained the scar on Mattie's mouth.

Mattie sighed. "Missus, she don't know all there is about those babies either." She glanced down. "Guess I don't need to go into that."

Certain she knew what Mattie meant, Hannah let the remark pass. "What about your other daughter?"

Mattie's face clouded again. "Master sold May some six years back when she was just twelve year old. I don't know where she went 'cause he took her to the auction and never told me who bought her. He wanted to break young Master from gambling, and since the boy had an eye for May, Master sold her to pay his debts. Didn't do the boy no good, 'cause he still gamble."

She looked up at Hannah, her eyes beseeching. "Miz Jacobs, could you help me find my May? I would give up my chance at freedom and go back for a beating if I could just know where she is and hear she's all right."

Hannah felt her heart lurch, just as when she met Jewel. How unacceptably horrible that people should suffer so much. "I wouldn't know where to begin, but we'll ask Mrs. Childers. Since your son is free, we might have more success finding him. Do you know where he might be?"

"All I know is Master sold him to somebody, and they was to bring him to Massachusetts and set him free. Least that's what I hear. They like him to sing and play his tambourine, so maybe he's doing that to earn his bread. I told him not to leave Massachusetts 'cause it's a free state and he's got papers and nobody can make my Pip a slave again."

Triumph shone in her face now, as though this one victory gave her hope for the future. "Ma'am, are you ill? All sudden, you look poorly."

Hannah trembled and clasped her hands to her face. It couldn't be the same Pip, could it? If the child who had adored Ahab truly was Mattie's son, how could she ever tell her that Pip had died aboard the *Pequod?*

"Ma'am?" Mattie rushed to Hannah and grasped her shoulders. "You gonna be sick?"

"I'm fine." Hannah struggled to regain her composure. She reached for her handkerchief but recalled leaving it with Mrs. Macy, so she used her sleeve. "It's just been a long day. Mattie, I'm so sorry about your children. We'll ask Mrs. Childers for help. Now please go eat something, then get a good night's rest."

Still eyeing Hannah with concern, Mattie stood. "I plan to earn my keep, Miz Jacobs. You tell me what to do, and no matter what it is, I'll do it."

"I know you will, Mattie. We'll think of something tomorrow."

In bed later, Hannah considered all the human suffering she had seen in just two days. She longed to talk to her father for, despite his frailty, he had been wise and would know just what to do for

Clara, Jewel, and Mattie. Papa would give his last dime, his last breath, to ease the pain of others.

As she drifted off to sleep, she wondered vaguely why it was her father instead of Ahab whose counsel and reassuring embrace she longed for.

In the morning, Mattie came to Hannah's room to help her dress. Although Hannah had always dressed herself, she saw how handy a lady's maid would be. With Mattie, she did not have to go through the usual contortions to fasten her corset or dress. Mattie even had a talent for brushing and curling Hannah's hair into the latest fashion.

This would be another busy day. Florence would bring more clothes for fitting, and Clara would arrive for a job, which Hannah had yet to arrange. Somewhere between breakfast with Timothy and approving of Patience's dinner menu, the obvious answer came to her. Clara could work for Florence; that is, if she arrived clean and properly dressed.

Clara did come in a modest, dark brown dress. Her newly washed hair was parted in the middle and pulled into two rolls over her ears. Her attitude also had improved, as though she remembered the good manners her mother had taught her. No longer defiant, she seemed an innocent girl. Satisfied with Clara's appearance, Hannah instructed Bridget to give her breakfast in the kitchen, where she was to wait until summoned.

Florence arrived at the back door with several large packages tied up in brown paper. With elaborate ritual, she laid out on Hannah's bed three new dresses: a soft green piqué walking dress, a dark blue muslin morning dress, and a burgundy gown of silk for Sunday wear. Then she set out a collection of nearly completed underpinnings. Through it all, she stammered apologies for the delayed delivery.

"I understand," Hannah said. "Without sufficient help, you couldn't be expected to do more."

"Oh, madam, I make no excuses. I'll work around the clock to finish in time for your departure to Europe."

"But still, you need help. I met a wonderful seamstress just yesterday, and I wonder if you would consider hiring her?"

Florence wrinkled her brow and then smiled broadly. "I would be delighted to hire a competent seamstress at your recommendation." Then doubt clouded her face. "You're certain she can sew?"

"You can give Clara a short trial. If she can always sew as well as she did on the work I've seen, I think you'll want to keep her. But you'll be under no obligation. I'll ring for her."

The meeting of the two seamstresses proceeded as comfortably as the subsequent fitting of Hannah's new clothes. Florence agreed to take Clara with her to begin work that very day. Her first project would be Hannah's underpinnings. If those were well done, Florence said, she would be permitted to assist with outer garments.

As she left with Florence by the back door, Clara turned to Hannah. "I owe you so much. You and me, we're gonna keep Jewel off the streets."

"Yes, we will, Clara. And I want her to go to school, so I'll send over some books for her."

Clara's eyes shone. "If you ever need anything, *anything*, you tell me." She gave Hannah a knowing nod and then hurried after Florence, balancing two large, brown-wrapped bundles as if they were breakable treasures.

Pleased with her success, Hannah puckered up to whistle one of her father's old tunes. Surely within her own walls, she could flout convention when her heart bubbled up with such happiness. Before she could blow her first note, Bridget rushed down the hallway.

"Mum, there's that gentleman to see you, the captain who came the other day, and he brung another with him. One of them slave catchers, I'm sure, despite him being dressed like a gentleman. I showed them into the front parlor, and Master Timothy, he popped in there before I could catch him. He's got their attention, so I suppose it's good, but—"

"Calm down. I'm sure you're mistaken about the man's being a slave catcher. Captain Longwood has just come to visit." Despite her words, Hannah felt her face heating up. The captain had agreed to limit his attentions so that her reputation would be protected. Why was he returning so soon, and why was he bringing another gentleman?

"Bridget, please have Patience prepare some tea cakes and lemonade." Hannah started toward the parlor but then turned back. "And have Mattie hurry after Florence with the mending. I forgot to send it with her."

Bridget curtsied. "Aye, mum. Right away."

With a deep, calming breath, Hannah ambled toward the front parlor. Surely the captain would not dare bring a slave catcher to her home. But if so, she would do everything within her power to protect Mattie, even if it meant she had to buy the woman's freedom.

At the sound of Timothy's voice, she paused at the wide parlor door. Her son stood in front of the two seated gentlemen, who listened as the boy explained about his bothersome playmate.

"So Mother said it was all right if I asked you—do you think I ought to hit him just once real hard to teach him a lesson?"

The stranger, a burly, well-dressed man, seemed annoyed at Timothy's chatter, but Captain Longwood reached out to clasp the boy on the shoulder.

"What a fine lad you are, Master Timothy. Most boys would have struck back without a question. Your restraint demonstrates remarkable self-control, an excellent quality. But, as to this Charles, what shall we do? Mr. Simons, what do you recommend?"

The other man snorted impatiently. "I didn't come here to play nursemaid to a pampered brat. Where are those Negroes?"

"Mr. Simons, my young friend here is no brat. He's a fine boy." Captain Longwood spoke in a light tone, but his dark scowl warned. "Ah, Mrs. Jacobs, you are more beautiful every day."

When she entered, the two men stood to greet her. The stranger's stare raked over her, his eyes narrowed, and his mouth formed a thin, frowning line. Although the captain smiled, his expression was harder to read. His stare seemed to bore into her, searching.

"Good morning, gentlemen. I see my son has been entertaining you." Hannah strolled toward them, drew Timothy to her side, and gave Longwood a questioning look.

His face relaxed, and he took her offered hand and kissed it. "Mrs. Jacobs, may I present Mr. Simons. He is a businessman here in Boston."

"Mr. Simons." Hannah nodded to the man but did not offer her hand. "Please, sit down. I've instructed my housekeeper to bring refreshments." Hannah turned to Timothy. "Run, find Jemima, and be sure she's had her morning milk."

"But, Mother ..." Timothy glanced at the captain, his eyes appealing for reprieve.

"Obey your mother, my lad. You must always do your duty by those entrusted to your care." Longwood patted the boy's shoulder. "We'll decide about Charles later."

"Yes, sir." Timothy glared at Mr. Simons before trudging out of the room.

After Hannah seated herself on the divan, the men reclaimed their chairs, although Simons sat on the edge and fidgeted.

"Captain Longwood, I must say, after our discussion yesterday, I thought we had an understanding. You've caught me in the middle of things that simply must be attended to this morning." She spoke slowly, sweetly, gazing into his handsome face.

A slight frown crossed his brow. "Of course. I will come right to the point. I fear you have been deceived by Mrs. Childers."

"What? Why, how could you think such a thing? She and I have been friends since our school days. I would trust her with my life. What on earth are you talking about?"

"She harbors runaway slaves. That's what we're talking about." Simons's tone was harsh. "And she—"

"Sir." Captain Longwood stiffened and turned to the other man. "Mrs. Jacobs is a lady. You will temper your voice in her presence."

As he spoke, Hannah studied her hands and put on a wounded expression to give herself time to think. But no helpful thoughts would come. She had no idea what to do. Slowly, she lifted her gaze and, ignoring Simons, appealed to the captain with her eyes. "I know you would never deliberately do anything to offend me, but I am deeply hurt that you would bring this man to my home—"

"The law of the United States Congress brings me here, lady, and—"

"Simons!" The captain's voice boomed, and Simons bristled but shut his mouth. Even Hannah drew back. "Sir, I will remove you from this house if you do not amend your manners immediately."

Longwood turned to Hannah, and she marveled that, although he had thundered at Simons, he held himself in complete control.

"Mrs. Jacobs, it is my unfortunate duty to inform you that you may be the victim of unscrupulous people who are engaged in the illegal, treasonous activity of transferring stolen property out of the country. The property of which I speak is, of course, those misguided chattels who have left their rightful owners and come North to escape their duty to God and man, enticed and deceived by those who tempt them here for who knows what purpose. Mrs.

Childers is known to be one of those who give assistance to these foolish individuals, hiding them perhaps in this very house. I came to ascertain whether that maid she sent you is this woman."

He pulled a paper from the front fold of his jacket and held it out to her. The picture was rough but, without doubt, it was of Mattie. The face, however unflatteringly drawn, showed her scarred lip and an open, simpleton-like grin that revealed missing teeth. Worst of all, her large, luminous, intelligent eyes had been given a wild cast. Hannah felt the blood drain from her face, and she clenched her jaw to control her temper. Scenes from the Douglass book darted through her mind, scenes that had enraged her as she read them.

Longwood moved to a chair beside her and took her hands. "Your anger is justified, but please do not make yourself ill. I'm sure you must feel betrayed, but you must permit me to handle this situation." He gazed into her eyes, a gentle smile gracing his lips. "Didn't we agree yesterday that I must take care of you? Summon the girl, and we'll return her to her rightful owners. There now, see how you're trembling."

"I ... will ... not ..." Hannah tried to choke out the words to dismiss these intruders.

"Mrs. Jacobs." Bridget entered the room, her brisk, cheery voice cutting into the tension. "Here's the lemonade and cakes you asked for. Oh, saints, mum, you're looking poorly. Sure, and these gentlemen will excuse you—"

"Hush, girl," Captain Longwood hissed. "You see, my dear, you even permit such insolence in your servants that this person should interrupt you when you have guests. Girl, put the tray down and run along."

Bridget placed the tray on the coffee table but stood by the door, watching Hannah.

"Very well, stay then. Mrs. Jacobs may need your assistance." He poured a glass of lemonade and held it out to Hannah. "Please take this. I'll see to everything. The law permits Mr. Simons to search the premises, but I will be with him in every room."

Declining the drink, Hannah ventured a look at Bridget, who gave her a placid smile. Hannah turned back to Longwood.

"How can you call yourself my friend and then bring this ruffian here? I'll not have my home violated this way—"

"But, dearest, you have no choice. It is the law. Surely you don't want a fugitive in your home. If it turns out your lady's maid is not this woman, all will be well. But if it is she, how can you be certain she will not bring harm to you and your son, being the outlaw that she is? These people become dangerous when cornered, like wild animals."

"May I see the likeness, mum?" Bridget did not wait for permission, but approached Hannah and glanced at the picture. "Oh, that one. Shall I fetch her, mum?"

The housekeeper's face wore a curious blend of annoyance and simplicity, the latter surely feigned.

"Yes, please. It seems we have no choice."

As Bridget turned to go, Simons strode across the room and grabbed her arm. "Not so fast, missy. You'll not be giving anybody a warning. I'll go with you."

"Take your hands off me …" Bridget twisted out of his grasp.

"Mr. Simons, I insist …" Hannah rose to her feet.

"Sir, I have warned you." Captain Longwood stood and took a step toward the other man.

The three spoke and moved at once, and their chorus stopped the offender. He turned to Longwood.

"We came here to get this woman, and I'll be da …" He cut off his own words. "I won't leave until I have her."

Longwood turned to Hannah with an apologetic frown. "With your permission?"

"You have made it very clear that I have no choice in this matter. Bridget, take both of these gentlemen to Mattie's room. And, if my son is still indoors, send him to me at once."

"Aye, mum." Bridget curtsied, did a saucy turn, and, with a glance over her shoulder, glared at Simons. "This way, your lordships."

When they left the room, Hannah slumped down into her chair, grabbed a fan from the nearby table, and waved it rapidly. She would never forgive Captain Longwood. How dare he! How *dare* he! She stood and strode to the front window, still fanning, but unable to cool her burning cheeks or quiet her tormented soul.

"Dear God," she prayed, though her heart felt no faith to back the desperate plea, "please help Mattie get away. Please protect her from these cruel people." She stopped fanning and brushed away tears with her sleeve. Wasn't there something she could do to save Mattie?

Peace.

The word, spoken to her troubled heart by a silent voice, carried with it the very feeling it named. Throughout her entire being swirled an unfamiliar elation, calming her wrath, lifting her soul. She felt a presence stand near and enfold her in loving arms. Her father. No. Her Father. At her feeble cry, God Himself had soothed her anxious spirit, for surely it could be no other.

"Thank You, Lord," she whispered.

All is well, sighed the voice within.

And she believed it.

Chapter Seventeen

⁘

Hannah turned at the loud thumps of hurried, descending footfalls. An angry Mr. Simons stopped at the base of the staircase, looking first toward the front entry, then to the rear. His eyes narrowed, and he dashed through the hallway and down the back stairs toward the first floor. Captain Longwood descended more slowly and, after glancing into the parlor and casting a sad frown at Hannah, followed Simons. They soon returned, with Simons herding Patience and John into the parlor.

"Your name," Simons demanded of Patience.

"I am Patience Hancock." Her voice was firm and her gaze even.

"Your papers."

"I am a free woman, born in Massachusetts. My parents were free, and theirs too. You have no right to ask me for papers."

Simons cursed and almost spat on the floor at her feet, but Longwood's growl of indignation stopped him.

"You." Simons now accosted John, whose face was creased with fear.

"John McAdam, sir." The old man reached into his jacket and pulled out papers.

Simons seized the sheets in his fist, scanned them, then thrust them in a wad back into John's shaking hands. The gentle old man seemed to age before Hannah's eyes.

"Bought your way out, eh?" He turned to Hannah. "Any others?"

"Why, uhm…"

Longwood bent near. "The little light-colored girl, where is she?"

"She's got her half-day off," Bridget said. "She's not here."

Simons uttered another oath and stormed to the entry hall, slamming the front door behind him. While Hannah dismissed John and Patience, Longwood watched the man leave, then crossed the room and took Hannah's hand.

"How distressing this must be for you. Please sit with me so I may be assured you are well." He led Hannah to the divan and sat close beside her, then turned to Bridget. "Bring water for Mrs. Jacobs."

"I'm all right." Hannah stared into his brilliant blue eyes, eyes filled with deep conviction, sincerity, and an almost childlike innocence. She could see he believed he was doing right before God and man. Unlike Simons, he would gain nothing from Mattie's capture except the satisfaction of seeing stolen property returned to one he deemed its rightful owner.

His eyes glistened. "Last evening, when I saw the handbill, I feared you had been led into illegal activities by Mrs. Childers. But now, seeing only serenity in your eyes, I know you are guiltless. Ah, Hannah, my dear ..." He raised her hand to his lips and held it there for a long moment.

Hannah studied his face. He was not an evil man, only terribly misguided. Yet everything he had claimed as truth about slavery and the character of the Negro race had been dispelled to her satisfaction by her short acquaintance with her household servants and Mattie, *and* by reading Frederick Douglass's book. Could she ever make him see how wrong his ideas were?

Bridget sneezed, and both Hannah and Longwood jumped.

"Beg pardon, mum." The housekeeper curtsied her apology. "Something in the air, I think. What would you like me to do, mum? That person they was after just disappeared clean away and took all her belongings too, what little there was of them. Shall I have Leah tidy up the room when she gets back?"

Longwood started to speak, but Hannah touched his arm to stop him.

"It's all right. Yes, Bridget, do that."

The girl gave her a pert smile, scooped up the forgotten lemonade tray, and left.

Longwood shook his head. "Dearest, I cannot bear to see your servant behave with such impudence. If she were my employee …"

Hannah laughed, her heart soaring. Bridget's so-called impudence had said far more than he realized. Mattie not only had escaped without making a sound, but she had also taken her few belongings. What miracle had been accomplished here, and how?

"Ah, yes, you would discipline her, or even fire her. Perhaps that's the difference between the slave and the paid employee. The slave does his work in fear. The employee can always find another job."

"Hannah, this is hardly a laughing matter."

He looked deeply wounded, but rather than apologize, she scooted back and leaned against the arm of the divan.

"See here, Captain Longwood, when did I give you permission to use my Christian name?"

He gave her a sheepish grin. "I hoped you would not object. Forgive me for taking such liberty. I will amend my ways immediately. But perhaps in the future …" His grin became a winsome smile.

Glancing down, she murmured, "Perhaps," knowing now that she would never permit it.

He reached over, reclaimed her hand, and set a gentle kiss on it. "When may I call again?"

She lifted her chin and arched her brow. "Certainly you don't consider today's intrusion a call?"

He grimaced. "But you understand that I was forced to come?"

She studied his handsome, frowning face for a moment before offering consolation. "Perhaps you may call next week."

Again, he pulled her hand to his lips. "Until then, my dear, dear Mrs. Jacobs."

The moment Hannah closed the front door behind Longwood, she began to tremble. Tears welled up and bubbled to the surface. With a strangled cry, she fled upstairs and flung herself on her bed, sobbing.

What was wrong with her? What had happened to that remarkable peace she just experienced, as though God Himself stood by her side through this crisis? Now she only felt abandoned, alone, and terribly frightened.

"Miz Jacobs?"

Mattie's soft whisper breezed into the storm of her tears. She sat up and stared at the woman as if seeing a ghost.

"Mattie." Jumping off the bed, Hannah pulled her into a frantic embrace. The two sobbing women clung to each other with equal measures of desperation.

At last, Hannah moved back and grasped Mattie's hands. "Where were you? You must leave right away. That horrible man may have followed you back here."

Mattie shook her head. "No, ma'am, he don't know I'm here."

"But where did you go?"

"I never left."

"What?"

"No, ma'am. Well, I did leave, but only next door."

"Next … ?" Hannah glanced beyond Mattie to see Bridget standing in the doorway, a triumphant grin on her face. "What are you up to?"

Bridget shrugged. "Oh, mum, it's best not too many know about it. If I don't tell you, you won't let it slip to your handsome captain."

"Bridget, this is my home, and I demand to know what's happening here."

Bridget bit her lip. "I don't have Mrs. Childers's leave to tell you, but seeing as how you are the lady of the house now, and she did tell me to mind you, I suppose you've a right to know." She hesitated, and a frown crinkled her brow.

"Go on."

"You see, mum, not meaning to disobey your instructions to send Mattie after Florence with the mending, but that would have put her out in plain sight. Them slave catchers work in pairs most times, with one waiting outside while the other goes in to search, and she'd have been sunk, that's sure."

"Oh, dear." Hannah turned to Mattie, who appeared as horrified as Hannah felt. "To think I would have sent you right into their hands …"

"No matter, mum," Bridget continued. "As it turns out, there's this gentleman next door who's an abolitionist."

"Ah! A friend of Mrs. Childers?"

"Yes, mum."

Hannah turned to Mattie. "But how did you get downstairs and around to his house without being seen or heard?"

Bridget giggled. "That's just it, mum. There's panels, secret ones, between his house and this one."

"What on earth … what are you telling me? You mean some man could just come into my home at any time through secret panels, and I would have no protection for myself or my son?"

"Oh, no, it's not like that. The only goings and comings through them panels is when people need to be hidden."

Hannah sank down on her bed and stared from Bridget to Mattie and back again. "Oh, my stars."

The other two women watched her, uncertainty on the face of one and fear on the face of the other.

"Captain Longwood was right. Mrs. Childers has deceived me. Bridget, send John for Mrs. Childers immediately, and tell him not to come back without her."

"It's only two little sliding doors, dear, one in the basement and one in the attic. Both are disguised so no one can find them." Nan perched on the divan, regal and triumphant. Having just endured Hannah's angry lecture, she sipped her tea with remarkable composure.

"But there's a man living next door who can enter my house any time he wishes, and I have no protection."

"Nonsense. He's a gentleman. Besides, he's rarely home, so you won't be disturbed. Now, Hannah, don't you dare go telling anyone our secret. This is not a game. It is life and death to the people who depend on our help, people like Mattie."

"But you never asked me if I wanted to help. You never considered my son's safety. How could you assume I would permit or participate in illegal activities in my own home?"

Nan regarded her for a moment. "I was planning to tell you soon. I had no idea Mattie would be forced to leave Kerry's house. Hannah, it didn't take long for me to realize you're the same good-hearted person I knew before. So when I needed someone to live here, and you arrived in town, I knew you were the one. I should have told you. Please forgive me. I will understand completely if you pack up and leave. I only ask that you keep this secret as well as you did my deepest secrets back in school."

Nan glanced away and wiped a tear from the corner of her eye. "Oh, what silly things I thought important back then, all those girlish dreams and fancies. Now to think I have the lives of needy people in my care." Her cheeks moist, she turned back to Hannah and cleared her throat.

"You must not let my tears move you, but rather be moved by the tears of children torn from their mothers' arms and sold like cattle, and by the tears of those mothers who are beaten for mourning the loss. Men, women, and the smallest children forced to work in slavery, *slavery*, Hannah. Can you even imagine how evil it is? Shall I take you to the South and show you how they suffer?"

Despite Nan's words, Hannah indeed felt moved. Yet, despite her disgust for Mr. Simons's trade, she was dismayed to see Nan break the law. How could she permit herself to be involved? Every instinct warned her to take Timothy and flee on the next ship to England.

"But why must you have someone living here? Why not just close the house?"

"This house is indispensable, and you can imagine the suspicions if no one lived here but the servants. Of course they're indispensable to our operation too, but no house can be without a master or, in your case, a mistress."

"*Our* operation? Oh, yes. The master next door. The very idea." Hannah huffed, outraged once again to think some strange man had access to her home. "You've expressed your trust in me, but how do I know I can trust you or this unnamed person?"

"Why, silly girl, it's David Lazarus, of course. But surely you knew that. Who else would it be?"

"Oh. Oh, thank heaven." Hannah slumped back in her chair. David. She trusted him as much as she trusted Jeremiah. She sat up again. "Oh, my goodness. That means he's an abolitionist."

"But surely you knew. Why do you think he makes all those trips to Norfolk when a competent crew could transport cotton without him?"

"Oh, of all the …" How Hannah wished she could run to her room and hide or retreat to the safety of her relatives' Indiana farm.

"I cannot understand your lack of interest in this matter, Hannah. You grew up in New Bedford, where abolitionists openly help fleeing slaves. Surely you knew of their work or at least read about their public meetings to decry slavery. Did you never hear of such things?"

Hannah nodded slightly. "Oh, I suppose I heard of them. But my father never was involved, despite his propensity for charitable works. No, I do not ever recall our having a conversation about abolition, though I do not think he condoned slavery." She thought for a moment. "No, I am certain he would not condone such evil."

"Hmm. Well, you mark my words, it won't be long before every thinking Christian in this country can proudly proclaim himself an abolitionist." Nan gazed toward the window, a soft glow of conviction brightening her face. "Every person must decide, and soon, whether to stand on God's side in this matter, or on the side of evil."

Her friend's searching stare made Hannah shift in her chair. "Of course I disapprove of slavery. Didn't I protect Mattie, without any prior warning and despite your careless deception?"

Still Nan's stare pinioned Hannah. "Disapprove is a very mild word."

"What would you have me say? That I hate slavery as much as you do? How can I hate it when I'm just beginning to learn about its worst aspects?"

"Isn't it enough to know that many millions of people, *millions*, Hannah, are held in bondage right here in this free country of ours? That they are forced to work to make profits for others yet never reap the rewards of their own labors? That children are sold like pieces of merchandise, never to see their parents again? That mothers—"

"Yes, I know that. I've been reading Mr. Douglass's book, and in it he relates many tragic things. But what do you expect me to do about it? I'm a widow with a son to rear. He is my only obligation in this world."

"And what kind of world is this when other little boys who are not so fortunate work in servitude from the time they are three or four years old, never free to run or play or be children?"

"Oh, Nan, that's the way things are. Even in the Bible, there were slaves. Didn't the apostle Paul tell slaves to be obedient to their masters? Didn't he warn masters to care for their slaves, just as God cares for us all?"

"Ah. I see our good Captain Longwood has swayed you, fine Christian man that he is." Nan's nostrils flared, and her lips curled with angry sarcasm. "I suppose he told you that his 'people' are as dear to him as family?"

Hannah frowned. Captain Longwood had said exactly that, and she knew he believed it. "Surely many Southern families do care for their slaves. What harm is there in such benevolence? The slaves may not be paid for their labors, but they are provided for. It's the way of things. It cannot be changed."

Nan fixed another intense gaze on Hannah. "But it can be changed. It will be changed. And you must decide whether or not you will help to change it."

Hannah covered her face. Why couldn't Nan just let things be? She sighed deeply. "I will not join you, but I will do what I can for Mattie. Is there any way I can buy her freedom without anyone knowing I did it?"

"Coward," Nan said, but her face lit up.

"You'll take care of it?"

"Consider it accomplished."

The triumph in Nan's expression seemed mingled with a measure of slyness. Hannah had a vague feeling she had just purchased Mattie's freedom at the price of her own.

Chapter Eighteen

ﻬ

For some time after Nan's visit, Hannah sat in her bedroom window seat and tried to dispel her anxiety. She looked down on Louisburg Square's grassy park, where two boys played fetch with their dog. On the sidewalk, a nanny escorted a young girl dressed in pink, perhaps heading for a shopping trip on Beacon Hill. Hannah gazed at the child with an ache in her heart. She dearly loved her son, but how she longed to have a daughter too.

As the nanny and child rounded the corner and disappeared, Hannah sighed. Perhaps it was not that she wanted to have another child, but rather to be a child again. Then she would not have to worry about Nan and her abolitionist work.

She leaned back against the window frame, clutched a small pillow for comfort, and pondered the thought. How good it would be to return to childhood, that long-ago time when her father had doted on her. He had let her explore her world, but with watchful eyes kept her safe and with gentle words guided her. How good and wise he had been. Had he ever felt the same uncertainties as a parent that she now felt? What had he thought of slavery? Of abolition? What would he do in her place?

How could Nan think to drag her into illegal activities? Nan had no child to worry about, only herself. And to think, not only did David Lazarus live next door, he also was Nan's accomplice in breaking the law. No wonder he thought so little of her interest in Captain Longwood. He was working to destroy the backbone of Longwood's family fortune. Now she understood why he continued to trade with the plantation owners. He transported more from their plantations than cotton.

A wave of confusing emotions surged through Hannah as she considered gentle-hearted David in this new light. She could not help but admire him even more than before. No wonder he challenged her to examine her beliefs about slavery. And no wonder he and Nan seemed to have an understanding. They shared in a bold vision and a dangerous work, work Hannah wanted no part of.

Once again, she felt the urge to pack up Timothy and flee this city that now threatened to entrap her. But an impulsive departure to Europe might put them in worse danger if she chose the wrong ship on which to sail or landed in a port where influenza was rampant. Returning to the Indiana wilderness would mean an inferior education for Timothy. The only other place to consider was Nantucket, but she could not take her son where he would be lured into the whaling life and where he would face the taunts of those who condemned Ahab.

As if summoned by her thoughts of him, Timothy wandered into the room, carrying Jemima under one arm and rubbing sleep from his eyes with the other hand. He smiled lazily, leaned against her, and set the placid cat in Hannah's lap.

"Did you have a good rest?" Hannah brushed his unruly hair back from his face and placed a kiss on his forehead.

"Hmm." He burrowed his head in her shoulder for a moment, then reclaimed Jemima and sat beside Hannah in the window seat. "Will you watch Jem for me while I go play with Charles?"

"Ah, so we're going to play with him again. I thought we decided not to."

"Captain Longwood said to give him another chance."

"Captain Longwood? When did you speak with him?"

He grinned, as if pleased with his own cleverness. "After you sent me out this morning, I waited for him on the front steps. Waited a long time. Finally, when he came out, I asked him about Charles again."

A wave of dizziness surged through Hannah. Mattie had come out of hiding and stood near this front window, and all the while, the captain had been on Hannah's front stoop.

"He said it's not wrong to defend myself 'cause sometimes a bully needs to be hit, same as Estevam said." Timothy's tone was casual, but he watched her.

She wanted to give him a smile of encouragement, or at least acceptance, but she could only frown.

He matched her frown but continued in the same casual tone. "He's going to teach me how to defend myself like a gentleman." Once again, he looked to her for approval.

"Oh. How nice."

Hannah heard the strain in her own voice, and Timothy's frown deepened. He stood and set Jemima on the floor, then placed his hands on Hannah's shoulders and stared into her eyes.

"Mother, sometimes we men have to do things you women just don't understand."

His earnest declaration summoned memories of Ahab's compulsion for his violent quest, something she would never understand. Tears stung her eyes, and she reached out to pull her son close.

"I know. I know."

He endured her tight embrace for a moment, then pushed back and held her face in his small hands. "I'll be all right. I promise. I'll never fight, I mean really fight, unless it's important. Captain Longwood says a gentleman should only fight for a righteous cause."

Hannah surrendered a short, ironic laugh. "Oh, he did, did he?"

Timothy watched her in confusion, his head cocked. "Are you angry at Captain Longwood?"

Her heart twisted. She could not involve Timothy in all that had happened this day. "No, darling, I'm not angry at him. I'm just surprised. Are you sure he said 'righteous'?"

"Yes, ma'am."

"Do you know what that word means?"

He thought for a moment. "Uncle Jeremiah sometimes says it when he talks to everyone in church. I think it means when something's righteous, it's God's work."

Hannah considered his words. "Yes. I think that's a very good definition. So, if you hit Charles back, just once, maybe not so very hard, do you think it would be righteous?"

He gave her another solemn nod. "It'll teach him it's wrong to pick on other people. Even if he hits me back and we have to fight a little, he'll know I won't let him bully me."

The earnestness in his voice brought more tears to Hannah's eyes, but she refused to cry. What a good, brave son she had, as brave as his father, as good as her own. Now she took his face in her hands.

"Then listen carefully, for this is very hard for me to say. You have my permission to hit Charles back, but only if he hits you again."

Timothy's face brightened with a broad grin. He threw his arms around her and kissed her.

"I promise not to beat him up too bad."

She sighed. He seemed so confident he could master the older boy. "That's good. Now run along and play."

"'Bye." Timothy scooped up Jemima and ran toward the door, but stopped and gazed back at her. His boyish grin and sparkling dark eyes warmed her like sunshine. Then he dashed out.

At the sound of the front door slamming, she peered out the window to watch Timothy skip along the sidewalk toward the Atwoods' house. She chuckled to see Jemima draped over his shoulder. How he did love his cat. He had decided to take her with him after all.

Oh, to return to childhood, where life's dilemmas can be so simply solved.

"What a silly thought," she whispered. For, if she were a little girl again, she would not have her own wonderful child who brought so much joy to her life.

Still, she often wondered if she could raise him as wisely as her father had raised her, though one could hardly compare a father bringing up a daughter with a mother bringing up a son. Boys seemed to require far more complicated instruction on how to get along in the world, as the problem with Charles proved. It all seemed so confounding. She would not be able to protect Timothy forever from such evils.

If only Ahab were still alive to help her. Ever since Tishtega had scolded her to provide a masculine example for the boy, the challenge had haunted her thoughts. But whom could she trust? She was grateful that Captain Longwood had advised Timothy on a matter that only distressed her. But she certainly would not permit him to advise her son on every dilemma in life, some of which were even more distressing, such as slavery. But if not Captain Longwood, then who?

Her weighty pondering ceased at the sight of a tall figure striding up the Louisburg Square sidewalk. The man wore a dark suit and a black seaman's cap. As he drew near, Hannah's heart began to beat faster. David Lazarus, back so soon from Norfolk. Well, she certainly had much to say to this surprise neighbor. Why had he never mentioned living next door to Nan's vacant house?

Without thinking, she rapped on her window and was rewarded with his upward glance, which was followed by a shocked but pleased expression. He waved, then took another step toward his own residence, but Hannah rapped again, beckoned him closer, and pointed down to her own door. He hesitated, but nodded and moved to comply with her command.

She rose from the window seat, her cheeks on fire. If anyone had seen her audacious invitation just now, they would be scandalized by such unladylike behavior. But she would not let another moment pass without interrogating him about this business of hiding slaves. More than that, she would demand to know why he had been Nan's accomplice in embroiling her in their illegal operation. With every intention of scolding him as soundly as she had Nan, Hannah hurried downstairs and threw open the front door. But at the sight of him, she stood speechless.

She had forgotten how imposing his stature could be, especially when a two-weeks' beard growth, sun-bronzed complexion, and formidable bearing gave him the appearance of a victorious Viking just returned from a plundering foray into some foreign land.

For a moment, he stared at her, hat in hand, his gray eyes blazing with a look she could not decipher. Yet her own inexpressible joy at seeing him confounded her even more. Her heart felt near to bursting.

"Good afternoon, Hannah. How good to see you. Was there something you wished to say to me?"

She gave her head a slight shake. "Yes. Please come in." She stood back to make way for him.

"Ah, perhaps I could return later. I've just returned from my voyage and have yet to, eh, to …" He brushed a hand through his thick beard and tilted his head in apology.

"No, please. I want to talk to you right away. Never mind the, um, the sea salt you're wearing. If you recall, I was married to a whaling captain." She managed a ladylike laugh when a giggle would have expressed her feelings more accurately. He truly did smell of the sea and hard work. Still, she would not let him go without a scolding.

"You must come in and sit down, and never mind the furniture."

"If you insist." David grimaced. His discomfort gave him a charming appearance, and Hannah almost relented. Almost.

"I insist." She spun around and led him to the front parlor. "Sit!" She pointed to a chair and sat herself in one across from it.

"Yes, ma'am."

He complied with her order, and his deep chuckle brought a smile to her spirits, which she forcefully denied admittance to her face. The battle was so fierce, she could not speak. But, oh, how she struggled to be angry with this pleasant, agreeable man.

He relaxed into the chair, leaned one elbow on its arm, and thoughtfully posted his chin on his fist. "You have me at a disadvantage. I fear I'm being called on the carpet, and I wonder what the cause of my offense might be." He gazed at her with youthful winsomeness, his sun-bleached eyebrows arched with questions, his firm lips curved into a half-smile.

Warm affection surged through her, defeating all attempts at anger. Without one doubt or reservation, she believed this man merited both her trust and her honesty.

"David, I know about the remarkable enterprise you and Nan are involved in, and I know how our two houses are linked to assist the operation."

His pleasant expression faded into a severe frown, his posture stiffened, and his gaze became a wary stare.

"And?"

His tone seemed to challenge, to accuse. Now she felt called on the carpet, and at last her anger surfaced.

"And …" She echoed his tone. "… I am not some silly schoolgirl who needs to be shielded from secrets, but a grown woman with a child, and we have been put in a very dangerous position."

David's expression softened, and concern replaced severity. "What happened while I was away?"

Hannah recounted to him Dorice's animosity toward Mattie, Mattie's flight to Louisburg Square, and Bridget's vague remarks about helping people. She treaded lightly when relating Captain Longwood's two visits, yet noticed David's jaw tighten at the first mention of the naval officer's name. Then, as she told of Mr. Simons's participation in that morning's events, David stood abruptly and strode to the fireplace, where he rested one hand on the mantel, ran the other through his hair, and muttered to himself.

Hannah paused in her story. She had never seen David like this before. Should she continue her story?

He took a deep breath and turned back to her, his anger gone. "Forgive me. I would never have put you in this position, nor would Mrs. Childers. We would never, ever endanger you or Timothy. Things were not supposed to happen this way."

She nodded. "I know."

He reclaimed his chair and leaned forward, his eyes searching hers. "To think your Captain Longwood would bring that Simons fellow here. That barbarian. ... Forgive me, Hannah. I know you are kindly disposed toward the captain." He studied his hands for a moment before looking back at her. "I have no need to ask if you have discussed the slavery issue with him. His actions surely reveal the man to you."

She shook her head. "I'm not entirely convinced he is unredeemable in this matter."

He continued to gaze at her. "And what of you, Hannah? What have you decided?"

She took a turn at staring down at her hands. "I have been reading the Douglass narrative, but as compelling as it is, I still do not believe this issue can be resolved. The economy of our Southern states depends on the people who work the land. Slavery is a fact, a necessary evil. It cannot be changed."

He heaved a weary groan, and she glared at him, annoyed.

"I will never betray you, David. I will never betray any of the people who come through here. Upon my life, I will not."

He started to respond, but a noisy rapping of the front door knocker interrupted. Bridget swept past the parlor door toward the front entry and soon reappeared, followed by Mademoiselle Trudeau and a dirty, rumpled Timothy. Before the housekeeper could announce her, the governess stepped forward wringing her hands. Hannah rushed to kneel and grasp her son, who grinned at her despite his bloody lip.

"Oh, my word, what happened?" Hannah stared at Timothy, then Mademoiselle Trudeau.

"Oh, Madame, forgive me. I was sent by Madame Atwood to deliver to you your son. She said I was to tell you he must never darken her door again. It is not my words, you understand, but she command me to say exactly as she spoke."

"But what happened?" Why was she asking? Hannah knew exactly what had transpired. If she had any doubts, her son's pleased grin explained it all.

"Oh, Madame, the boys will be the boys. They play, and they make the loudness, and they tumble on the floor, on the ground, and …" As she spoke, she churned her hands about for emphasis.

"Yes, of course. But why did Mrs. Atwood send Timothy home? And where did you get this lip?" She directed her last question to her son, holding his chin firmly to inspect his injury. "Oh, dear, a loose tooth, but a baby one. And this cut on your lip …"

He jerked his chin away. "Aw, it's not bad. You should see Charles …"

Hannah glanced at Mademoiselle Trudeau, who rolled her eyes and shrugged.

"It is certain Master Charles receive more than he give. It is about the time." The governess pursed her lips, obviously fighting a smile. "Oh, Madame Jacobs, I repeat my previous plea. If you ever need the governess for this wonderful, brave boy, ah, well, I am not with the contract at Madame Atwood's."

Hannah stood and stared at the French girl. "May I ask, is Charles truly hurt?"

The governess shrugged again, this time more dramatically. "Bah. He screams like the stuck pig, but he will live."

Hannah sighed. "Thank you, Mademoiselle. Please convey my apologies to Mrs. Atwood."

"Oh, Madame, it is she who should apologize for being the bad mother who never say no to her spoiled boy. Nevertheless, I will say all the words you tell me. *Au revoir, Madame. Au revoir, mon chéri.*" She blew Timothy a kiss and sailed out the door.

"And you, you little rascal." Hannah struggled to keep the laughter from her voice. "Go upstairs at once and wash. And change your clothes."

"Captain Lazarus, you're back." Timothy hopped over to his old friend, who leaned with crossed arms against the open parlor pocket door. "You shoulda been there, Captain. I really let him have it."

David set his hand on Timothy's shoulder and looked at Hannah. She imitated Mademoiselle Trudeau's elaborate shrug, and David chuckled. He crouched down to eye level with the boy. "Hello, Timothy. It's good to see you again. Too bad about your getting into a fight, but it sounds like you didn't have much choice in this situation with Charles."

"No, sir. I tried not to, but Captain Longwood said I should hit him once real hard just to let him know he can't bully me."

"Hmm." David scratched his beard thoughtfully. "Never thought I would agree with …" He stopped, then patted Timothy on the shoulder. "That was good advice, and it looks as though it worked out."

"Oh, you men are just so pleased with yourselves, aren't you? You, young man, march upstairs. And don't come down until you're all clean, and in fresh clothes too."

"Yes, ma'am," Timothy chirped.

"Oh, mum, I'd be happy to help him." Bridget appeared from the back hallway, her proud grin revealing she had watched everything.

"Thank you, Bridget."

After giving David an impulsive hug, Timothy raced up the stairs, with Bridget close behind.

Halfway up the stairs, Bridget turned back. "Captain Lazarus, sir, there's a wagon out back, and John is helping unload some trunks."

"Ah, yes. Thank you, Bridget."

She gave him a nod before turning back to follow her young charge.

"If you'll excuse me, Hannah, this is something I need to supervise. We can continue our discussion later, if you like. Tomorrow, perhaps?"

"Most definitely, and the sooner the better."

He returned to the parlor to retrieve his hat, and she followed, wishing for a reason to entice him to stay.

"If it's only trunks, can't the servants manage?"

He regarded her for a moment, as if trying to decide how to answer. "The shipment is fragile. I should supervise."

"Oh," she said. "Of course. Please go right away. You can go out the back door if you like. No need to go clear around through your house."

He took her hand and bent over it to place a gentle kiss on her fingertips. Then, as when he first appeared on her doorstep, his face radiated with an intense glow she could not decipher. Against her will, her heart responded with an unnamable, glorious elation.

"Welcome home, David," she managed to whisper. "My good friend."

She saw him to the back door and watched him cross to his own yard. What an astonishing, courageous man, one worthy of her highest regard and admiration. She wondered what other hidden qualities she might learn about him and found herself wanting to know all there was to know. But she should not feel this way. She forbade herself. This remarkable man had an understanding with her beloved friend.

Chapter Nineteen

&

At the supper table, Timothy's face glowed with confidence born of his successful scuffle with Charles. Although Hannah loathed the necessity of such an unpleasant exchange, she felt proud of him. David's stamp of approval proved she had made the right decision to let Timothy fight back.

"Patience has prepared your favorite: chicken and dumplings." Hannah supervised as he laid his napkin across his lap in proper form, noting the broken skin on his knuckles. But how could she expect him to grow up without scars? She herself bore several reminders of childhood antics.

"Can I have the drumstick?"

"Yes, my sweetheart, you *may* have the drumstick. But remember, you may not pick it up with your fingers. When the chicken is in a stew, you must use your knife and fork."

"I know. I just like the drumstick best." He watched as she served his plate and gave her a crooked grin. "More please. I really like chicken and dumplings."

"You finish that much, and we'll see if you're still hungry."

"Yes, ma'am." He dug into his supper with enthusiasm, but after a moment, he glanced up. "Don't watch me."

"Was I watching you?" Hannah turned back to her own plate and suppressed a smile, but looked his way once more.

"Yes, ma'am. You're afraid I won't mind my manners." He placed a large dumpling in his mouth and gave her another grin, then barely managed to catch in his napkin the gravy that ran down his chin. "Umph. 'Scuse me."

"Hmm. There's one little boy who's not ready for supper in polite company."

He shrugged and wrinkled his nose as he munched.

"But at least you don't feed Jemima under the table anymore."

He swallowed with a gulp, and his face went pale. "Jem. I forgot Jem." He jumped up from his chair and started toward the door.

"Timothy, stop. Come back here."

He turned and stared at her, terror written across his young face. "But I forgot Jem. When Charles pulled her tail, she ran away. That's when I hit him, and—"

"She'll come home. She knows the way to our house, and she's already been out exploring often enough to—"

"No, but never that far. Never across the park. And there's dogs out there, and I gotta go find her."

He stood in the dining-room doorway, his dark eyes pleading and his whole frame shaking, as though he struggled with whether or not to obey.

His intense anguish sent Hannah to embrace him. "Don't worry. We'll find her together. Patience, please take care of the food," she called over her shoulder as they ran upstairs to the parlor floor.

The long, midsummer's day still provided enough sunlight for their search. Hannah and Timothy rushed out their front door just as David Lazarus emerged from his. Freshly bathed and shaved, he wore his usual black business suit and tall hat.

"Ah, Hannah, I was just about to come—"

"Captain Lazarus," Timothy wailed, rushing to him. "My cat's lost. I don't know where she is. Help us find her, please."

"Timothy …"

"It's all right, Hannah." He squatted down to the boy's level. "Let's see what we can do. When did you last see her, and where?"

While Timothy repeated his story to David, Hannah felt her heart swell with gratitude at how quickly the captain had set aside his own plans and involved himself in her son's plight. But she marveled even more when he placed his strong hands on Timothy's shoulders and began to pray.

"Lord, You know where Jemima is, but we don't. Please help us find her, or bring her safely home on her own."

Hannah's eyes burned with sudden tears. That was exactly what her father had always done, prayed right away and out loud for any dilemma, whether his own or a friend's. Then he would always say …

"God knows best, and we must trust Him."

Hannah breathed out a short, shocked laugh. David spoke almost the same words her father often had said.

He glanced up at her, his eyes questioning.

"Thank you. That's just what we needed." Rather, just what she needed to calm herself so she could help her son.

"Let's *go!*" Timothy cried. He grasped David's hand and tried to drag him down the sidewalk toward the Atwoods'.

Before they could take two steps, Bridget called from the front door. "Mrs. Jacobs, could you please come see something out back?"

David and Hannah turned back. Even Timothy was stopped by the sharp, shrill tone in the housekeeper's voice. Then some wild instinct seemed to take hold of him.

"Jemima!" He raced back to the house and tore past Bridget's grasping hands.

"No, Master Timothy. You mustn't. Oh, mum, he mustn't see it."

She raced after the boy, with Hannah and David only short steps behind. They dashed through the house and out the back door just in time for Bridget to tackle Timothy and wrestle him to the ground. But though she tried to shield the struggling boy's view with her body, he screamed out his rage at the sight that horrified them all.

A long clump of bloody fur hung from the back gate, barely recognizable as Timothy's beloved Jemima. Only the distinctive golden blonde color identified it. Timothy twisted out of Bridget's grasp and ran, shaking and sobbing, to unhook the noose looped over the fence post and to lay his pet gently on the ground.

The creature twitched and jerked, and a low, strangled growl came from its throat. All three adults knelt by the weeping boy, who wiped his tears on his sleeve and looked from one to the other, his eyes filled with desperate hope.

"You can save her? Mother, you can, can't you? She's still alive. You can fix her. Captain Lazarus, please save her."

Hannah stared at David through her tears and, for a moment, hope sprang up in her breast. He was a whaling captain. Like Ahab, he had often been forced by necessity to doctor the men on his ship. Could he save this pitiful creature? Surely he could save it.

But his eyes told another story, and she understood why. The cat had not merely been hanged, it had also been tortured in ways that almost made Hannah swoon. With such brutal injuries, it should already be dead.

"You have to save her." Timothy's voice was weak, all hope gone from it. With silent sobs, he reached out to touch Jemima, but a wild growl warned him back.

David reached over and drew Timothy into his arms. "You can see there's nothing we can do for her. She's hurt too badly. I know you don't want her to suffer. Let me …"

He paused and looked at Hannah. She shuddered and nodded.

"Let me put her to rest so she won't be in pain anymore."

"No!" Timothy tore away from him, slumped on the ground, and reached out again to stroke Jemima's head. She swatted weakly, claws bared and eyes glazed with shock. The savage growl turned to a tortured, breathy hum, almost a purr.

Timothy raised his eyes to meet the captain's sad gaze. "I want to be with her. I want to know what you do to her."

David looked at Hannah again. "I don't know if he should."

"I want to be with her," Timothy repeated, his tone so much older than his years. Hannah could not deny him. She nodded to David.

He pulled a large white handkerchief from his pocket and wrapped it around the cat's head. "Perhaps you would prefer to ..."

She turned away, grasping Timothy while he watched the captain over her shoulder. The terrible crunch of the cat's neck being wrung almost made Hannah wretch, and she could feel Timothy struggle not to vomit as a violent shudder ran through his body.

Bracing herself, she loosened him and turned back to see David tenderly wrapping the dead cat in his handkerchief. As large as the elegant linen cloth was, it could not cover the whole length, so he gathered tail and limbs and swaddled the carcass, making Jemima appear more like a baby in a blanket than a corpse in a makeshift shroud. He laid it in Timothy's waiting arms, sat back on his heels, and wiped his bloody hands on his trousers.

Timothy raised the bundle to his chest and caressed it. He stared off into nothingness for a moment, but gradually his vacant expression darkened. Now his eyes focused on some unseen object, his brow curved downward into a scowl, and his lips formed a grim line. Hannah watched with sinking heart as Ahab's vengeful pride wrote itself across his son's countenance.

"Do you want me to help you bury her?" David's gentle voice drew Hannah's anxious thoughts back to reality.

"Oh, that would be so kind. Don't you think so, Timothy?" She reached out to touch her son and was alarmed by his rigid, almost brittle posture.

"Here. You bury her. I'm gonna ..." He thrust the corpse into David's hands, stood, and started away.

Hannah reached to him. "Where are you going?"

He stopped. "I'm going to see Charles."

"Oh, no, you're not."

"Son, don't …" David set his burden on the ground and gripped Timothy's shoulders, staring into his eyes. "This has become more than a boyish quarrel. If Charles did this cruel thing to your pet, there's something wrong inside him. You can't solve anything by going back to fight with him again."

Timothy regarded him for a moment. "I gotta do something back to him."

"I understand why you feel that way. And there's something you can do, the very best thing of all."

Timothy lifted his chin, inviting more information.

"You can pray for him, and you can forgive him."

Timothy snorted and jerked away. His tender, childish lips curled into a sneer. "I'm going to ask Captain Longwood what to do. He knows how to fight."

"Timothy." Hannah jumped to her feet. "You will apologize right this minute."

"Sorry," he mumbled. With one last glance at what had been his treasured pet, he turned and ran into the house.

"Mum, shall I make sure he doesn't go out?" Bridget said.

"Yes. Thank you. And thank you for trying to keep him from seeing …"

"Yes, mum."

As the housekeeper disappeared indoors, Hannah turned back to David. He had retrieved the tragic little bundle and now stood waiting for her.

"I don't know how to thank you, David." Her eyes misted over, and she suddenly felt exhausted. "What will you do with that?"

"We could wait until tomorrow and take it out into the country to bury it. Perhaps say a prayer over it, for Timothy's sake."

She gazed up at him in the deepening twilight. He seemed exhausted too. His voyage must have required much effort.

"Look at you. Your clean suit's all bloody." She could not keep a little sob from her voice. "And your lovely linen handkerchief ..."

He shrugged. "They're only things. It's Timothy I'm worried about."

"Thank you. Thank you so much. I hope he's able to forget this in a few days."

"I will pray for him."

"It gives me great comfort to know that you will."

They stood quietly, comfortably for another moment. "Shall I ...?" He held forth the bundle.

"Yes. Please find a place to bury it."

For the second time that day, Bridget scrubbed Timothy clean and bundled his clothing off to the laundry basket. Hannah sat on his bedside and brushed his damp hair away from his face, yet he stared off into the darkness, refusing to acknowledge her presence. Perhaps the light from the candle she held made his glower seem so hostile, so Ahab-like, but the sight chilled her. Would he clutch his rage as fiercely as his father had and seek some sort of revenge against Charles? She hoped he would not. But what would she have him do? Could a six-year-old boy be expected to forgive and forget such an awful deed? Only time would tell. For now, her entire being ached to soothe his anguish.

"We can get you another kitten."

"No. I never want another cat." He turned away, his mouth pursed with belligerence.

Why wasn't he crying? She had expected to console him, but he would not grant her admittance to his grief. He would not even give vent to it, but rather seemed to lock it up inside himself and thereby to suffer more profoundly.

Like Ahab. Like Ahab! Dear God, please don't let my son be like Ahab.

The thought shocked her but, with all her heart, she meant it.

The next morning, Hannah felt grateful to see the servants sharing Timothy's grief, although it created a somber mood throughout the household. Bridget forsook her usual teasing of the young master. Quiet Leah seemed to regard him with a special understanding. Patience made him flapjacks shaped like little men and heaped on extra butter and syrup, and for a moment it seemed his sad countenance might lighten. But when he took a small piece of bacon and glanced down beneath the table, he choked back a whimper, and his appetite fled, for no kitten reached up to take the forbidden bite.

After breakfast, their man-of-all-work, John, invited the boy to sit on the back steps and whittle.

"Come on, sugar, set out here with me," the old, gray-haired man said. "A fella can do a heap of good thinking while he sets a-whittling."

Hannah wondered about the wisdom of letting Timothy use a knife, but his passive acceptance of John's invitation kept her silent. Jonathan Lazarus had already given him some woodworking lessons, so he probably had more experience with knives than she knew. Whittling might be just the thing to keep him busy, and John's calm demeanor would surely soothe him. Her own spirits low, Hannah sat watching out the back parlor window as the former slave schooled her son in the harmless, manly pastime.

Should she go to Mrs. Atwood and tell her the malicious thing Charles had done? From the few visits they had shared, Hannah could see the woman thought her son beyond reproach. Every time the two boys had the slightest disagreement within their hearing, Mrs. Atwood would smile with maternal indulgence, give Hannah a knowing look, and make some remark about Timothy still having much to learn about getting along with other children. Hannah passed it off at the time because Charles did seem to have such good manners. How could she have known what subtle wickedness lay beneath the surface?

And now, just the thought of his vicious deed was so overwhelming, Hannah wondered if she could control herself in a confrontation. In her present state of mind, she had no idea what she might say to the other woman. Perhaps she should ask Captain Lazarus to advise her. His characteristic serenity could only help.

While she considered whether to go next door to ask his advice or to wait for his next visit, Bridget hurried into the parlor. Seamus Callahan followed close behind her, but the affectionate sparks recently visible between the two young people were noticeably absent.

"Sorry to disturb you, mum, but Seamus was sent to fetch you to Reverend Harris's," said Bridget. "More bad news, I'm afraid."

"What news? Is Kerry … ?"

"Still with us, mum, but just barely." Seamus coughed back his emotions. "She's asking for you, and Master Timothy as well."

"Dear God, please …" Head bowed, Hannah clasped her hands over her heart. "Please, please."

Bridget hurried to her. "Are you all right, mum? Shall I fetch the salts?"

Hannah shook her head sharply to clear her senses. She would not faint. Not now. "No. I'll be fine. Please tell Timothy to come in at once, and send Leah to bring down our hats."

Chapter Twenty

છ

"Is Aunt Kerry going to die?" Fear etched wrinkles across Timothy's young face, but he seemed determined not to cry.

Hannah held on to him with one hand and the side of the phaeton with the other as Seamus urged the horse to a brisk trot. Seamus and Bridget had ceased their whispering when Hannah and Timothy came out to the waiting carriage. He appeared reluctant to give Hannah more than his initial message that Kerry had asked for her.

"We must pray that she doesn't leave us."

Despite her own weak faith, Hannah longed for Timothy to bring his petitions to God. Perhaps the Lord would hear a child's plea. But Timothy frowned and looked away, and his whole body drooped. Only those few words were spoken during their pell-mell race through Boston's busy morning traffic.

They arrived at a house already in mourning, not for Kerry but for her tiny, ill-formed son who had been dead within his mother for untold days before being cast out reluctantly by her weak, ailing body. Tishtega pulled Hannah aside at the front door to whisper news of the loss and to say Kerry now rested. As Hannah breathed out her relief, Tishtega stooped to gather Timothy in her arms.

"What face is this, that you should grieve what you do not understand?" Tishtega brushed unruly hair from Timothy's forehead, and her dark eyes searched his. She glanced at Hannah, questioning.

The boy returned her gaze, and a flicker of trust lit his expression. "Charles murdered my cat. She's dead. Will Aunt Kerry die too?"

"This, too, is deep sorrow. Jemima was your friend. But of our Miss Kerenhappuch, we cannot yet know."

He sunk his face in her shoulder, yet still did not cry.

She's like a grandmother to him, thought Hannah, who had never known her own grandparents.

A moment later, when Jeremiah came downstairs, his shoulders were slumped, his blue eyes rimmed with red, and his steps heavy. Hannah had never seen him like this: no tie, no coat covering his wrinkled shirt, unshaven for countless days, but most of all, depressed, listless, and resigned. As she stepped toward him, he looked up, surprised to see her. He closed the few steps between them, drew her into his arms, and sagged against her wordlessly as silent sobs wracked them both.

"Pray, Hannah," he whispered. "Please pray. I can't lose her."

As if God would hear my prayers rather than yours. "Of course. I haven't stopped praying since she became ill."

He drew back and held her shoulders, a trace of brightness flashing in his gaze—his searching, pastoral gaze. "Truly? You've prayed?"

"Of course I have. Surely you know how much I care."

"But do you trust that God can do all things?"

"He can do all things, but ..." Why was Jeremiah concerned about her faith when he was suffering so much?

A soft, groaning sigh escaped him. "Our Heavenly Father never makes a mistake."

Words so typical of him, but Hannah wondered if he said them for her or himself.

"No. He doesn't." She voiced agreement, but her heart could not affirm that belief. She had seen too many wretched things in life.

"Timothy, I'm so glad you came." Jeremiah blinked his face into a paternal smile. "When Aunt Kerry wakes up from her nap, she'll want to see you."

"Me too. May I go see Lacy now?"

"I suppose it's all right," said Jeremiah. "Miss Ellen has the girls in the nursery. You may go play with them."

Timothy shook his head. "I don't want to play. I want to help take care of them."

"Oh." Jeremiah's voice broke, and he coughed to clear it. "Yes, of course. I know Miss Ellen will appreciate that."

After Hannah gave an approving nod, Timothy took care to walk quietly up the stairs.

"What an exceptional son you have, Hannah. Such an exceptional boy. You are truly blessed." Jeremiah's eyes reflected no bitterness, but Hannah could not but wonder if he were thinking of his own lost boy.

"Kerry is resting, and Mother Charity is with her," Jeremiah said. "Tishtega, if you're not too exhausted from last night, could you please look in on them? Let me know if there is any change."

Tishtega nodded and followed Timothy up the stairs.

"Come, Hannah, sit with me in the parlor."

"Don't you want to rest? You must have been up all night. I could sit with Kerry so Aunt Charity and Tishtega can rest too."

He considered the offer and then shook his head. "No. I couldn't possibly sleep."

Despite his words, he soon fell into heavy slumber on the parlor's long divan. Hannah removed his shoes and put a pillow under his head, observing that in repose his face assumed a peaceful, boyish appearance, as if he had not a care in the world.

When she had embraced him, she could feel his ribs. Clearly, he was not eating enough. Wondering how to remedy that situation, she found Mrs. Cook at the kitchen worktable, cutting carrots and potatoes for one of her hearty stews. Bread baked in the oven, filling the kitchen with a mouth-watering aroma, and three apple pies cooled on a side table.

"All I can do is cook it, ma'am. Most the time, he barely touches it, him being so worried about the missus and trying to keep up at the mission and all."

"I know you're doing your best. Perhaps I can get him to eat when he wakes up. He needs to be strong for Kerry and the girls."

Hannah then checked on Dorice and found her diligently dusting the back parlor. Without being asked, the housemaid reported to Hannah which daily tasks she had completed so far that morning and which she would be doing next. Her tone was pleasant, and she seemed eager to let Hannah know she was doing her part to keep this home running smoothly. In spite of Hannah's suspicions that Dorice's jealousy had forced Mattie to flee, she could see the girl loved her gentle mistress and longed to see her recover.

Hannah returned to the front parlor to check on Jeremiah. Satisfied he was getting some much-needed rest, she decided to relieve the sickroom helpers. As she passed the front door on her way to the stairs, a soft tap caught her attention. Through the glass, she saw David and quickly opened the door to let him in.

"Bridget gave me the news." As he entered, his gray eyes exuded deep sorrow. "Is there anything I can do?"

"How good of you to offer. I don't know of anything right now. Jeremiah's asleep, but when he awakens, perhaps he'll want to talk." Hannah gazed up at David, recalling how wise and kind he had been with Timothy the night before. "I don't know of anyone who could minister to him as well as you."

"I would be pleased to. People often think fathers do not grieve the loss of an infant as much as mothers, but we do."

Hannah questioned him with her eyes.

"Eliza and I had a stillborn son. Had he lived, he would be a young man now."

"Oh, I didn't know. Eliza never told me. I'm so sorry."

"Thank you." He gave her a gentle smile and continued to look into her eyes. "If there's nothing I can do here, I'll go over to the mission and see if Jonathan needs help. My good brother keeps the grounds and building shipshape, but he has no sympathy for mariners who fail to toe the mark."

Hannah wished he would not leave, but she cut short that foolish thought. "When you can, would you go visit Nan? She'll want to know about Kerry."

"Ah, yes, of course. I just visited with Mrs. Childers early this morning. But that was before I heard the news from here."

"Oh." Despite the midsummer heat, Hannah felt as if cold water had been thrown in her face. He did not need her prompting. No, he already had visited Nan. And early in the morning. But just how early? Or should she wonder if his visit began the night before? Now hot shame blasted away the chill of unreasoning disappointment. How could she think such a thing about her friends?

"Are you ill?" David studied her face, concern written across his own. He reached out and touched her arm, causing another wave of mortification to flood her face. "Perhaps you should sit down."

She took a small step back. "Oh, no. I'm fine. It's just become a very hot day. Do go now. I don't want to keep you." *Not true. I do want to keep you here.*

His caring frown deepened her embarrassment. In the midst of Kerry's and Jeremiah's suffering, she was behaving as if she were a jealous schoolgirl.

"I'm fine. Truly I am."

After David left, she continued to chide herself. Why did she give place to these feelings she could not even define? She should simply take Timothy and leave Boston now. But, as she went up the stairs and stood outside Kerry's door, she shook off her troubling thoughts. David and Nan were adults. They could see to themselves. In this house, her help was needed in many ways.

Hannah opened the door with care and peered in. The darkened room no longer smelled of sickness, and all signs of last night's agonizing loss had been removed. Tishtega dozed in a large armchair, and Aunt Charity stood beside the freshly made bed, helping Kerry take a drink of water. The patient had been bathed, and her dull, blonde hair brushed back from her pale face.

"Hannah." Kerry spoke in a croaking whisper, but her eyes brightened. Aunt Charity greeted Hannah and beckoned her to come closer.

Hannah hurried to obey and bent to kiss Kerry. "How are you, my dear?" She resisted an almost overwhelming urge to embrace her fragile friend.

Kerry released a little sob and shook her head. "Oh, so sad. So very sad. He was so little, his tiny body so damaged." Her voice broke, and tears coursed down her sunken cheeks. "And now the doctor says I must not have another child."

"Shh." Hannah sat on the edge of the bed and held her.

Aunt Charity moved to sit on the other side and reached out to hold Kerry's hand. "Doctors don't know everything. These Boston doctors surely don't know Nantucket women. Thou wilt mend, daughter. Thy color has already improved."

Hannah studied Kerry's face. Indeed, her color had improved. "Mrs. Cook is preparing her wonderful stew. You must make an effort to eat. And Jeremiah too."

"Oh, Hannah, he's lost so much weight, I'm frightened for him." Kerry's voice was weak, and her eyes exuded anxiety. "Promise me thou wilt take care of Jeremiah if anything happens …"

"Shh. You mustn't say that. Nothing's going to happen to you. Jeremiah needs you. Your girls need you. You must not give in to despair."

"Nevertheless, promise me."

A hint of her old determination flickered across Kerry's countenance as she made her demand, and Hannah almost laughed with relief. She glanced again at Aunt Charity, who gave her a brief nod and a shadow of a smile. The two agreed. Kerry would survive.

"If you insist, I promise. Now you get some more rest, and I'll see how our children are doing." Hannah stood and bent to kiss Kerry's cheek again and was startled as her friend's youthful cheek sank beneath her touch. This illness not only had claimed a precious baby, but also several teeth. Hiding her involuntary shudder, she turned to leave the room and was rewarded by a glimmer of approval in Tishtega's eyes.

At the far end of the hall, Hannah carefully opened the nursery door. Ellen sat rocking baby Daisy, while Lacy and Molly napped. Timothy was nowhere in sight.

"He said he was going to the mission," Ellen whispered in response to Hannah's questioning look. "I told him to ask your permission. Didn't he?"

Hannah shook her head, and her heart beat faster. It was not like her son to disobey. She rushed downstairs as quietly as possible and checked with Dorice and Cook before dashing out the door, past the chapel, and into the five-story mission building.

In the great parlor, several seamen glanced up from their reading as she scanned the room. Next, she hurried into the galley where Jonathan's two daughters were setting the long tables for the noon meal.

"Have you seen my son? Have you seen Timothy?"

"Yes, ma'am," sixteen-year-old Teresa said. "He's out back with Paolo and Estevam. They was awful pleased to see him."

"Oh." Hannah breathed out her relief. "Thank you." Her words were as much a grateful prayer as they were good manners toward Teresa. She smiled at her own foolishness. Timothy still felt at home here on the mission grounds. While he had not minded Ellen or asked Hannah's permission, she could not blame him for seeking his good friends, trustworthy boys who, unlike Charles, would do him no harm.

She walked through the swinging doors into the kitchen and greeted Mrs. Lazarus. "Everything smells wonderful, Maria. If it wouldn't annoy Mrs. Cook, I would insist on eating here."

"Oh, Mrs. Jacobs, is good to see you. We miss you here. You should come see us more." The short, plump woman handed Hannah a buttered biscuit. "Eat this. Is better than Cook's any day."

Aware of the women's friendly competition, Hannah chuckled as she took the biscuit. At first taste, she realized how hungry she was. It disappeared in three bites. "I'd better collect my son and get him fed."

"Is Mrs. Kerry ... ?" Maria's worried expression finished her question.

"She's resting, and her color is improving. I think losing ..." Hannah bit her lip. How tragic but true that Kerry might survive, but only because she had lost her child.

"Si, I understand." Maria crossed herself and sniffed back tears, then rolled out more biscuit dough. "You come back more."

"Thank you, Maria. I will."

Hannah looked out the kitchen window and watched the three boys tossing rocks in the air and hitting them with long sticks, then checking to see whose rock had flown the farthest. Estevam seemed to have won because his rock landed behind the chapel. But Paolo and Timothy cheered for his success.

Hannah walked out of the kitchen to the back hallway door just as David and Jonathan came down the back stairs, almost colliding with her. Both men quickly apologized and bowed their greetings to her, while her face flamed at the unexpected encounter.

"Good to see you, Mrs. Jacobs. We've missed you and your boy around here." Jonathan glanced out the back-door window. "I see the lads are keeping themselves out of trouble."

Hannah followed his gaze, trying not to look at David. "Yes, it would seem so. Please excuse me. I don't mean to be rude, but …"

She reached for the doorknob, but David anticipated her intentions, pulled open the door, and stepped out of her way.

"Permit me?"

Manners forced her to gaze up into his kind gray eyes, and her cheeks continued to burn.

"Thank you." Hannah nodded to both men before making her exit.

The boys had disappeared, but she followed the sound of their noisy chatter around the corner of the building. She tried to focus on how to scold Timothy without being too harsh, but visions of the striking stature of the Lazarus brothers would not leave her. Their appearance and demeanor differed vastly. Not only did Jonathan have the appearance of a large brown bear, he also carried himself like one, perhaps by design. For in his presence, seamen staying at the mission seldom needed to be reminded to watch their manners. Fair-haired and clean-shaven David exuded an equal but more genteel authority, developed through his years as a seafaring captain. Yet the brothers shared an easy camaraderie, just like Jonathan's sons. For all their outward differences, the entire Lazarus family impressed her now that she knew them better.

Just as Hannah rounded the corner of the mission, Estevam dashed her way and barely managed to avoid running into her. Paolo and Timothy, in hot pursuit, were not so careful. They both slammed into her, almost knocking her over. She managed to catch herself against the building.

Without missing a beat or offering his mother an apology, Timothy hopped about and grinned with pleasure. "Guess what Estevam told me?"

"Oh, goodness." Hannah gasped to recover from the collision with the two boys. She started to scold, but the joy on Timothy's face stopped her. He had seen too much sorrow these days for her to cut short this elation. "What on earth did he say to make you so happy?"

Timothy stopped jumping and beamed up at her. "He said those dumb ol' street boys still talk about what a tough varmint I am." He folded his arms into a proud pose. "I'm plenty tough. What do you think of that?"

Hannah felt the wind go out of her for a second time in less than a minute. "Oh, my goodness." Wouldn't Ahab be proud that his son's reputation resembled his own? But she was not proud of it. Perhaps Timothy should not play with these rough boys after all. "Come along then, my tough little man. We're expected for lunch."

Yet, as she and Timothy walked toward the house, Hannah's appetite disappeared, replaced by churning anxiety deep in the pit of her stomach.

Chapter Twenty-one

❧

"Captain Lazarus tells me Reverend Harris was back to his old self in the church service yesterday." Nan sat adjacent to Hannah, her dark blue gown draped gracefully across the divan in Hannah's parlor. "What a relief to hear that good news."

"Yes, he looked wonderful and sounded even better. After church, Timothy and I visited with Kerry, and she's recovering quickly. I'm sure that's the reason for his improvement." Hannah glanced at David, who had chosen to sit in a chair nearer her rather than beside Nan on the large sofa, perhaps to avoid sitting on her gown. "Despite their sorrow about their loss, they both seem to possess such amazing peace. One wonders how they can be so serene this soon."

"Mmm, yes." David nodded. "Their faith is an example to us all, isn't it? And, thank the Lord, we still have Mrs. Harris with us."

"Yes. If we had lost Kerry …" Hannah shook her head. " … many people would feel bereaved, not just her family. When I think of everyone to whom she ministers so unselfishly …"

David and Nan traded one of their private glances. David cleared his throat, as if preparing to speak, but Nan spoke first.

"Each of us has only one lifetime in which to do the right thing, Hannah. Kerry simply makes the most of the time God has given her."

"Mrs. Childers, permit me …" David began.

"No, Captain." Nan held up her hand to silence him. "You must let me say this my way. Now, listen to me, Hannah. We have all our pleasantries out of the way, and it's time to get down to business."

"Nan, how rude," said Hannah.

"Never mind. You and I were always able to be perfectly honest with each other. That's why we got along so well as girls, and neither of us has changed in that regard." Nan drew in a deep breath and blew it out, as though preparing for a speech.

"You understand what we are doing here. We are transporting to safety people who have fled slavery. When we can, we find them gainful employment and a safe place to live, which is what each and every one of them desires. When we cannot find such work and home, we help them on to Canada or other places beyond the reaches of those greedy scoundrels who would return them to bondage."

"Of course I understand that. I have known about it for close to a week, at which time I received the shock of my life—"

"Never mind," Nan repeated her pet phrase. "You've obviously recovered. What I want to know is what you're going to do about being here."

Hannah turned to David, who shrugged an apology for Nan's bluntness.

"Are you saying that, after aggressively pursuing me to live here, you want me to move out?"

"Oh, you silly girl, of course not. I simply want you to jump in and help out with our operation."

"Simply? Oh, Nan, it is *not* simple. How can you ask me to do such a thing? I have a son to rear."

"Now, Hannah, I don't see how you can refuse. Look at the people within this house and tell me you can desert them."

"Desert them? What do you mean? Patience is freeborn, and John has papers to prove he's purchased his freedom. That just leaves Leah, and she—"

"Ah, yes. Leah." Nan sighed. "There's much more to that little girl than meets the eye. For one thing, Leah is not her real name, but one we chose to help hide her slave identity. The dear child is very clever. Do you know that she can read and do her sums and that she wants to be a teacher? Think of her potential, Hannah, and what she can do for others. We must be careful about her. Keep her close to home and don't expose her to the likes of that Longwood person again."

"And you never even told me all this to begin with." Hannah felt her temper rising. "What if I had unwittingly said something? And how can you ask me to be a part of lying and lawbreaking? Think of my son."

David touched Hannah's arm. "We understand your concerns. We aren't asking you to do anything dangerous for either Timothy or you. In fact, you don't really have to do anything. Just remain here and perhaps occasionally provide, shall we say, diversions. I promise you that, in the unlikely event some difficulty arises, I will protect you both with my life."

His gray eyes exuded a gentle, probing intensity, and a slight smile graced his lips. When he looked at her this way, she felt comfortable, safe, and immeasurably reassured. She gave Nan a self-conscious glance and was surprised to see her friend grinning at her in a peculiar manner.

"Well, what do you say?" Nan seemed to be stifling a laugh. "Will you join—"

"I would say," David interrupted, "that we need to give Hannah time to think about it."

"Humph. Very well, then." Nan wagged a finger at Hannah. "But don't take too long. Now I must be running along. You two have a pleasant morning. Good day."

She rose without ceremony, and David stood to give her a chivalrous bow.

"Good day, Mrs. Childers."

Hannah rose to follow her to the door, but Nan held up her hand. "Really, dear, I can see myself out. You just stay still." She sailed from the room and out the front door.

"Well." Hannah turned to David, at a loss for any other words.

He chuckled. "There's no one quite like our Mrs. Childers, is there?"

Hannah nodded, and her heart seemed to drop. His words and warm tone confirmed what she had suspected. If they were not formally betrothed, they seemed to have an understanding. Hannah knew she should not sit back down, for to do so would invite David to stay, but Nan's visit had worn her out. Feeling desperately disloyal, she dropped back down into her chair, and, as expected, he reclaimed his too.

"How has Timothy been these past few days?"

Again, his gentle gaze breached Hannah's weak defenses. She must stop feeling this way. Why had Nan left them alone? Why had he stayed? How certain they must be of one another.

"He's doing as well as can be expected."

"Has he given up his idea of revenge against Charles?"

Revenge. The word stirred painful memories of Ahab's unreasoning rage. But, relieved to be diverted from her foolish feelings toward David, she straightened in her chair and shook her head. "I don't know. He doesn't talk about it. Oh, I just remembered something. The day after his poor kitty died, I thought perhaps I should ask you what to do about Charles. Do you think I should go to Mrs. Atwood and tell her what her son did?"

David propped his chin on his fist and considered her question for a few moments. "I wonder. I've only met Mr. Atwood once. He seems distracted by business, as ambitious young bankers often are, but perhaps I could speak to him."

"How good you are to try to protect us. But don't you think I should handle this myself?"

He chuckled and shrugged. "Forgive me. I didn't mean to assume … that is … yes, perhaps you should think about speaking to Mrs. Atwood." He grew serious again. "She should know what her son is capable of. I'll pray the meeting will produce good results for all concerned, but especially for the boys."

"Thank you, David."

To Hannah's sad relief, a tapping on the parlor doorjamb interrupted another moment of mutual, pleasant gazing.

"Mrs. Jacobs, mum, there's that Clara girl at the back door. I told her you were busy, but she insists on seeing you now. Shall I send her away?"

"Oh, dear. I hope …" Hannah stopped. "No, Bridget, I should see her. Please tell her I'll be there in a moment. David, would you mind waiting?" Another pause. She had meant to release him to leave, but her unthinking words betrayed her true wish.

"No, not at all. I'll wait here."

David rose with Hannah, and she started from the room. But before she could take two steps, Clara barged in, followed closely by Bridget.

"Now, you see here, girl …"

Bridget grabbed for Clara's arm, but Clara eluded her and strode toward Hannah.

"Mrs. Jacobs, there's trouble, and I came to warn you."

At her words, Bridget froze, and David stepped close to where Hannah stood.

"What kind of trouble, miss?" David's firm, quiet tone was that of a man used to being in authority, and Hannah felt a foolish but pleasant thrill dart down her spine.

Clara's eyes widened at both his presence and his words. "I'm sorry, Mrs. Jacobs, I never would have intruded."

Hannah glanced at David before responding. "It's all right, Clara. Oh, my dear, what happened to your cheek?"

The girl self-consciously touched a large purple bruise by her left eye. "It ain't nothing, ma'am. Just a clumsy accident." She eyed David with uncertainty.

"Captain Lazarus, this is Clara Macy, my new friend. Clara, this is Captain Lazarus."

David gave the girl a slight bow and a kind but guarded smile. "Miss Macy."

Also on her guard, Clara nodded.

"Come sit down, Clara." Hannah led her to the divan and sat beside her. David returned to his chair, and Bridget lingered nearby. "You may speak freely, dear. Tell me what trouble you're referring to."

Perched on the edge of her seat in obvious discomfort, Clara wet her lips. "I would have gone right to the mission, ma'am, but there's too many, uh, too many sailors I might, I mean, who might know me, and I didn't want to shame anyone." Clara's face grew red, and she glanced with embarrassment in David's direction as she spoke.

Hannah saw comprehension in his eyes, and she gave him a slight nod. He responded by staring at Hannah with obvious admiration, though she could not guess why. She reached out to touch Clara's arm.

"But what trouble were you speaking of?"

Clara wrung her hands. "These people down at the docks have this scheme to get sailors' money right after the ships come in and the men have their pockets full and are hungry for ... for company. It ain't enough just to sell 'em drinks or for the ladies to give 'em ..." She blushed even redder than before. "... guess the best thing to say is give 'em a little companionship."

Now Hannah felt her own face grow warm, and she labored not to look at David.

"Go on."

Clara bit her lip for a moment and continued to wring her hands. "So there's this scheme where they have these rooms at this tavern, the Blue Buoy, for a girl to take a sailor for companionship. And there's these secret panels—they call 'em crib panels—and they's set low on the wall beside the chair where the mark, the sailor, puts his clothes. Then when he's drunk and, um, happy, he falls asleep, and the girl signals her boss, and he reaches in and takes everything the poor fool has in his pockets. Then sometimes they drag him out and dump him in some side street in the same condition by which he came into this world. And none of his shipmates at the tavern knows a thing about it."

She spoke quickly, as if her shameful revelation could only be accomplished by rushing through it.

"Good heavens." Hannah wished for her fan, but it lay on the table across the room, so she took a quiet, deep breath. "And so you came to tell me this so I could help in some way?"

Clara lowered her head and shrugged an apology. "Yes, ma'am. I figured you could tell the reverend, and he could get the word out, maybe call in the law."

David breathed out a quiet sigh. "And how did you come by this information, Miss Macy?"

Clara's eyes widened with fear, and she turned to stare at him.

"It's all right, Clara." Hannah set a calming hand on the girl's clenched fingers. "Captain Lazarus works with the mission and has his own ships as well. This information may affect some of his own men."

The girl nodded her acceptance and relaxed a little. Then she straightened and lifted her chin. "I used to work that tavern. Until last week. Until Mrs. Jacobs got me a decent job. When Buzzer, my old boss, came around looking for me last night, I told him I was through. He didn't like that much." Unconsciously, she lifted the back of her hand to her bruised cheek.

"And so he hit you." David's fair eyes turned stormy.

"Yes, sir. He said he'd get me back to work one way or the other. That's when I knew I had to shut him down. That's why I came." Clara's posture drooped as she turned back to Hannah. "I know it seems like payback, and maybe it is. But I owe the reverend and his missus for being kind to Ma and Jewel, and I always pay my debts. I figured if I told you, you could tell the reverend. Like I said, I don't see going to the mission myself."

Hannah squeezed Clara's hand. "I'll tell Reverend Harris. It was good of you to do this. Why don't you go out to the kitchen with Bridget and have something to eat? I'm sure Florence will wonder where you are. If she is concerned about your tardiness, I'll vouch for you."

Clara lowered her head. "Thank you, ma'am. I am hungry."

Hannah leaned close and whispered, "I'll send something over for your mother and Jewel too. And I'll send those books I promised Jewel."

Clara's eyes glistened as she whispered back, "Thank you." She glanced toward David and gave him a grateful grin. "Sir."

He smiled. "You're a brave girl, Miss Macy."

The compliment, or perhaps his kind expression, seemed too much. She ducked her head and shook it, then rose and dashed from the room, followed by Bridget.

"You never cease to amaze me, Hannah. When did you begin this ministry to women of … women like Miss Macy?"

"I didn't exactly choose it. It was Kerry who influenced me."

"But you accepted the challenge. It shows you have the heart of a servant."

For a moment, she feared he would pressure her into adding his escaped slaves to her ministries, but his countenance bore no trace of coerciveness. Just as she began to wonder what to say next, he stood.

"I should go see Jeremiah right away. Then he can get the word out about the Blue Buoy."

As Hannah rose, she eyed him. "Keeping my promises for me?"

David grinned with sudden awareness. "Ah, I did it again, didn't I?"

"I forgive you. In any event, it's probably better, even more appropriate, for you to do it."

She walked him to the front door, where he claimed his hat from the hall tree, yet made no move to put it on.

"Give Timothy my regards, and let me know how your visit with Mrs. Atwood goes."

"I will."

He still hesitated.

"Yes?"

He lifted one shoulder in a slight shrug and stared out the side-light glass. "Oh, I don't know. It just seems …" He turned back and leveled a steady, tranquil gaze at her. "It seems we could work well together." He stepped outside. "Good morning, Hannah."

"Good morning, David."

After shutting the door behind him, she permitted herself one moment of sweet serenity before shaking off her deep, covetous longing for her friend's beau.

The time for action had come, but not what David and Nan would design for her. In spite of her discussion with David, she would not bother with Mrs. Atwood. No, she would take a different course. With Kerry past danger, Hannah had to make plans. She would send a message to Captain Longwood and ask him to help complete arrangements for her long-overdue trip to Europe.

Chapter Twenty-two

ℰ℧

For two days, Hannah struggled to write a letter to Captain Longwood, but the right words eluded her. Each attempt only led to wasted paper and ink as she sought ways to solicit his assistance for her voyage without encouraging his affections. In a moment of confusing pique, she wondered if those affections no longer posed a problem, for he certainly had kept his distance since last week when he had brought that awful Mr. Simons to search for Mattie. Never mind that she had told Longwood to visit less often.

At last, in frustration, she decided to abandon her task and go to the mission, even though a light rain had fallen intermittently all morning. Timothy had been asking to see Paolo and Estevam again, and now that he would be leaving Boston, a few more play-times with the Lazarus boys could do no permanent damage to his manners or his grammar. Dismissing guilty feelings for her unfair assessment of the good-hearted boys, Hannah grabbed her bonnet from the bedroom wardrobe and went to Timothy's room.

He sat on the floor with wooden blocks strewn around him as he built a large, complicated edifice. Another guilty twinge flickered through Hannah. Jonathan Lazarus had taught Timothy how to make all these blocks, from designing and sawing to sanding and painting, until he had several dozen of them in various shapes and colors. Along with the skill to do the actual handiwork Jonathan exhibited the patience needed to stick to the task, a quality to which Hannah made little claim but which she desired to see in

Timothy. The Lazarus family, all of them, had been good friends to Hannah and her son.

And there he sat now, his eyes glued on his creation. Not even an eyebrow wiggled to acknowledge her presence as he set a trapezoidal block at the apex of his creation. Once he successfully crowned it, he slowly removed his hand and slid backward, straightened his shoulders, and gave her a satisfied grin.

"Oh, it's lovely. Is this the house you would like to live in?" She carefully knelt beside him to inspect his work.

"Yes, ma'am." Timothy nodded and bent down near the floor to look into one of the side windows. "See, there's different rooms. And there's the little people John helped me carve."

Ignoring his improper grammar, Hannah laid her head on the carpet and peeked in the window on the opposite side. "Isn't that remarkable? Aren't you clever?"

She sat up to see sadness fill his eyes.

"I couldn't build anything this big before 'cause Jem would knock it down."

Hannah reached over to pull him into her arms, but he shrugged her off and started to play aimlessly with the unused blocks. She breathed out a quiet, sad sigh. He was growing up much too fast.

"Would you like to go to the mission?"

Timothy brightened. "Yes." He jumped up and ran to his wardrobe. "Wait till I get my hat."

"Oh, you'll need to do more than put your hat on. You need to wash your face and hands and change into your play clothes."

"That's dumb. Why do I have to wash if I'm gonna play. I'll just get dirty again."

Hannah stood up and glared at him. He ducked his head.

"I'm sorry. I'll wash up."

"That's my good boy. I'll send John to hitch Belle to the buggy. Meet me downstairs as soon as you're ready." As Hannah descended the front stairs, the music of his happy, childish singsong lifted her spirits.

She found John on the back porch oiling Belle's harness and sent him for the phaeton. After a few instructions to Bridget regarding household needs, she settled herself in the front parlor to wait, only to be interrupted by the tinkling of the doorbell.

"Bridget, I'll see to that." Hannah made her way to the front hall, then froze in shock upon seeing Mrs. Atwood and Charles through the sidelight. For a moment, she thought to refuse them entrance, but Mrs. Atwood had already spied her and offered a tentative smile while folding down her umbrella.

Hannah opened the door but did not invite them in.

"Mrs. Atwood," was all she could say, and that without returning a smile.

The other woman's eyes misted, but she squared her shoulders and lifted her chin. "Good afternoon, Mrs. Jacobs." She glanced up at Hannah's bonnet. "I see you're about to go out, but if we could have just a moment of your time, I would be so grateful. I've come to ask your forgiveness for the message I sent with Mademoiselle Trudeau last week regarding your son's welcome in my home. And Charles has come to ask Timothy's forgiveness for his rude behavior."

Hannah's mind seemed to go blank, and she tried not to let her mouth fall open in astonishment. "Oh."

Mrs. Atwood pulled her son up beside her and, with difficulty, continued. "It seems Charles has been the instigator of their troubles."

"Yes, ma'am." The boy nodded and stared at Hannah with wide, solemn eyes.

"Indeed?" Hannah stood still for another moment before remembering her manners. "Please come in."

After Mrs. Atwood placed her damp umbrella in the hall tree,

Hannah led them into the front parlor, offered them the divan, and then took a chair opposite. Staring at Charles, she tried to believe he was as repentant as his sorrowful expression suggested. But how could a nine-year-old boy brutally kill a cat, then expect it to be forgotten? With difficulty, she said, "Please go on."

Her arm still around her son, Mrs. Atwood glanced at him before speaking. "Charles has begged me for several days to let Timothy come play again. He misses him terribly. When I reminded him that Timothy was the one who had ..." She raised her eyebrows in the manner of a defensive mother. " ... who had given him several bruises and scrapes ..." She stopped and took Charles's chin in her hand, turning his face so Hannah could see the remnant of a serious bruise, now yellow and purple against his pale cheek. "There. You see. Your son did that."

Hannah felt her temper rise, and she almost stood to dismiss these intruders.

"But Charles says he deserved it, says he had been provoking Timothy since they met, the way boys always do. Timothy was just defending himself, though I hardly think he needed to go this far." Mrs. Atwood's eyes scanned the bruise once more, and she bit her lip, then turned back to Hannah. "Nonetheless, boys will be boys." A hint of a smile played at the corner of her mouth. "Can you believe it? Charles was actually proud of his bruises. He showed them off to his father who, of course, had to tell of his own boyhood scrapes. Can you imagine my chagrin when I heard them laughing about it? And here I had broken our budding friendship over all this boyish nonsense."

Her eyes misted again. "I like you, Mrs. Jacobs. You're a good person. Boston society can be very cold to newcomers, as you may have found. But we can form our own pleasant little society and—"

"Charles! You rat! You murderer!"

Timothy ran into the room screaming, tearing toward Charles with a vengeance. Mrs. Atwood threw herself across her son while Hannah jumped up, seized Timothy, and clung to him with all her strength.

"Stop it, Timothy. What are you doing? Stop it this instant." Hannah jerked him around to face her and shook him hard.

"He killed Jem. He murdered her. He cut her and hung her and …" Timothy threw himself against Hannah, and his sobs wracked them both.

"I didn't …" Charles stared, wide-eyed, first at Timothy, then Hannah, and last at his mother. "I didn't kill that dumb old cat. I pulled her tail, that's all. I swear it."

Mrs. Atwood's face was ashen. "Well, it seems I've made a terrible mistake in coming here. It's clear whose son needs correction, and it isn't mine. Come, Charles." She stood, grasped his hand, and started toward the door.

"No." Charles dug his heels into the carpet and pulled against her firm grip. "No, I'm not going. I didn't kill any cat, and I'm gonna make Timothy say he's lying."

"I'm not lying."

"You hush." Hannah glared at Timothy. "And you two sit down," she barked at Mrs. Atwood and Charles as she thumped her son down into a chair beside her own.

Charles planted himself back on the couch, a determined glower on his face. Perhaps Hannah's greater height felt intimidating to the diminutive Mrs. Atwood, for she also took her seat, though a little more slowly than her son.

"Now let's get to the bottom of this." Arms crossed over her bosom, Hannah remained standing. "Mrs. Atwood, last Friday evening, which would have been the last day Timothy visited Charles, the day they had their altercation, someone brutally injured my son's cat and hung her half-dead on our back fence.

Now Timothy had taken Jemima with him when he went to visit Charles, and Charles admits pulling her tail. According to Timothy …" She glanced at him for confirmation, and he gave her a scowling nod. " … according to Timothy, he took it upon himself to defend his pet and …"

She stopped, unable to find a polite way to describe her son's aggression. "In any event, right after supper that same evening, we found poor Jemima on the back fence."

"Oh, I'm so sorry." Mrs. Atwood's glistening eyes confirmed the truth of her words. "Poor little kitty. I've always loved cats, but Mr. Atwood won't have one in the house. But surely, Timothy, you can't believe Charles would do that?"

"I didn't. I swear." Charles was crying now.

Mrs. Atwood pulled her son into her arms. "No. In fact, he couldn't have. As soon as Mademoiselle Trudeau returned from escorting Timothy home, she cleaned Charles up and gave him his music lessons. He didn't go out again that day."

Hannah studied her for a moment, and her arms fell to her side. The woman was not lying. Hannah looked down at Timothy, who sat slumped back in his chair, staring at Charles, utter desolation written across his face.

"But if you didn't kill her, who did?" Timothy sniffed back his tears and wiped his nose with his fist.

Hannah grabbed her handkerchief from her sleeve and thrust it at him, not bothering to check whether he used it or not. With a heavy sigh, she sat back down.

"Mrs. Atwood, it is my turn to apologize to both you and Charles. I don't know what came over me just now. I don't ordinarily treat my guests in such a rude manner."

Mrs. Atwood gave her a rueful, forgiving look. "It seems we've both been under a great deal of stress." She reached up to smooth Charles's hair, but he brushed her hand away. She turned back to Hannah. "These boys are not easy to bring up, are they?"

Hannah shook her head. "No, they're not." She glanced at Timothy, who seemed lost in thought. "But I wouldn't change it for anything."

Charles wiggled impatiently to the front of his seat. "So can Timothy come over and play again?"

Timothy brightened and gave him a crooked grin before turning to Hannah. "Can I?" Annoyance crossed his face. "I mean, may I?"

The two women exchanged looks.

"Yes, you may, but not today. We're going to the mission, remember?" Hannah glanced out the front window. "John has brought the buggy around."

"Oh, yes, of course." Mrs. Atwood stood and reached out for Charles's hand. "I'm sorry for interrupting your schedule."

"But I'm so glad you came."

Hannah and Timothy saw the Atwoods to the front door, with the boys trading playful punches all the way and both mothers trading resigned looks along with their pleasantries.

Thankful to have the situation resolved, Hannah felt at peace as she drove Belle through the busy streets. Her happiness, however, was tempered by Timothy's lingering sadness, for now they had no idea who killed Jemima.

After greeting Aunt Charity and Tishtega, who were busy sewing new dresses for the girls, Hannah found Kerry in her room, sitting by an open bedroom window with Daisy curled in one arm. Kerry held a book with the other hand and was reading to her daughters when Hannah and Timothy entered.

"Hannah, Timothy, do come in. How nice to see you."

"Timofee," cried two-year-old Molly as she ran to embrace him. Lacy, almost four, walked to meet him, but also gave him a hug. He endured their affection with good humor and then looked at his mother, the usual question in his eyes.

"Don't you think you should ask Aunt Kerry how she feels?"

Timothy's eyes widened, and he grinned. "Sorry." He walked over to Kerry's chair and hugged her and Daisy as one. "How do you feel, Aunt Kerry?"

"So much better, my dear boy, now that I've seen you today. And how are you?"

"Fine, thank you." He looked at his mother. "Now, may I go?"

Hannah glanced at Lacy and Molly, who had followed him across the room like adoring puppies, and questioned him with an arched eyebrow. He rolled his eyes, and his shoulders slumped in resignation. Hannah and Kerry traded smiles.

"I suppose," said Hannah. "Run along. I'll come get you when it's time to go."

"Thanks, Mother. 'Bye, Aunt Kerry. 'Bye." He waved to the girls and dashed out.

Hannah took a seat beside Kerry, pulled Molly up on her lap, and put an arm around Lacy, while Kerry finished reading the story. Then the two women helped the older girls use blunt wooden needles to thread brightly colored yarn through flower designs on paperboard. Amazed at the patience the girls showed with the intricate work, Hannah once again wished for her own daughter to teach such skills.

In time, Ellen came to take the girls for their nap, and Tishtega appeared to insist on rest for Kerry. Hannah reluctantly left her friend, whose lingering sadness had not faded from her eyes, though neither had mentioned her stillborn son.

When Hannah entered the mission, she was drawn down the front hallway by the sound of familiar male voices. In the library, Jeremiah sat talking with a police constable, who wrote the minister's comments in a small notebook. Nearby sat Seamus

Callahan and Jonathan Lazarus, with David leaning against the wall, his arms crossed.

"I think we have enough evidence to keep that Buzzer fellow in the calaboose for a long while." The constable closed his notebook. "He'll send for his pettifogger cronies who'll try to get him off but, thank the Lord, we have a few honest judges to give them what for, despite all their crooked money."

The officer stood and straightened his jacket, then took in the other men with a sweeping glare. "Now a word to all you fine Christian gentlemen. The next time you discover a den of thieves, leave it up to the law to raid the place instead of going there yourselves, or else you may come out of it with more than these few bruises."

David, Jeremiah, and Jonathan glanced at one another sheepishly, but Seamus leveled a stare at the officer.

"Meaning no disrespect, your honor, but if it was your own baby brother who'd lost his shirt and nearly his life in one of them panel cribs, you'd be glad for friends like these to help you out."

The constable puckered away a grin. "Nonetheless, the next time, you give me a call. Good day, gentlemen."

As he made his way toward the door, he put on his hat, only to doff it again upon seeing Hannah.

"Ma'am." He edged past her and departed.

"Hannah." Jeremiah was the first to find his voice upon realizing she had witnessed their deposition to the lawman. The others once again appeared like guilty boys, with Seamus and Jonathan each mumbling that it was time for them to return to duties.

"You'll excuse me?"

"Begging your pardon, mum."

A curious blend of emotions churned through Hannah, with embarrassment over her own eavesdropping only a little overshadowed by her vexation at the appalling behavior of these friends.

She worked to control her temper as she entered the library, staring first at Jeremiah, then at David.

"David, I thought you intended only to inform Jeremiah of what Clara told us, not take the law into your own hands. And you, Jeremiah, with a wife, three children, and a mission to take care of, how could you do something so dangerous? Would it not have sufficed to enlighten the mariners who come here? Would it not have sufficed to have them pass the word among their shipmates, and let the sinners beware?"

As she spoke, Hannah copied the stern tone that her long-ago boarding-school headmistress had always used with mischievous students, for these men had surely been up to mischief. Further fueling her anger was the knowledge that it was partly her fault for entrusting Clara's message to David rather than delivering it herself. She might have ceased her reprimand, but as she walked closer, their facial injuries became apparent. David's square jaw bore a jagged red cut over one of several darkening bruises, and Jeremiah's patrician nose was red and swollen.

"Oh, my goodness, look at you." Hannah stamped her foot, and her face burned with anger. "How could you do that, getting into all that trouble? Has Kerry seen you?"

Jeremiah blew out a sigh. "No. It just happened this morning." He gave Hannah a boyish grimace, reached up to touch his nose, and winced. "You should have seen it before Maria put a cool cloth on it." Then he grew serious again. "But we didn't have any choice in this matter. Seamus was worried about his brother. He's been trying to get Paddy to come to the mission, but the boy just won't have anything to do with God. He has a weakness for drink, and a certain young lady, and the bad judgment to return to that partic-ular tavern, despite previous misfortunes."

Remembering all the hidden meanings of Clara's story, Hannah felt another surge of warmth in her face, this time the heat of embarrassment. But she forged ahead with her scolding. "And so you took it upon yourselves to sweep in like avenging angels and rescue the prodigal son?"

David peered down at her with a soft smile. "To do nothing in the face of such evil would have been a greater sin."

Hannah gazed up into his gray eyes, eyes that always seemed to say more than his words. Was he referring to today's escapade, or was he urging her once again to join his other enterprise? Steeling herself against all the mixed emotions David's presence caused, she lifted her chin again and focused on Jeremiah.

"But haven't I heard you preach, 'Vengeance is mine; I will repay, sayeth the *Lord*'?"

"Of course, but this wasn't vengeance. It was more like the time the Lord sent Abraham to rescue Lot from the heathen kings. Remember, Hannah, both righteous anger and righteous boldness have their place."

Hannah studied one, then the other, and heaved a sigh. "Well then, you've thoroughly excused yourselves. There's nothing more to say. I'll just collect my son and depart for a more peaceful abode."

She turned to leave, but David gently touched her arm, and a strange shiver streaked up her shoulder and across her neck.

"Please set your mind at ease, Hannah. God was watching over us." He gave her a reassuring smile. "May I see you home?"

Hannah swallowed hard, but no plausible refusal for his offer came to mind. Surely it would be all right to enjoy his company until she left for Europe.

"Thank you," she mumbled as she walked out into the hallway. Hearing him take his leave of Jeremiah, she tried not to be too pleased when he followed her out the back door.

They found Estevam peering about, first behind the woodpile and next into a shed. Giggles erupted when the boy pulled his younger brother out into the open.

"Now let's find Tim," Estevam said.

The two boys dashed about, checking hiding spots Estevam had already searched. Paolo spied the adults and ran to them.

"Mrs. Jacobs, Tim's the best hider. We never find him. Uncle David, will you help us?"

Hannah and David chuckled together, and she permitted herself to enjoy this carefree moment of camaraderie.

"Of course we'll help." She lifted her skirts to keep them from dragging in the dirt and walked around the corner to search between the buildings and out front.

Her enjoyment of the childish game soon disappeared, for when they all met in front of the mission, where Belle waited patiently to return home, none of them had found Timothy. After several minutes of calling, even the boys seemed worried, especially Estevam.

"Mrs. Jacobs, if he's gone someplace, it might be my fault."

A chill swept through her. "Why do you say that?"

Estevam and Paolo looked at each other and then back at her.

"I told him who killed his cat," said Estevam.

This time, Hannah swayed, leaning against David without apology. He gripped her with one hand and set the other hand on the boy's shoulder.

"Tell us everything, son."

Estevam pulled himself up tall and stared evenly at his uncle. "We found out those street boys were mad at Timothy 'cause he's just six and he can beat some of them up. 'Course they started it, but they always do. He was just defending himself."

"But they haven't seen him in weeks." Hannah regained her composure. "We live across town. How did they … ?"

Estevam frowned. "Street boys can sneak around and get the particulars on anybody. They found out where you live and went over there. They were bragging all about how they …" He gave

Hannah an apologetic grimace. "'Scuse me, ma'am, but they killed the cat and hung it on your fence."

"Do you think Timothy might have gone looking for them?" David asked.

Again Hannah swayed against him. "Oh, please, Lord, no."

A muffled sob behind them drew their attention to the phaeton. David steadied Hannah and then stepped over to open the trap door. Dirty and sweaty, Timothy tumbled out, his face streaked with muddy tears. Hannah rushed to stoop down and pull him into her arms.

"Oh, my darling, I was so afraid you had gone after those boys."

He leaned into her, shaking his head. "No, ma'am. I knew they'd gang up and lick me bad."

David knelt down beside them and gently touched Timothy's back. "That was wise, Timothy."

"You don't think I'm a chicken?"

David shook his head. "Not at all. You're a fine, brave boy. But a wise man once wrote, 'the better part of valor is discretion, in the which better part I have saved my life.'"

Timothy gave him a puzzled look.

Estevam nudged Timothy. "My Uncle David's always saying stuff like that."

David chuckled. "I mean you knew it would not be wise to go after those ruffians, even though they deserve to be punished. You're not a chicken when you save yourself from needless injury."

"I guess so." Timothy nodded.

Hannah gripped the phaeton wheel and pulled herself up. "Timothy, go get your hat. It's time for us to go home."

After a few token protests, he rushed off to obey, with his friends close behind him. When they were out of earshot, Hannah turned to David and tried to be stern, despite her giddy relief that Timothy was safe.

"Really, David. Comparing my son's behavior to Falstaff's cowardice on the battlefield with Henry V?"

He chuckled. "Not at all. Just quoting Shakespeare. Don't you think there's an application of the idea in this instance?"

Hannah gave him a prim glare. "Indeed. Perhaps." But his literary reference tempered her scolding. Had she at last found a friend with whom to discuss her beloved Shakespeare? This David Lazarus never ceased to amaze her.

Chapter Twenty-three

ಬಂ

David's large frame filled more than half of the buggy seat as he drove Belle across town toward Louisburg Square. Hannah held Timothy on her lap, letting his head rest on her shoulder while he dozed lightly in the late-afternoon heat. She was glad for his napping, for it kept conversation with David to a minimum. It also gave her time to think.

Why had she never realized that the box under the buggy seat provided a perfect hiding place? Two children or a medium-sized adult could easily curl up and hide there, though it would be a stuffy ride. She wondered if those slender, diagonal slits on each side could supply enough ventilation to keep a person from suffocating on a hot day like this one.

A strange thrill surged through her as she imagined someone being in the box right now, hiding from Mr. Simons. How gladly she would break the law to keep Mattie from his kind. But just as quickly as she thought it, she rejected the idea. Mattie was safely tucked away in David's attic while they awaited word from Nan about buying her freedom. Hannah would not have to put her son in danger.

"How interesting you knew the Shakespeare reference." David spoke softly, leaning down near Hannah's ear so as not to awaken Timothy. "Do you like to read all his works?"

"Oh, yes," she breathed out, recovering with difficulty from the shiver his close whisper had given her. If Captain Longwood ever murmured in her ear that way, she would be certain he hoped for such a reaction. But David's eyes radiated no hidden meaning, only kind curiosity. "When I was in boarding school, my greatest joy was portraying Portia in *The Merchant of Venice*. I'm not sure how well I performed the role, but my height gave me the advantage in securing the part."

"Ah, yes. I recall Mrs. Childers telling me about that. She said you played the part so well, one could easily mistake you for the wealthy young lady of Belmont, 'fair, and, fairer than that word, of wondrous virtues.'"

Hannah's face grew warm, but his mention of their mutual friend tempered her enjoyment of the conversation. "But did she confess to portraying Shylock in that same play? It was a difficult role, but she executed it admirably."

"Why, no, she did not. I shall have to call her into account for that omission."

How odd for Nan not to mention her own success. "The play is a delightful memory from our girlhood. For me, it ensured a life-long devotion to the Bard. Sometimes, my dear husband and I read Shakespeare's sonnets to each other, as well as the plays."

David nodded. "Eliza enjoyed more recent authors such as Miss Austen and Miss Burney. I carried several of those books on my voyages, but none moved me like the intelligence and wit of Shakespeare."

Hannah cast him a sidelong glance. How interesting that he was moved by fine literature. How she wished they could sit and discuss their favorite books. But her better judgment once again took hold.

"Ahab carried a library on his voyages too, though not on his last one," she murmured with a wistful tone.

Timothy looked up at Hannah through sleep-laden eyes. "Mother, you said 'Ahab.' Is our game over? Can we use our real name now?"

Hannah glanced at David, whose eyes radiated understanding.

"No, our game isn't over yet. But Captain Lazarus knew your father, just like Aunt Kerry and Uncle Jeremiah did, so it's permissible to say our real last name when we're with him, unless someone else is around."

Timothy's sleepy, troubled pout wrenched Hannah, and she held her son closer.

"Sir, was my father a bad man? I mean, was he wicked? Is that why we don't say his name?"

Hannah drew in a sharp breath, but David reached over and gently tweaked Timothy's nose.

"When a man saves your life, it's impossible to think him bad."

Timothy sat up, his eyes round. "My father saved your life?"

"Certainly did." A twinkle lit David's eyes.

Timothy slumped back against Hannah's shoulder, grinning. "Well, criminy, don't that just beat the devil."

"Timothy. Where did you learn such words?" Hannah gave him a little shake.

"I fear my nephews might be to blame." David answered for Timothy. "I should speak to my brother about it, for his poor hearing prevents him from noticing some of the language they've picked up from the sailors. And, of course, Maria still struggles with English, so she doesn't understand everything they say."

"Oh, dear." Hannah sighed. She would not criticize David's relatives, but she certainly would correct her son's language. "Please don't say that again, my darling. It doesn't sound nice."

Timothy wrinkled his nose. "Yes, ma'am."

Hannah's shock at his inappropriate words had been tempered by David's clever deflection of Timothy's question about Ahab, although it was one she often asked herself. Had Ahab been a wicked man? She could not believe that, yet she wished to keep their son from following his footsteps, especially his last, fatal act. On this pleasant day, however, her gratitude to David outweighed her concerns, for it seemed that, in his presence, every challenge met its match.

The rest of the ride home was filled with easy conversation, despite the hot weather. When they arrived in front of their connected houses, David secured Belle's harness to the post and lifted Timothy down.

"Mother, may I go play with Charles?" Timothy took a few steps down the sidewalk in anticipation of an affirmative answer.

"No, darling. If I permitted you to go there all dirty like that, Mrs. Atwood would be appalled. Besides, it's too late in the day. Perhaps tomorrow you may go."

Timothy grimaced with displeasure and heaved an impatient sigh. David chuckled as he helped Hannah down from the buggy.

"Tomorrow seems so far away, doesn't it, lad?"

"Yessir." Timothy's tone reflected his disappointment as he trudged up the front stairs.

"Won't you come in for some lemonade?" The words were out before Hannah could stop herself. Why couldn't she ever think before speaking? This was betrayal.

David seemed pleased, however. He glanced toward his house, rubbed his chin, and nodded. "Thank you. That would be refreshing after our dusty drive."

With Bridget dispatched to help Timothy wash up, John sent to tend Belle, and Patience instructed to bring lemonade, Hannah removed her hat and led David into the front parlor. Despite the dust that clung to both of them, she dismissed his concerns about her furniture and insisted they sit for a chat.

This one last time, she would permit herself to lean on David, to seek his wisdom, before shutting him out of her life. He belonged to Nan, Hannah reminded herself, and she would do nothing to try to change that.

"You cannot imagine how grateful I am to you, David, for the way you redirected Timothy's attention when he asked about his father."

David's gray eyes were warm with kindness.

"Hannah, when you first came to Boston, I promised you that no one would ever hear an unfavorable opinion from me about your husband, nor will I even harbor such a notion."

Hannah blinked back sudden tears. "But what if it's true?"

David moved from his place on the divan to the chair next to her. Encompassing her hands with his, he spoke softly. "Dearest friend, tell me what causes you to weep. What burdens your gentle soul?"

Through the mist of her tears, she returned his gaze. "What if he was evil? What if he was lost? What if he is in perdition this very moment?"

"Oh, dear friend, don't think of it. Don't let it torture you this way."

"But the *Pequod* survivor recounted that Ahab was intent upon revenge. And before Ahab left on the voyage, I heard him say—"

"Shh. Don't think of it, Hannah. You must rely upon the mercy of God and know He gives every man many chances for salvation, even unto the last moment of his life. That survivor, whoever he is, may not be a Christian. Or, if he is, he may not have been there to see Captain Ahab cry out to God in his last moments."

"I don't know if he saw Ahab …" Hannah bit back a sob. "… saw him die."

"There are many things that only God knows, but we can always trust Him to be merciful as well as righteous."

Hannah nodded, but her tears continued. "Perhaps if I had been older or wiser or somehow a better wife, he never would have sailed away on that last voyage."

"Never think that."

"But I do think just that. He was everything to me, but I was nothing more than an incidental diversion in his life."

"Not so, not so. I saw him in New Bedford soon after he met you. He was a changed man. No longer brooding or sullen, as he always was known to be, but cheerful and laughing. *Laughing,* Hannah. And what else was it but you and your love, and his love for you, that lightened his soul that way?"

"But what happened to that love?"

"I'm sure he loved you till the day, yes, even the moment he died. One can only imagine that when he was wounded, his horrible injury must have driven him mad with pain, perhaps so much so that he felt compelled to seek vengeance against the creature that wounded him. The compulsion for revenge can be an overpowering force, even when it's against a dumb beast. And from this force, sometimes not even the strongest human love can save a man.

"Oh, dearest friend, Captain Ahab was the best of men: brave, strong, a prudent leader. But he took too much on himself. He lived so long alone, relying only on his own resources, as we whaling captains do, that he did not know how to seek help from those who could ease his misery, neither God, nor man, nor the woman he loved."

How eager he seemed to comfort her, and he was succeeding. Right now, this moment, with all her being, she believed in the goodness and mercy of God, and without a doubt, she knew she had given her all to Ahab, and he had loved her in return.

"We grieve our lost loved ones and will grieve until we ourselves die. But you know they would wish us happiness while God grants us life. Be at peace, dear one, for surely your beloved would wish it so."

Hannah surrendered a soft sigh, willing herself to believe him. And, as she observed the earnestness in his eyes, she was mindful of the endearing names he had used. Was it just friendship he felt, or something deeper?

No, she must not think it. Her every thought and word must direct him toward Nan, whom he held in such reverence that he still addressed her as Mrs. Childers.

"Thank you, David. Your reassurances are so kind. I know what you say is true."

His intense gaze seemed to go even deeper, and she stared down at her hands.

"When you and Nan came to visit the other day, I thought she looked particularly lovely in that blue gown." Hannah reached for a glass of lemonade from the tray Patience had set before them.

David sat back, a look of bemusement spreading across his face, and Hannah felt heat rising to her cheeks once more.

"Did she?" Some dark understanding seemed to cross his brow. "Yes, of course. Blue looks very well on Mrs. Childers." He reached for the other glass and held it, but did not drink.

"Did you know Mr. Childers?" What a silly question, but all Hannah could think of to say.

"Yes. We became very close friends despite the short time we knew each other."

"I understand he had a weak heart."

Frowning, David pursed his lips and seemed to weigh his words. After a few moments, he set his drink down.

"Henry didn't have a weak heart. He told me to say that to Mrs. Childers as he lay dying."

"What?"

So David was the friend who had delivered Henry's last words to Nan.

"He did not want her to know ..." David shook his head and chewed his lip thoughtfully, then continued. "Hannah, Henry Childers was mortally wounded by slave catchers who chased him through a forest in Virginia as he was helping two men escape bondage. My ship was waiting off the coast, and his companions brought him aboard."

"Oh, merciful heavens." A wave of dizziness swept over Hannah. "But why are you telling me this?"

"Because I want you to know what some of us are willing to do to end slavery. As Mr. Emerson said, 'God offers to every mind its choice between truth and repose. Take which you please; you can never have both.' Henry Childers chose truth, and he died for it."

A pinpoint of rage stung Hannah for only an instant before confusion reclaimed her. "You're telling me, but you won't tell Nan how courageously he died?"

David shook his head. "She knows how courageous he was. She doesn't need to know he was shot."

"Oh." Hannah expelled a deep sigh, and a shadow seemed to fall across the room. All the comfort David had given her was displaced by great sorrow for Nan and greater confusion over why David had burdened her with this new revelation.

Before she could question him further, she heard a soft tapping on the parlor door. Timothy stood in the doorway, his freshly washed face solemn.

"Mother, may I ask Captain Lazarus a question?"

Hannah glanced at David, then back to her son. "Come here, my darling, and we'll see."

Timothy nudged himself into the chair beside Hannah. "Sir, you knew my father." His voice resonated too deeply for a six-year-old.

David nodded. "I'm proud to say I did."

"Would my father punish those boys for killing Jemima?"

"Timothy …" Hannah began.

"No. I want to know what Captain Lazarus says." Timothy's tone was not disrespectful, only insistent. "Would my father get revenge?"

David shook his head. "We can never know that. We can only remember how much he loved you and your mother. If he were still with us, he would take very good care of you. You believe that, don't you?"

Timothy's frowned deepened. "I guess so."

But Hannah believed something more. If Ahab were still alive, he would track those boys down and beat them within an inch of their lives, not because they had killed a kitten, but because they had hurt his son.

Chapter Twenty-four

ॐ

"Nan, I'm so glad to find you at home. Are you certain I'm not keeping you from something?" Hannah settled herself next to her friend on a pale blue brocade chair in the elegant Pemberton Square home.

"Not at all. It's wonderful to see you. You've brightened an already beautiful day. But won't you let me give you a cup of tea and a tour of the house? I'm so proud of my new décor." Nan's blonde corkscrew curls bounced against her dimpled cheeks. Her sunny disposition seemed especially bright today, and Hannah hated to spoil it.

"I mustn't keep John waiting out in the sun. I had him drive me here so your neighbors wouldn't be scandalized."

Nan's merry laugh rang out like a bell. "And a good thing too. Most of them are at their summer homes now, but the few remaining here in town would be shocked to see a lady of your position driving herself." She gave Hannah a knowing wink.

"And your wink would shock them as well. How do you manage to fit in here when you despise such strict social forms?" She gave a playful, haughty sniff. "Furthermore, I hardly care what Boston's elite society thinks of me. I won't be here that long."

"You keep saying that, but here you stay. Now tell me your exciting news."

Hannah's playfulness vanished. "Oh, how I wish it were exciting news, but it's actually a tragedy. Do you recall my mentioning Clara Macy, Kerry's young friend?"

"Ah, yes. The young woman who used to be a …" Nan's eyebrows wiggled upward. "Yes, I remember. You found her an honest job."

"And she's done very well at it, already earning Florence's trust with her sewing skill. Just yesterday, she brought more of my travel wardrobe for a fitting, and her work is exceptional."

"But what tragedy? And how can I help?"

"I knew you would say that. In fact, I know of no one else who could do so. Last night, Clara's mother and sister were burned out of their home."

"Oh, my word. How awful."

"That's not the worst. The fire was set deliberately by friends of a man known as Buzzer in retribution for Clara's informing on his illegal activities, which led to his being put in jail by the authorities. When the fire was started, Clara wasn't home, but her little sister, just a child, saw him through the front window. He and his friends had blocked the front door of the Macys' tiny house so poor, sick Mrs. Macy and Jewel could not escape. The scoundrels probably thought Clara was home too. And there is no doubt they meant to kill them all to pay Clara back for informing on them."

"Oh, Hannah, how horrible. But the family did escape?"

"Yes. Jewel woke her mother, and the two managed to break their back window and crawl out. So many people were drawn to the fire that those wicked men were surely afraid to do anything more to them. But the Macys lost everything, what little they had. When Clara came to me for help this morning, she said her mother is mostly grieving the loss of her husband's small gifts to her, a set of brightly painted crockery bowls from Mexico and his old sea chest, with lovely scrimshaw he had carved and inlaid on the lid."

Nan brushed away a tear that stole down her cheek. "Oh, how awful. How truly awful. But what can I do?"

"I'm not really certain what can be done. I know it wouldn't be wise to bring them to my house because of what goes on there."

"Oh, mercy, no. We have no idea of whether these women can be trusted about such things. Where are they now?"

"Clara pulled herself together and went to work, which I think was very brave. Florence has offered to let her sleep in the back room of her shop. Her mother and sister are staying in a nearby tenement, but the people who live there are afraid to keep them for long, for one never knows what those criminals will do if they find out. And those tenement dwellings are so small that two more people can be a terrible burden when they're all so poor to begin with."

Nan nodded. "Then we must do something quickly. Let me think a bit, and I'll devise a plan. Do you think either Mrs. Macy or the little sister—Jewel, is it?—could keep a job?"

"Not right away. Both of them have been quite ill for a long time. Perhaps it's the foul air in their neighborhood. It seems almost a miasma to me. Somehow, Clara has managed to avoid whatever afflicts them." She brushed away imaginary lint from her dark skirt. "You know, I believe it was desperation that drove Clara to her previous job rather than moral weakness."

"Hannah, you don't need to make Clara's excuses to me. She has begun a new life, and it's up to us to make certain she is not dragged back down."

"You're right. Now, what can we do to help?"

"Let me make a few inquiries. I'll be quick about it. You can count on me."

"I know. That's why I came." Hannah gave her a bright smile. "Now, before I go, you must tell me what brings about this happy mood of yours. You are positively radiant this morning, and I know it's not because of my visit."

Nan giggled like a schoolgirl. "Oh, I would have come to see you very soon to give you this good news. I'm engaged to be married!"

Hannah felt as if she had been struck. A soft "Oh" was all she could manage.

Nan shook her head, which sent her blonde curls bouncing again. "Oh? Is that all you can say? Aren't you happy for me?"

Hannah's eyes stung with sudden tears, and she snatched a handkerchief from her reticule. "Oh, yes. So happy. So very, very happy." She tried to think of a graceful way to hide her bitter shock but could only dab at her tears and try to keep more from coming.

"Don't worry that my fiancé will interfere with the help we give to Clara. Maurice is well aware of our charitable work. In fact, it was through our work that we met."

"Maurice?"

"Yes. He's simply wonderful. I never thought I could ever love anyone again after my beloved Henry died, but Maurice is a true man of God, and so very generous with ..." Nan patted Hannah's cheek. "Dear, are you ill? You're all flushed and breathless."

"Maurice?" Hannah managed to croak out. Could it be David's middle name? Was that what she called him when they were alone?

"Don't be angry with me. I know when we were girls we always promised to tell each other everything. But Maurice only recently completed his year of mourning after his wife's death. It would not have been appropriate for us to reveal our growing attachment any sooner. That is one social form I firmly believe in and will always abide by."

Unable to think straight, Hannah gave her a crooked grin. "Maurice?"

"Oh, you mean, what is his last name? It's Pendergast. Quite unusual, but who cares about things such as that? It's the man I'm marrying, not the name."

As Hannah's mind began to clear, she giggled. "Then this Maurice Pendergast is the reason you hesitated when I asked you to go to Europe with me?"

"Yes. I wasn't certain Maurice felt the same way I did, and I didn't want to leave Boston until I found out. I also didn't want to give some other woman a chance to set her cap for him. Oh, dearest, it's also why I've neglected you the way I have after thrusting you into the center of all our activities."

"I must say I wondered from time to time." Hannah leaned toward Nan and smiled through happy tears. "But, with this announcement, you cannot imagine how delighted I am for you."

"And you forgive me for not confiding in you?"

Hannah laughed, barely subduing the hysterical joy that bubbled about inside her. "Oh, my dearest, dearest Nan, there is nothing to forgive. Nothing, nothing to forgive. I have been such a fool."

"What on earth are you talking about?" Nan joined her laughter. "Why on earth a fool?"

Hannah hugged herself in an effort to gain a measure of self-control. "I have been a fool because I have been afraid to ..." She paused, choosing her words carefully. " ... afraid to be happy. But your happiness has set me free in ways you cannot imagine."

Nan gave her a knowing nod. "Oh, but I do imagine. It took me a long time to allow myself any kind of joy after Henry died. One feels almost guilty to be still alive, doesn't one? But our beloved husbands would not have wanted us to pine our lives away. Of this I am convinced. I can just imagine Henry peering down from heaven saying, 'Goodness, my little dumpling, what took you so long?'"

Seated in her parlor that afternoon, Hannah tried to read Mr. Douglass's compelling book about his life as a slave, but her eyes merely scanned the pages, imparting no information to her mind. Nan's revelation opened an entirely new world of thought for Hannah to explore, but not all her thoughts comforted her.

David must think her a ninny for the way she had acted. She had not seen him since his visit last week, except to exchange a friendly nod with him across the pews of the mission chapel on Sunday. After the service, he seemed busy conferring with Jeremiah, so she did not stop to talk. Rather, she took Timothy for a short visit with Kerry before going home. Now, with Nan's revelation of her engagement to Maurice, whom Hannah loved wildly even without meeting him, no impediment stood in the way of her accepting David's attentions. That is, if he wished to bestow them upon her. But how did she go about telling him? After her silly behavior, he might never come calling again.

No, that could not be. If nothing else, she was certain of his good opinion. Last Friday, after he had reassured both Timothy and her about Ahab's love for them, his leave-taking had been as pleasant as ever. Of course, that did not mean he wished to court her. But how else should she interpret all his kindnesses to her? And what of the endearing names he had used to console her? Surely those signified his affection for her. But she had put him off, almost rudely, and now must repair the situation.

What had she done to let Ahab know she desired his courtship? How had he ever seen beyond her naïve, girlish ways and fallen in love with her? From their first meeting, she had felt overwhelmed by his magnificent presence. Yet, though David was almost as tall and every bit as broad-shouldered as Ahab, his company always reassured her and gave her a sense of peace. Perhaps that was part of a more mature love.

Love? No, it was too soon to say she loved David, although her feelings for him involved something more than admiration and friendship. Perhaps, if he gave her another chance, and she made it easier for him to declare his intentions, friendship might lead to a deeper affection.

Hannah again picked up the Douglass narrative, and a slight chill swept through and tempered her joy. Accepting David meant accepting his work, perhaps even becoming deeply involved in it. Could she do that? Could any cause be worth placing her son in danger? Last week, David had promised to protect both Timothy and her, should she decide to help, but was that enough?

"Begging your pardon, mum." Bridget tapped on the open parlor door as she entered. "Not meaning to disturb you, but there's a message just arrived. I gave the boy a penny from the dish." She crossed the room and handed Hannah the missive.

"Thank you, Bridget." Hannah glanced at the envelope. Perhaps it came from Nan with a solution to the Macys' dilemma. "And while you're here, has Timothy come home from the Atwoods' yet?"

"No, mum. Would you like me to send John to fetch him?"

"Let's give him a little more time. He only seems to need a nap every few days, so we can let him play till suppertime."

"Very good, mum. Now, with your permission, I'll take my afternoon off, if there's nothing else you need."

"Certainly, Bridget." Hannah gave her a teasing smile. "But tell me, what will you do with your time?"

Bridget blushed scarlet beneath her freckles and stared down at the floor with a grin. "Mr. Callahan's waiting out back to take me for a walk, maybe buy me a bit of candy from the sweet shop down near the Common."

"Ah, so you've decided he's an acceptable suitor?"

Bridget nodded with enthusiasm. "Aye, mum. When you told me the whole story of how he rescued his brother—with the help of the captain and the reverend, of course—I realized he was a man of substance, not a man of the bottle at all. Do you think I'm doing the right thing?" Bridget's tone bespoke real concern for Hannah's opinion.

"My dear girl, I have learned if Reverend Harris and Captain Lazarus recommend a man, that man is worthy of every consideration one might wish to bestow upon him."

Bridget breathed out a happy sigh. "Aye, mum."

"Now you run along and have a wonderful afternoon. And next

week, don't wait so late to leave. It's after four o'clock. You've barely time for any fun."

"Aye, mum."

After she left the room, Hannah studied the ivory envelope in her hands. It was addressed to "Mrs. H. Jacobs" in a strong but graceful script. Turning it over, Hannah felt her heart leap, for pressed into the red wax seal was an elegantly shaped L. David had sent her a message. But why on earth had he not come in person? She slid her finger under the envelope flap to break the seal and pulled out two folded notes. The first one read:

"My dearest lady, I beg your indulgence. With the greatest urgency, I must ask you to meet me at the Bunker Hill monument this evening at six o'clock. I send this message with great desperation filling my heart, and you are my only hope of consolation. Your servant, DL. P. S. I have enclosed driving instructions."

If Hannah had not been seated, she might have swooned. David was forcing her to make a decision. Oh, not on purpose, of course. Without a doubt, an emergency had arisen, and he had no one to transport some fleeing slave, someone like Mattie or Leah, people for whom she deeply cared. But could she not send Seamus in her place? Surely David would approve of this substitution? After all, he had promised to protect her.

Energized by the thought, Hannah jumped up and ran through the house to the back door. Throwing it open, she scanned the alley, to no avail. Seamus and Bridget were nowhere in sight.

Her heart raced as she read the note again. Urgency. Desperation. These were not words David would use carelessly. She had no choice. She must go to him.

Willing or not, she would join his illegal beneficence and pray to God her precious son would not suffer because of it.

Chapter Twenty-five

ಬಿ

*B*elle seemed to sense Hannah's agitation, for she, too, was skittish as they drove through the busy evening traffic. At every dog bark or shout of a street vendor, the mare flinched, breaking her usual even gait until reined under control. But while Hannah might control the horse, she could not rein in her own anxious thoughts.

What extremity had forced David to call for her this way? How she feared for his sake, but what would the situation require of her? Before leaving home, she had resolved that, whether it be sin or not, she would lie to protect anyone put into her care, yet she trembled to think of what it might cost her. Could the authorities arrest her? Could they take Timothy away from her and put him in an orphanage? Surely Jeremiah would never permit that. But perhaps his association with her would taint his influence with those who made such decisions.

Her fear-laden thoughts distracted her, causing a wrong turn and much self-scolding. She glanced at David's directions, realized her error, and was forced to wait for several other carriages to pass before she could turn Belle back to the right course. The error cost precious minutes, and her fears increased. Her pin watch read one minute before six o'clock. Late! What if she did not arrive in time to help? But the summer sun was still high above the horizon, and she could not help but wonder why David would be moving an escaped slave from place to place in broad daylight.

She navigated over bumpy cobblestone streets, frequently glancing toward the Bunker Hill monument, whose great height made it visible from afar. With less than a mile to go, Hannah tried desperately to still her pounding heart. But her greatest challenge lay before her: taking Belle over the Charles River, for though she had crossed as a passenger, she had never driven a buggy across any bridge.

The link connecting Boston and Charlestown bore unending traffic of every sort: horse-drawn wagons, peddlers pushing carts, pedestrians from every walk of life, including numerous men in military uniforms. The latter caused Hannah almost as much consternation as the thought of Belle dumping this light buggy into the river below. What if these soldiers or sailors discovered what she was doing? Could they arrest her? Why on earth did David choose a meeting place so near the Navy Yard?

Biting back tears, Hannah headed the mare toward the bridge. She would not change her mind. She would go to David now, whatever the cost.

To her relief, the phaeton made the passage without incident, other than having to take a turn among the many others waiting to cross.

Once on the Charlestown side, Hannah again checked the page of directions, which were crumpled from being grasped in her fist, and noted that a short road going uphill on her left should lead to the appointed spot. But the drawing seemed not to reflect the reality, for ahead, under the shadow of the giant spire, sat some sort of pavilion, a slightly raised, canopied tent with dim lights glowing through its canvas walls. Worse, as she drew near, she could see several uniformed men milling about.

Hannah's foreboding erupted into stark terror, as her mind numbed and hot pinpoints of fear shot through her entire body. A wild spasm jolted her arms and, instead of reining Belle for a turn, she slapped the mare's haunches and sent her forward at an uneven trot. In desperation, Hannah pulled back hard just as a naval officer rushed toward her. The frightened mare reared on her hind legs, gave a chilling scream, and then lunged ahead. With shouts and calls, uniformed men swarmed the scene, all hands grasping at the horse. One man swung himself up on her back, and with great effort, drew her to a shuddering halt. He then dismounted, gripped the reins, and talked soothingly to the animal.

Surrounded, Hannah stared at the men, who were not so many as she first thought. The naval officer dashed to the buggy and, reaching up, grasped her hands. The rest dispersed, except for the man at Belle's head.

"Hannah, my dearest, thank heavens you were not injured. Whatever possessed you to drive yourself here?"

"Captain Longwood." Hannah could hear the almost hysterical squeak in her own voice, but she had no power to control it. What was this man doing here? Where was David? Had he already been arrested?

"Oh, my dear, if anything had happened to you, I would have beaten that man senseless for not driving you." Longwood tugged at her hands, drawing her to disembark from the buggy.

"What man?"

As he lifted her down, Hannah's mind refused to impart any sensible thoughts, just as her legs refused to support her. Why would Captain Longwood want David to bring her here?

Longwood caught her as her knees began to buckle, and he pulled her into his arms to steady her.

"Easy, my love. Rest a bit." Holding her firmly with one arm, Longwood pushed her bonnet back and kissed her flaming cheek. He then motioned for seating, which his subordinates hastened to bring. When he had placed her safely on one of the close-set chairs, he drew back with a great sigh and studied her for a moment. "There, all safe now."

"What man?" she demanded again. Nothing here made sense, but she would never give David away.

"Why, your manservant, of course. You see, it's just as I told you. These Northern Negroes have no idea how to care for you. He should have driven you here." He shook his head. "But you came."

"I came?" Hannah could not still her quivering body or her racing mind.

Longwood reached to pull her into his arms again, placing another gentle kiss on her temple. "Shh. There. Don't tremble so. Yes, you came. For a few desperate moments, I feared you would not. Whatever possessed your mare to start as she did? Never mind. You're safe with me." His low laugh revealed his relief.

Hannah struggled to hide the hysteria that clamored for release from her heaving chest. The note had not been from David Lazarus at all, but from Duncan Longwood. DL. Why had she never noticed their matching initials?

Longwood leaned back, chuckling, but Hannah could see it required effort for him to appear relaxed. And, despite her own inner struggles, she could call his expression nothing but raw vulnerability.

"But you came." He repeated the words in a hushed, awestruck tone, and tears glistened in his eyes, almost disarming her.

"How could I not?" she managed to say.

"I should never have doubted that you return my lo—"

"No, of course not. I could never refuse a friend who sent such an urgent message. Now what could possibly have you in such a dither, Captain Longwood?" Her voice sounded harsh, but she would not apologize.

He ran his hands through his hair and heaved another sigh. "The message was written in such haste, I have no idea what I said."

"Indeed? Here then, have a look." Hannah pulled the folded note from her reticule and thrust it at him. Her pulse had begun to slow from its fearful pace, but her temper was beginning to rise.

Longwood chuckled softly. "Ah, yes, yes. I recall it now. And, my dear, I mean every word of it. You are my only hope of consolation."

She studied his face. Again his expression revealed his vulnerability. Without doubt, he was in love with her. And, without doubt, though her heart ached for him, she knew she must regain self-control and permit him to go no further.

"I hardly think so, Captain. You must remember who you are: a man of great responsibility. Not only does your family depend on you, but our country depends on you. Your new command is proof of your courage, your patriotism, your leadership. Why, just think—"

"Please, dear lady." Longwood waved her compliments aside. "This is not my purpose in begging for your company in such a juvenile manner. There is a method to my madness." He glanced toward the pavilion. "If you can walk now, won't you come see what I've prepared for you?"

"Prepared? For me?"

"Why, yes. Our picnic." He laughed. "Don't tell me you've forgotten."

Hannah drew in a breath. "Oh, dear." She hoped her voice conveyed her dismay.

"Did you think I was the one who had forgotten?"

"I must admit, since you have not come calling recently, I assumed you had found other interests." Oh, foolish words. He was sure to misunderstand her meaning.

But he merely grimaced. "Oh, no. How stupid of me." Clasping her hands again, he drew them up to kiss. "Oh, my darling, I thought to play the wounded lover. I thought if I withdrew my attentions for a short while, you might discover your own feelings for me, for surely you must admit you've displayed the most genteel reticence to my courting."

Hannah pulled her hands back and turned to stare out across Boston Harbor. "Please don't misunderstand ..."

Longwood reclaimed one hand, but only held it. "How could I misunderstand? You came. You responded to my urgent plea. And now you must permit me to take you to our picnic where I shall explain everything to you."

He stood, and a reluctant Hannah rose too, allowing him to take her arm. Their walk somewhat steadied her legs, and by the time they reached the white-canvas pavilion, she had regained a measure of control.

Once inside the tent, Longwood watched as she surveyed the elegantly prepared supper. A half-dozen silver candelabras lighted the shadowed shelter, and food enough for a shipload of sailors was spread out on a linen-covered table. But no ordinary seaman ever tasted such an array of delicacies, for it was a banquet fit for royalty. A large, juicy beef roast and several baked chickens sat on silver trays, ready to be carved by the uniformed black man behind the table. Three kinds of fish simmered in chafing dishes, the aromas of their seasonings blending to cause Hannah's stomach to murmur in appreciation. She could not count the number of vegetables, fruits, and desserts in the all-too-lavish, all-too-inviting presentation. But how could she eat at a time like this?

"Captain, you shouldn't have done all this." She managed a little laugh. "So much food, and I fear my incident with poor Belle has chased my appetite away." She swallowed discreetly so her watering mouth would not expose her lie.

Longwood's hand slipped from her arm to her waist. "Come sit down, my dear. I'm certain that once you've tasted my chef's appetizers, you'll be as hungry as a starving sailor."

He guided her to a small table set for two with sparkling crystal, elegant bone china, and an assortment of gleaming silver utensils. Even with boarding-school training, Hannah had no idea which implement to use for each course. Still, she could think of no reason to refuse his offering when a wave of dizziness reinforced her need to eat.

While they ate appetizers—large mushrooms stuffed with spicy breading and topped with tiny shrimp—Longwood chatted about his recent activities. With his new ship, he had been assigned new officers and sailors, some of them entirely green, so he had supervised their training. A new contingent of marines had come aboard, all in readiness for the USS *Lanier Wingate's* voyage to the war in Mexico. He had spent time with his superior officers and learned of the progress of the conflict and his part in upcoming campaigns.

With each course, as he continued to impart information, Hannah saw that once more he was forcing himself to appear nonchalant while a current of nervous restlessness flowed beneath the surface. Gradually, she came to realize the direction of his news. Before he spoke the words, she knew his departure was imminent.

"And so, instead of a month or more, I have only these few days to accomplish all I had hoped to do here in Boston."

Abruptly, he stopped, and unguarded hope glistened in his brilliant blue eyes. Not since their first meeting had Hannah been so moved by his astonishing masculine beauty. But, whereas attraction had characterized that meeting, compassion was all she felt now. She turned from him and through the tent opening spied the spire of the Old North Church across the river. *Lord, grant me wisdom*, she prayed.

Longwood reached across the table and took her hand. "Now you understand why I've asked you here and why there was so much urgency in my message."

Hannah retrieved her hand. "But we must do more than this. Why, Jeremiah would be terribly hurt if you didn't permit him to give a reception for those of your men who have been attending the mission services. He regards them as quite his special little flock, you know. I'll go and speak to him first thing in the morning. And since

Kerry is still on the mend, I'll take full responsibility for arranging the details. We won't be able to match this beautiful spread, but I'm sure Maria and her daughters can prepare an excellent banquet."

Longwood's face revealed his bemusement, and for the first time since meeting him, Hannah thought him struck speechless. As he took in her words, though, appreciation replaced confusion.

"Ah, Hannah, you are the most thoughtful, gracious lady I have ever known, apart from my sainted mother."

She shrugged lightly. "Nonsense. Now I'm really quite stuffed, and I must return to my son, so would you be so kind …"

His eyes widened with alarm, and he leaned forward. "Please, Hannah, listen to me. I didn't ask you here only for supper. You must know how I feel about you."

"Please …"

"From the moment I first saw you, I have loved you. Every passing day, every meeting with you, has caused that love to grow. Beloved, please understand. I don't have time for a proper courtship before I must return to my duty to our great country. But surely you can see from this small offering …" He waved his arm to include the very large supper spread. " … I would do anything, everything, to win your love. Only say the word, and my ship's chaplain will arrange our wedding—"

"Stop. Oh, stop. I demand it." Tears scalded Hannah's eyes, but whether from anger or pity toward him, she could not tell.

He obeyed, wincing without artifice, staring down at his hands, and shaking his head. "I've wasted all this time when I might have won you. I shall never forgive myself."

They sat in silence for several moments while both stared unseeing at their untouched desserts. At last, Hannah lifted her eyes to see his dejected posture and clenched jaw. What had she done to make him think he had a chance with her?

"We really would not suit, you know."

Longwood's head jerked back up, denial written across his face. "But indeed we would. We could. Doesn't every marriage need a time of adjustment? You must know this."

Hannah sighed. What one thing would make him realize how different their life philosophies were? The answer came immediately.

"Do you recall the woman who came to be my lady's maid?"

His frown deepened. "Yes, of course. Why do you ask? Was she discovered and returned to her owner?"

"Whether or not she was found, I cannot say. But I have discovered a way to send word to her master that I would like to buy—"

Longwood sat up, a laugh of relief escaping him. "Ah, you see. You do understand the way things should be. But of course you'll have to move from Massachusetts once you acquire her, due to this state's laws. May I suggest Virginia? Somewhere near Richmond?" A charming smile played across his lips. "My family would be only too happy to assist you—"

"Will you ever permit me to finish a sentence?" At her sharp tone, Hannah was gratified to see true repentance return to his face.

"Forgive me."

She blew out a sigh of exasperation. "I plan to buy Mattie's freedom and that of her children, if I can locate them."

Understanding began to creep into his eyes. "Ah. I see. And once they are free, what will you do? Will you buy them a house? Will you supply them with food? For surely you must realize that without guidance and care, these Negroes will have no way to take care of themselves." He bit his lip and glanced away for a moment, but quickly relented. "Oh, Hannah, forgive me. You haven't been schooled in these things. Let me teach you … let my family show you—"

"Captain Longwood, I seem to recall asking you to use my married name, yet still you persist in a familiarity for which I have not granted permission."

At last, full understanding settled into his countenance. His eyes reddened, but he nodded. "Again I beg your forgiveness, Mrs. Jacobs. Please understand that I spoke from a heart overflowing with the purest devotion and affection."

Hannah finally permitted her own tears to slip down her cheeks. She could not despise this man, regardless of his views toward slavery or his impertinence in pursuing her. He merely lived what he had been taught. And he had certainly humbled himself before her, which called for some response. Had she time, she might have tried to persuade him from his views. But it was more than their disagreement over slavery that prevented her from accepting him. Before she began to care for David Lazarus, she had known she could never love Duncan Longwood.

She stood, replaced her bonnet, and collected her gloves and reticule. He was quick to stand and motion for a servant.

"Will you see me to my carriage?"

"Of course. In fact, please permit me to accompany you. It's growing late, and it's not safe or acceptable that you should drive yourself home." Doubt clouded his face. "Or, if you prefer, I could send a mounted escort instead."

Hannah gave him what she hoped was a maternal smile, one she would give Timothy for doing something kind or good. "I would be pleased if you would see me home, Captain Longwood. But an escort would also be appropriate."

To her relief, he merely nodded and gave her a rueful smile of defeat.

Chapter Twenty-six

ᴇᴐ

*D*uring the ride home, Hannah tried not to lean against Longwood, but she could not avoid brushing her shoulder against his arm when they drove around corners. Exhausted from her ordeal, constricted by her corset, and embarrassed for both of them, she sat stiffly clinging to the buggy's side. Longwood, however, seemed to have regained his composure, for his posture was relaxed and his mood affable.

Perhaps he felt conscious of their escort, three armed and mounted marines in dress uniforms, and wished to save face. She certainly could not deny him that. But to her, the drive home seemed to go on forever. Whether Longwood drove slowly to spend more time with her or whether he was being careful of his own horse, tied to the back of the buggy, she could not guess.

Traffic had lessened as evening drew on. Lamplighters walked the streets, lighting the whale oil lamps at every corner. Few people were out this time of night. None too soon for Hannah, they climbed Beacon Hill to Mount Vernon Street and turned into Louisburg Square.

Longwood reined Belle close to the curb while one of the marines dismounted and took charge of securing the mare to the post. Longwood disembarked and offered his hand to Hannah. But as she scooted to the edge of the seat, he gripped her waist, forcing her to grasp his shoulders while he slowly lifted her down. Then he placed a kiss on her cheek.

"You'll not deny me that," he whispered in her ear. "Will you?"

Hannah tried not to stiffen and back away. She would not embarrass him in front of his men.

"Don't you *ever* do that again," she whispered back.

He laughed, as though she had told him a private joke, but his eyes flickered with hurt. "May I see you to the door?"

Without answering, Hannah turned, eager to end this foolishness. Then she gasped. At her open front door stood David and Timothy.

The boy whooped and jumped down the front stairs, racing into Longwood's open arms with a happy shout. "Captain Longwood."

While Longwood lifted him up into the air and swung him about, Hannah stared at David across the few yards that separated them. In the dim evening light, his face seemed a mask.

"Mrs. Jacobs." He nodded to her, unsmiling, as he came down the front steps.

"David, did you need to see me?"

"It was nothing important."

Now she saw the dismay in his eyes, even while she heard the happy chatter of Timothy and Longwood behind her.

"But won't you stay?" Hannah reached out to touch his arm, but he bowed away from her and shook his head.

"You will excuse me. I have an appointment."

"Mother, Captain Longwood says you've had a grand picnic at Bunker Hill." Timothy clung to Longwood's hand and dragged him toward her.

"Yes, we did." Hannah stared at Longwood, willing him to know he must stop.

Longwood responded with a cheerful laugh. "Don't be angry, my dear. I'm afraid I've given away our secret." He took her hand and bowed to kiss her fingertips. His grip was too firm for her to retrieve it without a scene, but she stepped back, only to have him step closer. "Now, dear, don't forget that you promised to speak to Reverend Harris about our little matter first thing in the morning."

Before she could answer, he looked beyond her. "Why, Captain Lazarus, is that you? How are you, sir?" He released Hannah and reached his hand toward David.

David lifted his chin slightly, a grimace playing across his lips while they shook hands. "As well as can be expected, sir."

"Are you ill then?" Longwood's concern sounded sincere.

"Not at all. Merely enduring the heat."

"Ah, yes. Yet it is my understanding June is not the hottest month in Boston."

"Hot enough this year, I think." David gave Hannah a slight bow. "Now, if you'll excuse me."

"Of course. Good evening, David."

With sinking heart, she watched him turn and stride down the street until Timothy claimed her attention. "Can Captain Longwood come in for tea? Please, Mother?"

Hannah glanced at Longwood, who appeared about to accept the boy's invitation.

"No," she said quickly. "He's needed elsewhere. Back to duty, didn't you say, Captain?" She glared at him, daring him to contradict her.

"Oh." Timothy gazed at Longwood with nothing short of adoration, to Hannah's dismay. Her son loved this man, but only with a child's understanding.

"It seems I had better be going, my boy." He started to tousle Timothy's hair but apparently changed his mind and shook the boy's hand instead.

Timothy beamed with pleasure and straightened up tall, as he did when anyone accorded him adult honors. "But you can come back another day?"

Longwood looked at Hannah, the same question in his eyes. She gave her head a quick little shake no, but said, "We'll see. Now, into the house with you, my darling. It's close to bedtime."

"Aw, do I have to?" Timothy slumped his displeasure and appealed to Longwood with a look.

Longwood set his hand on Timothy's shoulder. "Now, lad, is that any way to speak to your mother? If she says you must go to bed, then you must. You cannot be a leader until you learn to obey."

His words seemed to please the boy. "Yes, sir." He grinned and saluted Longwood, who returned the gesture. "Yes, ma'am." He ran up the front steps, turning back to wave. "See you later, Captain Longwood."

"Well, aren't you pleased with yourself?" Hannah turned to follow her son, but Longwood gently gripped her arm.

"Please don't be angry." His earnest, winsome expression affected her far differently than he must have hoped.

Hannah jerked her arm from his grasp and hissed, "You have no idea how angry I am. Good night, sir." She spun away from him and hurried into the house.

Hannah sent John to tend Belle and then searched for Bridget, finding her upstairs preparing Timothy for bed. The two were in a playful disagreement over which nightshirt he would wear.

"Never mind, Bridget. I'll put him to bed."

"Aye, mum." Bridget tweaked Timothy's nose. "He's a right lively lad tonight."

Timothy giggled and mischievously batted her hand away. "Did you see the captain's fancy uniform, Bridget? Captain Longwood, I mean? Captain Lazarus doesn't have a uniform."

Hannah frowned. "Bridget, what did Captain Lazarus want? Is everything all right?" Her eyes asked more questions than her words.

"Aye, mum." Bridget's manner seemed guarded. "He just wanted to see how everything was. When he found you were out, he visited with Master Timothy for a few minutes and was leaving when you came home."

How disappointing. David had come to visit her, and if she had not been so foolish as to mistake Captain Longwood's message, she might have found some way this very evening to let him know she would welcome his attentions.

She pulled a clean nightshirt over Timothy's head. "What did you and Captain Lazarus talk about?"

Timothy's head popped through the neck opening of the nightshirt, and he frowned at her. "Nothing important."

Hannah glanced again at Bridget, who shrugged.

"What was it?"

"Oh, he has this dumb idea about starting a Bible class for those street boys down near the mission. He asked me what I thought about it."

"But it's a wonderful idea. That would take a lot of his time, and he's a very busy man. And it wouldn't be easy either. Don't you think he's very generous to do something like that?"

Timothy scowled. "They don't deserve something good done for them. They killed Jem. And they didn't just kill her like they do stray cats. They came all the way over here and did it 'cause I licked 'em and they're cowards. They oughta be punished."

Hannah led her son to a chair and drew him up on her lap. "What they did was cruel and wicked. But if no one is ever kind to those boys, what will happen to them?"

He shrugged. "I don't know."

"They'll probably grow up to be very bad men and do many more wicked things. Captain Lazarus hopes to redeem them by teaching them about God's love."

Timothy considered her words for several moments. "But then I couldn't pay them back."

"Begging your pardon, mum, may I say something?" Bridget came and knelt by their chair.

Hannah nodded to her.

"Master Timothy, if you forgive those boys and let go of your anger, it's not for them you do it."

"It's not?" He looked at Bridget, as puzzled as Hannah.

"It's for yourself, my lad. Hatred and anger stored up in the heart hurt the one who carries 'em far more than the one who's hated."

"Oh, Bridget, how true. How wise." Hannah hugged her son close. "You understand that what she says is right?"

He slowly nodded, but Hannah could see that, deep inside, he was not convinced.

Hannah sat at the dressing table brushing her hair in the dim candlelight. What an exhausting day this had been, and how she longed to talk with someone about her ordeal with Captain Longwood. However, Bridget seemed preoccupied, probably with thoughts of Seamus Callahan. And even Mattie, who sometimes slipped over from next door to help her undress, did not come this evening. Ah, well, perhaps tomorrow she could visit Kerry and receive some much-needed consolation. After all, she must go to the mission anyway and speak with Jeremiah about a reception for the departing sailors and marines.

Once in bed, she could not sleep, for the day's events refused to release her. In rehearsing all that had happened, especially the last few hours, she could not entirely acquit herself.

Her error regarding the note from Longwood could be dismissed. But once at the appointed spot, she should have insisted on coming home immediately. How foolish to give in to her hunger, no matter how tempting the lavish supper. By dining with Longwood, she had encouraged his later audacity at her door, for he obviously did not believe she had rejected him in earnest.

An image came to mind, giving her heart a twist. When she reached out to David, he had moved away from her. Not that she blamed him, but still it hurt. Would she ever be able to make him understand why she had been with Longwood?

Unreasoning rage welled up inside, and she sat up and thumped her pillow with clenched fists. How dare David be angry with her! Hadn't she risked everything—her safety, her son, her very life—to come to his aid?

But what a foolish thought. He had not summoned her at all, so her actions proved nothing to him, although she had risked all for his sake. She slumped back down on her bed and let her tears flow freely.

But then, inexplicably, Hannah felt the burden lifted from her. Perhaps she had proved something, after all, for now she understood her own capabilities. As fearful as the experience had been, she knew without doubt she would do it again. Not for David. Not for Nan. But for all the people like Mattie and Pip, John and Leah, and all the unknown slaves who had the courage to flee their evil bonds. Yes, and for Clara, who had escaped another kind of slavery. And for Mrs. Macy and Jewel, who still paid the price for Ahab's revenge. And most of all, for Timothy, so he would not follow in his father's footsteps.

Indeed, she had proved something of great worth to herself this day. No longer would she be dependent on another person for strength. Not on a husband, for as much as she had loved Ahab, she must now break his hold on her and leave him in the past. And not on a friend, no matter how dear. But rather, like her father, she would depend only on God, for He had tested and tried her, and she had come through the furnace like gold.

She dried her tears on the sheets and smiled up into the darkness with a whispered prayer of thanks.

The time had come for Hannah to begin a new life, not with adventures abroad but with far more important adventures right here at home.

Chapter Twenty-seven

❦

*H*annah awakened early the next morning with a feeling of serene anticipation. What the next days and months and years would bring, she would not try to guess. But her decision of the previous night had only grown stronger during her restful sleep.

Even her unpleasant recollections of Captain Longwood's actions had mellowed into compassion. Everything in his countenance and demeanor bespoke great love for her, albeit a love she neither desired nor returned. But with his imminent departure for the war in Mexico, his aggressive behavior was understandable and even forgivable. She knew him to be a man of honor, and one day he would reflect on his misdeeds and perhaps feel ashamed. To let him know she harbored no ill feelings, Hannah would keep her promise to arrange a reception for his crewmembers.

More exciting things lay ahead, however. After visiting Kerry and making plans with Jeremiah, she would call on Nan and tell her of this new resolve to devote her life to helping people escape slavery in its many forms. Nan and David would show her where she could help the most.

Even Hannah's fears regarding Timothy had receded in the night. She awoke realizing she had the power to designate a guardian for him, should anything happen to her. In fact, she was foolish not to have a will already. Ahab, in spite of all his rage against his misfortune, had written a liberal will giving her power of attorney to inherit his money and raise their son, without which the authorities in Nantucket could have done as they wished with both. Now she must further ensure Timothy's care, and no one could be trusted more than Jeremiah. She would be certain to discuss it with her dear friend this very morning.

To her surprise, Mattie did not come help her dress. And, although the usual morning pitcher of hot water sat on the nightstand, Bridget did not knock on the door for morning instructions. Still, Hannah felt that ritual was honorary, since Bridget had managed the household before Hannah moved in. Perhaps the housekeeper was down the hall helping Timothy dress. All the servants loved her son and went out of their way to take care of him.

No sounds came from Timothy's room or any other on the third floor. But muted voices drifted up from downstairs, so Hannah descended to the first-floor dining room, where Timothy was quizzing Patience about the possibility of helping her make gingersnaps that day. The cook threw her head back and laughed heartily.

"Oh, you know you can, Master Timothy. I'll let you know when I'm getting started." Patience then turned and saw Hannah, and her smile faded. "Mrs. Jacobs." She nodded and swept out of the room to the kitchen.

Hannah bit her lip. Patience seemed upset with her. Was it because she had prepared a lovely supper last evening, only to have Hannah leave before eating?

"Patience says I can help her make gingersnaps. Do you want to help too?"

"That would be fun. I used to help make cookies when I was your age. But this morning, you and I are going to visit the mission and do some other errands. Will you be too disappointed to miss out on the cookie making?"

Timothy weighed the options for only half an instant before letting out a little whoop. "Yippee. The mission. I've gotta tell Paolo and Estevam about Captain Longwood's visit."

Hannah suppressed a grimace. The heroic captain certainly had captured her son's heart, or at least his imagination.

"I'm sure they've seen many brave officers and sailors at the mission services. Now, let's sit down and have breakfast."

After they had eaten, Hannah sent Timothy to his room to get ready for their excursion. As she followed him upstairs, she pondered the behavior of her servants. From the moment she had moved into this house, they had treated her with warm respect, but today the atmosphere was strangely different. No smile greeted her when she asked John to fetch the phaeton. Patience served her usual tasty eggs, bacon, biscuits, and honey, but she wore a frown. Bridget announced her departure on a household shopping trip in cool, though respectful tones, and Leah was nowhere to be seen.

Were they all coming down with some sickness? If so, it was too late to remove Timothy to a safer location. If he became ill, she simply would have to manage. That thought surprised Hannah, for it was quite different from her former attitude of protecting him before anything else. Perhaps her decision to engage in a noble cause somehow strengthened her faith that God would send them no needless suffering.

Carrying her gloves, bonnet, and reticule toward the stairs, Hannah called to Timothy not to linger over his toys. As she descended, however, she saw Nan through the sidelight and hastened to open the door.

"Nan, how good to see you. I was coming to call on you later this morning. Don't you look beautiful? It must be love." Hannah laughed. Nan always was a beauty, and today her azure gown lit her blue eyes and made them sparkle. But seen closer, Nan's face seemed more flushed than radiant. Was she ill too?

"Thank you. Judging from your glowing face, I surmise you might have a bit of the same affliction." Nan bustled through the door and faced Hannah.

"Oh, it's not …" Hannah looped her arm through Nan's and drew her toward the parlor.

"Nonsense. It's written all over your face." Nan tapped Hannah's hand playfully with her fan and withdrew her arm. "And sometime you must tell me every detail about it. But I can only stay a moment, and I have come to apologize to you."

"Apologize? Whatever for?"

"Why, keeping you here all this time. I've been selfish to insist you stay when all you want to do is take a simple trip to Europe, one you were denied as a bride, while I was fortunate enough to see all those wondrous sights."

"But—"

"No, let me finish. I further think that, while you plan your trip, you must move back into the Harris house. Now that Aunt Charity and Tishtega have returned to Nantucket, Kerry could use your help until she is on her feet again. You won't mind, will you?"

"I hadn't thought of that. Well, I suppose if that's where I'm needed most right now—"

"Without question, it is." Nan still had not seated herself and seemed inclined not to do so. "I would make all haste to get over there. That nursemaid Ellen takes on too much authority and needs a bit of comeuppance. I'm sure you've noticed."

Hannah shook her head. "I think she only wants to prove herself capable. But if you think I should go—"

"Oh, yes. The sooner, the better. Tomorrow won't be too soon. I'll instruct Bridget to pack your trunks. With all your new gowns, you have much more than you brought, so it will take a while."

Hannah laughed. "Don't you think I should ask Kerry and Jeremiah if I may move back over there?"

Nan stiffened, and her smile was strained. "How could your old friends turn you down?"

Hannah studied Nan's face. "Are you ill? You don't seem yourself today."

Nan's laugh sounded brittle. "Not at all. I have many things to do and can't stand around chatting."

"No, of course not. With your upcoming wedding—"

"Yes, that's it. Just too much to do. Now, if you'll excuse me, I had best be going."

"Do sit a minute. I have some important news that just won't wait." Hannah gripped Nan's hand and tried to tug her friend down on to the divan, with no success.

"But it must wait. I'm sure it's very lovely news, but we'll have to make it another time." Nan twisted her hand out of Hannah's grasp and stalked out of the parlor, meeting Timothy at the base of the stairs. She stopped and drew in a breath, and her eyes were filled with sadness as she reached out to caress his cheek.

"Dear boy." Nan's voice broke, and before Hannah could stop her, she fled out the front door.

Timothy rubbed his cheek and cocked his head. "Is something wrong with Mrs. Childers?"

Hannah shrugged. "No, I don't think so. She has a lot on her mind." Now that Nan was getting married again, all her emotions seemed to be on the surface. Perhaps she was remembering her own lost son. "John has brought the buggy. Let's go to the mission."

With her visit to Nan now unnecessary, Hannah drove to the mission to discuss the reception with Jeremiah. John seemed relieved when she told him he could stay home, though he had never approved of her driving before.

The day seemed unusually hot and dry, and dust from the street swirled up into the buggy, making both mother and son cough.

Hannah was beginning to understand why most of her neighbors took refuge outside the city in their summer homes. The unpleasant trip across town seemed endless, but at last they arrived.

Kerry welcomed Hannah with a loving embrace, and Jeremiah joined the two women in the parlor for midmorning lemonade and cookies. Once Timothy had pocketed several treats for the Lazarus boys, he set out to find his friends.

"I miss your mother, Kerry." Hannah set down her lemonade, feeling refreshed already. "I'm sure you must too."

"Yes, but my sister-in-law will be giving her another grandchild within the month, so she must be there to help now that I'm well. Still, it seems we must say good-bye too often, doesn't it?"

"And here we're about to be faced with another parting," Jeremiah said. "Hannah, are you still determined to go to Europe with all the news we're hearing of epidemics and political unrest?"

Hannah shook her head. "When I arrived here less than two months ago, I would have scolded you for suggesting I postpone my trip, and I probably did scold. But now I think it's an excellent idea to stay here for a while."

"Indeed?" Jeremiah sat up, smiling.

"Truly, Hannah?" Kerry reached out and grasped Hannah's hand. "Oh, I couldn't be more pleased. And the girls will be delighted they won't have to say good-bye to their 'Timofee.'"

The three chuckled over Kerry's imitation of Molly's baby talk.

Jeremiah leaned forward, his eyebrows raised and a slanted grin on his lips. "But what changed your mind?"

"Yes, do tell us, Hannah. What's changed your mind?" Kerry raised her eyebrows and mimicked her husband's quizzing expression.

Hannah glanced from one to the other, blinking her confusion over their eager response. "Well, you see, I thought there might be things I could do here to help out. You know, with the charitable work everyone is involved in."

Her statement seemed to set them back, for they exchanged puzzled looks.

"That's commendable, of course, but is that the only change you expect in coming days?" Jeremiah assumed his pastoral posture and voice, but a grin still played at the corner of his mouth.

Hannah breathed out a sigh of annoyance. "Don't tell me our good captain has spoken with you already."

"No, dear," Kerry said. "But it was just a matter of time before this happened."

"At least so we thought," added Jeremiah.

"And so we hoped." Kerry squeezed Hannah's hand again.

Hannah frowned, her confusion growing. "But we all knew the *Lanier Wingate* would be sailing to the war in Mexico. And I know how much the conversions of the men from the ship meant to both you and Captain Longwood. That's why I suggested you might like to give a small reception for them. But he seems to have come here before me and arranged it already. Still, I know he did not tell you this: I would like to help with expenses, since this would be beyond the normal budget of the mission."

Jeremiah nodded, but he now appeared puzzled. "A truly generous offer. Thank you, Hannah."

"Yes. Very generous." Kerry glanced at Jeremiah and then at Hannah. "But I don't think we have been speaking of the same matter. Captain Longwood has not been here to arrange a reception or any other event, has he, Jeremiah?"

"Not at all. What is it? There's something else about Captain Longwood, isn't there?"

Hannah studied her hands. A lady should never feed her own vanity by revealing a rejected suitor's proposal. But Hannah needed to unburden herself to her pastor. Still, she could not bring herself to tarnish Longwood's reputation. After all, he was a Christian man, just a very misguided one when it came to slavery ... and women.

"He proposed marriage to me last night, and I—"

"Oh, Hannah." Kerry leaned back and shook her head.

Jeremiah frowned darkly. "And you said … ?"

"Why, no, of course. I don't love him. And I certainly don't … oh, that's enough. I simply said no."

"Ah, praise the Lord." Kerry produced a fan and began using it in earnest.

Jeremiah chuckled, then laughed aloud, and then struggled to produce a more proper reaction. "Poor Captain Longwood. He was defeated before he began." He shook his head and pursed his lips, but his eyes sparkled. "I don't mean the good captain ill will. It's just that the two of you would never suit. It was obvious, at least to all your friends. It's also sadly obvious that he is blind to the truth."

Kerry huffed her indignation. "Indeed, husband, it's more than that. I would never have our Hannah yoked to such a man, and she's proven how wise she is for having seen beyond his handsome face and Southern charm."

Jeremiah ceased his laughter and grew serious, though he continued to gaze at Hannah fondly. "One can always count on our Hannah to know when a man only desires to win her as some sort of trophy."

Hannah's face grew warm. Did Kerry know Jeremiah once sought her hand? Observing the love these two now shared, she knew her rejection of this wonderful man all those years ago had been a wise decision. But such musings were best dismissed, so Hannah turned to Kerry.

"But you said it was only a matter of time 'before this happened.' If you did not speak of the captain proposing to me, what on earth did you refer to?"

"Ah, Hannah," Jeremiah answered for his wife. "We were indeed speaking of the captain proposing, but we were speaking of a different captain."

"Jeremiah." Kerry tried to scold, but her own merry mood broke her composure, and she laughed. "Darling, this is not for us to say. He must declare for himself."

Hannah sat back, stunned. This time, she could not mistake their meaning. They were convinced David cared for her. But if he did, after last evening, he surely must now question those feelings, or at least her worthiness to receive them.

Now the full force of Longwood's behavior struck her. He purposely had made a show of possessive affection, surely knowing all the while that David stood watching. And who else might have seen him lift her down from the buggy and kiss her cheek? Did all of Louisburg Square think she somehow belonged to Captain Longwood?

She could not imagine being so cruel as to gossip about rejecting him, but how else could she preserve her own reputation? How else could she let David know she was free to receive his attentions, not to mention joining his noble cause of rescuing slaves?

Chapter Twenty-eight

&

This was no game. Nor was it merely a matter of two men vying for her affections. Life or death hung in the balance for the people David and Nan helped. And despite Captain Longwood's claim that his "chattels" were considered part of the family, there was even a chance David had delivered some of them to freedom. That thought both elated and sobered Hannah.

Yet she still could not bring herself to broadcast her rejection of Longwood's proposal. His desperation had caused him to behave in an ungentlemanly fashion, but she refused to sink to his level. People would simply have to realize through observing her actions that she was above reproach.

The only concession Hannah would make to this resolve was to interrupt Nan's busy wedding preparations and tell her oldest friend what she had told Kerry and Jeremiah. Never mind that Nan's neighbors might be scandalized to see a lady driving her own phaeton into Pemberton Square.

But even as she drove toward her friend's home, Hannah wondered if David's meeting the previous evening had been with Nan. The memory of his gray eyes clouded with disappointment, and worst of all, his refusal to take her hand, haunted her and stirred up dismal imaginings. Why else would Nan be in such a hurry for her to move from her house? Why else would the servants be suddenly distant? In her excitement about the decision to join their operation, she had misread and dismissed all their actions. They surely must think her a traitor.

"Are we in a hurry?" Timothy held on to the side of the buggy but gave her a crooked grin, clearly enjoying their rapid pace.

Quickly, Hannah reined Belle to a walk. "Oh, my, I was lost in thought. Thank you for saying something. I'm not so good a driver that I can take such a risk. Driving is a big responsibility, especially with my own sweet treasure by my side."

"I like going fast." Timothy embraced her and then rested his head against her with lazy contentment. His playtime with the Lazarus boys had tired him, and if she did not feel compelled to visit Nan, Hannah would take him home for a quick dinner and a lengthy nap.

As she reined Belle toward the curb in front of Nan's house, Hannah glanced up and thought she saw her friend's blonde curls bouncing away from an upstairs window. But when Hannah rang the front doorbell, the butler informed her that Mrs. Childers was not in. His formal stance and frosty tone first chilled Hannah and then angered her.

"Very well, you can tell Mrs. Childers that I have no intention of moving out of her Louisburg Square house."

"Very well, Madame. I shall inform her." The butler retreated within.

Hannah gripped Timothy's hand and turned to leave, but Nan flung open the door and ordered, "Come back here."

Hannah obeyed without a word. She and Timothy were soon seated on the divan in Nan's parlor, but the diminutive blonde stood unsmiling in front of the hearth.

"Timothy, wouldn't you like to go with Mary to the kitchen for a cookie?" Nan nodded toward the serving girl in the doorway.

"No, thank you, ma'am." Timothy sat solemn and wary, his dark Ahab look heavy on his brow and his mother's hand held tight.

Hannah felt near to tears but refused to surrender to them. Her son's grip on her hand was not for any fear of his own but to reassure her. When had he become so intuitive, so protective? She would not send him away, but with him in the room she must take particular care in explaining things to Nan. Still, it seemed best not to evade unpleasantness.

"Please explain why you refused to receive me."

Nan lifted her chin, still offering no smile. "As I told you this morning, I'm busy with wedding preparations."

"No, it was I who suggested your wedding preparations were cutting short your visit to me."

Doubt flickered in Nan's eyes, but only for an instant. "Nonetheless, it's true. I have many things to do."

"Then why can't I help you?"

Again, Nan hesitated. "You have your trip to plan. I'm sure you want to be sailing for England soon."

"No, not at all. I've decided to stay."

Nan started, but before she could respond, Hannah continued.

"I have decided to join your charitable work."

At this, Nan's eyes narrowed, and her lips drew up in a tight little line. She took a step toward the divan, her eyes now blazing. "Have you really? Well, I'm not so certain that's a good idea, considering—"

"Oh, but I have considered. I have thought of all that your work entails and made my decision. Other influences notwithstanding, I believe in what you are doing with all my heart."

"But—"

"Appearances can be deceiving. You *know* my heart, dear friend."

Nan's eyes filled with tears, and she shook her head. "I have always thought so, but …"

Hannah squeezed Timothy's hand and kissed his cheek, then released him. She went to Nan, grasped her shoulders, and leaned near her ear.

"I have completely rejected Captain Longwood's attentions," she whispered, "and his way of life."

Nan flung herself into Hannah's arms and wept. "Oh, thank God. Thank You, God. Oh, Hannah, if only you knew …"

Hannah released her own tears and held Nan fast. "But I do know, my dear. And now all is well."

After a few moments of emotional release and mutual comforting, Nan produced a handkerchief from her pocket, and Hannah found one in her own sleeve. They stood wiping tears and laughing softly for a few moments, until Timothy claimed their attention. He sat slumped back on the divan, humming in monotone, swinging his legs and lightly brushing the coffee table with his foot. The expression on his face bespoke active boredom, and both women laughed again.

"All right, we can leave. I know you're hungry."

"Oh, but you must have dinner with me," cried Nan. "I have so much to tell you. And besides, you must help me with my wedding plans."

Hannah lay on her fainting couch feeling anything but faint. Her visit with Nan had solved several problems, and now she felt almost giddy with happiness. Although the two of them had spoken carefully so Timothy would hear no censure of Longwood, Hannah learned important information and could once again happily anticipate her new life. First, she learned that Nan's Maurice had volunteered to take Mrs. Macy and Jewel to his country home where they could escape the miasma of their tenement neighborhood and perhaps regain their health. This Maurice sounded wonderfully kind and generous, and Hannah looked forward to meeting him.

Then Nan promised to stay close to Hannah during the social so she would not find herself alone with Longwood—*that person*, as Nan referred to him.

Nan also said David had come to see her the night before and then had left for another location, one unknown to her, to arrange safe passage for Mattie and the others hiding at his Louisburg Square residence. Nan did not know when he would return. This news cut deeply, but Hannah understood his actions. She would have to wait to tell him of her true decision about Longwood, but with the offending party sailing to war in three days, she could afford to be patient awhile longer. With a mischievous laugh, Nan promised not to interfere, but to let Hannah tell David herself.

Nan also asked Hannah to deliver a message to Bridget. Although it confused Hannah, Bridget's sunny Irish disposition returned when she heard the words, "My rose has bloomed." Hannah had not known Nan grew roses.

More than thirty sailors and marines from the USS *Lanier Wingate* had attended services at Grace Seaman's Mission since being assigned to the warship in the early spring. Some resided in the mission dormitory, while others only attended Sunday services. All had abandoned the taverns and seedy establishments on the water-front, swayed by Jeremiah's preaching and godly example to a more spiritual life. With this part of his flock soon to be thrust into war, Jeremiah felt the sorrow of a father saying good-bye to his beloved children. Whether the seaman was a newly enlisted boy of sixteen or a weathered old salt of fifty, officer or common sailor, each received the same paternal care and guidance.

For this reason, Kerry, Hannah, and Nan worked to make the farewell reception as pleasurable as possible. Kerry chose a luncheon menu with foods the men could not enjoy at sea: fresh roast beef and lamb sandwiches, fresh summer vegetables and fruit, and a wide selection of desserts. Nan hired a stringed ensemble to play and confided to Hannah with a surreptitious wink that if some of the men felt lively enough, they might tap their toes and no one would scold. Even Timothy, Paolo, and Estevam participated in the event, their boyish antics charming the men who had already bid farewell to their own sons.

As the instigator of the event, Hannah considered herself responsible for its success, but when the room began to fill with early guests, she grew nervous. Captain Longwood would come, of course, and she had no idea how she would respond to seeing him again. She must not be rude, but she also must not permit him to display unwanted affection for her. With Nan and Kerry by her side, she began greeting guests.

In addition to navy men, Jeremiah had invited several of the other mariners who resided at the mission, merchant sailors like Seamus Callahan and several whalers awaiting the call to their next adventure in the South Seas. For appearances, the men in the naval uniforms had the advantage over the others in their diverse dress. Not only were their black trousers, snow-white shirts, and neck scarves crisply ironed, but they also were clean-shaven, and their hair was always neatly trimmed. Still, they could share a friendly joke or spiritual blessing with the other, less-regimented men of the sea.

Captain Longwood was punctual, arriving on the hour of one o'clock. As he entered, he was accorded proper military respect from his men and a handshake from Jeremiah, but the atmosphere of the room quickly relaxed.

By the time Longwood entered, Hannah had moved from receiving guests to arranging sandwich trays on the buffet luncheon table. She was near the spot where she had stood when he had made his previous grand entrance into the room. This time, however, few ladies were present to swoon over his handsome face and heroic form. And all Hannah felt was dread, for Kerry and Nan had busied themselves in other quarters.

True to her fears, Longwood gazed at her across the room. But rather than approach, he nodded, gave her a sad smile, and turned to enter the library across the hall. Then Hannah noticed another tall figure leaning against the library hearth, his arms crossed and a pensive glower on his strong, Viking face. So David had returned from his mysterious mission. Hannah's heart seemed to skip a beat, then drop in disappointment when he seemed deliberately to look away from her. Could he not see that she and Longwood had no connection?

Hannah forced herself to concentrate on making sure the food table remained supplied with full trays until boyish giggles drew her attention back to the library. The unmistakable alto voice of her son was mingled with those of his two friends, and the three of them seemed about to get out of hand. With a maternal sigh, she marched across the hallway just in time to see Timothy and Paolo at the center of a group of men who goaded the boys on in a fencing duel undertaken with long sticks.

Her anger flared, both at her son and the men who watched their antics. She looked at David, still at his post by the hearth and wearing a frown of concern. But it was Captain Longwood who grasped the giggling Timothy about the waist and lifted him in the air with a hearty laugh.

"I think I'll sign this sailor to serve on board my ship. If all my crew fights with this determination, we'll have the war won in no time."

The men chuckled as Longwood sat down, holding Timothy close.

"What do you say, lad?" Longwood said to the boy. "Will you sign aboard my ship?"

"Don't know." Timothy's eyes sparkled with mischief.

"Don't know. Don't know what?" Longwood demanded with mock sternness.

"Don't know if I wanna be a sailor."

Longwood glanced about the room. "Did you hear that, men? The boy doesn't know if he wants to be a sailor. But, lad, you would make a fine one. Where else should a brave man serve?"

Calmer now, Timothy stared at Longwood with round, innocent eyes. "Maybe I'll be a whaler."

For one heartbeat, the room was silent. Then laughter broke out, with Longwood's laugh the heartiest. Timothy glanced about, his dark eyes growing stormy, his mouth drawing down into a frown. Longwood seemed not to notice.

"Why, lad, whaling's no life for a fine boy like you. It's a dirty business with no glory and few rewards." Longwood waved his arm to take in the assembly. "Now, see what fine sailors we have here. Wouldn't you like to wear one of these grand uniforms, perhaps attend the Naval Academy and become an officer? These brave men serve our country and keep us free. What good are whalers?"

Timothy's lower jaw clenched, and his lips twitched with anger.

"Listen, my lad, and let me tell you what whaling does to a man. Why, not long ago, just a year or two, I think, a crazy, one-legged whaling captain took his whole crew down to Davy Jones's locker because he was bent on killing a particular bull whale out in the Pacific. Never mind that there were a thousand whales all around that he could have had. This mad captain, who didn't deserve the title, if you ask me, said he would have that bull whale, and none other. What did it get him? The whole crew lost, except one poor fool who can only sit around seaside taverns in a drunken stupor and tell his tale. Mad, both of them, lad. That's what whaling does to a man. Now if you want to go to sea, the United States Navy ..."

Longwood was so caught up in his tale, he no longer seemed to notice his reluctant captive. But Timothy glared at him, and tears had begun to slip down his cheeks. Hannah, stunned as she was over Longwood's cruel speech, tried to shake off her shock, tried to rescue her child, but was too horrified to move. Perhaps this was the best way to bring to an end her son's affection for the man.

Then a nearby movement drew her attention. David Lazarus sauntered toward Longwood and his young prisoner. Just as Timothy seemed about to blurt out his fury at Longwood, David took a chair beside them and tugged Timothy into his arms.

"Well, now, Captain, I must defend my chosen profession. I was a whaler for many years, yet no one has ever accused me of being mad, nor do I know any other whaler to be mad. As for the captain you speak of, I knew the man, and the story that drunken survivor tells, well, I think it's just a whale of a tale."

The crowd of men chuckled. Hannah drew in a careful breath, and her dizziness began to fade.

Longwood glanced at Hannah, and a smirk crossed his lips. "Indeed, sir? Perhaps. But mad or not, you must agree there is no match for the courage and abilities of a sailor fighting for his country aboard a United States warship."

David scratched his chin. "I'll not disparage your bravery, Captain, or that of your crew. But I would assert that it takes more courage for a man to ride the back of a giant sperm whale to harvest oil for our lamps than to stand behind a broadside of cannon firing on a distant enemy."

The assembly of seamen now hummed with disapproval, except for the few whalers in the group, who took their turn at chuckling.

Longwood stood suddenly and burst out with an ironic laugh. "Indeed?"

David slowly stood and with great care scooted Timothy away. The boy rushed to Hannah's arms and turned back to watch the two men.

"Yes, indeed." David's voice was low and calm. "In fact, I would like to challenge you …" He paused, and the room became silent again.

"Sir, I hardly think …" Longwood began.

"Captain Lazarus …" Jeremiah moved between the men, disapproval in his eyes.

"No, don't stop me, Reverend Harris." David held up his hand. "I'll accept no apology. In fact, I demand satisfaction." Despite his grave words, his tone was light, and he gave his adversary an easy-going smile.

Jeremiah saw his look and, with an expression Hannah knew well, stifled a grin and stepped aside. "If you're determined, then I won't stand in your way."

Hannah slumped down in a chair, her dizziness returning. What madness possessed Jeremiah that he would let this continue? And David. Did he truly mean to engage in a duel?

Longwood licked his lips, rested his left hand on the hilt of his sword, and stared hard at David. "What do you propose, sir?"

David cleared his throat, scratched his chin again, and studied the ceiling for a moment. "Hmm, well, I'm trying to think of something appropriate for the occasion, and the nearest feat to riding a whale that I can come up with is a log-rolling contest in Boston Harbor. Last man standing on the slippery log wins. The loser acknowledges the superior agility, if not the superior courage, of the winner."

Longwood glared at him in obvious disbelief while the men around them laughed their relief and good humor.

"I fear I must decline, sir. We sail for Mexico tomorrow. Perhaps our challenge could be deferred until my return?"

"Not at all, sir." David put his hands in his pocket and rocked back on his heels, appearing anything but menacing. "We can go right now. My ship is berthed at Commercial Wharf, just a short distance from here, and it will take little effort to find a suitable log to test our mettle."

"Really, Lazarus, I don't think …"

"Aw, go on, Captain," cried one sailor.

"Don't let this whaler best you, sir," a junior officer added.

Longwood shot him an angry look. Then he glanced around at the assembly and, aping David, scratched his chin. "Hmm. Looks as if I've no other choice."

"Name the time, sir."

Longwood's chuckle seemed forced, but he stuck out his hand. "Five o'clock. Commercial Wharf. You will excuse me while I return to my ship to change out of my dress uniform and put on something more appropriate."

"By all means." David clasped his hand and gave him a crooked grin. "We wouldn't want any of those brass buttons to lose their shine."

Longwood gave him a quizzing frown, then shook his head. He glanced at Hannah, and one eyebrow cocked upward.

"Perhaps this whole assembly would like to attend our farce? What do you think, Mrs. Jacobs?"

Before Hannah could find her voice, Nan stepped in front of her.

"Why, Captain Longwood, we wouldn't miss it for the world."

Chapter Twenty-nine

ဢ

*H*annah, Timothy, and Nan were among the last arrivals at the "dueling grounds," as Nan dubbed Commercial Wharf. Despite Hannah's reluctance to attend, Nan had insisted on driving both mother and son to the spectacle.

"You need to see what these men are made of, dear. And our Timothy needs to see it too."

Nan's remarks nettled Hannah, for she could not imagine a more childish activity than for these two Christian men to engage in a public brawl. That she herself might be the true object of their conflict only added to her discomfort. Rather than argue, however, she held her son close and studied his face. His solemn mood had not changed, nor had he spoken since the confrontation at the mission. But then, Nan's happy chatter had dominated the entire drive, and Timothy was learning not to interrupt adults.

Upon arrival at the wharf, their first surprise was to see how many people had gathered to watch the unusual event. More than a hundred sailors, whalers, and other seamen crowded the docks and nearby vessels. Nan and Hannah found themselves the only ladies present, for Kerry had elected to stay home.

Hannah's biggest shock came when she saw David's ship. The *Hannah Rose* sat berthed in the harbor, as trim and beautiful as when she had sailed from New Bedford on her last, lengthy whaling voyage in 1837. Despite Hannah's instructions when he returned safely in 1844, David had not sold the whale ship. Obviously, he had bought the *Hannah Rose* himself, and he now transported a far more precious cargo than whale oil within her hold.

That her namesake could be such a vessel of grace soothed Hannah's spirit for the first time since they left the mission. How pleased her father would have been to know his last ship was being used for such a grand, though clandestine, purpose.

Hannah's attention was soon drawn to the event they had come to witness. Captain Longwood appeared dashing, as always, in his crisply ironed navy trousers, a blousy white shirt with full sleeves, a bright red sash around his waist, and shiny black half-boots. David emerged from his ship wearing nondescript black trousers, low-cut shoes, and a formfitting shirt that made his arms appear all the more tanned because it was white and all the more muscular because it had no sleeves. At the sight of him, Hannah felt her face burning, and she shifted in her seat. She had not realized how finely structured this Viking was.

Before anyone had left the mission, Jeremiah had designated himself as referee, and he had brought along Seamus to attend the ladies. The jovial Irishman jogged to their buggy, ready for duty.

"They couldn't find a proper log, so they're using a rowboat." Seamus's enjoyment of the event was evident in his laughing tone and his inability to stand still as he spoke. "Captain Lazarus thought it might be more sport to swamp the boat and try to balance on the wet hull, but Captain Longwood thought it would work just fine top side up."

"And, of course, our Captain Lazarus conceded, being ever the gentleman," Nan quipped.

"Aye, mum, that he did." Seamus turned to Timothy, "Say, lad, would you like to sit on my shoulder and watch the proceedings?"

"Yes, sir." Timothy jumped up from the buggy seat and reached out to Seamus, but Hannah pulled him back.

"No, thank you." Hannah sat her son back down beside her.

"But, Mother ..." Timothy's face wore an uncharacteristic pout.

"Oh, Hannah, why not?" Nan nudged her. "Seamus won't let anything happen to him."

Timothy grinned at his ally, then appealed to Hannah with round, beseeching eyes. "Please?"

Before Hannah could answer him, Jeremiah called out to the assembled company. "Gentlemen ..."

He paused, glancing up from where he stood on the dock. "I beg your pardon. I should say, '*Ladies* and Gentlemen.'" He raised his hat and bowed toward Hannah and Nan.

Nan gave him a discreet nod, but Hannah glared at her old friend, her face burning with embarrassment. How could a godly pastor like Jeremiah be involved in this foolishness? But a memory darted across her mind. Years ago, Jeremiah had spent some time on the frontier, and there he had encountered all sorts of rough men. He had called it his initiation into manhood, something his genteel upbringing, and even his youthful voyage as a cabin boy on his grandfather's whale ship, had lacked. Hannah trusted Jeremiah without question. He must believe some good would come from this contest.

"The matter is not so much courage," Jeremiah was saying. "For we all know of the courage required in any seafaring man. No, I think we're assembled here today—"

"Belay the sermon, preacher," a voice called from the motley ranks, and everyone, including Jeremiah, laughed.

"All right then. Here are the simple rules for our contest. Each man will be given a harpoon as an instrument with which to dump his opponent into the harbor. Because you are both gentlemen, I need not remind you that there will be no prodding or hooking one another with your weapons."

Already positioned in the boat, David and Captain Longwood nodded to Jeremiah and then shook hands with each other.

Jeremiah handed each a long, wooden-handled harpoon with a dangerous iron point and hook on one end. At Jeremiah's signal, they gripped the poles with both hands and began their duel. Cheers erupted from the gathering, with sailors and whalers calling encouragement to their respective captains.

Eyes locked on his opponent, each man tapped his harpoon lightly against the other's, checking strengths and weaknesses. David applied sudden pressure to one foot, and the skiff's gunwale dipped near the water's surface. Longwood answered with a similar dip to the other side. Sweat beaded on both men's brows. Friendly smiles drew down into grim, determined lines. The harpoon strikes increased, along with the raucous cheers of the onlookers.

Although David was taller and broader in the shoulder, Longwood held his own. The men traded blow for blow, dip for dip, until, oddly, their harpoon hooks locked. With a swift rotation, David spun his weapon away from Longwood's and with its staff, caught his opponent by the ankle and lifted upward, at the same time dipping the skiff for a deep drink of water. Off-balance, Longwood lost his weapon and flailed his arms to regain footing, to no avail. David dropped his harpoon and reached out just in time to catch Longwood's head before it struck the opposite gunwale. For an instant, it seemed the bobbing skiff would swamp, but David deftly balanced it and then used both hands to toss his rival into the harbor.

A hearty cheer went up from the crowd, with sailors shouting their approval of David's heroics as loudly as the whalers. Nan laughed and applauded, Timothy and Seamus sent up hurrahs, and even Hannah gave a yip of happiness before remembering herself. She remembered herself all too well.

"Take me home, Nan."

"What? You don't want to kiss the conquering gladiator?"

Hannah's face burned, and her temper rose. "I want to go home *now*."

"Oh, my, look," Nan cried.

She pointed back to the action, where David was offering his hand to the laughing Captain Longwood. The navy man seemed about to pull himself back up into the skiff, but with a sudden jerk, he grasped David's hand with both of his and pulled hard, landing David in the water beside him.

Hannah gasped and would have jumped from the phaeton if Seamus had not put out a restraining hand.

"Never you mind, mum. He'll be all right. Look."

She followed his gaze.

David bobbed back to the surface and swam toward the dock, where he and Longwood helped one another out of the water, guffawing and slapping each other's backs all the while.

Timothy jumped up and down in his seat, clapping his hands and shouting. Seamus put his fingers to his mouth and whistled a piercing cheer. Nan giggled merrily. Hannah could bear it no longer.

"Now, Nan. Take me home now."

"But, Hannah, dearest, you take this much too seriously." Nan sat in the Louisburg Square parlor, stirring her tea and tapping her foot impatiently. "Even Timothy seems to understand it was nothing more than masculine high jinks."

Hannah took a sip of her own tea. It was true that Timothy seemed to have forgotten Captain Longwood's unintentional insult to his father that had begun all the nonsense. Even now, he was upstairs with Bridget getting ready for bed, probably still chattering to the housekeeper about the way Captain Lazarus had dumped Captain Longwood into the harbor.

"Furthermore," Nan continued, "I think it was marvelous—

might I say, noble—that our Captain Lazarus stuck up for the whalers, although he's retired from that occupation."

Hannah gazed at her friend, her heart overflowing with affection. For once, Nan did not know everything about the circumstances, though her choice of words was more than appropriate. Yes, David Lazarus, a man of humble origins, had displayed a nobility that far outshone the aristocratic lineage of the unsuspecting Longwood.

"And furthermore, again ..." Nan pointed her teaspoon at Hannah. " ... wasn't it clever the way he stepped into the conversation and removed Timothy? It was very cruel for Captain Longwood to disparage the occupation your son is interested in. Couldn't he see our darling boy was getting upset? Little boys get fanciful ideas all the time, and there was no need for it. Today he may want to be a whaler. Tomorrow he may want to be a banker. Captain Longwood simply has no sense of how to treat children, or anyone else. Now, Captain Lazarus ..."

Hannah sighed. "Oh, Nan, you need not say anything more. I agree with you that Captain Lazarus is the superior man, and certainly not just because he bested Captain Longwood in a silly contest of agility."

Nan eyed her knowingly. "Ah, now I see. You're concerned about your reputation. But nothing in our captain's behavior cast any aspersions on you *or* your son. Pretty clever, I would say, though you and I are not the only ones who might guess what the real contest was. Now, as I was saying, our Captain Lazarus—"

"Enough. Please, Nan, enough. You've made your case. I agree that Captain Lazarus is a good, wise, noble man. But I fear it will be some time before he trusts me again."

Nan wrinkled her brow, considering Hannah's words. "Perhaps so, perhaps not. Although I did not see him arrive at the reception and didn't have a chance to speak with him, surely he realized by the way I was behaving toward you that you have not lost my trust. Oh, and the way you kept your distance from Longwood—"

"I hardly think he had a chance to observe my interactions with others, or lack thereof. To him, I'm probably still a traitor, and if that is true, his kindness to Timothy was all the more remarkable."

"Hmm. Perhaps you're right. I should go next door right this minute and set him straight." Nan set down her teacup and picked up her reticule.

"Oh, I cannot bear to have him think ill of me." Hannah's voice caught as all the emotions of the past two days burst free, and she surrendered to her tears.

Nan hurried to embrace her. "There, there, my dear, go ahead and cry, if you like. But we'll soon have it all set straight."

"But for a lady to visit a gentleman's house, and in the evening, of all things, oh, Nan, it simply is not done."

"Nonsense. You just wait right here."

After drying Hannah's tears, Nan scurried next door only to return in a few moments to report that David was not at home. "I'm sure he needed far more time to dry off after today's little, um, event. But never mind, dear, I'll make sure he knows, and just as soon as possible. For now, I had best borrow John to see me home. Do you mind?"

Hannah gladly sent her manservant with Nan. Her friend had already stayed too far into the evening, and after the day's excitement, they both needed rest.

For Hannah, however, rest refused to come. She lay in bed rethinking recent days and wondering what she could have done differently that would have prevented David's censure. Would he ever understand her mistake regarding Longwood's urgent message? Would he ever comprehend what she had been willing to lose for his sake? And if he did, would it make any difference to him other than just knowing he now had a new compatriot in his courageous endeavors? All these questions churned about in her mind, fore-stalling sleep for what seemed like hours.

When at last she began to drift off, the jangle of the doorbell echoed up the stairway, jarring her awake. David. Finally, he had come home, and now she could tell him everything. She jumped out of bed and, with only a slight pause to consider her modesty, grabbed her summer dressing gown and threw it over her chemise. It would be too dark for David to see how thin her garments were, but she must make haste, or he might leave. Not taking time to light a candle, she dashed down the familiar stairs and flung open the front door.

"Captain Longwood!" Hannah stepped back in horror.

Her surprise visitor obviously mistook her gesture, for he strode boldly into the foyer and pulled her into his arms.

"Hannah, my darling, I feared you would not answer. I must speak with you, my love. I set sail with the morning tide, so surely you won't deny me this?"

Hannah pushed both hands against his chest and, for an instant, in the dim light, she could read shock on his face. An admiring smile stole across his lips, and his hand moved down her back.

"My dear, you're in your nightclothes."

With some difficulty, Hannah twisted out of his grasp and faced him, trembling. "How dare you … !"

Longwood shook his head, properly shamed. "Oh, dear heavens, I've done it again. Is there no right thing I can do in your company? It's all your fault, you realize. You drive me mad with love and then refuse to acknowledge your own feelings for me."

"I do not love you. I have never loved you. Why do you insist upon pursuing me?" *Dear Lord, why can't David help me now?*

"Ah, Hannah, I don't think you know your own mind. From the first moment I met you, I saw true passion in your eyes. Yes, passion. Feelings far beyond the silly women around you, feelings worthy of my own. You stood out from all the rest. How could I not love you? How could I not desire you? Will you deny you found something in me to draw your admiration and perhaps even your affection?"

He took a step toward her, one arm extended, and she retreated further, backing up against the staircase newel post and holding up her hand to forestall his aggression.

"Listen to me, Captain Longwood, and do not fail to hear me. You fell in love with the woman you wanted me to be, not the woman I am. You say you saw passion in my eyes. What a silly bit of nonsense. It was the lighting in the room, or the dress I wore, or perhaps the whiskey you drank before you came to the mission. But I do not love you, and if you were not so possessed by your own passions, you would realize you do not love me."

"But, Hannah …"

From deep within, anger welled up so consuming that Hannah did not recognize her own voice growling out with animal-like rage. "Dear Lord in heaven, what will it take to convince you? I … do … not … want … you!"

Longwood drew back, stunned. He gave his head a little shake, as if to deny what he heard. Then, slowly, so very slowly, he bowed in silent acquiescence.

"I see. Forgive me. I thought perhaps your reticence was designed to encourage—"

"No, it was not."

"Ah, yes …" Longwood stared at her, then beyond her. Even in the dim light, Hannah could see his expression change, from hurt to shock to deep, deep sorrow. She turned to see what finally defeated him. Standing in the darkened hallway was Bridget, armed with a broom. Behind her stood John and Patience, one with a rake, the other with a rolling pin. Even Leah, whose freedom had not yet been assured, stood ready to defend her mistress.

"Did you really think I meant to harm you, that you should need such pathetic defenders?" Tears glistened in the captain's eyes, and his voice was choked with emotion. "I would die for you, Mrs. Jacobs. And even now, I swear, if you ever need anything, *anything*, any time in the future, I will be your willing servant."

"Good-bye, Captain Longwood. May God keep you as you serve our country."

He bowed his head in defeat, withdrew out the door, and stood for a moment on the front stoop. Then he turned and blew a kiss to her before slowly walking to his horse to depart.

As Hannah shut the door behind him, she heard the muted sound of another door closing through the wall to her right. Slumping to the floor, she wept bitterly. Had David once again watched Longwood's inappropriate, late-night visit and misinterpreted what he saw?

Chapter Thirty

ॐ

Hannah felt Bridget lift her up from the floor with a firm grip. She leaned against the housekeeper, barely hearing her murmured words of comfort, or those of the other servants.

"Miz Jacobs, that man is walking evil," Leah said.

"Shh. Help me take her upstairs." Bridget braced Hannah's arm over her own shoulder and grasped her about the waist. "John, bolt the door. Patience, get the laudanum."

"No, no laudanum." Hannah shook her head, straightened, and gently removed herself from Bridget's grip. "Thank you. Thank you all. I can manage. Just a glass of water, please. I must check Timothy to see if he was disturbed."

With legs still atremble, Hannah ascended the stairs and peered into her son's room. To her relief, he slept soundly. She would not be able to claim that privilege for herself.

Far into the night, she rehearsed in her mind every contact she had had with Captain Longwood. What kind of passion had he seen in her that he would take such liberties? Surely he could not accuse her of some wanton lack of restraint, for she had always refused his advances. Yet she feared it was more than his own pride that had prompted his remarks ... and his actions.

Long ago, Ahab had told her he had seen passion in her eyes, and in her girlish innocence she had felt no shame for it. Directed toward her beloved husband, her unbound feelings had been a good thing because she loved him with all her heart and mind and body. But he was gone from her forever, and now she must subdue such feelings so no other man would misread her intentions.

In the dark of night, belated shame made her face grow warm. At her age, how could she still be so naïve, so ignorant of her effect on men? Captain Longwood had regarded her polite interest as affection. No wonder he had been so persistent. Still, she could not accept all the blame. Once she said no, he never should have mistaken her rejection for coy reticence.

Was Leah right? Was Longwood an evil man? Only God knew. In a moment of ironic humor, Hannah thought it a good thing to send such a persistent man to war, for surely he would never surrender to the country's enemies. But his aggressive tactics had been more than out of place with her.

He was gone now. She could be at peace. But why would sleep not come? David, of course. Through no fault of her own, she had lost his trust. And, even though Nan had promised to clear her name, David had seen Longwood leave her home at a very late hour *and* blow her a kiss. Oh, but, maybe he hadn't seen it. But maybe he had.

Hannah's heart ached. How could she bear it if she truly had lost David's good opinion?

Sleep came at last, a dreamless void. Long after first light, Bridget tapped on her door and brought in a pitcher of water for Hannah's morning ablutions.

"Mum, would you like for me to take Master Timothy over to say good-bye to Master Charles? You'll recall this is the day the Atwoods are leaving for their country home."

"Oh, dear. I had forgotten." Hannah sat up in bed, feeling anything but rested. "Yes, Bridget, that would be wonderful. Be sure to give my apologies to Mrs. Atwood for not coming myself."

"I'll do that, mum. Now you just take your rest."

Hannah wished she could accept that advice, but waking had only stirred up her mind with anxious thoughts from the night before. She rose, washed her face, dressed, and then sat for some time listlessly brushing her hair. Her reflection in the mirror was not pleasing, for dark circles hung under her eyes, set off to disadvantage by her black dress. She looked awful. She felt awful. This would not be a good day.

Should she go to David and explain herself? No. Despite Nan's actions the night before, a lady simply did not go calling on a gentleman alone, even an old friend, even one who lived next door. And then, what did she have to explain that, in the explanation, would not make her sound foolish? She must not presume to know what he was thinking or what he had seen.

A tapping at her door broke into her sleepy, fretful reverie.

"Mrs. Jacobs?" Patience opened the door and peered into the room. "Captain Lazarus is downstairs. May I tell him you'll be down?"

Hannah gasped, fully awake now. "Oh, my, yes. Oh, yes. I'll be right down."

She studied her reflection in the mirror. How dreadful she looked. How haggard her often-praised green eyes appeared, eyes that had shed far too many tears of late. This would be one time the gentleman in question would not be moved by her so-called beauty. With a shrug of acceptance over her unchangeable appearance and a strange, giddy lilt in her heart, she placed the last hairpin in her hair and hurried out the bedroom door.

Hannah paused on the bottom step and peered into the front parlor. David stood in profile staring out the front window, and to her surprise and distress, his jaw clenched and unclenched, as though he were angry. She hurried down the last step and shoved the half-open pocket door down its track and into the wall with a thunk.

"Good morning, David." She injected as much teasing good humor into her voice as possible. "I do hope you have thoroughly dried out from last evening's foolishness."

He eyed her coldly, but offered a formal half-bow. "Hann … Mrs. Jacobs. Good morning. I hope I'm not disturbing you. I would not have troubled you except that I was concerned that Timothy … about last evening … that he might still be upset. Is he at home?"

He looked beyond her toward the parlor door as if trying to avoid seeing her. And she did not fail to notice that he addressed her as Mrs. Jacobs after all these months of using her Christian name.

"No, he's visiting the Atwoods." Despite her dismay over his attitude, she retained her sunny smile. "But since you're here, I hope you understand that I'm quite put out with you for participating in a … a *duel*, however harmlessly it ended."

"You put out with me? I would hardly think you have reason. After all, your Captain Longwood is quite safe. I did not injure him, beyond a little damage to his overblown pride. I'm sure that once you two are happily married and settled at Longwood Plantation, you'll both look back and have a good laugh about the whole incident." Now he glared at her, his mouth a grim line, his eyebrows bent in disapproval.

Hannah sauntered across the room. "Married? To Captain Longwood?"

"Yes, married to Captain Longwood. He made it clear, and you did nothing to dispel the implication, that you were promised to each other."

"Oh, dear." Hannah sighed. So David had in truth misinterpreted Longwood's reprehensible behavior—twice—at her front door and had inferred that she and Longwood were betrothed. "Poor man, he's always so sure of himself, but now we've both dealt him a blow. After you bested him in your little contest, I finally convinced him last night that I was truly rejecting his proposal."

"Do you mean you broke your engagement?"

"We were never engaged. I rejected him twice, and he seemed to have difficulty believing I meant no."

Lazarus blinked, relaxing his posture somewhat. He seemed unable to adjust to what she had told him.

"And so, David," she said softly, "would you like to wait here until Timothy returns home? I'm sure he'll be happy to see you. Last night, it was difficult to get him to go to sleep. He couldn't stop bragging about the way you tumbled Captain Longwood into the harbor."

"Indeed?" A smile crept across his lips.

"Oh, yes. Now, that's not to say that you don't deserve a scolding for such behavior."

He chuckled. "A scolding?"

"Oh, yes, a scolding. David, far too many people depend on you for their well-being for you to take such a risk on such a foolish activity. That's not to say I did not appreciate the way you rescued my son from revealing the truth about his father to Captain Longwood in front of everyone at the reception. But, on the other hand, you carried it entirely too far. Think of those poor people who are rescued from the likes of Captain Longwood because of your involvement in our organization."

"Ah." David's gray eyes exuded understanding. "It would seem that appearances have deceived me in more ways than one. You have made your decision?"

She nodded.

He gazed down at her. "I know it was a difficult choice, but one you will not regret. What changed your mind?"

"Sit down, dear friend, and I shall tell you."

She motioned him to the divan and took her seat at the far end. Then she revealed to him how deeply she had been affected by his story of Henry Childers's death while helping slaves escape, how reading the Douglass narrative had persuaded her of the depravity and self-deception of slaveholders, and how her brief acquaintance with Mattie and her own household servants had convinced her of the full humanity of the Negro race, contrary to Longwood's assertions. Despite all these compelling reasons, however, she still could not think of continuing to endanger Timothy by hiding people in her home. She then told him about Longwood's urgent message and her own mistake in thinking he had sent it.

"Of course, I was frightened. Yet I knew that if my dear friend desperately needed my help, I must go, whatever it might cost me, and I would depend upon God to protect my son."

She continued a brief, much-subdued account of her frantic trip to Bunker Hill, but his countenance nevertheless displayed alarm, and his eyes glistened. When she finished, his expression grew stormy for a moment. "When I think of Longwood's devious, possessive behavior when he brought you home that evening, I would like to …" He glanced away and shook his head, then reached across the divan and took her hand. "Dear friend. Dear, brave friend."

Her face grew warm at the admiration glowing in his eyes and the emotion evident in his voice.

"Despite my error in thinking you had sent for me, I now realize I cannot refuse to do what God so clearly wills for me. In accordance with Mr. Emerson's words, which you so kindly used to challenge me, I have made my choice between truth and repose. As a result, I have postponed my tour of Europe until a later time." She did not add that she would follow Nan's example of staying in Boston to see what might become of a certain friendship.

"Ah. Interesting. Actually, I've been thinking of traveling to Europe myself."

"Oh? You mean when the danger of influenza and insurgency has passed?"

"Yes." He still held her hand and, after a moment of silence, he spoke again. "I must tell you something, Hannah."

"Yes?"

"I hope you will forgive me for speaking in such a personal manner."

"Please go on."

"When you first arrived in Boston, when Jeremiah first told me of all you and Timothy had suffered after your husband's death, I felt great concern for you."

"Thank you. You're very kind."

"But then I saw you that first day at the mission. I saw your remarkable zeal for life reflected in your lovely eyes, and I knew you could face the future with courage and endurance."

Zeal for life? Is that what David had seen? Not some inappropriate passion or unconsciously predatory behavior? Perhaps she bore no responsibility for Captain Longwood's faulty interpretation of her after all.

"Without my friends, I fear I could not manage."

"Hannah, I wish to be the best of friends to you. Do you recall that just the other day I suggested we would work well together?"

"Yes." She held her breath. Surely he would not propose this soon.

He studied her for a moment. "We cannot tell where God will lead us, but it is my prayer that His plan might include one future for the two of us."

She breathed out a sigh of relief. "I will join you in that prayer." *And I believe with all my heart that God will answer.*

He moved closer to her, and his eyes twinkled with understanding. He drew her hand up to his lips. How pleasant it was to sit with him this way. How warm and safe and secure. Surely this friendship would prove to be far more enduring than some flash-fire of passion.

Neither of them seemed willing to break their gaze, even when the front door opened. Together, they turned to see Bridget wink and giggle, while Timothy rushed forward.

"Captain Lazarus!"

David released Hannah's hand, caught Timothy, and pulled him into his lap.

"Timothy, how are you today?" David's tone was light, and Hannah wondered if her son would appreciate the depth of his question.

The boy beamed with happiness. "I am well, thank you. You were very brave yesterday. You dunked Captain Longwood right into the water." He giggled more loudly than necessary, but Hannah decided not to scold.

Timothy looked back and forth between them, suddenly troubled. "I didn't like what he said about …" He stopped, peering back at Bridget.

"About whalers?" David asked.

"Yes, sir. But he was talking about my father too. I didn't like that. Was my father crazy, like Captain Longwood said?"

David glanced at Hannah, and she nodded, trusting him to say the right thing. So far, he had not disappointed her.

"My dear lad, we three—you, your mother, and I—have nothing but admiration for your father. And none of us will ever forget him. What others may think will never change that."

Content with this answer, Timothy flung his arms around David's neck and gave him a fierce hug, which was returned with considerably more gentleness. "Then you may take my mother's hand again." He jumped down from the divan and ran to Bridget. "Did Patience bake gingersnaps this morning?"

"Aye, she did. This way to the kitchen, Master Timothy." She took his hand and led him out of the room, sending an approving glance over her shoulder.

Hannah stared into the cold hearth, her flaming face more than making up for its lack of fire.

David chuckled and reached out to her. "I suppose we must do as he says."

In full agreement, she was very pleased to place her hand in his.

Readers' Guide

ഇ

*H*istorical fiction takes us away from our daily lives to another time and place, "the good old days," when life was simpler, morality and manners were the mainstays of social order, and everyone knew his or her place. But were those times truly better than today? In the pre-Civil War nineteenth century, people faced devastating difficulties. Life expectancy was short due to disease and lack of medical knowledge, and many children never reached maturity. All over the Eastern seaboard, thousands of immigrants poured into America from Europe seeking better lives, competing with and threatening the livelihoods of lifelong residents of English descent. And our nation was faced with an impending conflict as people of conscience formed the abolitionist movement to eliminate slavery, which formed the backbone of the wealthy Southern economy.

Against this turbulent backdrop, widowed Hannah Ahab must make decisions that will affect her son's future and her own. No longer the naïve young woman who had married dashing, dangerous Captain Ahab, Hannah has developed a strength that often surprises her, although her friends know she has what it takes to go beyond herself and live for others.

The power of a story such as this is the reader's ability to live the experiences of the characters. Hopefully, you have enjoyed walking with Hannah and Timothy through their uncertain journey, and relished their reunion with friends Jeremiah and Kerry Harris, Captain David Lazarus, Aunt Charity, and Tishtega.

Reflect on the following questions as you continue your journey with Hannah Rose.

1. Although Hannah's faith is almost destroyed by Ahab's death, she manages to keep up a façade of belief for her son and her friends. How do you think her spiritual life would have progressed had Ahab returned alive and successful from killing Moby Dick?

2. Hannah has always despised lies, yet she devises a drastic deception to protect Timothy when she changes their last name. Was she justified in making this decision? Was this fabrication morally different from the lies the abolitionists told to protect runaway slaves?

3. The story begins with a playful scuffle between Timothy and his cousin and ends with a good-natured "duel" between David Lazarus and Captain Longwood. In between those two harmless altercations, Timothy, David, and even the pastor, Jeremiah, engage in some very real fights, all three of whom justified their actions as necessary. What do you think?

4. Hannah resists helping David and Nan in their illegal transport of escaping slaves, yet when she thinks David has summoned her in desperation, she goes to him with only a moment of hesitation. What does that reveal about her true character?

5. Imagine that you are Nan or David, trusting Hannah to make the right decision about helping with their clandestine, life-or-death activities. Without knowing Hannah's thoughts, how would you react to seeing her interactions with Captain

Longwood? Would you have trusted her, or would you have withdrawn from her, as they did? Why?

6. Still influenced by her great love for Ahab, as well as the mystical bond she felt with him, Hannah resists as her family and friends urge her to consider remarriage. What loosens Ahab's hold on her? Whose influences replace that hold? How?

7. Kerry challenges Hannah to minister to wayward young women like Clara, asking, "Beloved, ask thyself, what would thy Father have thee do?" Yet Hannah interprets her words to mean her earthly father. At this point in her life, why is this a more persuasive appeal to Hannah?

8. Hannah continues to encounter people whose lives have been damaged by Ahab's fatal decision. Why does she feel compelled to make amends for his actions? Is this an appropriate motivation for her good works? Why or why not?

9. Hannah has two suitors: a handsome, heroic military man who desires to sweep her off her feet and treat her as a fragile flower, and a humble, taciturn former whaling captain who expects her to be strong and live her life for the benefit of others. Early in the story, before you learn more about each man, if you had been her friend and advisor, which man would you counsel her to receive? Why?

10. Hannah felt that God had not heard her prayers for Ahab because He did not save him from death. When our prayers are not answered as we want them to be, what happens to our trust in God? Does our faith depend on getting what we ask for?

Additional copies of *HANNAH ROSE*
and other River Oak titles are available
from your local bookseller.

If you have enjoyed this book,
or if it has had an impact on your life,
we would like to hear from you.

Please contact us at:

RIVER OAK BOOKS
Cook Communications Ministries, Dept. 201
4050 Lee Vance View
Colorado Springs, CO 80918
Or visit our Web site: www.cookministries.com

RIVEROAK®
Good News in Fiction